The Omega's Secret Pregnancy

ANNA WINEHEART

This novel contains graphic sexual content between two men. Intended for mature readers only.

Warnings: Self-lubricated butts, angst

ISBN: 1548720399
ISBN-13: 978-1548720391

For two Really Stubborn guys.

Special thanks to my mentor, Jessica Mueller,
for all she has done.

1
Felix

Meadowfall, California

IT'S TWO days into spring, and Meadowfall is *freezing.*

Felix huffs into his palms, the paper bag crinkling under his arm. Behind him, the pharmacy's cool fluorescent lights glow from the windows, chasing away the shadows of the parking lot. The pharmacist, Sue, flips the sign from Open to Closed. She waves at him; he smiles crookedly, waving back.

It had been a pain, remembering his pills so late. Felix winces. He's been through heats ten thousand times, but somehow he forgets the suppressants, even though he's right on the cusp of the next heat. He can't remember anything, and he should be better with these. He used to be.

His body hums, flushed with warmth. Once he takes the suppressants, at least he won't be desperately in need of sex.

He should have gotten the pills earlier. He'll be interviewing for that cashiering job tomorrow, in that gas station down by the expressway. No need for some alpha tool to scent his pheromones and start sneering about attracting customers.

"Come on already," he mutters, fishing his phone from his pocket. "It can't take you thirty minutes to pick me up."

A second later, the phone buzzes, its screen glowing. *Sorry!* his brother texts. *Work things came up. Running out of house. Ask dad to pick you up? Sorry! Going dark in a min.*

"No," Felix groans. It's midnight. He can't possibly ring his father, of all people, to make the drive across town. "Really, Taylor? Call Dad?"

He's had enough of calling his father for favors. If it weren't for him, Felix would still be back in Highton, mired in late loft rents and a towering pile of unsold watercolor paintings. He bites his lip, scrolling through his phone contacts for a friendly name. *Hi, Jane, haven't heard from you in a while! Are you still in Meadowfall? I kind of need a favor if you're still awake. I took a bus downtown for some meds and need to get home.*

"No. No way," Felix says, shoving his phone back into his pocket. He's done asking for favors. Three miles isn't much of a walk, and he'll probably get home by 1 AM.

He tucks the paper bag under his chin, pulls the hood of his jacket down, and folds his hands under his arms, trudging along the sidewalk. Tomorrow, he'll hopefully have a new job. He'll be able to pay rent, and invite Taylor over for dinner in two weeks. If Taylor is even in town at all.

And that's all Felix allows himself to think about Meadowfall: his brother, his father, and the familiar schools and craft shops he abandoned five years ago. Not the other people—person—he left behind. He sucks in a deep breath, pushing the thoughts out of his mind. He had left, and he doesn't need a reason for it.

His heat seeps into his limbs like an ache. He thinks about pulling the paper bag open, popping a pill dry. He doesn't *need* the suppressant. It'll save him eighty cents, and he'll use it on another day when he'll need it more. Like tomorrow.

Still, a hot water bottle would be nice.

Thunder rumbles half a mile away. It's no ordinary thunder, though, because it draws steadily closer like a motorbike. Felix turns, watching the busy roads to see if a biker's going to roar down this street. It gives him a little thrill, seeing them. *I just like bikes. That's all.*

The bike skims through the intersections, weaving between cars. Its model is familiar under the orange streetlights: chrome with gleaming black paint, its single headlight blazing a path straight ahead. Except it slows, tipping slightly to the right to change lanes, and it's purring down this road, on the lane right next to his sidewalk.

He slows his footsteps to watch, the machine's roar vibrating in his heart. The bike rolls to a stop next to him, and suddenly Felix isn't looking at the bike anymore. He's looking at its rider: leather jacket clinging to his biceps, dark jeans wrapped around his bulging thighs, and his face—

His heart slams into his ribs.

Sharp mahogany eyes, strong jaw, dark hair scattered across his forehead. It's a face Felix knows far too well. Because of course he has to bump into

Kaden Brentwood again, and of course Kade can smell him from anywhere in town.

Kade's gaze flickers over him, down his chest and hips and legs, pausing on his ratty sneakers, then darting back to meet his eyes. His nostrils flare. Felix hopes that Kade can't smell him over the bike's oily exhaust, but he picks out the familiar pine-and-cedar scent anyway, Kade's musk. The ache in his body intensifies. Kade's eyes darken.

Two days back in Meadowfall, and Felix has to meet the one person whose body he knows better than his own. The one person who had proposed, and he had dropped everything to run from.

Shit. He forces a smile, says, "Hi," and spins on his heels, striding down the sidewalk. He should turn the other way, go somewhere Kade can't follow.

The bike revs. Kade rolls alongside Felix on the pavement, eyes fixed on him. "I didn't know you were back," Kade says, his voice rumbling just the same as Felix remembers, curling into his ears. "Saw some ads of your work on the internet."

Heat crawls up Felix's cheeks. *You've been following news about me?* His heart flutters, at the same time his stomach twists. *I never forgot about you,* he thinks, staring at the weeds along the sidewalk. *I never wanted to leave.* "Oh."

"You staying long this time?"

It means *I want to see you around.* Felix swallows. He can still read this man, five years after he fled. "I don't know," he says. "Just a while, I guess. I'm moving away soon. Meadowfall is a small place."

If Kade reads through his lies, he doesn't say. But he follows on his bike, three feet from Felix, and checks the road when they approach a street corner. Felix doesn't know why this man is still with him, why he's not taking off yet, disgust scrawled across his face.

The streets yawn empty to either side, so he crosses the road, Kade inching along on his bike.

"You're not staying with family?" Kade glances at the street sign, and Felix hears his thoughts clicking together. "New place?"

He shrugs. They shouldn't be talking so easily. He's hurt Kade, more than he can repair, and Kade is still here, his visor pushed up on his helmet.

"Want a ride?" Kade asks. He's not asking about sex, but Felix can't help thinking it anyway. He smells the cleanness of Kade's scent, the way he hasn't marked himself with another person recently. Kade can probably smell the same on him, too. It teases his heat, makes his body remember those broad shoulders, Kade's warmth soaking into his skin. "It's gonna get colder out."

Felix swallows. It'll be an hour of uncomfortable walking out in this cold, his body longing for heat and touch. Kade's not asking for sex, he's not asking to pick up where they left off. Felix bites his lip. *Is that all you're offering? A ride home?* "Why?"

For a long moment, Kade studies him, eyes flickering over his face. He opens his mouth, closes it, and glances off to the side. "No reason. Just thought it'll be faster if you ride. You won't freeze as quick on the bike. I'm headed north anyway."

It's not where Kade's family home used to be. Felix winces. If he'd known earlier, he wouldn't have rented this place. "You moved?"

Kade shrugs, his eyes unreadable. "Are you jumping on, or not?"

The thought of sitting on the cruiser, so close to Kade, makes blood rush down between his legs. Felix gulps. He should run as far from Kade as possible, before Kade really smells him. He should hurt Kade so Kade recoils, speeding away. Instead, Felix says, "Yeah. I am. Just... because it's cold."

Kade turns the ignition off and hands over the ring of keys. "Helmet's in the trunk."

Felix's fingers brush his callused hand, a spark sizzling down his skin. Kade's nostrils flare. *You smell like lavender,* Kade once murmured in his ear. *Sweet, but not like honey. Just right.*

He gulps and pops the trunk open, grabbing the only other helmet there. *Why do you have a spare helmet? Is it for someone else?* There used to be one for him, but it's been five years, and plenty has changed. *Are you seeing someone else now?*

Felix pulls the helmet onto his head, buckling it. The foam inside smells like different people—the woodsy aroma of alphas, the grassy scent of betas, the sweet floral note of omegas—and he can't tell if any one person has been using it more than the rest. He locks the trunk and hands the keys back, heart thumping. *I can't believe I'm doing this. With Kade.*

Kade flips down the passenger foot pegs for him, then restarts the engine. The bike roars. Felix sets a hand gingerly on the trunk, steps onto one peg, and swings his other leg over the leather seat.

It's surprising how his body still remembers this, fitting on a motorbike up against his former mate. He pushes the thought away, settling two inches behind Kade, and his heart aches at that distance. They used to be closer.

"Ready?" Kade asks.

Felix curls his fingers into the edges of the pillion seat, careful to keep his thighs away from Kade's. Kade is broad—shoulders, chest, waist. *Never thought you'd be between my legs again.* "Yeah," Felix says.

"Where are you staying?"

"Walnut Street. Three miles down, next to Sally's Grocery. It's tucked in with a bunch of other smaller houses."

Kade punches in the address on his GPS. Felix barely registers the new device, when he's looking at the expanse of Kade's back, the breadth of his shoulders, all hidden within his jacket. *It's been so long.* Kade twists the throttle, and the bike lunges forward, sending Felix's back thumping against the trunk.

In hindsight, he should have flipped the visor down. But he forgot, and the wind whips around them, sending Kade's scent right into his face, the mellow, familiar bite of it. Felix breathes it deep into his lungs, remembers the times when he was pressed under this man, back arched, fingers clawing into worn sheets.

Kade's scent goes right down to his cock, sets his nerves alight. The aching throb of his heat flares like wildfire in his limbs, burning low in his stomach. He leans in close, sniffing, growing damp, his pants stretching too tight around his hips. It's been five years, and his body still reacts the exact same way. *I can't go into heat right now!*

Kade glances down the side streets, watching for traffic. Behind him, Felix's throat runs dry. He squirms, trying to find a more comfortable position, but it's hard to when his alpha sits inches away, and all Felix wants is for Kade to bend him over, to mount him and knot in him. It'll feel like things are back as they were. Felix yearns for that. He has told himself repeatedly that he doesn't need Kade in his life.

Felix is so, so wrong.

He breathes in Kade's scent, inching closer on the leather seat. He wants to spread his legs even though Kade's not looking. He wants Kade to know. Wants him to stop, turn around, pin him up against a wall. Felix shouldn't be wanting this. He should've taken those goddamn pills, but nothing will change what he feels for this man.

He curls his fingers into the seat, heat throbbing between his legs.

Whatever Kade wants tonight, Felix will freely yield to him.

2
Kade

FIVE YEARS.

Five fucking years, and Kade has to find Felix huddled on the street, clutching a little paper bag that's probably full of pills. It's chilly, and of course the idiot is out by himself, walking three miles with a thin jacket on.

He won't slam his fist on his bike. Instead, he grits his teeth and rides, the warmth of Felix's body seeping through the scant space between them, tempting. Kade sucks his breath in slowly, tries not to think about his lavender scent, the times Felix writhed under him and hauled him in for a kiss.

Felix had looked surprised tonight, eyes wide, mouth open. Kade had smelled him four streets away and ridden up. Few omegas smell like lavender, and he'd thought... He'd been hoping for a familiar face.

Felix rides behind him now, something Kade has been hoping to see for the last five years.

His heart pounds in his chest, full of betrayal and longing. He doesn't know what he should do. If he should do anything at all. Felix had smelled purely himself, no markings from anyone, the cuff of his jacket pulled over his scar. *Have you been alone? Did anyone else mark you? Why did you return?*

The questions flood Kade's mind. He concentrates on following the fuchsia line of the GPS, trying not to think about Felix's legs open around him, trying not to think about pulling his omega close, sliding his hand inside his pants. If Felix is anywhere near the same person as the one Kade knew, he'd enjoy that.

He pushes the thoughts out of his head, the wind skimming along his helmet, and rides through twisting roads, into a part of town with smaller, shoddier houses.

The house the GPS leads him to is tiny, windows bare, no lights on at the front door. The headlight illuminates the broken front porch. Kade pulls into his driveway, turning off the ignition. A rat scurries through the bushes. He pushes his visor up, twisting slightly in his seat. "This your new place?"

"Yeah." Felix tenses, then slips off the bike, his paper bag crinkling in his hands. He tugs at the buckle under his chin. "I won't be here for long, though."

Kade climbs off his bike, turning to look him over. The moment he does, Felix's scent slams into him like a wave, heady and musky. It winds fingers into his instincts and *hauls,* and in three seconds, he triggers Kade's rut. Kade's heart pounds. His blood surges down, and he's rock-hard in his pants before he thinks, *You're in heat?*

Felix's throat works. He looks away, his tongue darting out to wet his lips. "Do you... want a drink? I've got tea and water inside."

"Yeah." His voice comes out gravelly. Kade doesn't even know where he's finding his words, when he's staring at the hard line in Felix's pants, the shadows it casts from the weak streetlights. It makes him leak, and he needs to feel Felix against him, needs to mark him with his scent. "Didn't think I was thirsty."

He can't help looking at Felix's wrist again, but it's hidden behind a thick wool sleeve. So he follows Felix to the front door, breathing him in, the fresh sweat in his hair, the musk of his body, the sweet, sharp tang of his arousal.

Felix's key trembles against the keyhole. His nostrils flare, too, and Kade knows what he smells, sees the way his throat works. "I'll get you something to drink. Just... just make yourself at home."

The door opens, welcoming them like a refuge. Kade follows him past the stacks of sealed cardboard boxes, Felix's footsteps loud in his ears. Felix taps the switch, and warm light bounces off his golden hair, lights up his green eyes. He looks away, his lips glistening, his throat pale. Kade knows he shouldn't be touching this man. Felix made it clear that Kade wasn't good enough, and that memory still stings.

So Kade follows him to the empty kitchen, his body quivering with need, his boxers damp. With Felix's back turned, he reaches into his shirt, tugs off the chain around his neck, barely glancing at the silver ring on it before shoving it into his jean pocket. Then he pulls his jacket open, so it won't be so damn hot inside.

"I have tea," Felix says, his voice lowering by

a notch. He glances at Kade from the corner of his eye, his gaze flickering down Kade's chest, to the tent in his pants. Felix's breath rushes out of him. "Or... or water. Or coffee. Whatever you want."

Kade swallows. "What if I want something else?"

"We'll find a solution for it," Felix says. He lifts his chin to expose his throat. *Taste me,* Kade reads, and he's crossing the five feet between them, curling his hand around Felix's narrow waist, dipping his head to mesh their lips together.

Felix tastes the same, like lavender. Kade groans into his mouth, brushing his lips over Felix's, and he stops thinking. He slips a hand down Felix's chest, pulling his jacket open, rubbing his hard nipples. Felix moans, hips bucking.

Kade slides against his tongue, smoothing his hand down Felix's abdomen to his cock. Felix's breath hitches. He presses heavily into Kade's palm, so hard it's as though he hasn't fucked anyone in years. Kade growls. Felix tastes the same, like nothing has changed. Kade rucks his shirt up, dragging his hand down Felix's back, down his chest, grinding the scent gland at his wrist against Felix's skin. He wants Felix to smell like him, wants everyone to know Felix is his, even though Felix hasn't been for years.

His omega writhes. Kade shoves him up against the wall, his need spiking when Felix groans softly, his hands coming up to tug at his own pants. Kade knocks his hands away, hooks a thumb into his waistband. He wants to pleasure Felix, see the way Felix craves his touch.

Felix gulps, panting when Kade kisses along

his jaw, down his throat, sucking lightly. Kade licks over his pulse, feels the way it jumps against his tongue. He kisses down the base of Felix's throat, where his scent gland is, and drags his teeth against it.

Felix cries out. He tugs Kade's shirt free, flattening his hands against his bare abs. Then he reaches down to squeeze Kade's cock, and pleasure hums in his body. "Kade," he breathes, his voice low and rasping. "Kade, please."

"Please what?" Kade presses him harder against the wall, pushes his hand down Felix's pants, barely squeezing it in. His fingers brush over the smooth, damp length of his cock. Felix throws his head back, his tip smearing against Kade's palm. Kade throbs, the pressure at his groin spiking.

"Bedroom," Felix hisses, rutting against his hand, his musk so thick that Kade can almost drink it. And so Kade grinds his wrist against Felix's cock, marking him with his scent, dragging his wrist down to his groin, over his hips. "Need—need you inside."

He growls, hearing those words. Kade wraps his arms around Felix's smaller frame, hefts him up by his ass, and his fingers press into the damp fabric of Felix's jeans. *You're so damn wet.* Felix spreads his thighs, wraps his arms around Kade's shoulders, and for a breathless moment, all Kade wants to do is heft him against the wall and push inside him, just like that.

"D'you have a condom?" Kade asks. "Don't wanna knock you up. That'll be a mess."

Felix winces, and Kade regrets asking. He

doesn't want to remind Felix about the past.

"I don't," Felix says, his forehead wrinkling. "I—I'm on BC."

So Kade drags Felix down his chest, the bulge of Felix's pants rubbing against his abs, along his cock. Felix trembles, his jeans drenching through. Kade swears. He finds the bedroom, flicks the light on, and throws Felix onto the bed, pulling their shoes off, then Felix's pants.

Felix squirms, lifting his hips to help. The moist, heavy scent of his arousal swamps over Kade. His cock throbs in his pants, and he flings Felix's jeans to the side, grasping his pale, thin thighs, pinning them apart to lap between his glistening cheeks.

It's been five years since Kade last saw him, and Felix still tastes the same; salty, musky. Kade flicks his tongue against his damp hole, the ring of muscle rough against his tongue. Then he pushes inside that tight heat to taste him. Felix's strangled cry fills the corners of the room. He squirms against Kade, cock straining. Kade licks up his soft balls, sniffing at their musk, before lapping along his cock, his nostrils flaring at his own cedar scent on Felix, the way Felix's cock smells like *his.*

Pulsing, Kade crawls up the bed, straddling him, tugging Felix's shirt and jacket up over his head. Felix slips out of them, naked beneath him, his skin pale, his cock leaking onto his abdomen. He looks so *vulnerable.*

Kade tosses his clothes to the side, gaze trailing over the growing flush on Felix's chest, down his thin arms, to the teeth-shaped scar on Felix's wrist, left from a smaller jaw an age ago. *You haven't belonged to anyone else,* Kade thinks, and triumph roars in his chest, chasing through his limbs.

Felix turns his wrist against the bed, looking away.

But he can't hide the fact that no one else has claimed him. Kade shrugs out of his clothes, his breath puffing through his nose. Felix's eyes rake over his chest, down his abs, to his thick, heavy cock. He squirms, spreading his legs, relaxing his hole.

The moment Kade is just as naked, he climbs atop his omega, kissing him deep. Felix accepts him into his mouth, his hands fluttering up Kade's sides, tracing him with his own scent. It feels like acceptance, somehow. Kade grinds their cocks together, leaking precum onto Felix's skin, slicking them both. Felix mewls.

It isn't enough. Kade rubs their bodies together, chest-to-chest, his hands smoothing over Felix's back, down his arms, marking along his sides. He drips, just having Felix in his arms again, smelling like he's *his.*

Mine, he almost growls, but he swallows it, pushing his cock against Felix's, licking into his mouth, claiming his mate again. And Felix arches against him, nails biting into his shoulders, throwing his head back so Kade sucks on his throat, trailing slow, wet kisses down to his scent gland.

He sinks his teeth into it. Felix shudders, his breath rushing out. "Kade," he gasps, spreading his legs, rutting up at him. "Inside, please."

Kade pries himself off just enough to flip

Felix over, onto his knees, pushing his legs apart to expose his hole. "What do you want in here?" he rasps, rubbing his thumb down Felix's ass, wedging it between his cheeks. Felix gasps. Kade circles his hole, reaching down to fondle his balls, stroke his flushed, straining cock. Felix moans, pushing into his hand, leaving a trail of precum along his palm. "One finger?"

"No," Felix says, rocking against his palm. Kade grasps the skin hooding his tip, pulling it down to expose that pink, gleaming head. Felix gasps. Kade strokes over the sensitive tip of his cock, again and again, until Felix squirms, dripping onto his fingers, his limbs trembling. "Oh, gods, Kade."

"Tell me what you want," Kade says, dragging his fist down Felix's cock, pumping him slow.

Felix shudders, his back arching, his thighs spreading further, trails of slick streaking down their insides. "Your cock. Please. Fuck me with it."

The catch in his breath makes Kade pulse. He growls, crawling over Felix, chest to back, fitting his cock against Felix's ass. Felix trembles against him, pushes his ass up high to lodge him between his cheeks. And so Kade grinds deeper, against his hole. Felix moans under him. "Here?"

"Fill me, please," Felix gasps. Kade groans, dragging his cock against him to smear it with slick. He reaches down, pushes two fingers into Felix's hot, tight hole, before wiping that slick over his own cock. Then he fits his tip against Felix's hole, feels the way it gives under him, the way Felix stretches to take him, and he fucks in slow and hard, pushing all the way to his hilt.

Felix shudders, his ass snug around Kade. Kade can't think for a full minute. All he feels is the heat of Felix's body, the way Felix rolls his hips back, pushing up at him for more. He shoves in deep, building a momentum that sends Felix's back arching, makes his nails dig into the mattress.

"Kade, Kade," he moans, and when Kade reaches around to touch him, Felix's cock is so hard it has to hurt. *He needs me.* Kade thrusts in deeper, fitting every inch inside, and it feels like he's coming home, when Felix trembles and rides his cock desperately, his breathing short, sharp pants. Kade slings an arm against his sweat-slicked chest, rolls his hips to pull out, then fuck back in. Felix gasps, his cock dripping.

Their bodies meet over and over, Felix tensing beneath him, his cock taut as Kade strokes him again. *He likes this,* Kade thinks, and the thought hurls him over the edge. Pleasure rips through his body like a tidal wave, and he jolts, pumping his cum into Felix.

He tightens his fist around Felix's cock, stroking hard, pushing him over the edge. A ragged cry tears from his omega's throat. Felix *jerks* against him, pulsing, spurting cum all over his mattress, sheets fisted in his hands. Kade presses his forehead to Felix's back, memorizing his broken moan, the way Felix's skin clings to his body, the way they fit so well together.

It's only when he feels himself start to swell that he rolls his hips, to pull away before his knot forms inside Felix. They aren't ready for that yet. They haven't talked in five years.

Felix closes his fingers around Kade's wrist. *Stay.*

And Kade hesitates, his pulse stuttering. Sex with your bonded mate is far different from fucking anyone else. Above their familiarity, above the way their bodies mesh, mating with *his* omega feels like intimacy, like a promise.

I swore an oath to you when we bonded, Kade thinks, closing his eyes. He slides back in, blood pumping into the base of his cock. Felix stretches around him, locked against his body, and he hisses with pleasure. *What did I do wrong? Why did you really leave?*

Beneath him, Felix pants, the blond mop of his hair a mess. Kade breathes in the lavender of his scent, finding the constellation of scars across his shoulders; marks he left years back, when they were younger, and Felix had laughed and threaded his fingers through his hair.

He scoops Felix flush against him, rolling them onto their sides. Felix sighs. Kade buries his nose in his hair, savoring his presence.

He doesn't know if Felix will leave again, and he can't make him stay. Part of him feels like a failure, unable to keep his omega by his side.

His hand slips down toward Felix's wrist, and Kade catches himself. He wants to touch that bonding mark. He shouldn't. They haven't made up yet—this was only something they did to resolve Felix's heat, and the rut it triggered in himself. He thinks about the ring in his jeans pocket, trailing his fingers down Felix's side instead. Then he caresses Felix's abdomen, thinking it's not as intimate as touching Felix's bonding mark, or his chest.

It isn't enough if I say sorry, is it?

Felix keeps silent. They breathe together, their heartbeats synchronizing, Felix a bundle of warmth and comfort in Kade's arms. When his knot recedes, Kade slips out. Felix tips his head back, a tiny smile on his mouth. Kade's breath catches.

This time, when he pulls away, Felix doesn't beg him to stay. He keeps still on his side. Kade pulls his clothes on, the rustle of fabric loud in the room. It smells like sweat and sex in here, like afternoons from their past, and Kade breathes it deep into his lungs. "I'm leaving now," he says.

Felix nods, a bare movement of his head. He looks at the far wall.

When he shuts the front door behind him, it feels as though Kade's leaving a part of himself behind, all over again.

3
Felix

FELIX WAKES the next morning feeling like utter crap.

The curtains are too thin. The heater is cranked too high. The bed sheets are too rough. His ass is sore, and when he relaxes, thick fluid oozes from his hole.

He frowns, reaching down. His heat makes him drip thin, colorless slick, and... The smear on his fingers is a pearly white.

The memories from last night slam back into him: Kade bending him over, his cock thick against Felix's ass, his blunt tip pushing in. Kade, his teeth dragging sharp against Felix's throat. Kade, filling him up, knotting inside him. Felix lingers on the sensations of being stretched, the way Kade fucks him like no one else can.

It makes his body flush with warmth, makes him hard. When he pushes his fingers inside, he finds more of Kade's cum, thick and sticky.

He groans, turning over in his bed, grinding against his sheets. He fucks into his hand, but it's nothing like Kade's callused palm stroking down his cock. He's had other lovers over the years, of course, but none of them had enticed him to return, and Kade... Kade had driven the breath from his lungs, made him come so hard his vision blurred.

Felix climaxes with a hoarse cry, spilling onto his sheets. He huffs into his pillow, wipes his hands off on the bed, and slowly gathers his thoughts.

His heat feels better today. It lingers as a faint warmth in his limbs, a low throb in his belly. Last night had helped, and so had the semen Kade left inside him. The bedroom smells like pine and cedar, like the musk of sex. He smells Kade in the sheets, on his skin. Kade had ground his scent into Felix's cock. Heat creeps up his cheeks. He hadn't thought that Kade would want to mark him again.

Felix pulls himself slowly up in bed. He hadn't seen Kade in years. Kade still looks the same: broad, muscular, his eyes sharp, as though he can see through anything Felix does. As though if he looks hard enough, he'll see why Felix had tried so hard to flee. Felix gulps, reaching for the water glass on his bedside table.

And there, next to the glass, his birth control pills sit on a stack of notepaper. There are three rows of ten white pills, black marks colored onto three plastic bubbles. He hasn't taken them in three days.

"I forgot?" Felix whispers, air punching out of his lungs. He glances down at his belly, thinking about the white streaks on his fingers. Kade had asked about condoms last night, and Felix had been positive he'd taken the pills. All he'd had to do was look at the bedside table, but what had he done instead? He'd gone and spread his legs and Kade had knotted inside him.

What if I'm pregnant? It's not... very possible. He hasn't been pregnant before. And it'll take a week before a test confirms anything. "I can't be pregnant," Felix says, staring down at his abdomen. "I'm not pregnant. The odds are too big."

But it had also been his bondmate inside him. The chances with another alpha would be smaller, but it had been Kade, and Kade had filled him thoroughly last night.

He sets his palm gingerly on his belly, staring down at his pale skin. But it's flat, and there's nothing to say he'll be pregnant for sure. How could he have forgotten the pills? First the suppressants, and now the BC. *I hate my brain so much.*

"I'm not ready for a baby," Felix says, groaning into his hands. "I can't be pregnant."

But what if I am? The thought sends a chill through his stomach. *What if Kade's child is growing inside me?*

The bedroom spins around him. If he gets pregnant... if he's swollen with child and Kade sees... if Kade thinks Felix is back to ruin his life a second time... *That'll be a mess,* Kade had said. Kade had never wanted a child, even from before Felix left.

What if he thinks I tricked him? Felix whimpers, sagging back into his bed. *I can't keep the baby. I can't afford it. And it'll only have one parent. Kade never even agreed to it.*

I should wait, he thinks. *I shouldn't panic. Maybe I'm not pregnant. Maybe... maybe abortion might be an option.*

But it'll also be *Kade's* child, a piece of Kade that'll stay with Felix, when he finally discovers what Felix did five years ago, and turns his back on him for good. Felix bites hard on his lip, cradling his belly. If last night was the final time he slept with Kade, then he can't regret a child. He'll have a piece of Kade with him when he leaves Meadowfall again, someone to remember him by. He'll be gone before Kade even discovers the pregnancy.

Kade will find another mate to replace Felix, someone who won't hurt him again, and he'll have a good life after that.

Felix buries his face in the pillow, his face crumpling.

AN HOUR later, Felix pops a heat suppressant and gets ready for his interview.

At the gas station, the burly alpha manager looks him over, bushy brows drawn low, thick lips pulled in a sneer. But he nods after Felix answers *What work experience do you have?* Rick shoves his hands in his pockets. "You'll do," he says. "You look decent enough. We need to increase the sales here—costs are rising."

It's not like Felix does any good with sales, when his own paintings have been collecting dust, hidden under rags in a spare bedroom. A job is still a job, and it'll give him shelter for now. "When can I start?"

"Tomorrow. Uniforms are in the back," the manager says. "I'll leave the forms here and you'll fill them in. Don't be late. Susan will tell you what to do." He heads out the doors in a rush of bitter-wood, turning past the storefront posters with a glower. *He waddles like a duck,* Felix thinks.

Behind the counter, the beta cashier shrugs, offering a commiserating smile. She smells like fresh-cut grass, her presence calming, and tension drains out of Felix's shoulders when the manager doesn't return.

"It's a lot better when he isn't around," Susan says, tucking wavy auburn hair behind her ear. "And you've been marked, which helps you avoid harassment. All you have to do is renew the scenting."

Felix cringes. He's forgotten about that little bonus, after last night with Kade. It always feels like he's lost his privacy when people can smell who he's slept with. "Really? Is Rick that bad?"

"Sometimes." Susan purses her lips. "I'm not an omega, though. It might be a different case with you—it's just been me and that slacker kid here for a while."

Felix sighs. *That figures.* At least omegas get treated better in Highton, where employers don't demand that he have an alpha partner. Here... he'll figure things out somehow. He doesn't want to depend on Kade or anyone else. Even if he's spent most of his time here *with* Kade. "Have you been working here long?"

"A few years," Susan says, glancing along the low shelves lining the store, filled with muffins, pretzels, notebooks, campfire starters. "I'd like to move out of this place, though. Better opportunities out in Highton."

Of course there are. Felix sighs, hugging

himself. "Same here."

Mostly, though, he just wants to leave Meadowfall. It's a place of mistakes: Kade, and Felix's dad. *Why couldn't you not be an asshole for once, Father? If you weren't, then maybe I could have stayed here.* He picks at the folds of his shirt, touching his belly. *Please don't let me be pregnant. I can't face Kade if I am.*

"New here?" Susan asks.

"I've been away for a while," Felix says, looking up as the doors slide open. A man walks in, covered in road dust and smelling like burnt bark. He glances at Felix, looking him over. Felix sighs, touching his stomach again. *You'll need to eat an extra egg, orange, and a glass of milk to feed the baby,* a pregnancy website said. *It'll cost an extra dollar a day.* "I have to go. See you tomorrow?"

"See you," Susan says, her gaze drifting over to the gas station customer. She gives a small wave. "Take care, okay?"

"I'll try," Felix says.

A WEEK later, he finds out he's pregnant.

Sitting on the toilet, Felix tries not to glance at his phone clock. His heart thuds with dread. He tries playing a game, making a mustached man jump over little red birds. He tries crossword games. He tries connecting jewels in a row, but his stomach twists, and his gaze flickers over and over to the three sticks sitting on the tiled counter, drops of urine scattered between them.

When the timer goes off, jangling and vibrating the phone, he jumps. The phone clatters across the floor. *Damn it,* Felix thinks. *Do something right, for once.*

He swipes his hands on his shorts, gulping, before scooping the phone up, its warm weight comforting in his hands. Then he closes his eyes, trying not to look at the tests while he approaches the counter, letting his hand trail along cool tile to guide him.

I won't be pregnant. I'll open my eyes and it'll just be a hallucination. I can still be honest if I bump into Kade.

But deep down, in his gut, he knows his new alertness isn't normal. That his body's new sensitivity to sounds, to heat and light, aren't happening because he ate something bad.

Felix presses his hand to his belly and opens his eyes.

On all three test kits—white, pastel green, egg-yellow—the results are the same. Two crossed lines replicated across three oval windows. *Plus. Plus. Plus. Congratulations, you're pregnant.*

His fingers dig into his abdomen. He staggers to the wall, glancing down at his belly, disbelieving even now. "No," Felix says. "I'm not."

He gathers the sticks, drops them in the trash, and ties the bag up. Walks out to rid it in the dumpster.

He can't be pregnant. He doesn't even have money to feed himself. He wants to throw up, to hide, to crawl along Kade's body and beg him for a pity fuck.

Felix squashes the thoughts down. It should be easy enough to forget. He's been forgetting everything else. But the same sick dread wells up in his throat like bile, and he doesn't know how he should feel.

A baby brings untold joy to a family, the TV ads jangle in his mind. Felix closes his eyes, thinking about faded posters in the Meadowfall shops, the cheerful advertisements along the town hall. *You'll never regret having yours.*

"I don't have a family," Felix whispers. He has his brother, who flies out of town without notice, and his father, who frowns and wears smiling masks for his business partners. And Kade... he can't tell Kade. How can Kade possibly grin at this news, when Felix had slapped that ring from his hand five years ago?

He wanders into the empty living room, weaving between stacks of cardboard boxes. Felix squeezes himself between a wall and a pile of boxes labeled "dishes". *This isn't happening.*

He stares at the empty corners of the house, at the dirty cream carpet, and touches his belly again. It doesn't feel any different. It's still flat, solid with muscle. There won't be a second pulse beating in him. He'll continue living life as normal, and nothing has changed.

After a while, the pretense fades. Felix sucks in a deep breath, then another. He cradles his phone in his hand, unlocking the screen.

Taylor answers on the second ring, his voice tinted with worry. "Felix?"

"Hey," Felix says, feeling as though all his energy has been wrung out of his body. "Are you busy?"

A pause. If Taylor's answering, then he has time to talk right now. Felix imagines his brother in a safehouse, eyes on the closed doors and curtained windows, leaning back against a wall. Taylor has always been the one their father favors. He does so much more than Felix can, and he's so much more capable, even if he's away most of the time.

"You aren't calling to tell me your pancakes burnt," Taylor says.

Felix sighs. He's only rung his brother twice while he's on a job. "I'm pregnant."

"What?"

"I'm not saying it again."

Taylor's voice sharpens. "Who did it?"

Felix sucks his lip into his mouth, closing his eyes. In his mind, he sees Kade grinning at him. Kade's face, frozen with hurt. "Who else?" he says, and his voice is bitter, sharp-edged. "You bastard, you left me at the pharmacy. He picked me up."

Down the line, Taylor sighs, long-suffering. "I told you, I got an emergency call. You went willingly into it?"

Felix wants to laugh. "I've never been unwilling with him," he says, and to his horror, his voice breaks. "I didn't expect to see him again, Taylor. I didn't... I thought I could go without a heat suppressant for just one night. I didn't... I missed him."

Seven days after that encounter, and Kade's scent is fading from his skin. Felix doesn't like that it's going, but he needs to forget Kade. He's been trying to forget him for an eternity. *So much for that. I guess I have a part of you now.* He dashes the tears away from his eyes.

"Thanks for telling me," Taylor says. Felix imagines him setting a revolver on his thigh, ears pricked for any unnatural sound. Taylor works for a private, secretive organization. And in his new rented house, all Felix has are some paintings and a flimsy contract for a gas station job.

He tugs at the ragged clumps of carpet at his feet. "It was my fault. I forgot the BC pills for three days straight. I don't want to start them again."

Silence stretches between them for a few moments. "You're keeping the baby?"

"Yeah."

"And you're going to tell Kade after this, right?"

"No. I'm leaving Meadowfall as soon as I've got some money saved up."

"Felix. *No.*"

Felix sniffs. "I bankrupted his family, Taylor. He won't want... I can't do this."

His brother exhales heavily down the line. "Okay, we'll set that aside for now. Your scent is going to change. Do you have a suppressant for it?"

Because everyone's going to smell the pregnancy otherwise, especially Kade. Felix can't risk that. But he can't deal with remembering so many things, either. He covers his face. "More pills? I can't keep track of all of them, Taylor."

"Get a pill dispenser. It's easy. You know what, go to my place. I've got some lying around. The scent suppressants are in the study. Second drawer in the desk. I've labeled them."

Felix sighs. "How are we both omega and you're so much better at life?"

Taylor pauses, contemplative. "I'm not trying to forget things, Felix."

He flinches.

"Look, while you're over at my place, grab some cash. You know the safe combination."

"Yeah. But I can't—"

"You need to eat better. You know that."

Felix pushes his forehead against the wall, closing his eyes. "I'm supposed to invite you over to my new place for dinner, not have you pay for everything."

"Take the money," Taylor says. "It's not doing anything sitting in a safe."

"I love you and hate you at the same time."

"That's okay. But remember to feed yourself and the baby. I can't believe I'm going to be an uncle!"

"I'm going to be a father," Felix says, groaning. It sounds like a humongous mountain he doesn't know how to climb. "I'm not dad material."

"You'll be a good one," Taylor says, his tone gentle. Felix closes his eyes, knowing his brother means *You'll be a better dad than our father is.*

"Thanks," he mumbles, looking back down at his stomach. He imagines the little cluster of cells making its way through his body, attaching itself to him. The embryo that's half him and half Kade, and he wishes he had Kade's arms around him right now, pulling him close. Wishes he could hear Kade say *I'll help you through this.*

"I've got to go," Taylor says, his voice hushed. "Take care, okay?"

Felix gulps. "Will do."

The line cuts off. Felix stares at his phone, his cheeks wet. Slowly, he peels himself off the floor, wiping his face. He has goals now. A baby to care for. He can't disappoint his child, too.

4
Kade

THE BIKE purrs beneath him, a docile, humming beast. Kade turns off the highway, squeezing the brakes to slow down. Next to him, the beginnings of rush-hour traffic cluster at the stoplight, a cacophony of engines growling around him. He flares his nostrils, huffing to rid the oily exhaust fumes in his nose.

It's been a week since he saw Felix. A week since he last got any decent sleep, and it makes him uneasy, not knowing when Felix will leave Meadowfall again. He doesn't know what Felix thinks of him, doesn't think he should have left, that night. What alpha sleeps with his bondmate and leaves him alone in bed after?

He rubs the scar on his wrist, thinking about Felix covered in his scent. It's been years, but the idea of Felix as his gives him comfort, like a missing puzzle piece in his life settling back into place.

Clearly, Felix hadn't wanted him to stay the night. Kade had assumed too much years ago, thought he'd known Felix thoroughly, when he hadn't. He doesn't even know where Felix is right now. Which is how Felix meant it to be, if he's not saying anything about meeting again.

Kade sighs, glancing up when the stoplight changes to green. On the dashboard of his bike, the fuel light comes on, glowing orange. He flicks his turn signal to change lanes, before rolling into the nearest gas station.

He smells that trace of lavender again, faint as a strand of hair lost on the sheets. He has to get home, pull out the laptop and finish debugging his work's new application. But he knows that scent. *Felix.*

He rides between the filling stations, sniffing. No blonds next to the cars, none lingering outside the convenience store. Kade parks the bike by the door, shuts off the ignition, and strides up, pulse thumping. He can't possibly expect to see Felix, can't expect Felix to want to see him again. That had been just a fling.

The doors hiss open, but the lavender scent lingers, like Felix had visited briefly and left traces of his presence.

"You don't have to do much with the credit cards," a female voice says. "The important thing is that we only take these few, and they're only for purchases ten dollars or more."

"What if they only have a different card?" another voice asks, soft and familiar. It settles the nervous patter of Kade's heart, even before he glimpses the man behind the counter, the way his green eyes widen.

Kade's pulse hammers to life. He sees only Felix, the pink of his lips, the point of his chin, the way his maroon uniform sags loosely around his shoulders. Felix's throat works. He opens his mouth but doesn't say anything, and it feels like the first time Kade finds him after five lonely years, like an oasis in a desert.

The woman next to Felix looks between them, and her eyebrows rise. "Oh."

Felix's gaze drops to Kade's jacket, his jeans, and he's gulping, anchoring his eyes on the register. "The credit cards, Susan. Could you explain it again?"

Susan glances at Kade, then looks back down at the register. "If they don't have a credit card..."

Kade wanders around the store, squeezing between the narrow aisles. It feels as though the place was built for kids, or people without broad shoulders. The chip packets rustle against his elbows, and the price-tagged ends of product hooks reach out to gouge his skin. He squeezes through the shelves, grabs a bottle of soda from the fridges, and heads back to the counter.

"Want to practice ringing it up?" Susan asks.

Felix gulps. Kade can't help smirking a little, at the way things have worked out. Even if he doesn't have Felix back, his bondmate still has to talk to him, and it's a relief after days of not hearing his voice.

"Hello," Felix chirps, in that high, fake tone of his. "How's your day?"

"Better," Kade says, sniffing at him again. It's only then that the thrill of seeing Felix wears off, and he realizes: "Your smell is gone." It feels damn weird, only smelling a fraction of Felix's scent, when the last days of his heat should be intensifying it. Or was he on the tail end of his heat when Kade met him?

Felix's shoulders tense. "I thought it would be better not to have a scent," he says, beeping the soda with a handheld scanner. His eyes lock on the register. "Is that all for you?"

It feels wrong, like Felix is avoiding him somehow. Kade bristles. "No," he says. "There's more."

Forest-green eyes flicker up to his, wary. Kade studies the brittle way Felix holds himself, the mask of his face. It's not something Kade should mention at his workplace. "How can I help you?" Felix asks, strained.

"When do you get off work?" Kade says, because to hell with workplace boundaries. Felix is—was—his bondmate.

Felix opens his mouth, hesitating.

A guy steps through the doors with a swagger, short with a gray mustache, his shirt stretched over his pot-belly. An alpha, but a lesser one, even lower-ranked than Kade is in this town. He smells like bitter-wood, like decay. Kade steps instinctively between him and Felix.

The man sniffs, beady eyes snapping toward the counter. "You," he says, stepping around Kade to jerk his chin at Felix. "Where's your smell?"

Felix stares. The other cashier frowns, and Kade's mouth twitches. *Guy's a damn asshole.*

"Suppressed it," Felix says, his expression full of thinly-veiled distaste. "Sir."

He's your boss? How dare he talk down to you?

"I hired you because you're an omega," the man says, mustache quivering. "But at least smell like something. Where's your alpha, huh?"

"Here," Kade snarls, heat surging up through his chest. *How dare you threaten my omega?* He rounds on the manager, pulling his shoulders back, baring his teeth.

The man's eyes widen. He backs away, pasting on a cajoling smile. "Come on, now. He's just an omega."

"He's mine," Kade says, advancing on him. The manager holds his hands up, still smiling. Kade wants to punch him in the jaw. "I mark him however I want."

The moment it leaves his lips, he knows the reaction Felix will have: glowering, frowning. They aren't together anymore. Kade doesn't have the right to even lie about him.

But pink sweeps up Felix's neck. Kade stares. *What?*

Kade fishes some change from his pocket, dropping it into Felix's outstretched palm. His fingertips skim Felix's skin, sending a thrill down his nerves.

Felix shivers. He counts the coins, drops them in the register, then presses a nickel of change into Kade's palm. His fingers linger warm against Kade's skin. "Four," Felix says, glancing at the clock just above the counter. "Thank you."

"You know how to keep him disciplined, of course," the manager says behind Kade. "He's a rude one. I almost regret hiring him."

Kade whirs on the manager, glaring, and the other alpha backs down, lowering his stare.

"Touch him, and I'll break your neck," Kade growls. He stalks out the door, the manager's stare an itch on his skin.

HE SPENDS the next hour regretting his words. Felix has always let him stake his claim in front of the other alphas, because that's what it is—protection. A defense mechanism to stop people from pestering them. Now, Kade isn't sure. They aren't together anymore, and maybe Felix wouldn't be okay with him saying that.

Once he refuels the bike, he rides down the street, taking a long loop to kill the minutes. His uncertainty dulls along the way; Felix agreed to meet with him. It's more time together, and Kade will gladly accept it.

Some pair we are, he thinks, tipping his head back to face the cloudless sky. *I'm not in control at all.*

By the time he pulls back into the gas station, the sun has sunken lower, and more cars have pulled up to the pumps. Kade waits by the side of the convenience store, looking up when Felix rounds the corner, stormy green eyes searching him out. Kade hands the spare helmet over. "Did he harass you again?"

Felix shrugs, turning the helmet around in his hands. But he keeps his eyes down, looking at the pavement. "It went okay."

"About earlier," Kade says, his pulse thudding. "I was just talking. About the alpha thing."

A wave of pink creeps up Felix's neck. *You never got off on that before.* They didn't have a regular alpha-omega bond. Never had.

And Felix's mouth pulls up in a tiny smile. "I understand. But don't do that again. We're not..."

Not bonded anymore.

Kade swallows, his heart aching. "Yeah, sure."

They stand together, traffic rolling down the streets around them, not looking at each other.

"Want a ride?" Kade asks. He remembers a week ago, and where that question had led. Heat trickles through his torso.

Something eases between them when Felix grins again, warmth flickering in his gaze. He doesn't look directly at Kade, and his smile doesn't reach his eyes, but he's staying around, and he's still holding on to the helmet. "Actually, I need to get to the thrift store, if that's okay. I ran out of time before my shift started."

"Sure. Which one?" Kade buckles his helmet. Felix slides onto the seat behind him, thighs bumping against Kade's. His body hums.

"Rosie's," Felix says. "It's five blocks down this street, on the left."

"Okay." Kade twists the key. "Ready?"

"Yeah."

Felix's heat pulls close as they join the traffic, a familiar, soothing warmth. Felix touches his fingers to Kade's waist. Then his hand curves against Kade's side, and Kade shouldn't feel this thrilled. He can't help it, though, when Felix squeezes his hip and his helmet bumps into Kade's, as though he's leaning in. As though he wants Kade closer.

He's half-hard when they reach the thrift store. They've had sex once, and Kade can't stop thinking about pinning him against a wall, kissing him senseless. He wants to mark Felix again, so he doesn't smell like *nothing*.

"I'll find my way home from here," Felix says, slipping off the pillion seat. "Thanks."

An icy jolt skims down Kade's spine. He's not leaving this soon. "I'm coming in with you."

Felix's eyes flicker up to meet his, forest-green and surprised. He sets the helmet down on the seat. "You really don't have to."

But Kade's swinging his leg off the bike, tucking his own helmet into the trunk. "I'll head in and look around. Friend's birthday coming up."

Which is a lie, but he's learned enough from Felix to manage it. Sometimes, he doesn't know if his tells originated from himself, or if they're habits he's picked up from Felix since their early years. At thirty, they seem so old, now.

Felix looks away, shrugging. "Fine, I guess."

It isn't fine, though. Felix holds his arms close, as though shrinking from everything else. Kade thinks about pulling off his own jacket and setting it over Felix's shoulders, but hesitates. He doesn't want the jacket shrugged off, slapped away.

So he tucks his hands in his pockets, following Felix into the store. Inside, the fluorescent lights shine down on cramped, circular clothes racks, shirts and sweaters and pants jammed together. Sunlight slants through the glass door, lighting books on the far wall. A jumble of picture frames, bowls, and lamps cluster on the shelves to the sides.

Felix glances over, as though wary that Kade would judge him. Kade shrugs. He's been to thrift stores more often than he'd like, himself. "What do you need?" Kade asks.

"Sweaters, I guess. And some shirts."

Felix pulls shirts off the racks at random. First a lumpy, knitted sweater, then a thin T-shirt three sizes too big for himself. He checks their price tags, then slings both over his shoulder, flipping through the rack. Once, he pauses at a white button-down shirt that would fit him perfectly, but he glances at the price tag, and passes.

"You're changing your style?" Kade asks. He's never seen Felix wear anything but fitting clothes; pants that cling to his legs, shirts that hug his chest.

Felix looks away, his mouth pulling into a tight line. "Yeah."

"Why?"

"No reason." Felix steps over to the next rack, extracting a collared shirt, his eyes anchored on the clothes. It feels like a lie.

"You could just borrow mine," Kade says, and swears inwardly. It's not like Felix wants anything to do with him.

Felix flips through the clothes faster, his neck turning pink."You should go."

"You're not... you don't even look excited about these." Kade frowns. Does Felix... like that idea? Wearing Kade's clothes? Because the thought of Felix in *his* shirts sure as hell makes him want to mark his omega. Hold him close. It would make some of this right again.

While Felix sifts through the clothes, Kade returns to the previous rack, pulling out the button-down shirt Felix paused at. *Five bucks. You're not spending this money on yourself?*

When he wanders back to Felix, his

bondmate has a stack of lumpy, too-large shirts draped over his shoulder, like a mountain about to topple off. Kade thinks about the oversized work shirt Felix wore at the gas station, the way he'd blushed when Kade claimed him in front of the manager.

It doesn't make sense next to his indifference, the way he refused to look at Kade while he worked. "Something happened?" Kade asks. "You don't look okay."

Felix's bottom lip trembles, and tears well in his eyes. "I'm fine."

"Bullshit," Kade says, but he's stepping over, slipping his arms around his bondmate's narrow back, pulling him against his chest.

The pile of clothes on Felix's shoulder tips sideways, spilling onto the floor in a ragged heap. Felix sucks in a shuddering breath against Kade's collarbone, his hands fisting in his shirt. Kade holds him close, as though if he doesn't, Felix will slip away like a leaf on the wind.

5
Felix

ALL DAY, the secret has built in Felix's chest. *I'm pregnant. I'm carrying Kade's child. Kade doesn't know.* Even when he tries to quell those thoughts, they bubble up in his mind, lurking in the background. *What will he say? Will he think I tricked him?*

If he's hiding the pregnancy, he'll have to start now, not months from now, when his belly swells and he'll have to change his clothes to fit. So he pulls the baggiest shirts from the thrift store racks, flipping through them for both sweaters and thin shirts. His brother's money sits heavy in his wallet. *I have no way to pay you back right now.*

Taylor had sent a text after the call. *Promise me you're going to eat well.*

It means setting aside some money for the child, buying groceries other than frozen pizzas, making sure he takes the scent suppressants in the mornings. Felix wants to drink, to forget, but he can't do that to his—their—child. So he curls in on himself, the weight of all those words compressing his heart.

Then Kade had said "You don't look okay," and of course he doesn't look okay. He isn't okay.

He doesn't want to be back in Meadowfall, doesn't want to be pregnant, doesn't want to be next to Kade when Kade can say *You expect me to trust you again, after you embarrassed me?* and Felix has never felt more alone in his life.

His vision blurs before he knows it, a hole in his chest gaping open. He needs to get out of this place, needs to not let Kade see him break like this. But he can't move, can't see the floor to step away, and Kade's in front of him, pulling him close, tucking Felix's head under his chin.

Felix chokes on his breath, shaking. *Why are you doing this? We're not back together and you don't owe me anything.* But he sucks in a breath, and all he smells is cedar and pine and *Kade.*

Kade's arms slip around him, strong and warm, holding him together like a cocoon. It feels like all the other times Kade has held him—when he failed his math classes, when the bullies taunted him, when he said *I promise to be yours.* Felix can't hope for them to return to that time.

The whimpers he hears don't sound like his own. He struggles to breathe, thinking about the bundle of life growing inside him, and he aches to say *I'm pregnant. It's ours.* But Kade won't want the child—never wanted to have a child—and Felix is entirely responsible for this.

He presses his face into Kade's shirt, sobbing until the wave of self-pity passes. Kade strokes a soothing hand down his back, and Felix shakes harder, knowing Kade will reject him if he finds out. He doesn't want to lose this.

Kade's arms tighten around him.

When Felix gathers himself back together, he

feels wrung out, hollow. His nose has stopped, his eyes still prickling.

"Better?" Kade murmurs. His nose brushes through Felix's hair, lips trailing against Felix's forehead. Felix shivers.

"Yeah," he croaks. "Sorry."

"You gonna tell me what's wrong?" Kade's breath feathers through his hair, damp and warm.

Felix shakes his head. "It's nothing."

Kade snorts. "Nothing, huh?"

But his arms curl around Felix, pulling him against his strong chest. Felix releases a shuddering breath. "I'm fine." *I will be fine.*

Kade threads his fingers through Felix's hair, massaging his scalp with slow, careful strokes. Felix's eyelids flutter shut. He tilts his head into Kade's touch, luxuriating in it.

He hasn't had this in a while. No one touches—knows—him like Kade does, and he's comfortable, safe in his alpha's arms.

"Shop's closing," a man's voice calls from the other side of the store. "Take your necking elsewhere."

Felix jerks away from Kade, heat creeping up his cheeks. That hadn't been anything important. Just a hug. But Kade's touch had sent a thrill through his body, just like back at the gas station, when Kade had said *He's mine.*

Felix steps away, looking down when his foot catches in a pile of clothes. They fell off his shoulder when Kade hugged him.

"We'll go somewhere else if you don't have enough," Kade says.

Felix shakes his head. "That's plenty."

The man at the counter—omega, by his apple blossom scent—scans the tags on Felix's clothes, before bundling them into a large plastic bag. "That'll be forty-seven fifty, sir."

Felix peels his wallet open. Kade's gaze prickles along his skin, and he tries to ignore it, pulling crisp ten-dollar bills out, the smallest denominations he found in Taylor's safe. *You'd better take a thousand at least,* Taylor had texted. Felix had compromised and withdrawn five hundred dollars.

A minute later, they step out of the shop into the cool evening air. Felix blinks at the royal-blue sky, and the streaks of pink-edged clouds floating overhead. "I didn't think it was this late."

Kade hands the spare helmet over. "You took your time picking clothes." After a pause, he asks, "That enough for you? You weren't ready to leave."

Felix thinks about the tiny paycheck he'll receive for this week, and shrugs. "I'll get more next week," he says. "This is enough for now."

Kade studies him with narrowed eyes. "Tell me if you need a ride anywhere."

"I shouldn't. I've been imposing." But the offer makes his pulse quicken anyway. He hadn't thought Kade would want to see him again.

Kade clicks his tongue. "Like a ride is imposing."

It reminds him of the last time he'd had a ride, and heat slips down his body. He doesn't need that to happen again. He's gotten into enough trouble because that had been *just one ride.* And now he's pregnant.

He tugs his helmet on, then climbs onto the bike behind Kade, swallowing when their thighs bump. He wants more of that warmth. It doesn't seem like enough, now that Kade has touched him and held him. Kade's woodsy, musky scent steals into his nose. The plastic bag of clothes sits bulky and rustling between them, pressing Felix back against the motorbike trunk.

At least I can't rub up against you this way.

The ride home passes too quickly. He leaves the visor open, breathing in the wisps of Kade's scent carrying into his helmet. Felix sags when they pull into the driveway of his house, its windows dark, the stairs leading up his porch warped and ugly. He slides off the bike with a sigh. "Thanks for the ride."

"Do you still have my number?" Kade's eyes linger on his face, then dart down his body, pausing at the bag of clothes at his feet.

Felix bites his lip. He'd etched Kade's cellphone number into his mind, back when he was still contemplating a call. He'd hit the End Call button before he could confess what he'd done. Now, with Kade's gaze on him, he pulls out his phone, handing it over.

Kade studies the painting on the home screen—a red-roofed cottage in the countryside, surrounded by trees. They'd talked about a home countless times in the past, with a vegetable garden and birch trees on the edges of the property, and a wooden bridge arching over a stream.

"I've been meaning to put that one on sale," Felix says. "Hopefully it'll land a buyer."

"You're not keeping it?" Kade pulls up the

phone contacts screen, tapping out his name and number—still the same.

"I should... let go of some things." Felix shrugs. "I've got too many paintings lying around."

Kade stares at the cottage again, then hands the phone back. "They should sell for a lot. You're good."

Felix's heart flutters. He tries not to look at the bonding mark on Kade's wrist. There's only one there, left from two decades ago. "It doesn't matter if I'm good. They're not selling, and I need the money."

"People knew you in Highton. Your work will probably sell if you get them some exposure."

Felix sighs. It's not as though he hasn't thought about it. "It's difficult. There are a million artists out there."

"But—"

"You should be getting home," he says, glancing at the inky sky. The streetlights have been on since they pulled in, and a wintry chill creeps up his sleeves, marching goosebumps across his skin. "It's late."

Kade sighs. He reaches slowly for the ignition, his gaze still on Felix. "Fine. See you around?"

"I guess." Felix gathers his bag of clothes in his arms, skirting around the bike as it roars to life. Kade backs out of the driveway, waving.

Felix waves back. The moment Kade rides down the street, Felix slips into the house, shutting the door behind himself.

He drops the bag of clothes on the floor.

Leans against the door, one hand coming up to cradle his belly. There's a baby in there. His child.

"I guess I should say hi at some point," Felix murmurs, pulling his shirt up. His belly is still flat, still pale. "I'm your dad."

His breath snags. He'll be a father. He'll be a dad, and he hasn't thought about it, ever since he left Kade five years ago. Felix can't imagine himself with a tiny child, holding one, having a person who won't remember him for all his mistakes.

It feels like relief, fathering a child who won't judge him. His throat tightens. "I think I'm really glad to have you," Felix says, rubbing a thumb over his skin. It feels like a second chance to make things right. "I'll do my best for you."

And he will.

6
Kade

"WANT A painting, Mom?" Kade asks three days later, looking up from his bowl of leek and potato soup. "I heard there's some for sale."

Across the tiny square table, his mother raises her eyebrows, surveying the carved plates hanging on the kitchen walls. Her red-brown eyes sparkle. "We might have space. Are they watercolors?"

"Yeah. Landscapes."

"Really? You know I'll always have space for those." She glances out the kitchen doorway, where framed paintings line the foyer and hall. "Do you know the artist? We could visit and look at some."

"Yeah. I know him." Kade swallows. He shouldn't be nervous about telling his mom, when she's listened to him vent in the past. But mentioning his bondmate feels like picking an old wound open. "Actually... It's Felix. He's back and selling his watercolors."

To ease the ache in his chest, he looks at the polished teak counters, the way his mom has scrubbed them until they shine. The edges of the fridge gleam, and the stovetop shines in the sunlight.

They've done well ever since the bankruptcy. This house is halfway paid off, and they have hot meals in their stomachs and laughter around the table. Most of his savings had gone into helping his parents recover. While he and his brothers were working extra jobs, his dad had passed away. Then Chris and Sam had moved out of Meadowfall, leaving his mom with just him for support. Kade and his mother have been recovering, though, just like they've recovered from almost everything else.

"Felix? I thought you said he was in Highton. When did he get back?"

Kade shrugs, scooping soup into his mouth. "He moved back about a week ago. I don't think he's unpacked yet."

"That's nice. Right?" A line grows on her brow. When Kade doesn't answer, she asks, "Are you upset?"

I don't know. Kade stirs the soup in his bowl, thinking about that first night, then the time he's spent lying awake in bed since, wondering if Felix will disappear from his life again. That's not within his control. "Maybe."

Mom leans in, her voice hushed. "Is he... with anyone else?"

He chuckles then, low and unexpectedly bitter. Felix has no new markings, but his lavender scent had also faded. There's not much Kade discerned other than there's only one scar on his wrist. "I don't know. Don't think so."

"I'm sorry," she says. "But that means there's hope, right?"

"Guess so." He sighs, lifting his soup bowl to drain it. *Can't do anything right now.* "He's working at the gas station just off the 95."

"At least you'll get a chance to see him. Does he want to be friends?"

"Maybe. I gave him my number." Kade stands to rinse their bowls at the sink. "Gotta go, though. Working at the office today. Damn debugging fixes."

"If Felix is still selling those paintings, I'd love to see them," she says, getting to her feet. "And... well, I hope you'll be able to right things with him somehow."

Kade shrugs. When he turns, his mother wraps her arms around him. He stoops to return the hug, breathing in the reassuring lilac scent of her hair. The silvery strands glint in the sunlight, tucked between cinnamon-brown.

"Do tell him that he's welcome here anytime," she says. "I just hope he's doing well."

"I will." The thought of Felix stepping through this house, looking with awe at the paintings on the walls, cheers Kade up. He kisses his mother on the cheek, turning to leave. The bike needs a fill-up; he'll take a detour there. The thought shouldn't make his stomach flip, should it?

HE FINDS Felix alone at the register, his lavender scent still oddly muted. Felix's eyes brighten when Kade steps in, his mouth pulling into a tiny smile. "Hello."

"You doing okay?" Kade asks, glancing over his uniform. No bruises on his arms, no markings. What little he can smell of the lavender is untarnished, and it sends a spark of triumph roaring through his chest.

"Not too bad," Felix says. He lowers his gaze, tidying a stack of rubber bands so they fall into a neat circle.

Kade looks around. "No one else on this shift?"

"It's just me right now." Felix straightens the stationery around the register. "I guess they trust me enough to run this place for a few hours."

"You'll do fine," Kade says. Felix's ears turn pink, and he smiles, looking away. Kade's pulse quickens. "I told my mom about your paintings." He wanders over to a shelf, picking up a bag of chips. It crinkles in his hand, lightweight and overpriced, but it's a reason to stop by instead of going to the office. "She likes them."

"She used to," Felix says. After a pause, he asks, "How is she?"

"Not bad. We moved. Got a new house and all that." And it's not like Felix wants to know, but Kade says, "Better than before."

Felix sighs deeply, his shoulders relaxing. "I'm glad to hear that."

Kade shrugs. It's not as though Felix knows anything about their difficulties, anyway. He'd left before most of it happened. "What about you? How was Highton?"

"Not bad, I guess." Felix rubs his arm, his loose shirt wrinkling. "The paintings sold well for a while. I had a loft apartment. It was the prettiest place—large windows, sheer curtains. I—I think you'd have liked to see it."

Felix doesn't say *It's just like what we talked*

about in the past, for our own home, but Kade hears it, hears the regret echoing between them.

And he shouldn't be asking, when they're no longer lovers, but he wants to hear about those years Felix spent in Highton. He wants to know if Felix missed him. "What else did you like about it?"

"The kitchen. It was wide and open. It had an island counter, one of those nice ones you see in catalogs, you know? With the row of hanging lamps in the middle, a silver fridge, and racks on the walls for the spatulas... And the ceilings were so high. It felt like I was living in a cathedral, almost. When the breeze blew in, the curtains fluttered in the living room, and I... It was lovely."

Felix looks away. Kade stares at the chips in his hands. Classic ruffle cut. Reduced sodium.

Chips are one thing, but a loft like that? He's got a decent job, but he's never truly had enough to pay for the sort of houses they discussed. At least, not yet. *Did you find someone who can buy you that?* Kade swallows. The ring sits warm against his chest, and he reaches up, touching it through his shirt. "So why'd you come back?"

Felix purses his lips. His eyes dart up to Kade's, then away. "I wasn't doing that well. Like I said, the paintings stopped selling."

Kade sighs. Felix has all the talent to be successful. "Was that all you did? Selling paintings?"

Felix's green eyes sweep over the store, and he turns his hands, palms facing up. "For a while, yes. I should be better at selling my things. It just... didn't work out, somehow. Maybe I didn't have enough connections."

"But your dad knows people, doesn't he?"

Felix winces. "I'd rather not talk to them, if I can."

Kade remembers Felix's dad. Tall, imposing, never smiling. Felix rarely brought Kade to his family home, and the times he did, they were careful to avoid the grand rooms in the mansion, full of sprawling tables and arched hallways. Lots of voices had come from their closed doors, polite, quiet laughter that spoke of formal business meetings.

"Have you listed them on the internet?" Kade asks. "Auction sites, craft sites, that sort of thing?"

Felix looks at the register. "I'm not so great with those."

"I can help," Kade says before he thinks about it. "Shouldn't be difficult for me."

Felix bites his lip, uncertain. Kade thinks about his shabby new house, the falling-apart porch, and Felix in this gas station job. He can't afford a better place like that. And as his bondmate, Kade wants to help somehow. Even if they aren't building a home together. Felix sneaks a glance at him. "If it isn't inconvenient, I'd... appreciate it."

Kade keeps his expression calm, even though his pulse shoots all the way to sixty miles an hour. "When are you off?"

"This Saturday. Anytime is fine, I guess."

"9 AM?"

"Sure. I, uh, kind of don't have a computer. I sold mine." Felix blushes.

Kade shrugs. "It's fine. I've got a couple from my job."

Felix smiles shyly, stretching a rubber band between his fingers. "Still programming?"

"Yeah. I might be getting a promotion soon." He's been taking on new projects since he finished debugging that damn app, and it's nice, having a pile of jobs at work so he isn't daydreaming about Felix.

"Really?" Felix's grin widens. "I'm glad."

"Yeah, well." *I'd be happier if we were back together.* But he won't say no to seeing Felix smile. He's gone without it for too long, and it sends a slow, joyful warmth curling through his veins. "You've unpacked, right?"

"Some." Felix winces. "I'll try to get a table set up. Or there's the bed, I guess. That functions as a table, right?"

Kade snorts, turning the packet of chips in his hands. "I don't work on beds."

A crimson tint sweeps up Felix's cheeks. Kade is suddenly aware of what he's thinking, about what they do on beds instead. They've spent years of their history pressed together behind closed doors, sweat soaking into worn mattresses. "I'm sure you don't," Felix says. "You'd save your bed for more... suitable things."

"Like what?" Kade's voice dips, a kindling heat sinking down his body, gathering at his groin. He wants Felix pinned beneath him again, wants to smell the full weight of Felix's scent, the musk of his arousal. "You know what I use my bed for?"

Green eyes darken. Felix's gaze coasts down Kade's body, lingering on his chest, his arms, his hips. Kade feels himself grow full in response, his pants stretching tight, and how did that happen, when he hasn't moved from the convenience store racks, the packet of chips still in his hand?

Across the counter, Felix shifts as though his pants are too tight. "I'm sure you could enlighten me," he croaks. "About your bed."

Kade's throat goes sandpaper-dry. He thinks about Felix arched under him, sees the way Felix's nostrils flare to catch his scent, the way he reaches down to adjust his pants. Kade can't help sliding a hand down his abs, tracing a finger along the hard line at his groin, from base to tip.

Felix groans. "Don't do that."

"Why?" Kade steps closer, closing the distance between them. Felix's gaze clings to him, to the bulge in his pants. "I'm getting comfortable."

Felix drags his eyes away, squirming. And there, just beneath the trace of lavender, Kade smells his musk. "We shouldn't.... shouldn't be talking about this."

"You're hard," Kade murmurs, watching as Felix's throat works. More quietly, "And I can fuck you up against the wall."

Felix squeezes his eyes shut, his fingertips whitening against the counter. "Kade, please."

Kade almost tastes the tang of his arousal. His own cock swells, and he almost crushes the bag of chips in his hand, setting it roughly on the counter. "You sell lube in this store?"

"I..." Felix bites down on his lip, turning it red. "I'll look for it."

And he turns, circling out from behind the counter, a hard line at the front of his pants. Kade trails behind him through the shelves, breathing in his musk, and he almost can't wait for the weekend. Felix walks down one aisle, then the next. Kade's attention snags on the jeans of his pants, the way it hugs the curve of his ass.

"Here," Felix says, bending to snatch a bottle off a lower shelf. Kade keeps his arms to his side, fighting down the urge to grab his hips, to press up against him, let his omega feel his cock.

Felix sets the bottle in Kade's hand when he straightens, fingertips caressing his palm. An electric sizzle shoots under Kade's skin, and Felix shivers. Kade snags his wrist. "Wait," he says. "You're gonna just smell like sex right now."

Felix squeezes his eyes shut, sucking in a shaky breath. "Damn it. That bastard's going to come in and check on me."

Bottle in hand, Kade rubs their wrists together, scent glands brushing, before dragging his wrist just under Felix's jaw. Then, along the sides of his neck and down his shirt. Felix gulps. Kade reaches lower, grinding his wrist against the front of Felix's pants, just over his cock. Felix flushes a deep shade of scarlet, rocking up against his wrist. He's so hard behind his pants. Kade wants to push him up against the shelves.

Mine, he wants to growl. He pulls his wrist away, and Felix tries to follow with his hips.

"I'll find a use for this," Kade says, shaking the lube.

Felix pants, pupils blown. "Is there.... anything else you need?"

"Just this," Kade says, following him back to the counter. "And the chips." *And you.*

Felix scans the lube and chips with trembling hands. His breaths puff short and quick. Something in Kade's chest settles, seeing his omega this aroused all because of *him*. It's as though their past doesn't matter.

"Six-eighty," Felix says, glancing at the register. "Do you need a bag?"

"Nah." Kade drops a few notes into his hand, fingertips brushing against Felix's palm. They both shiver at the contact. "Gotta find a use for the lube, though. See you Saturday."

Felix gulps. He sets the change in Kade's palm, his fingers lingering. Felix drags his gaze away. "Okay. See you then."

Something must be going right, if Kade's got Felix agreeing to see him again. He walks out of the store, his scent strong on his omega. Maybe Felix doesn't find him a disappointment. Maybe they can repair their relationship. Maybe things will work out this time.

7
Felix

THE STORE smells like Kade. Felix smells like him, too, but it isn't as noticeable as the musk lingering between the shelves, and at the counter where Kade had grown hard. All Felix had wanted was to drop to his knees and drag Kade's pants down.

It's not right that his instincts scream to please Kade, to rub himself against his alpha. In Highton, there had been groups protesting along the streets about omega rights. Felix knows the chants: *Pay us equally. We have choices too. Omegas do not need an alpha.*

But it's not that between Kade and himself. He wants to screw Kade senseless because it's always been the two of them, and Felix hadn't known a time when Kade hadn't been by his side, offering his protection and his body.

Kade has always been there, and how does Felix repay it? He ruins Kade's life.

His cock throbs uncomfortably in his pants. He looks at his hands, throat dry, needing release. So he forces the thoughts out of his mind, stepping out around the counter, grabbing a set of newspapers to fan the scents out the door. Some of the people at the filling stations look over.

He thinks about the baby instead, the minuscule ball of cells growing inside him. It's been two weeks since that first night. A week since the baby fastened itself inside his body, and he still can't believe that there's another life inside him, that part of Kade is in his belly.

If Kade found out... He would narrow his eyes. He would say, *You told me you were on BC. Why did you lie? Are you using me again?* Felix winces. It hadn't been a lie. If he can forget his birth control pills, why can't he forget about the baby?

Years ago, Kade had told him, *I don't think we're suited for kids.*

"It's really not your fault," Felix murmurs at his abdomen, touching it. Somewhere in there, his baby needs love. Felix will be damned before he neglects his own child. "I promise to love you."

Ten minutes later, he steps outside. He sucks in a deep breath, then steps back into the store. It smells vaguely like cedar and pine now, a little like musk, as though a couple of horny teenagers had loitered for a while.

At the door, he tries swinging his arms like a windmill, cycling the old air out of the store. Three minutes in, Susan walks in from the side.

Felix jumps, heat crawling up his cheeks. "Sorry. I didn't think you'd be early."

She raises her eyebrows, looking pointedly at his arms. "The bus was earlier than usual. What were you doing? Exercising?"

What do I say? "Yes? I... thought it would be an opportunity to stretch."

But Susan lifts her chin, sniffing. "Smells like

sex in here."

Felix's cheeks burn. "It was two teenagers," he says. "A couple of boys."

"Smells kind of familiar." Susan heads to the back room, her nostrils flared. Felix looks down the front of his pants. *At least it's not obvious now.* When Susan pops back out, she says, "I've never seen anyone hook up in the store, and I've been here four years. It almost... Your alpha didn't visit, did he? You smell like an alpha."

Shit. Felix gulps, thinking about Kade's finger tracing down his jeans. That was all it had taken. Kade had rubbed his wrist on him for half a minute, but they'd both been hard by then, and smelling enough to fill the store with musk. "Uh."

"There's a back room, you know," Susan says, her eyes twinkling. She sobers a moment later. "I don't think I need to warn you about Rick, though."

Felix remembers the manager's waddle, shaking his head. "I'd really rather not get in trouble with him." He rubs his arms, suddenly missing Kade, the way he'd snarled at Felix's boss. "But Kade—that alpha—he's... not really mine. Just... so you know."

It hurts to say it.

Susan cocks her head. "He isn't? I thought... When he came in here the other day and snapped at Rick, you didn't say anything."

He'd been too surprised that Kade would even defend him. "It felt safer not to."

"Yeah, I understand." Susan's gaze falls to Felix's wrist, where the bonding scar is. He holds himself still, fighting his instincts to hide it. But

Susan steps closer, sniffing again.

Felix realizes what it must look like then—the scar means he's bonded, and he smells like an alpha he says isn't his. He cringes. "Don't judge me, okay? Kade and I... it's complicated."

"A good sort of complicated, or a bad sort?"

He glances down at his belly. "I don't know."

"Oh, honey." Susan sets a gentle hand on his arm. "I'm here if you ever need to talk, okay?"

Felix relaxes, the tension in his shoulders seeping away. They haven't known each other long, but it's comforting to know that he has a friend in his workplace. "Thank you. I appreciate it."

She grins, wrapping an arm around his shoulder. Felix smiles down at his hands. Maybe his new job will be enjoyable, after all.

FELIX WAKES to birds twittering outside the window. At first, he squints at the sunlight shining over the landscape posters on the wall, pulling his covers over his head. It's way too early on a Saturday. All he wants is to huddle in bed until it gets too warm, then crawl out to feed himself.

He hasn't missed this, working a salaried job where he has to be at the gas station seven to four, six days a week. When he gets off work and the bus drops him near his house, it's close to evening, and by the time he reaches home, he doesn't want to cook at all.

He doesn't have enough time to himself on the weekdays, so it's *nice,* lying here, watching the dust motes in the sunlight. He doesn't have to worry about catching the bus, being on time, making his baggy work shirt fit right...

It doesn't fit right because he changed his clothing style, because he doesn't want anyone to notice when he swells with child, and he's *pregnant.*

His stomach plummets. Felix whimpers, sliding a hand over his abdomen.

He still can't believe it. He's been talking to the fetus, and it's been a week. And his body is still the same, except the sun is a little too bright, and there's a new, strange note of honey alongside his lavender scent.

Felix groans, rolling over in bed. "This isn't happening," he says. "Can't this be a dream?"

He grabs the glass of water from the bedside table, gulping a mouthful. Then another, and he looks at his trusty digital clock, scuffed with age. 8:48 AM. *Kade will be here at 9.*

"Fuck," he yelps, wobbling. The room spins, and he's toppling onto the floor in a tangle of sheets, bumping his head on the bedside table, water spilling everywhere. "You're thirty years old. Why can't you do things right, goddamn it?"

Tears prickle in his eyes. He scrambles out of the blanket, throwing it back onto the bed. He dashes into the bathroom, twisting the knob of the shower, squeezing toothpaste onto his toothbrush. The entire house smells like lavender and honey. Like a pregnant person. Felix swears, running through the rooms to throw the windows open.

The scent doesn't dissipate fast enough. He doesn't have fans to blow the air out, so he hurries back to the bathroom, fumbling through the drawer. Aftershave. Cologne. Air freshener. Window cleaner.

Toothbrush in his mouth, he plods through the rooms, juggling the bottles in his arm. Three pumps of window cleaner in the corners. A splash of aftershave in the doorways. Cologne in the kitchen. Air freshener in every damn room. By the time he's done, he's reeling from all the smells, his stomach roiling.

Felix staggers back to the bathroom to rinse his mouth, stepping under the scalding shower. He scrubs himself clean, heart thumping, and drips water all over the floor trying to reach his bath towel. *Holy fucking hell, Felix, why do you do this to yourself?*

"I don't know," Felix says. Will Kade still smell him after the shower? *The scent suppressant.* He stumbles to the front door, where Taylor's pill dispenser sits in a crooked, half-full bookcase, plucking today's tab open. He swallows the round white pill dry. Something rumbles outside, then stops.

Heartbeats later, the doorbell rings.

He almost chokes on the pill. *It's seven minutes to nine!* Felix turns to the window, towel around his neck, and peers past the ratty curtains. And there, on his doorstep, Kade's dressed in a smart red shirt and jeans, his hair combed down, a laptop under his arm.

I can't let him stand and wait, Felix thinks. *What if he gets tired of waiting and leaves?* Because he doesn't want Kade to leave, doesn't want him turning away. Even if the entire house stinks, and his hair is a mess.

He pads to the front door, his toes wet against the foyer floor, and pulls it open.

Kade meets his eyes. Water drips off Felix's bangs, sliding down his cheek. "Um," Felix says.

Mahogany eyes flicker along his body, then coast back up. Cool air prickles along his skin.

Something is wrong. Felix looks down, and realizes the towel draped across his shoulders should be wrapped around his waist. He's wearing *nothing but a towel.* Its ends accentuate a vertical strip of his chest, all the way down to his groin.

His cheeks burn. *You aren't supposed to see me like that!*

Kade raises an eyebrow. "I interrupted something?"

"My... my shower," Felix gasps. "You, um, came early."

Kade's gaze rakes back down his body, heavy and lingering. Felix should be pulling the towel from his shoulders, holding it over his hips to make himself decent. But that's where Kade's attention anchors. Felix's cock twitches in response.

"Traffic was light," Kade says, gaze dragging up Felix's body to meet his eyes. "But I never plan on coming early."

Kill me right now. Felix spins on his heels, tugging his towel down before Kade sees the telling rise of his cock. But Kade's attention prickles on him, on the bare skin of his back, his ass, his legs, and Felix can't decide if this was a bad idea, letting him come over.

The front door clicks shut, sealing him and Kade into the same house. *I'm doomed in here,* Felix thinks.

Kade coughs violently. "The hell? Stinks in here."

Felix cringes. *Guess you won't smell me now.* Relief sweeps through him. "Really? I was... doing some cleaning."

"What the fuck," Kade says. He coughs again, huffing to clear his nostrils. Felix ducks into his bedroom to dry off his wet limbs, his face burning.

I can't believe I answered the door naked. In front of Kade. He pulls his underwear and clothes out of his closet, stepping into them. They cling damply to his skin, and he squirms, trying to get comfortable.

When the hem of his bulky, knitted sweater falls below his erection, Felix steps out, looking cautiously into the living room. Kade stands in the middle of the unpacked boxes, studying them. Felix winces. He'd said he was going to unpack, hadn't he? He can't even be trusted to make promises.

"I'm going to make some coffee," Felix says. "I haven't had breakfast yet. Have you?"

Kade turns, raising his brows. He flicks his gaze over Felix's fresh clothes, lingering on the sleeves falling past his fingers, and the gaping neckline of the sweater. Felix had bought it from the thrift store they visited. "I've eaten, but coffee's fine. Thanks."

"Right. I won't be long." Felix ducks into the kitchen, his skin too tight. Why did he even answer the door? They've got nothing to talk about. Things are over between them. And Kade has absolutely nothing to do with the child inside him.

Felix heats two mugs of water in the

microwave. While it whirs, he folds his sleeves up and cracks eggs into a pan. *Two for me, one for you. Although I'm sure you'll only need more when you get bigger.* He pokes his flat abdomen. It still doesn't look like there's a child inside him, even if the tests had all chimed positive.

"Mind if I sit?" Kade says, stepping into the kitchen. Felix shrugs.

Sturdy chairs flank the kitchen table, each chair with castor wheels. Kade plants his laptop over some older burns on the table, his fingers tapping over the keys. While he waits for it to start up, he looks over. It feels as though Kade can read through him, even though his baby bump isn't showing yet, even though his sweater is far too bulky to reveal anything.

"You look better today," Kade says.

"Oh. Really?"

"Yeah. You're not as tense."

He looks back down, wondering how Kade always sees things he can't discern about himself. "I didn't realize."

Kade shrugs. He connects the laptop cable to a wall socket, before tugging his phone from his pocket. Felix pulls the mugs from the microwave when it beeps.

"Black coffee?"

"Yeah. Thanks."

While the eggs sizzle, Felix turns slightly, peeking at Kade. He hasn't truly looked at his alpha since he returned to Meadowfall, hasn't just watched him being busy, because Kade's attention had been laser-sharp on him.

Now, Kade's fingers fly over the keyboard.

Felix realizes that he hasn't seen this in five years: Kade in his kitchen, focused on something on the screen. It had been one of his dreams of his future, sharing a home with this man.

A lump rises in his throat.

Felix swallows, tugging his sleeves down. He scoops instant coffee granules into the mugs, gives them a stir, and sets Kade's mug beside him. "There."

"Thanks." Kade watches him, contemplative.

His heart thumps. *Why are you still here?* he wants to ask. Instead, Felix returns to the stove, fiddling with the pans.

Hiding is what he does best. But now that Kade has found him again, all he can do is soldier on.

8
Kade

"SMELLS LIKE cologne in here," Kade says, looking up when Felix brings eggs, and then cereal over to the kitchen table. He turns his laptop to face them both.

Felix blushes. "I spilled some. Sorry about the smells."

"It's fine. Just really stinks." Which would be tolerable, really, if it didn't strike him that Felix is trying to hide the scent of something. *Did you have someone else over?* He draws a deep breath, but all he smells is the sting of cleaning fluid, the chemical sweetness of air freshener. He wrinkles his nose, wishing a breeze would clear the air between them.

Felix heads over with a mug of milk coffee. He settles down next to Kade, their knees bumping. "I'll avoid spilling everything the next time."

"Don't worry about that." Kade looks over the plates of food, raising an eyebrow. Felix has always liked sweet coffee, but Kade has never seen him eat more than a bowl of cereal for breakfast. "You're hungry?"

Felix shrugs. "I guess."

Their knees bump again. Kade focuses on

why he's here—Felix needs help selling his paintings. He shouldn't be distracted by his omega's warmth, or the image of him naked at the front door. Most of all, Kade just wants to smell him again. He can't pick out that familiar lavender scent, and part of him wants to shift his chair closer to Felix, wants to bury his nose in Felix's neck.

"So, your paintings," Kade says, yanking his thoughts back to the laptop screen. "I did some research on them."

"You did?" A hint of pink dusts Felix's cheeks. "That's... very nice of you."

But *that's very nice* doesn't mean Felix wants anything to do with him, so Kade focuses on the motorbike on his laptop wallpaper, pulling up a search engine. "I've looked up some sites. There's places where you can sell prints of your paintings, then there's sites where you can auction them off. I made a list. Do you have pictures of the canvases?"

Felix stares at him, wonder in his eye. Kade's cheeks prickle with heat. It's been five years since Felix looked at him like that.

"I do," Felix says between bites of egg. "On my website." He reaches over to the laptop, his fingers peeking out from his sweater sleeves. Kade wants to pull those sleeves back, wants to nose at Felix's bonding mark. The one he'd left almost two decades ago.

"There," Felix says, hitting the Enter key. "It's not much of a site, though. I didn't really know what I was doing."

Kade keeps a straight face. The website is terrible—the overlapping buttons, the low-contrast font colors, the outdated storefront...

"I kind of slapped together some basic HTML," Felix says, smiling sheepishly. "Sorry it looks ugly."

"It won't help you like that." Kade sighs. Does Felix really think this will sell his paintings?

"I've mostly done the sales in person," Felix says, as though reading his thoughts. "At farmers' markets in Highton, or at galleries. They weren't too bad."

"But people need a way to search for you online." Kade gulps a mouthful of coffee. *Still using Baker's Brew?*

Felix sighs. "I know."

"Why don't I redo the site for you?" Kade asks, his breath catching when Felix's eyes brighten. Felix hasn't needed him in a while. "Email me your hosting details. In the meantime, we'll set up accounts on the other sales sites."

"Okay," Felix says. He shifts his chair closer to Kade, its castor wheels rumbling against the kitchen floor. Kade can't help turning to sniff at him.

Felix's arm presses against his, the heat of it dulled by his sweater, but Kade doesn't mention it. Instead, he takes Felix through the art sites, the auction sites, and even some collectors' forums so he'll have a better idea who he can sell his paintings to. Through it all, Felix crunches on his cereal, a trickle of milk collecting on his lower lip.

"So that's the easier stuff done," Kade says, closing the internet browsers. "You'll have to remember to sign in and actually talk to the people on the forum."

Felix chuckles. "I'll try. I don't remember a

lot."

Kade looks at him in question, but he doesn't elaborate. And now that the godawful scents have drifted out of the windows, Kade smells him a little better.

He leans closer, sniffing at Felix's ear, then his neck. Felix's eyes widen, but he doesn't move away. Kade presses his nose to the loose neckline of his sweater. There's no sharp, woodsy scent, no smell of grass, only a faint lavender; Felix hasn't been with anyone lately. Kade relaxes. He hadn't known he'd been worried about it.

You smell good, he wants to say, but he doesn't. Instead, he trails his nose up along Felix's neck, along his jaw. Felix shivers against him.

"We should be working," Felix whispers. But his nostrils flare, and Kade licks a slow stripe up his throat, kissing his pulse. It flutters against his lips, and he sucks lightly on the skin there. Felix inhales sharply, lifting his chin to allow him access. It means he wants Kade's touch, even after he rejected the proposal. Kade's heart thumps.

After all he's seen this week—Felix hard at the gas station, Felix bending over, Felix standing naked in his doorway—the thought of touching his omega sends desire humming through his body. He slips his hand between Felix's knees, stroking up his thigh. Felix's breath hitches.

"Something you want?" Kade murmurs, letting his warmth soak through the rough fabric of Felix's pants. Felix lifts his hips, his legs spreading further apart. Kade cups his balls through his jeans, runs his thumb lightly along the bulge of his cock.

"Maybe," Felix whispers, and when Kade

glances up, he finds Felix's pupils dilated, his mouth falling open.

He leans in, trailing the tip of his tongue along Felix's lip, stealing the droplet of milk. Felix shivers. He isn't in heat. He's not desperate for alpha cock, and this means he's interested in *Kade.* For a moment, Kade can't breathe.

Do you really want this? Kade leans in carefully, kissing the corner of Felix's mouth. His omega could reject him at any time.

"Tell me what you want," Kade whispers, his pulse in his throat.

Felix moves his lips. He doesn't answer, instead locking his gaze with Kade's. So Kade presses their mouths together, licking at the seam of his lips. And Felix parts for him.

Felix wants him closer. Kade growls, slipping his tongue inside. Felix meets him with his own, wet and warm, tasting like milk and coffee. He moans into Kade's mouth, his tongue sliding hungrily along Kade's, his fingers pushing Kade's hand down against his growing cock.

It makes Kade hard, his omega's cock sliding urgently against him. He slips an arm around Felix's waist, tugging him closer, holding his legs open. Felix sucks in a sharp breath.

"You're hungry," Kade says. Felix's soft, damp lips drag against his own. "I want to see you hard for me."

And Felix trembles, his nails digging into Kade's wrist when Kade unbuttons his pants, pulling the zipper open with a harsh rasp. He hooks his thumb into Felix's briefs, his knuckle brushing down the side of Felix's cock. When he tugs Felix's pants down, his cock juts up, thick and pink, betraying his arousal.

In the sunlight reflecting off the kitchen walls, the very tip of Felix's cock pushes out of his foreskin, dusky, a bead of clear fluid gathering at its slit. Kade touches his fingertip to it, smearing precum along the opening of his foreskin.

"I'm... I'm..." Felix wets his lips, watching as Kade swirls his thumb around his tip, rubbing him through his skin. This hasn't changed, either—Felix likes to be played with. Kade slides his skin down to expose his blunt, gleaming head.

"What do you want?" Kade asks, curling his fingers around Felix's cock, pumping him lightly. Felix thrusts up at his hand, musk rolling in tiny waves off his skin. It's stronger than his lavender scent. Kade leans in to nose at the scent gland at his shoulder, dragging his teeth lightly over it.

Felix hisses, his hips jerking up, his cock sliding heavy and hot against Kade's fingers. "More."

"If I feel like it." Kade smears the next droplet over Felix's tip, working his finger under his skin so it stretches around him. It's lewd like that, watching Felix's skin take him in, clinging hungrily around his fingertip. Felix trembles. Kade slides his finger around his head, coating it with precum. Felix bites hard on his lip.

Kade releases him, slipping his fingers into the open V of Felix's pants. He cradles Felix's balls in his fingers, lifting them out so they rest on light blue denim, their skin soft and warm.

"Want to see you," Kade growls.

"This isn't enough?" Felix whispers. He looks

down at himself, his cock and balls exposed, the rest of him all covered up, save for a thin sliver of his hips.

"No. Feet up." Kade taps on his inner thigh. Felix pulls his legs up onto the seat, spreading them open. He looks vulnerable like that, the sensitive parts of him exposed. Kade smirks, reaching between his legs to trail his fingers along Felix's cock. "Open my jeans."

A wave of scarlet sweeps up Felix's throat. He reaches over, tugging on Kade's belt, then his zipper. Kade opens his legs, groaning when Felix pushes his small hand into his pants, cool fingers wrapping around his cock. Felix purrs. "Was I supposed to find this?"

"Fuck yeah." Kade rocks up into his hand, fucking against his palm. Felix's eyelids flutter shut. He eases Kade out of his jeans, his hand sliding soft and firm down Kade's cock, and for a breathless moment, Kade forgets about everything, except Felix's hand, his mouth, Felix's tongue licking up his cock.

"So big," Felix whispers, his voice hoarse with longing. He slides his palm down the underside of Kade's cock, to his base, then back up.

"Jack me off," Kade says. He gathers the wetness trickling down Felix's cock, reaching down to smear it over Felix's balls. Felix makes a soft, delighted sound in his throat, pushing his hips up. "C'mon."

Felix wraps his fingers around Kade, stroking him from base to tip, the crown of Kade's head catching on his fingers. He pulls his hand back, gathering his own precum on his fingertips, then smears it all over Kade's cock, his fingers working over Kade, falling into a rhythm that they've learned after years of touch. Then his touch feathers down, fingertips trailing along the ridge of Kade's cock, before massaging his underside. Pleasure hums through Kade's body. He swears, pushing up into Felix's hand. "Harder. Stroke me."

So Felix strokes him, licking his lips. Kade rewards him by rubbing his thumb over Felix's balls, squeezing them lightly, his fingers brushing down the back of them. Felix whines, low and needy, clear fluid dribbling down the fine veins of his neglected cock. "Kade, please."

And Kade takes his cock in hand, pumping him firmly, dragging his skin down to expose his flushed tip, circling it with his thumb. Felix chokes on his moan. His balls grow tight, and Kade grinds his fingertip against the underside of his head, so he jerks, shoving his cock up into Kade's grip.

Kade relaxes his hand then, leaning in to lick along the shell of Felix's ear. "I didn't say to stop jacking me," he growls, and Felix shivers, his fingers tightening around Kade's cock, pumping him. Kade increases the pace of his strokes, matching Felix's touch, breathing in the heady musk rolling off his omega.

When Felix trembles, Kade slows his pace, waiting as his bondmate's strokes slow to the same rhythm. Felix circles Kade's tip with his fingers; Kade mirrors that touch on him. Felix tips his head back, panting.

Felix's cock grows thick in his hand, heavy and slippery, and he's so damn close. So Kade takes his earlobe into his mouth, sucks on it, before he murmurs, "Come for me."

His omega comes with a ragged cry, spine arching, pulsing hard in his hand, spurts of white streaking onto his sweater, dribbling wet and warm down Kade's fingers. Kade strokes him slow, thumbing his head, milking him until the last drop oozes from his tip. Felix shudders. "S-stop," he hisses, trembling, his breaths coming in broken gasps. "Too—too sensitive."

But Kade knows that. He traces Felix's tip again, so his body jerks and he tightens his fist around Kade's cock, trying to hang on.

"Damn you, Kade." Felix rears up in his seat, eyes flashing. This, too, is familiar, when Felix leans in and closes his mouth around Kade's tip, sucking hard. A jolt sears through Kade's body. Felix slides his fist down Kade's cock, his lips dragging along his head, tongue working just under it. Pleasure spikes down Kade's nerves. He sucks in a sharp breath, throbbing, pushing Felix's head down. Felix yields, taking him deeper, his mouth hot, his other hand rubbing Kade's balls through his pants.

Felix hollows his cheeks. Kade thinks, *Can't believe you're sucking me off again* and his release crashes through his body like a punch, forcing the air out of his lungs. He spills into Felix's mouth, watches as Felix stays, swallowing his cum. He growls, dragging his wrist across Felix's cheek, down his throat, marking Felix with his scent. *Mine.*

He slips his hand down the neckline of Felix's sweater, rubbing his wrist along Felix's collarbones, down his chest, over his nipples. Felix moans around him, his tongue lapping over Kade's tip.

When he pulls off with a soft *pop,* Kade withdraws his hand and sets it on Felix's shoulder, leaning him upright. Felix allowed him close, and this feels like a little bit like forgiveness.

He leans in and kisses Felix softly, slipping his tongue into his mouth. Felix tastes like bitter musk and *mine.* Felix trails his hand down Kade's cock, a light, careful touch. The pressure in Kade's knot swells. As Felix slips his fingers around it, he massages Kade lightly, swirling his fingers around him like he used to.

Felix jerks away the next instant. Cool air rushes between them; Kade stares as Felix fixes his eyes on the empty plates, cheeks reddening. "Um. That... that wasn't supposed to happen."

"No shit," Kade says, reeling. Felix had been so receptive just a minute ago, and this feels like a slap, his bondmate refusing to even look at him. It feels like the night Kade picked him up, when Kade had knotted inside him. Felix had stared at the wall after. But maybe Kade had been wrong, coaxing him into sex. Felix had never contacted him when he was away. Why would he, when he'd all but told Kade that Kade wasn't good enough? "Look, I'm sorry."

"I should be the one sorry," Felix says, springing to his feet. He gathers the plate and bowl from the table, his cock still hanging out of his jeans. Kade follows him to the sink. "I shouldn't... I mean, I appreciate what you've done today. Thanks for coming over."

It sounds like a cue to leave. Kade doesn't

want to, not so soon after sex. The first time had been bad enough. He still remembers Felix alone on his bed, back turned to him. "Look, there's still more to do with the website," he says. "I can set it up here, and you can decide which options you want."

It's a pitiful excuse to stay, and he's certain that Felix can see through it. But Felix slows down, setting the dishes carefully in the sink. He fiddles with the front of his pants. Kade grimaces, fixing his own jeans. *We're bonded. This shouldn't feel like a damn dirty secret.*

When Felix turns around, his pants are buttoned, and the smears of cum on his sweater have been brushed off. "I... I guess you can stay," he says, looking at his belly. "Just for that."

Kade releases the breath he didn't know he was holding. "Okay. We'll get you set up, and then I'll leave."

Felix nods, looking back at the sink. While he washes the dishes, he tells Kade the details of his website—the hosting site, his username, his password.

"'arts&brushes'?" Kade asks, surprised. "You're still using the same password?"

"You've never tried logging into my accounts?" Felix says, and immediately ducks his head. "Well, no, I didn't mean it that way. Sorry."

Kade looks down at his laptop, stung. Felix had said he wasn't good enough, so he'd let Felix leave, thinking he'd return if he really wanted Kade in his life. After years of waiting, he'd realized that Felix was never coming back. And Felix has made it plenty clear that he's not staying permanently in

Meadowfall. "Should I have logged in?"

"I don't know."

Kade doesn't know, either. Even though so much of Felix has stayed the same—his mannerisms, his favorite food, his looks—there's a new, cautious side to him, and it unnerves Kade. "Anyway, I've signed in."

"Okay." The faucet runs in the background, and the crockery clatters together.

Kade taps through the site settings, wincing at the HTML Felix used. Felix has never been good with computers, even back when they were sitting through the basic lessons in school. While Kade made circles spin on animation programs, Felix had spent those classes drawing pigs and houses. Kade had animated them for him, boosting Felix's grades up to a B.

"Remember that group project?" Kade asks. "Back in middle school. The one where we had to make a website."

At the sink, Felix chuckles weakly. "The one where I drew flowers for the background and you made the site work?"

Kade snorts. But it eases the tension between them, and Felix's shoulders relax. "Yeah, that one. But see, I was thinking you could do something like that for your website. Get some graphics done for a banner, maybe a background."

"I don't have a computer, remember?"

"I'll leave this one with you."

Felix turns, staring at him wide-eyed. "Don't you need it?"

"I've got two."

And Felix droops. "Really? That's... that's

very nice."

"They're for my work." Kade shrugs. He may have work-related programs on this laptop, but he can access them on the other one, and he trusts Felix not to mess with them. He trusts Felix with his life. That much hasn't changed.

He preps the laptop for Felix, closing the programs he won't need. "Text me if you've got any questions."

"I'll probably have a buttload of questions," Felix says. He dries his hand on a dishcloth, smiling wryly. "Thanks for your help."

"Anytime." The silence that settles over them prickles at Kade's skin, and when Felix putters around the kitchen, avoiding the table, he winces. Felix probably doesn't want him around right now, even if he's not furious about the sex. "I should go," Kade says, checking his phone. "You've probably got things going on."

Felix's throat works. "Yeah. Thanks for coming over."

Kade follows him to the door. The house still smells like chemical crap, but Kade picks up his own scent on Felix. It settles his unease, knowing that it'll keep that bastard alpha manager away from his bondmate. "See you around?"

"I'll try to have the graphics done soon," Felix says. "Maybe in a week or two?"

"Sounds good." Kade steps out of the house. As Felix meets his eyes, sunlight caressing his cheeks, Kade itches to kiss him, just to smell him again. "Take care."

"I will. Thanks." Felix smiles then, his eyes warm. Kade's heart kicks.

I'll miss you, he wants to say. Instead, he steps toward his bike, Felix's gaze lingering on him the entire way.

9
Felix

A WEEK later, the doorbell rings.

Felix freezes in his kitchen, halfway through frying some eggs. *Kade?* He turns the stove off, heart pattering as he hurries to the door. Kade hasn't said anything about visiting. He holds his breath, checks the pill dispenser—yes, he's taken the scent suppressant—and then the peephole.

Instead of Kade's broad shoulders, he sees the slight frame of his brother, the same dark blond hair. Felix throws the door open and flying into Taylor's arms. "Taylor!"

"You're going to crush me to death," Taylor says, staggering backward.

Felix burrows his face in his brother's shoulder, gulping deep breaths of his familiar jasmine scent. His brother hasn't texted in two weeks, and Felix had worried. "I'm so glad you're alive."

"You always are." Taylor wraps his arms around him, and for a long minute, they stand on Felix's porch, hugging. Felix doesn't talk about the risks of Taylor's job, the risk that someday, he might not return. In a lower voice, Taylor asks,

"How are you?"

How is the baby? he means. Felix's stomach drops. He swallows, pulling away from his brother. "I'm fine."

Taylor follows him into the house, watching as he locks the door. His eyes dart around the place—windows, doors, obstructions. Felix holds his brother's hand, giving him a squeeze. Although Taylor has a well-paying job, and although their father likes him better, Felix doesn't envy his brother at all. Taylor's missions scare the hell out of him.

"Are you really fine?" Taylor asks.

Felix sighs. Some days, he forgets about the baby for a while, and it's a relief to be free of that burden. "It's not as scary as your job, but it's still pretty damn terrifying."

His brother studies him. "Kade?"

He shakes his head. "He doesn't know yet."

"*Felix.* He's the kid's dad."

"He'll murder me," Felix says, trudging to the kitchen. The eggs don't seem so delicious anymore, suddenly. "It's been a month since I screwed him."

"The longer you keep it from him, the more pissed he's going to be," Taylor says. He follows Felix into the kitchen, opening the cabinets until he finds a glass. He fills it with water. "Trust me on that."

"I'll leave before he notices," Felix says, biting his lip. Kade would discover him missing, and... He would be furious. Or glad. His heart thuds painfully. "He... never wanted children."

"He's your bondmate," Taylor says, flopping

into a chair. "He should know."

Felix winces and turns back to the stove. In his head, Kade's voice murmurs, *I don't think we're suited for kids.* "You still remember what happened five years ago, right?"

Taylor sighs. "If you actually talked to him about it, I'm sure he'd understand."

"They went bankrupt because of me, Taylor!" Felix glances out of the window, his heart pounding. But all he sees are the neighbor's closed windows, the weed-strewn dirt of his backyard. No Kade. Kade wouldn't be listening in, but just the mention of this makes his stomach constrict. "They'll all hate me if they found out."

"So what if his family hates you? You're still bonded to him, right?"

And that makes it worse, because Felix can't stand the thought of their accusing stares, can't stand the thought of Kade saying *You drove my family out of our home* and *How dare you call me your alpha?* He looks down at his flat belly, thinking the baby should be showing anytime, but it hasn't yet. "He can always find a new bondmate."

"Has he?"

Felix shakes his head. Kade smells only like himself when he visits the gas station, like cedar and pine, and Felix rues the days when Kade's scent fades from the store. "He will soon. I'm sure."

Taylor shakes his head, sniffing the air around them. "He should have. But he's been visiting you."

Felix shrugs. "He was only here to help with my website. And that was last week. My site sucks balls."

"Just tell him, damn it."

"No!"

"I look down gun barrels, Felix, and you're scared of Kade saying no?"

Put that way, it sounds like Felix is making excuses all over again. But he can't erase the guilt lurking in his chest. He's lived by himself for five years, thinking Kade will never forgive him, and he can't see why Kade would. "I wish you would stop working as a spy, Taylor. I don't want to lose you."

"I can't promise that. But come on, at least tell him," Taylor says. "Give him a chance to respond."

Felix winces. He turns the stove on again, poking at the half-cooked eggs with his spatula. "It'll kill me if he says no."

"And he hasn't smelled the pregnancy yet."

"I've been taking the suppressants, so no."

Taylor throws his arms in the air, exasperated. "You guys are idiots."

"Better an idiot than a divorcee," Felix mumbles, poking at the eggs. When they're done, he slides them onto a plate, then pours himself a bowl of cereal. "Things are better this way."

"Are they really?" Taylor props his chin on his hand, his eyes flickering toward the windows, then the doors. It's a habit, and Felix has learned to ignore it. He glances at the pale scar on his wrist, tiny tooth marks that have never really faded.

"Did you meet anyone cute?" Felix asks instead. "On your big, scary mission."

At that, Taylor laughs. "Maybe."

Felix brightens, glad to focus on something other than his own problems. "A big, handsome alpha?"

To his delight, his brother grins, warmth shining in his eyes. "Yeah, he's cute," he says. "Just that he's working for someone else, and we may or may not be on opposite sides."

"But did you fuck? I think that's the most important question," Felix says, and Taylor laughs.

"Yeah. Once so far."

"So far? You'll be seeing him again?" And Felix is truly glad for Taylor, because unlike himself, Taylor doesn't have a mark on his wrist, doesn't have a bondmate who will disappoint him. When Taylor shrugs, smiling, Felix scoots closer pulling his eggs along. "Okay, tell me about him," he says. "I want all the details!"

And Taylor grins, slinging an arm around his shoulder. "Of course."

KADE VISITS again the next Saturday. This time, Felix is expecting him, and the house smells like bacon and eggs when he opens the front door. Felix is dressed, too, in another bulky sweater and jeans, and he holds his breath when Kade's eyes flicker down his body, past his abdomen. *He didn't notice.*

"You look like you dropped out of a magazine," Kade says, meeting Felix's eyes.

Felix exhales, heat creeping up his cheeks. He wasn't expecting a compliment. "Thanks. Uh, I'm just making breakfast. Would you like to come inside? I—I mean. Oh, gods."

Kade's gaze darkens, as though he'd like to do just that. "Sure."

Felix gulps, swearing inwardly. "I didn't mean sex. Definitely not."

Kade deflates a little. Felix bites his lip. They really shouldn't fuck again. If they do, he'll forget that he's supposed to be keeping secrets from this man, that he'll be running from Kade at some point, leaving clueless about everything. Including the unborn child. It'll be better if they stop getting so close.

"Your laptop's in the kitchen," Felix says.

"Right." Kade follows him through the house, and Felix can't help the tingle on his skin, knowing that Kade's watching him.

In his mind, he hears Taylor's voice. *You can't keep this from him forever. He'll find out at some point.* Felix frowns at the bare kitchen walls, pulling a couple mugs from the cabinets. "Yes, I can," he mutters.

"What?" Kade glances over.

"Nothing." Felix fills the mugs with water, sliding them into the microwave. "The food's on the stove if you want any."

"Okay." Kade looks through the cabinet for a plate.

Felix watches him, his pulse pattering at having his alpha just three feet away. Over the past two weeks, Kade has visited the gas station four times, but he hasn't tried to kiss Felix again, hasn't been hard in the store.

Even though Felix knows it's a good thing, it makes him uneasy. He hadn't meant to reject Kade so suddenly the last time. He'd remembered the pregnancy while he touched Kade's knot, and his guilt had burned.

When Kade crosses over to the stove, Felix steps back. His scent is sharp and woodsy: a hint of sex, a hint of Kade. His bondmate's shoulders are broad, tapering down to his waist, and from the back, Felix admires the way his jeans cling to his ass, the way his thighs stretch his pants. He wants to crawl onto Kade, rub against him, and...

He snaps his gaze away when Kade turns, but Kade's eyes anchor on his face. Felix blushes, turning away to grab his own plate.

When he joins Kade at the table with steaming mugs of coffee, Kade smiles. "It's pretty good," he says. "Better than the stuff I make."

Felix shrugs, his breath catching. "They're simple things. Just eggs and bacon. It's not like I'm making cream of mushroom soup."

Kade's knee bumps into his when he sits. Felix swallows. "I still think you cook well. How are the website graphics going?"

"I have them on the laptop," Felix says. "I just need to know the dimensions to resize them."

Kade nods. He opens the laptop, glancing at the password he'd written down at the corner of the screen. "Did you have any problems using this?"

Felix shakes his head. Most of his issues had been figuring out the tools he needed, but he'd done that quickly. All the same, it's nice of Kade to ask, nice of him to care. "No, I did okay. It wasn't too bad."

"Okay."

They eat in silence, Kade's gaze flickering over to him, Felix anchoring his eyes on his food. They're almost done with breakfast when Kade says, "I was looking through the hosting site details. You're currently using the lowest pricing option, but that won't give you the best graphics. You'd want to host the larger image files so people can zoom in on the details."

Felix sighs, wincing. Between rent and setting aside money for moving, and the baby, he hasn't got much left. "How much is that going to be?"

"Looks like fifty bucks a year. It's not too bad." But Kade sees his wince and reaches for his wallet. "It's not that much."

"No, I'll pay for it," Felix says, rubbing his stomach. It roils slightly, as though he might be falling sick. "Do they take bank transfers?"

"Just credit cards, it looks like." Kade hesitates, glancing at the screen. "Pay me back some other time."

"I can't—"

Felix's gut heaves, and he swears, clapping a hand over his mouth. He stumbles out of the kitchen, swallowing desperately to delay the inevitable, and his knees barely hit the bathroom floor before his stomach empties itself into the toilet.

His eyes water. He clings onto the cool, glazed ceramic, the sour scent winding up his nose, making him retch further.

Felix barely registers the warm presence next to him, a large hand on his back, fingers smoothing across his forehead. He spits to get rid of the taste in his mouth, blinking his tears back. He hadn't thought this would happen so soon. It's been barely a month.

"You need to rest," Kade says next to him,

stroking down his back. He stands, and while Felix clutches the toilet, waiting for the rest of his nausea to pass, Kade fills a mug with water, handing it over.

Felix rinses out his mouth, before gulping down water to ease the sting in his throat. "Ugh."

"How're you feeling?" Kade asks, crouching next to him. He rubs down Felix's neck, brushing off the sweat prickling there. "Need to see the doctor?"

Heat rushes up Felix's cheeks; he hadn't even thought about seeing a doctor. *It's not like I need one to tell me I'm pregnant.* "No, I'll be fine."

"I thought you were doing okay," Kade says, scrutinizing him. He refills Felix's mug. "You were eating and all that."

Felix shrugs. He sucks in deep breaths of air, flushes the toilet, and pushes himself to his feet. Kade stands with him, slipping a warm hand around his elbow to provide support.

His chest tightens. Kade shouldn't be doing this. Felix will leave with their child, and Kade won't know it even exists. In fact, Kade should still remember how Felix had rejected him and turn away. *Why are you still here?* Felix wants to ask. He swallows the question instead. "I think I'll be fine after this."

But Kade presses the back of his hand to Felix's forehead, a cool, firm touch. "You're not running a fever."

Of course I'm not. Felix blushes anyway, his heart thudding. He looks at Kade through the bathroom mirror, at his drawn eyebrows, his full lips. *Will the baby look like you? I hope it does.* He doesn't notice Kade's hand until it touches his cheek, Kade's thumb brushing callused and warm along his lower lip. Felix sucks in a sharp breath.

"C'mon, you should sit down," Kade murmurs, setting his hand on the small of Felix's back. Just like when they'd been together. Felix's breath snags in his throat.

He follows Kade out of the bathroom, and the air in the hallway feels light and fresh in his nose.

You sat with me through the vomit stench, Felix thinks, his throat itchy. He traces the line of Kade's jaw with his eyes, leaning closer for warmth. In the kitchen, the air smells like bacon and eggs again, and the lingering scent of pine and cedar. His chest tightens.

Kade looks into the fridge. "Want something else to drink? Milk?"

"That'll be good," Felix says, looking at their cold cups of coffee, the plates of half-eaten food. "Sorry about breakfast."

Kade clicks his tongue. "Doesn't matter." He empties Felix's coffee in the sink, rinses the mug, and fills it half-full with milk. "That enough?"

"It's plenty. Thank you." Their fingers brush when Kade hands the mug over. Felix cradles it close, sipping.

When Kade settles back into the chair, he taps on the laptop touchpad so the screen lights up again. "Forgot about this," he says. "I'll pay for the hosting."

Felix winces. They don't even know if the paintings will sell, and whether they'll break even on the cost of the website. "I'll pay you back," he says. "When I get my next paycheck."

Kade huffs. He signs into the domain hosting site, though, and Felix watches as he taps his credit card details into the payment form. After a minute, the payment goes through. Kade clicks into the site options.

Felix rubs his fingertips against the condensation on his mug, looking down at his abdomen. All he sees is the lumpy white sweater—no visible sign of a child, no belly bump, nothing. Kade will hate him so much when he finds out.

"Why are you doing this?" Felix blurts. Immediately after, he wishes he could snatch his words back. He doesn't want to hear how Kade's in this to hurt him somehow. Felix deserves to be beaten up for what he's done.

Kade's eyes flicker to meet his. For a long moment, he rubs the silvery chain around his neck. Then he exhales, looking away. "Just because I can, I guess."

It doesn't explain anything. Felix bites his lip. Kade's throat works, and Felix picks at the hem of his sweater, squirming in the silence. He needs money, needs another job to cover all his expenses. The cash he borrowed from Taylor is dwindling—he has about three hundred dollars left.

"I should go," Kade says, looking at the kitchen window. "Most of the site's done. Just need to upload the graphics, and then focus on site traffic."

"Oh." But he doesn't want Kade to leave, when his limbs still hang weakly from the morning sickness. "I—I was... wondering if you want to stay? Just for a little while longer?"

Kade doesn't answer immediately. He purses his lips, as though torn between his decisions. Finally, he takes a deep breath and says, "Yeah, okay. I'll stay."

10
Felix

"I JUST had an idea," Felix says in the next heartbeat, twisting his fingers together. Kade lingers in his seat, still listening, so he says, "We could sell lemonade on the street corner."

Kade stares. "Lemonade?"

"It's going to be hot out, isn't it?" Felix checks his phone, brightening at the 90-degree weather on the forecast. It's the beginning of May, and people will be trawling through the neighborhood on a Saturday morning, looking for garage sales. "Come on, if we hurry, we'll be able to make some money off the traffic."

"Is this for your website?" Kade asks, incredulous. "Selling lemonade is for kids."

"Are you going to help, or not?"

Kade sighs, standing. "Okay, fine."

Felix smiles a little. Kade has always agreed to his ideas, even if they were insane: painting gigantic swirls on Kade's bedroom wall, building a three-story tree house in his backyard, cooking the grandest dinner for Kade's parents. They'd had fun, in the end—even Kade can't deny that. So Felix slides his chair back, thinking about the materials they'll need.

"No." Kade sets a hand on his shoulder, pushing him back into the cushioned seat. "You just puked. At least eat something first."

Why do you care so much? Felix covers his hot cheeks with his hands, watching from the corner of his eye as Kade opens the cupboards.

"You have enough sugar for three cups of lemonade," Kade says. "No lemons. And no plastic cups."

Felix breathes out, telling his heart to stop beating so fast. It's not as though Kade will visit him again. "I guess we'll need to buy them."

"It's almost 11 AM," Kade says, glancing at the wall clock. "Think anyone's gonna want lemonade?"

"If we get back before noon, yes."

"Do you even have any signboards for a stand?" Kade shuts the cupboards, looking over at Felix's plate. "You haven't been eating." He grabs the pan from the stove, shoving an egg and a slice of bacon down in front of him. "Eat."

"Yes, sir," Felix says, grinning. The roiling in his stomach has mostly faded by now, and it's nice, Kade serving him breakfast.

Kade rolls his eyes. While Felix stuffs the food into his mouth, Kade pulls his phone out, tapping on the screen while he checks the cupboards. Felix realizes he's making a list, and he wants to hug this man, suddenly. Wants to share an entire life with him.

He looks down at his abdomen and bites his lip.

Five minutes later, Kade settles back down in

his chair, placing his phone between them. "I've added up the stuff we need for a stand," he says. "We'll make a batch first, and if there's not enough, we'll make more."

"Sounds good." Felix scans the list: 10 lemons, 1 lb sugar, 40 cups, 40 straws, 4 signboards.

"You coming with me to the store?" Kade stops next to him, his heat radiating through the air between them.

Felix nods, scooping the last of the egg into his mouth. He isn't nauseous anymore. Maybe the morning sickness won't be so bad if he learns to anticipate it. "Are we taking the bike?"

"Walk if you want. I'm taking the bike," Kade says. Felix elbows him. "Hey, you asked."

Felix grins. He suppresses the urge to hug Kade, following him out of the house. In the driveway, Kade hands over the spare helmet. Felix pulls it on. This is starting to feel familiar again—buckling his helmet alongside his alpha, swinging his leg over the seat behind him.

When Kade turns the key, the bike roars to life, vibrating beneath them like a trembling beast. Their thighs bump, and Felix realizes that it isn't that big a deal now, when they've slept together twice, and Kade has been ferrying him between places. He swallows, thinking about the day he has to leave. He shoves that thought aside.

"Ready?" Kade asks over the engine's growl.

"Yeah." And Felix hesitates before slipping his arms around Kade's waist. He'll only be in Meadowfall for a couple of months. And Kade won't mind, will he, if he stayed with Felix through the morning sickness?

Kade turns at the contact, as though surprised, but his helmet hides his eyes. Felix edges closer, holds his breath, and hugs him a little tighter. Against his forearms, Kade's abs are warm and solid. Felix resists the urge to trail his fingers over them. Instead, he looks over Kade's shoulder, watching as he wheels them out of the driveway.

With a roar, they take off down the street, merging easily into the mid-morning traffic. The wind sweeps Kade's pinewood scent into Felix's helmet, and they ride along the roads, turning corner after corner until Kade pulls them into the department store's parking lot.

Inside the store, they pass glass cases of jewelry, sections of wicker chairs. Felix's heart thumps when they walk by the baby clothes. It takes all his willpower not to turn for a second look, when Kade watches him sideways. Felix clenches his fists, ignoring little pastel-colored dresses and tiny shoes, and his mind whispers *How much do the jumpers cost? Which shirt is the cutest?*

He releases his breath when they step into the kitchen utensils section. The mixing bowls gleam at him, cool and unsympathetic. Felix lowers his gaze. Kade hadn't wanted children, even before they broke up.

"Wanna grab the lemons? I'll get the sugar," Kade says, studying him.

Felix nods. He picks the lemons out, and when Kade returns with a packet of cane sugar, they head to the disposable goods aisle, where pastel-colored plates sit with plain white ones. Felix thinks about children's birthday parties, and how a child will fit in with other school kids if he has only one father. He glances down at his belly. *You'll forgive me for that, won't you?*

At the register, loaded up with placards and lemonade ingredients, Felix reaches for his wallet. Kade has his card out before Felix even blinks. "That's not fair," Felix says

Kade's gaze slides over to him. "I'll take the profits of whatever we make today. Sounds fair?"

It sounds like a decent deal, if a risky one. They have no idea how a lemonade stand will do. Kade could be losing his investment, and it would be Felix's fault. "Fine, I suppose."

Pulling his hand away from his wallet feels like defeat, so Felix makes a decision—a second plan he can rely on, if they don't earn anything off the lemonade. This decision he tucks away in his chest, hoarding it like a secret.

Back home, Kade mixes up the first batch of lemonade—heating water in the microwave, dissolving sugar. Felix paints thick black gouache onto the placards: *Lemonade: $1. Get yours now!*

He wants to say, *This would work better if I have a huge baby bump. People would stop by to chat and buy drinks,* but he swallows that, too. Instead, Felix cuts the larger placards into two, drawing arrows under the words "Lemonade for sale".

At the kitchen counter, Kade squeezes the lemon halves onto a glass juicer. Light glints off the trickling juice, and Kade's biceps bulge, stretching the sleeves of his shirt. Felix stares. He can't help it, when his alpha is more handsome than anyone else. Kade glances up, meeting his eyes.

Felix gulps. "I finished the signs," he says. "Give me a couple minutes, and I'll get the things for the stand."

Kade's still watching him as he leaves the kitchen. Felix hurries through the house, his pulse thudding in his ears. He finds two rickety folding chairs and a slim rectangular table, hefting them to the front door. Then, he gathers up an easel, some brushes, and his watercolors.

It's almost noon by the time they're ready to head out. Kade emerges from the kitchen with a jug of lemonade and a box of ice cubes. "Ready to go?"

"I am."

Kade stacks the chairs, placards, and easel onto the table. Felix holds the lemonade and ice cubes, cups and straws tucked into the painting supplies bag. Together, they make their way to a sidewalk corner one block down from a busy street. While Felix sets up the lemonade stand with the biggest, most colorful poster, Kade fastens the smaller signboards a block away, so passers-by would notice them and wander over.

The first few sales happen slowly: people who happen to drive by, and neighbors strolling along with their dogs. While they wait, Felix prepares his easel.

"Didn't think you were going to paint," Kade says, leaning back in his chair.

Felix scuffs the grassy boulevard under his shoe. "Figured I'd do something while we wait. Or, you know, draw some attention to my paintings. I work better this way."

Kade falls silent. Felix feels the light touch of his gaze as he sketches the street with a pencil, light lines that he'll erase later. He daubs water onto cyan paint, then fills the sky in with broad strokes of his brush. The sidewalk gets an ivory coat, the asphalt a gunmetal gray.

Through it all, Kade watches him. This feels familiar, too, Kade's unassuming attention on him as he works in silence. Felix almost wonders if he should speak, but Kade doesn't. So he keeps his mouth shut, and paints.

After a while, Kade says, "You got better with painting."

A lump rises in Felix's throat. He swallows and touches his brush tip to paper, watching as grass-green pigments bloom through white fiber. "Really?"

"Yeah. More detail. Or maybe you changed your style." Kade shrugs, straightening the stacks of cups on the table. His cheeks darken, though, and Felix can't look away.

Their next customer is a short girl with ponytails, six years old, reaching out with a handful of coins. Kade nods, pulling a blue plastic cup from a stack, before filling it with lemonade. While she waits, her mother wanders over to Felix, a smile on her face. "That's beautiful," she says. "You replicate the scenery so well."

Felix beams, handing her a postcard with his name and number on it. "Thanks! I do landscapes and custom portraits, if you find that you ever need a gift."

Mother and daughter thank them as they leave, both smelling like lilies, and the girl turns back to look at Felix's painting.

"You should be a little more friendly with children," Felix says to Kade. "They like nice people."

Kade raises his eyebrows. "I'm not nice enough?"

"I guess you are. But you need to smile at them, you know? Show them you're harmless." And at that, Felix begins to laugh, because Kade is the opposite of harmless. Kade has broken arms and snapped fingers, and that had been when they were ten, surrounded by bullies at the school playground.

I'll protect you, Kade had whispered. Felix swallows, swirling his paintbrush in its water glass.

"Sure," Kade says, but he narrows his eyes. "I'm not the one kids like."

Felix can't help touching his abdomen. *You'll have to smile, or you'll make our child cry.* He fans the painting to help the background colors dry. "We're running a business today, Kade. We have to be nice."

Kade snorts. "Why don't you sell the lemonade, then? Looks like I'm the one doing all the work here."

"I'm supervising." Felix laughs.

And Kade just stares, his eyes dark. If their separation didn't stand between them, Felix would have thought Kade was *hungry.* He turns back to the painting, and yelps when Kade smacks him lightly on the back of his thigh. "I should be supervising," Kade says. "This was your idea."

"You hit me," Felix says, but he smiling, glad that this part of their past has returned. That Kade can relax enough to touch him in public, that Kade even wants to touch him at all, without any expectations of sex.

"You were asking for it," Kade says,

smirking. Felix wriggles, taunting him. Kade's gaze flashes then, his fingers twitching, a second away from grabbing Felix, or slapping him on the ass. Felix gulps. He wants Kade to grab him and stroke him.

He turns to his painting instead, touching a finger to drying paper. "No, I wasn't," he says. "You volunteered to sit at the stand."

He almost hears Kade rolling his eyes. Felix grins. He daubs a darker brown along the arcing lines of trees, filling in wooden lampposts and door lintels, before rinsing his brush.

An alpha-omega couple jogs by next—two women with neon headbands and sports bras—and smile as they buy a cup of lemonade to share. They spend a minute admiring Felix's painting, smelling like sandalwood and rose, before heading down the quieter end of the street.

"We've never gone jogging," Felix says.

"We exercised other ways."

Felix doesn't have to look at Kade to know the glint in his eyes. He chuckles. "Always about the sex, huh?"

"No. You know that."

He does. Kade has joked with him, taken him out to art shows, followed him down steep hills for a picture, and he can't even begin to describe the relationship he'd left behind. So he mixes cyan and pink for a vibrant lilac shade, and dabs it across the canvas, spots of flowers speckled along the front lawns. "How have your parents been the past few years? I... haven't caught up with them."

Kade thinks on his words for a while. "My mom's doing okay. My dad died a couple years

back. So Chris and Sam left, the bastards."
Felix stills, the air whooshing out of his lungs. He's known Kade's father since he was ten, and Mr. Brentwood had been family to him. "Your dad died?"

11
Felix

FELIX CAN'T breathe. Kade's dad is dead. And he hadn't been there for Kade when he needed someone to lean on.

Only a failure does that. He bites hard on his lip, wondering how else he's failed his bondmate. Why is Kade staying around when he needs to find an omega better than Felix?

Kade shrugs, looking at the curb. Lines deepen around his mouth. "Yeah. We weren't doing that well after you left. My dad went back to being a mechanic—and... There was a workplace accident."

How? Felix wants to ask. He forces the question down, not wanting to put Kade through his grief again.

But he needs to know, too, because he's spent years with Kade's family. Kade's father bringing them all to the swimming pool. Kade's mother baking cookies for him. Kade's younger brothers had teased him for being omega, but Kade has always defended Felix. Kade has always been there for him.

Felix wants to cry, suddenly. "Oh."

Kade flicks a look at him. "Shit," he mutters, reaching out. "C'mon. Sit down."

"You... didn't say anything about it," Felix says, his voice strangled. Kade scoots to the other chair; Felix trudges over, sinking heavily into his warm seat.

"I thought you didn't want to know." But Kade watches him sidelong, and Felix's heart aches. How had he not found out? He's spent a month back in Meadowfall, and he had no idea...

He remembers the man—a tall, sturdy alpha with salt-and-pepper hair—who treated Felix as one of his own sons, playing volleyball with them in the yard, mussing Felix's hair while he grinned. Felix tries to imagine Kade after his father's death, crumpled, the light gone from his eyes, and he's gasping, fingers curling into the warm metal of the chair.

"Hey, don't cry," Kade says. He pulls Felix into a hug, and Felix trembles against him, his cheeks itchy with tears. "He went quickly. Car crashed into the mechanic shop. He was trapped under it. They said it was an instant death."

Something inside Felix rips apart, and he's sobbing into Kade's shoulder, little whimpers that don't sound like his own. He shouldn't even be this upset about it, but he is. Kade's hand on his back just makes him shake harder. How had he not been here when Kade needed him? How can Felix suck so much as a bondmate? How...?

"I'm fine now," Kade murmurs in his ear. "We're doing okay."

Felix snakes his hand between them, touching his own belly. The bump still isn't showing yet, and maybe all this is a hallucination. Maybe he's just imagining the pregnancy. He can't bear this child and still face Kade, when he's caused the bankruptcy, caused Kade's dad to return to work, caused his dad to die.

Felix deserves so much pain, and yet Kade's here, holding him, whispering into his ear. "Why?" he asks, and his voice rises high and thin, a pathetic whine. "Why—"

"Shh," Kade says. He strokes over Felix's back, and his scent is familiar and comforting against Felix's nose. "It's okay."

"It's not okay," Felix says, pulling away from him before he loses his resolve. "You shouldn't do this. I'm not—I'm not..."

I'm not fit to be your bondmate, he wants to say, but Kade kisses him.

It starts off slow and gentle, Kade's lips soft against his own, and Felix stills. *You shouldn't be doing this,* he thinks, but Kade's mouth caresses his, as though he's saying *You'll be fine.* Felix trembles.

Kade coaxes his lips open, slides in, and Felix needs him, has always needed this man. His fingers tangle in Kade's shirt, and he leans in, hungry for this intimacy, for the promise of safety and comfort. Kade drags his wrist over Felix's arms, marking his shoulders and his back, then his nape, his throat. Felix wants to say *I'm all yours,* except he can't.

"Why?" he whispers against Kade's lips, his breath hitching.

"Because—" But Kade doesn't continue. He threads his fingers through Felix's hair, brushing his scalp, rubbing the small of his back. His touch eases the misery that's been building in Felix's chest, untangling it, drawing it out of him, until Felix sags against his alpha, shaking and weak, his mind whirling.

"Uh, hi. Are you still selling lemonade?"

Felix startles, leaping out of his seat. Kade glances up at the gangling teenage boy standing to a side, a wince on his face. "Sorry," the boy says, blushing. "I, uh, just wanted to get my sis and I some drinks."

He waves at a girl in a sundress across the road. Felix looks back down at the lemonade stand, at the scatter of condensation on the lemonade jug, and the upside-down stack of colorful cups they've got in front of them. "Sure," he says. "I'm so sorry. How many cups did you want?"

"Two. Thanks." The boy hands over a bill and some coins. Kade drops them in the coin bowl, while Felix scoops ice into two cups. "Nice painting. I really like the colors."

"Thanks!" Felix swears inwardly. They're supposed to be here earning money for his website, not kissing or dissolving into a mess of tears. He tries to breathe through his stopped nose and gives up. "If you ever want some paintings done, feel free to contact me! I also do art lessons. My number and email are on this postcard."

"Thanks," the boy says. He raises a cup in a toast, then walks off.

Felix winces, swiping the wet trails off his cheeks. "Damn it."

"I'm here if you wanna talk," Kade says, watching him solemnly.

"Okay." Felix swallows, turning back to the

painting, mixing water with bright lemon yellow.

To the side, Kade leans back in his chair, tipping his face to the sky. "I haven't heard from Chris and Sam in a couple years."

Felix glances at him. "You haven't? But they're your brothers."

Kade shrugs. "They left after Dad died. I think they were trying to cope in their own way. They've been helping with the house payment, though. There's checks in the mail sometimes."

"That's nice," Felix says. He ducks his head, hiding his wince. He should have helped, too, but he'd been away in Highton, trying to secure buyers and art shows. "I should have been here."

He feels the prickle of Kade's gaze again, but Kade doesn't speak. So Felix paints, adding first the pastel greens and pinks, then the burnished hues of red roof tiles, and the spreading wings of fluttering birds.

While he layers finer details into the houses, he thinks about Kade's father, about Kade's loss, about all the things that could have gone right between them, but didn't. Neighbors and passers-by drive up to their lemonade stand, a steady trickle of people that walk up with smiles, and then head off with colorful cups of lemonade.

"It's doing better than I expected," Felix says when they're down to twenty plastic cups. The watercolor is done, a quick painting of this street, and he clips it to the back of the easel to dry. "I mean... I thought we'd just have five customers."

"We're gonna need another batch," Kade says, nodding at the almost-empty jug. "And some sunblock too. You're turning pink."

"I am?" Felix rubs his cheeks, frowning. Now that he's paying attention to himself, he feels the prickle of sunburn on his face. "Oops."

Kade sighs, glancing up at the sun. "It's just past three. Do you wanna go back and make another jug? And get a hat or something if you don't have sunblock."

"I have a hat," Felix says. "Do you need one too?" Kade shrugs, so Felix rests a tentative hand on his shoulder, squeezing lightly. Kade lets his hand stay. "Right. I'll be back with more lemonade."

Kade nods. Felix jogs home, thinking about the painting he left out to dry. Maybe he should have left a price on that with Kade, but in this neighborhood, he doesn't know if anyone would be interested in a painting. People had been more willing to pay for art back in Highton. He sighs, stumbling into his home, and heads for the kitchen.

The sun glares when he steps out ten minutes later, with a full jug of lemonade and hats under his arm. He hurries back to the lemonade stand, thinking they'll still have twenty plastic cups, maybe nineteen. Kade will be staring at the cars driving past, bored.

What he doesn't expect to find is an old man in a baggy T-shirt and trousers, peering at the painting through his glasses. He smells like fresh-cut grass.

"He's the one who painted it," Kade says, nodding when Felix steps closer. To Felix, he says, "This guy wants to buy your painting."

"Yes, it's beautiful," the man says, his rheumy eyes magnified by his glasses. He looks up at Felix, smiling brightly. "My husband and I have been living on this street for thirty years. I think he'll love this painting."

Felix smiles, his heart leaping. "That's really sweet. I'm very touched that you like it."

"How much do you want for it?" the man asks.

Felix hesitates. He doesn't want to price the painting too high, because it'll feel like he's cheating the old man of his money. Not everyone in this neighborhood can afford things like that. So he begins to say *Thirty,* but Kade cuts in. "Fifty."

Felix stares at his bondmate, eyes wide. *Fifty?*

Kade raises an eyebrow. *Are you gonna say no?*

"Fifty is a good price," the old beta says. Felix gapes at him. The man pulls out his wallet, thumbing through the bills inside. Felix sets the jug of lemonade down so he won't drop it. It's very generous of the man. He accepts the notes when the man hands it over, unclipping the painting from his easel. "You haven't signed it yet."

"I guess I haven't." He'd forgotten about that, too, while he'd been busy thinking about the lemonade. Both Kade and the old man watch as he scrawls his signature at the bottom of the painting, before handing it over with a flourish. "I hope you and your husband enjoy this painting! If you'd like to reach me, my phone number and email address are here."

The man accepts his postcards. Felix watches as he strolls back down the street, disappearing behind a wall of bougainvillea bushes.

"I feel bad about the price," Felix says,

sinking into the seat next to Kade. He stares at the notes in his hand—some crisp, some ragged—and rubs his thumb over them.

"He agreed to pay for it," Kade says. "People value things they sink money into."

He looks back at the money, thinking about the old man and his husband, about Kade and valuable things. "What if you didn't pay for something? Would you still value them?" *You didn't pay for me.*

Kade studies him quietly, as though he sees through Felix's question. Felix gulps. "Some things we don't pay for with cash," Kade murmurs, "but with everything else."

He doesn't know what Kade means by that, so he looks at his hands, folding the notes up. "Here, the fifty dollars for the website."

Kade's lips pull into a smile. "Keep it. I said I'm taking the profits from this, remember?"

"Well, I'd rather pay you back," Felix says, extending the stack of notes to him.

And Kade reaches over, closing his hand over Felix's. The heat of his palm soaks through Felix's skin. "Keep it."

Felix lowers his gaze, afraid to meet Kade's eyes. He nods, heat rushing up his cheeks, and tugs the hats from under his arm. "Here, I brought us hats. That's yours."

Kade snorts, but he wears the sunhat anyway, a flimsy woven thing that matches Felix's, from when he and Taylor had bought them at the beach. Five minutes later, Felix starts on his next painting.

When the sun begins to inch toward the

horizon, Kade gets up from his chair, stretching. "Want some food? I'll go to the store and grab something. And some vodka—we can sell that with lemonade."

Felix laughs. "We can sell that?"

Kade grins, rugged and handsome, and Felix's pulse thuds in his ears. "Sure."

Kade heads back to the house, roaring by a minute later on his bike. He waves at Felix when he passes; Felix waves back, before hiding his face. It feels like they're back to being friends, when they shouldn't be. He's pregnant, and Kade still doesn't know.

The minutes drag by without Kade. Some teenagers walk up to the stand, buying a few cups of lemonade, and more joggers pass by with their dogs. The next painting ends up being a sunset by the beach. Felix smiles while he paints, thinking about Kade's warmth, about his smile, Kade coming back to him. It feels a little bit like what they used to have.

Felix straightens when Kade returns, dropping a plastic bag on the table, before he rides off to park the bike. Curious, Felix picks through the bag—a bottle of vodka, a tuna sandwich, and a box of pasta salad. He pries open the tuna sandwich packet.

"Thought you hate fish," Kade says, settling into the chair next to him.

Felix pauses, the tuna sandwich halfway to his mouth. "I... don't know. I have an urge to try it. There, take the rest."

Kade looks at him oddly. Felix bites into the sandwich anyway, and the fishy scent of tuna isn't as awful as it usually is. He swallows, and takes another bite. Kade pushes the other half-sandwich back. "If you like it, have the rest."

"But the pasta," Felix says, guilt swirling in his stomach. "You don't like pasta all that much."

Kade rolls his eyes. "You ate my sandwich anyway."

Felix blushes. "It's fine. Have the other half."

They end up splitting the food between them, sharing a fork. Kade pops the bottle of vodka open. "Want some in your lemonade?"

Felix opens his mouth to say yes, then freezes. "No." Kade looks at him again, so he hurries to say, "I might have gotten hives once. When I was away and drunk. I'm just... I'd rather not be drinking again anytime soon."

Which is bullshit, another lie on the mountain of lies, but Felix forces himself to meet Kade's eyes.

In the end, Kade nods. "Sure."

Felix should have gotten used to the guilt by now. He prods at the pasta salad, sighing.

"Tired?" Kade asks. "You puked this morning."

Felix shakes his head. *I didn't think you were watching so closely.* "I'm fine. It's just been a long day."

"You feel better? Not sick or anything?"

"I'm fine." Felix grins. Kade smiles, bumping their arms together.

The altered signboards—*vodka lemonade: $7*—get them a few more sales, and by the time the sky turns a velvety blue and the streetlamps flicker on, Felix yawns, his eyelids drooping.

"Let's pack up," Kade says. "Not selling

anymore, anyway."

Felix nods. They clear the table, fold the chairs and easel, and trudge back to Felix's place, setting down the materials just inside the doorway.

"You're working tomorrow?" Kade glances at the closed front door. In the living room, only one lamp is on, its weak golden glow stretching into the shadowy corners. "It's late."

"I am." Felix rubs his eyes. He slips past Kade to the door, stifling his yawn. "I just..."

Kade steps up behind him, a sturdy heat. His arms whisper around Felix's waist, pulling him gently back against his chest. Felix's eyes snap open. They shouldn't be hugging. He isn't prepared for this. Neither is he prepared for Kade's lips brushing down his neck. His heart pounds, and he wants more.

Kade slides one hand up his chest, rubbing his nipples through his shirt. His other hand drags down Felix's abdomen, cradling him. Felix's stomach drops. He thinks, *Do you already know?* but Kade's fingers brush down to his groin, and cup him through his pants.

Felix moans. Kade kneads him slowly, working him, and maybe Felix shouldn't be hard already. He can't help it. Kade plays his body like a familiar instrument, unzipping his pants, teasing his cock out. He sucks lightly on the scent gland at Felix's neck, and pleasure jolts down his spine.

Kade pulls slow and firm on his cock, massaging him until he throbs with need. Then he relaxes his touch, fingers circling loosely around Felix.

Felix snaps his hips forward, shoving into his

hand, tension humming through his body. It feels wrong to plead right now, when Kade hasn't said a word, so he thrusts forward, then grinds back, his pulse thumping when he feels Kade hard in his pants. So Felix pushes up against his alpha, and Kade's breath hitches.

But Kade doesn't touch himself. It feels wrong that he isn't, because isn't this just about pleasure? He's expecting something after, isn't he? He tightens his grip around Felix, stroking steadily with precum-slick fingers. Felix tenses, pulsing with need.

Kade kisses his shoulder, cupping his other hand in front of Felix's cock. Felix hears *Come for me* above Kade's ragged breathing. Kade's teeth graze lightly against his scent gland, a firm, light pressure, and Felix comes, shuddering, pleasure surging through his body as he spills into Kade's palm.

Kade groans, milking him dry, before he brings his hand up and licks Felix's cum off his skin. Felix shivers, panting. Kade presses a damp kiss to his nape.

Before Felix can offer to return the favor, Kade growls, "I'll see you around."

He slips out the door, shutting it quietly behind himself.

What just happened? Felix staggers forward, leaning onto the door for support. What could Kade have gotten out of that, just touching him? Why didn't he want to stay? They aren't lovers anymore, but Felix is more than willing to touch him in return.

Don't go, he wants to say. The bike roars

outside, and he imagines Kade backing out the driveway, his eyes hidden behind his helmet. His laptop is still in the kitchen. Felix is certain he'll be back for it.

And no matter how many times Kade returns after this, Felix will be willing to spread for him, every time.

12
Kade

20 Years Ago

THE FIRST time Kade meets Felix, he's running late for art class.

He dashes into the classroom after splitting his lunch with his brothers, because they'd gone and lost theirs somewhere. And they'd almost spilled his lunchbox, too. So Kade dashes through the door three minutes after the bell clangs, hoping the art teacher isn't there yet.

"Sit down," Mrs. Penny says, frowning over the rim of her glasses. Kade scowls. Not his fault his brothers argued over *his* lunch.

All the seats are filled except one, at a table where a skinny blond boy is picking out pencils from a case. Kade drops into the chair next to his, blowing a sigh. He hates art class. Nothing he draws ever turns out decent.

"What's wrong?" the boy asks, looking over.

Sheets of blank paper cover his desk, and the pencils roll across them, all sharpened, their paint coating unchewed. Kade's never seen anyone with cared-for pencils like that. The boy smiles shyly.

"I guess you need some paper, too." He

slides a large sheet over, but not the pencils.

Kade stares down at the paper, still panting. Maybe he should've gotten here earlier. This blond kid isn't so bad. "What're we supposed to draw?"

The boy looks up at the chalkboard, where Mrs. Penny has written *Garden* in cursive letters. "Plants, I guess. What's your garden like?"

"My mom has a huge one," Kade says. "She likes the roses and the tulips most, but it's so hot in the summer that the tulips always wilt. She makes me dig them up. Bah."

The boy giggles. "It must be fun to dig up plants! I can't touch mine. The gardeners take care of our gardens, so they always look like the parks."

Kade shrugs. He only looks at flowers when his mom points them out to him. What sort of family can afford gardeners? "What's your name?"

"Felix." The boy picks up a pencil, tracing faint curves over the sheet. "What's yours?"

"Kade." He pulls his pencil case out of his bag, picking out a chewed, blunt pencil. "I don't like drawing. It's stupid."

Felix shrugs. "It's fun."

Kade tries to draw the roses along the front of his house, but they turn out looking like lumps of coal. He erases the drawing, scowling when the eraser leaves smudges of black across his paper. "Screw this."

His desk-mate looks over. "Here, why don't you use mine?"

He hands Kade a pink square, his own sheet covered in flower-dotted bushes, rocky paths, and a sky full of puffy clouds. Kade gapes.

In the same time Felix took to sketch that, he

had only drawn three flowers. "You just drew that... that garden."

Felix tilts his head. "Yes, I did."

"How?" The only other person who draws that well is Kade's mom, and she has some old sketches of horses and whales hanging on the walls at home. "That's really good."

A wave of red sweeps up Felix's cheeks. "Oh. Well, I practiced. It's the only thing I'm good at. At least, that's what my father says."

He's pretty, Kade thinks, staring at the forest-green of his eyes, the curve of his lips. "I'm good at lots of things," he says. "I've been helping my dad fix the computers at his work. They have ten of them there!"

"Wow." Felix's eyes grow round. "I'm not so good with computers. You must be clever."

Kade puffs his chest out. "'Course I am. I've been getting full marks on my tests. And my mom says I'm learning a lot."

Felix smiles, then looks down at his drawing. "I wish my father would say that. My brother's better at everything, and Father transferred him to a different school so he can learn faster."

Kade didn't know people learned at different speeds in other schools. He shrugs, leaning in to nudge Felix. "Well, you can come join me in the playground. I build my castles there in the mornings."

Felix brightens, his eyes shining. "Really?"

"Yeah," Kade says. "I need help building sandcastles. My dad says we gotta dream big. So I'm gonna dig holes into the playground and build all the things."

Felix giggles, and Kade grins along with him. "Okay."

13
Felix

Present Day

FELIX STEPS out of the employee washroom, wincing. Two months since the lemonade stand, and the morning sickness hasn't abated. He sniffs at his work shirt, trying to decide if the faint sour tang comes from the dregs of scents in his nose, or if his shirt really does smell like puke.

I guess that's what pregnancy and child-raising is. Puke and more puke.

The store is blissfully empty, and he finds Susan behind the counter, her eyes narrowed. "Please tell me he knows," she says.

Felix winces. His morning sickness rears its head during his morning shift sometimes, while Susan is around, and it's painfully obvious when he's been dashing to the bathroom with no warning at all. "You noticed?"

"I guessed it the second week in," she says, moving over when he rounds the counter. Felix cringes. "It's just painful watching you talk to him when you guys are, like, two-hundred percent smitten."

"We're not." Felix glances down at his baggy

shirt, to convince himself that the little bump of his abdomen isn't obvious. "I mean, we see each other occasionally. Like once every two weeks."

By "see", he really means "fuck", when Kade drops by his place to check on his website, and he ends up bending Felix over on the kitchen counters, sliding home. Felix cuts that thought off, in case it shows in his pants. Kade still hasn't taken his laptop back.

"And right after that, you come back here smelling like him. I mean, you smell like alpha, not omega. Do you know how weird that is?" Susan lifts her eyebrows. "I mean, you don't even look like an alpha—you're kind of slender. Narrow shoulders, pretty. Of course, Rick comes in and sniffs, and I try not to laugh at his expression when he smells you."

Felix winces, glancing around the shop and out the door. No manager. "He's nasty."

"Not the biggest jerk in Meadowfall, but a jerk anyway." Susan chuckles, but her smile fades. She pulls the store inventory off a shelf, flipping through it. "But back to your secret."

He groans. "Can we not talk about it?"

"You're going to have to. How long are you staying here?"

Felix bites his lip, counting the funds he's been setting aside. "Maybe another three months. More than that, and it'll be obvious. I guess I'll borrow off my brother if I really have to."

Susan shakes her head. "You're really not telling Kade?"

"I can't! I—Well, he won't be interested." He frowns when Susan rolls her eyes. She doesn't know all his other reasons. "He didn't consent to a child, so..."

"Oh, Felix. That's not how it goes." Susan drapes her arm around his shoulder, squeezing lightly. "Having a family is all about support. And I'm sure he'll be glad to know you're expecting."

"Oh gods, please don't mention it in front of him," Felix says, cringing. "He really can't find out."

Susan cocks her head. "It's not his?"

Felix wants to laugh. He hasn't slept with anyone else in a while. "It's *mine.*"

"Still."

"Promise you aren't going to tell," he says, sticking his pinky out. "Please. No mentions of babies or anything in front of him. Nothing about puking."

Susan stares warily at his finger. "He really should know."

"No, he really shouldn't."

She sighs, linking their fingers together. "Fine. But if he explodes, and I mean in a bad way, I'm saying it's your fault."

"Yeah, everything is my fault."Felix snorts. That's probably what Kade thinks, too.

An engine roars outside the store, the sound muffled by the glass doors. They look up at the same time. Felix's stomach flops. *It's not Kade, is it?* "Quick," he hisses. "Do I smell like puke?"

Susan sighs. Her nostrils flare, though, and she shakes her head. "You're good."

Felix nods, gulping some water. He grabs the delivery roster to keep busy, and Susan flips through the inventory, stepping away from the counter. Felix's neck prickles. He looks up, and he recognizes those broad shoulders through the glass doors, that leather jacket.

The doors trundle open. Kade steps in, looking him over, his gaze hot. Just like that, Felix is hard. He shouldn't be affected this easily. But he shouldn't be pregnant, either. And even though he's been seeing Kade for the past three months, his pulse still races at the sight of his alpha, those mahogany eyes sliding down his chest, to his hips.

The corners of Kade's mouth quirk up, and he meets Felix's eyes. "Hello," Felix says, breathless. "Haven't seen you in a while."

"Oh, jeez," Susan mutters. She steps away from the counter, weaving through the shelves to the back of the store. Abandoning him. Felix makes a face at her back.

"Hey," Kade says. His voice rumbles down Felix's spine, and Felix's pants strain tight around his hips. Kade steps closer to the counter. "Sorry. Had to work on the bike for a bit."

"You should be at work," Felix says. "It's kind of early, isn't it?"

Kade shrugs. "Didn't have to go in today. Just dropping by for a project meeting."

"How is work?"

"Not bad." Kade studies him, and it feels as though he can read all of Felix's secrets in one glance. "I'll drop by to help with your website this weekend. That okay?"

"Yeah, sure," Felix says, even though they both know it means they'll look at the site for half an hour, and Felix will be spreading for him twenty minutes later. Things have gone that way ever since the lemonade stand. Felix has no complaints about it. How can he, really, if his alpha has been fucking him delirious?

Behind the shelves, Susan coughs. Kade's gaze lingers on Felix.

He squirms to ease the discomfort of his pants. It doesn't help, so he reaches down, and Kade watches him nudge his erection sideways. Felix's throat runs dry. "I mean, the site isn't drawing a lot of traffic yet. It did get more clicks after we tried selling cookies, so we should try that again. Perhaps in a better neighborhood."

"Or even Highton?"

"Actually, that sounds good. Just to revive the business there." Felix tries smiling, and Kade returns it. Felix's pulse flutters.

"I've got a favor to ask, actually," Kade says a moment later.

Felix blinks. What could Kade possibly want from him, that he doesn't already have? "Really?"

"Yeah. Do you still have that watercolor of the bay?" Kade holds his gaze. "I think my dad really liked that one. I showed him a picture of it once. Not sure if I told you."

Felix bites his lip. He remembers the painting vaguely, a waterscape with a boardwalk outside a restaurant. Maybe he brought it along when he moved. "I'll look for it when I go home."

"Thanks."

Felix grins. "So are you buying anything, or did you just stop by to ask that?"

"Pump eight. Five gallons of middle-grade gas."

"Fourteen fifty-six."

Kade hands the cash over in notes and coins, his fingers brushing over Felix's palm. Felix breathes in deep just to catch his pine-and-cedar scent, and Kade brushes their wrists together, marking him. Felix blushes. Maybe he should question why Kade keeps scenting him, but Kade has also promised his protection. That has to be the only reason why Felix smells like his alpha.

He ignores the lump in his throat, tapping the keys to approve the transaction, before dropping the coins into the register. The register cranks out a receipt. Felix hands it over with Kade's change, unable to stop himself from touching Kade's fingers again.

"See you," Kade says, his eyes dark.

"See you," Felix answers, but he wishes Kade were staying longer, wishes he could burrow into Kade's arms. The weekend seems like a month away. To the baby, he thinks, *Your other dad is the most gorgeous man.*

Kade steps out of the store, and Felix wants to be right next to him, Kade's smile a promise for the future.

14
Felix

TWO DAYS later, Felix steps off a bus and follows the winding, orange-lit sidewalks up to his father's mansion.

He glances down at his phone. *I'd rather be at the gas station. But it's not as though I can find the painting anywhere else.* He wishes Taylor was with him. Taylor talks to their father and charms his attention away from Felix, but Taylor has gone dark again. Felix shivers in the cool breeze.

The things I do because of you, Kade.

Felix quells the uneasiness in his stomach as he walks up to the wrought-iron gates, nodding at the guards. They nod back and heave at the tall gates open, and they open like a giant's maw ready to swallow him down. He grits his teeth and steps in.

No one greets him along the ascending driveway, or at the towering front doors. Felix twists his key in the lock, holds his breath, and pushes the door open.

Inside, the marble-lined foyer stretches out before him, exquisite spotlights reflecting in their surfaces. Felix shuts the door softly behind him, listening to the quiet footfalls of the servants in the other hallways, the clink of dishes in the far-off kitchen. He takes the stairs on the right, treading on ivory carpets to mask his footsteps, and his heart thunders in his chest.

At the top of the stairs, he turns down a long corridor, following the carpet past carved wooden doors, the high ceilings arching over him. It feels like he's stepping through a hotel, almost, even though he lived here for the first twenty years of his life. He'd moved out and shared a home with Kade for five years—

"Sir," a voice says at his shoulder. Felix's heart slams into his chest. He jumps, guilt prickling his skin. He shouldn't be sneaking like a thief through his childhood home.

"James," he says, wheezing. The butler by his side smells like hay, calm eyes studying him. "I'm sorry. I didn't hear you."

"A good butler is never heard," James says, his mouth curving into a kindly smile. "Might you be looking for your father?"

"Actually, no. I was just back for a painting. Do you... know where my father is?" Felix relaxes his face like the thousand times he's seen his father grin for cameras, but he's certain that James can read beneath his smile, anyway.

"He has retired to his study for the night. I believe he has a meeting with the council tomorrow."

Which means he'll be occupied, not coming out to judge Felix. Felix sighs. "Thank you."

James nods, turning down the next hallway. Felix pads through more corridors, gaze darting to the closed doors for the slightest sign of movement.

He relaxes slightly when he turns into the west wing, where he and his brother had rooms on opposite sides of the hallway, and they'd wait until the lights were off, before tapping on each other's doors.

The silver doorknob to his room turns easily. He slips into the shadowy suite, flipping the light switch. The bed is made, and the room smells very slightly musty, as though no one has visited in months. Felix glances longingly at the bed, and heads instead for the row of framed paintings in the corner, next to a solid oak desk.

You're okay with this? Kade had asked a decade ago. *Leaving your dad's place to live with me? I can't... provide all of that.*

I don't care about furniture, Felix had said. *I care about you.*

Felix touches the curve of his abdomen through his sweater. "And look where that has gotten us," he murmurs. "It shouldn't have happened."

There had been no space in their tiny apartment for all his previous work. Felix pulls the thick sheet of cotton off the paintings, flipping through them: a whale surfacing in a harbor, a crooked log cabin tucked into a snowy pine forest, a shadowy boat shop with giant propellers on the floor.

"Look at these," Felix murmurs at his belly. He imagines a baby girl, with Kade's dark hair and eyes, laughing as she waves a paintbrush around. "I hope that when you grow up, you'll love to paint, too."

He finds the painting of the bay right at the

end, tucked into the awning of larger frames. Felix lifts it out carefully, studying the crooked planks of the boardwalk, the hazy people behind the restaurant window, the sea sparkling beyond the railings. He slips his phone out of his pocket, snaps a picture of it, and hesitates.

Kade had typed his number into the contacts list. Felix had never sent him a message or called, but... he wants to hear Kade's voice, suddenly.

He scrolls down the list, to where Kade had typed his name as "Kade Brentwood", as though Felix will label anyone else as just "Kade". Felix bites his lip. Before he second-guesses himself, he hits the call button.

The dial tone rings four times, and Kade answers. "Hey." His voice sounds tinny over the phone, and it steals Felix's breath, just hearing him again. "Felix?"

Felix's heart thuds. He hadn't realized that Kade has his number. He had to have seen it when they gave postcards out at the lemonade stand, but it isn't as though he can't look it up on the website. And so Felix can't pretend that he's calling the wrong number, or that this is a prank call. "I found the painting," he blurts. "I just wondered if you want a picture of it first."

"Sure. Thanks," Kade says. Felix wishes he would talk more, so he can close his eyes and listen to Kade's voice. "I'll pay for it."

"No, no. It's fine. I'll just give it to you." Because Kade never took the money from the lemonade stand like he said he would. Felix has tried shoving the bills in his pockets during the times he visits. And he always finds them tucked under his pillow, or in his kitchen cabinets, or somewhere he wouldn't look until after Kade leaves.

"Whatever you want. That painting's worth money, you know."

And I want you to be happy. That's worth more than money. Felix sighs. "I guess we'll see. I can drop it at your place or something, if you text me your address."

"Okay."

They fall silent. Felix cradles the phone against his ear, thinking about Kade on the other end of the line, holding the phone to *his* ear. Kade just listening, waiting for him to speak. He swallows, his chest aching. Kade has to be in his kitchen, or on his couch, the TV turned to mute.

"What are you doing now?" Felix asks, and regrets it immediately. It's not as though they're dating or anything.

"Watching the motor-cross races," Kade says. "You?"

Felix licks his lips, looking at the paintings. "At my dad's place. I thought I might find the painting here."

Kade mulls over his words. "Want me to pick you up?"

"No, no. It's fine," Felix says, because he shouldn't. He'll be leaving Meadowfall, and he doesn't need to fall in love with this man again. "I'm sorry—I have to go. It's getting late. I still have to get out without bumping into my dad."

"Okay. Call if you need anything," Kade says.

Felix glances at the door."Will do. Thank

you."

He hits the end call button so he doesn't linger on Kade's voice, shoving the phone back into his pocket. He has to leave. This place doesn't feel like home, and Felix wishes he could just teleport outside, but he can't.

Painting in hand, he shuts off the lights and cracks the door open. He makes it down three corridors, wooden frame bumping into his thigh, before a lock clicks. "Felix?"

He freezes, heart kicking against his ribs. Slowly, Felix pastes a smile on his face and turns. "Good evening, Father. I didn't expect to meet you."

Alastor Henry stands, tall and broad-shouldered, one hand on the doorknob of his study. This late at night, he's dressed in a starched shirt and a burgundy robe. Felix feels like a school kid in his shirt and jeans. With a frown, his father sniffs the air. "Where's your scent? You smell like that... Brentwood son, was it?"

Felix swallows. "Kade, yes."

His father frowns. Kade's family ranks nowhere near the Henry line, even if Alastor's two sons are both omegas. Alastor's status as an alpha mayor far overshadows Kade's, and for that reason, Felix's father has never liked Kade. *Neither you nor that Brentwood boy are competent enough to inherit the Henry line,* Alastor said once. *Taylor is far better suited to it.*

"Why are you suppressing your scent?" his father asks, looking down his nose at him.

Felix sighs, holding his arm at his side, even though he wants to touch his belly. The bonding mark at his wrist prickles. "I smell like an alpha. Isn't that enough?"

Alastor's lips thin. Felix wishes he were far away from Meadowfall. He shouldn't have turned to his father for help. "He's not good enough for you."

Felix almost laughs at that. *Really?* "His father has passed away. You know that, don't you?"

Alastor dips his chin. "I may have heard about it."

"You forced them into bankruptcy," Felix says, heat building in his chest. He's had two months to think about this, since that afternoon at the lemonade stand, and he's been regretting his decisions ever since. He—and his father—had caused Kade's dad to die. His voice wavers. "Mr. Brentwood had to return to work, and it killed him. I can't believe you asked for my help."

Because it was his father who had said, *I'm planning to rebrand some estates. Could you do some artist's impressions for higher-end housing?*

Felix had pored over those impressions for days, and his father had taken those drawings and marketed them to a wealthier crowd. Then, he had raised the rents for the existing community, sinking them into debt. Then the new tenants had started moving in, and Felix only realized then which community his father had been referring to. And Kade never found out who caused it, because the Henry line was never linked to the rental corporation.

"I'm sorry to hear about their loss," his father says, his face pulling into a solemn mask, like the countless times he's had to listen to the people's woes.

"You're not sorry at all," Felix mutters, his eyes burning. "You only care about money."

His father meets his gaze. Felix reads flinty disapproval, even now. "Do I?"

"I'm sorry my choices disappoint you," Felix says. The words clog up his throat. "I was just here to retrieve a painting."

"I see." His father's gaze flickers to the frame. "I hope you've been doing better in Meadowfall."

Barely. "I have, thank you. It's getting late. I hope you'll have a pleasant day tomorrow," Felix says, nodding. His skin itches. "Goodnight."

"Goodnight," his father says. "I'll see you again."

Felix walks stiffly to the end of the corridor. The moment he rounds the corner, he runs, his eyes stinging. He hates his father. Hates what he's done, hates himself for starting it all. He dashes along the carpets, feet thumping down the stairs, across the marble-lined foyer. Then he pushes out of the front door, and the night air is chilly against his skin.

Felix stumbles down the driveway, catching himself before he falls. His fingertips press white into the glass of the painting, and all he thinks about is Kade, Kade protecting him, Kade's warm arms curving around him and their child. *Don't wanna knock you up,* Kade had said.

I miss you, Felix thinks, but he doesn't have Kade to return home to, either.

15
Kade

KADE SETS the third bolt down on the concrete garage floor, glancing at the wall clock. 1:10PM. Felix still isn't here yet. He glances at the phone on the nearby stool, expecting it to buzz. Instead, it stays mutinously silent. With a sigh, he hooks his wrench around the fourth bolt on the air filter, loosening it.

He's heard nothing from Felix in the past two days.

The last time he did, Felix had been at his dad's place. He'd sent a snapshot of the bay painting the day after, then fallen silent. Kade assumes he isn't interested, since their communications so far have all taken place at the gas station, or at Felix's place.

The old air filter unhooks easily from the bike. He wipes the pipes down with a blackened rag, eyeing the new circular filter next to him, complete with chrome trim and gleaming black paint. It matches the rest of the bike, all sleek and streamlined, and yet... Kade sighs, setting his wrench down.

He had felt a twinge of guilt when he

splurged on a hundred-dollar filter. But he doesn't have much to pay for—he's just sharing a house with his mom right now, with no plans to settle into his own home. It would be different if he had a husband, or a family to consider.

Besides, Felix had said Kade wasn't good enough, five years ago. *Should've known that alpha rankings were important to you, too.*

Down the road, the neighbor's kids yell over basketball, and further away, a drill whines. Sunlight glints off his mom's car in the driveway. *It's a beautiful cornflower blue,* he imagines Felix saying.

Sweat trickles down his neck. With an exhale, he tugs his shirt off, tossing it over his phone. *Doesn't look like you're coming today,* Kade thinks, glancing down at the ring resting against his chest. *Doesn't look like I'll ever have a use for the ring, either.*

His throat aches with loss, so he pushes that thought aside, installing the new filter. Felix has been turning down his offers of a ride—going home from work, getting to places—and Kade misses having his omega's arms around his waist, Felix's warmth seeping through his clothes as he leans in, his fingers smoothing down Kade's abs.

Since the lemonade stand, they've gotten a little closer. They've made plans—selling cookies door-to-door, painting at crowded malls, looking at the website... except peering at the laptop is really an excuse to slide his hand down Felix's pants. Felix arches into his palm every time.

Kade swallows, pushing those thoughts aside. He's in the middle of installing his new filter, and the garage doors are wide open, facing the street. Not the best time to start jerking off.

So he wipes his hands on a clean rag, then fastens the filter on with the first bolt, then the second, leaving them halfway tight for further adjustments. A car zooms by outside, and Kade hums to himself, one of the older songs he'd listened to in the tree house with Felix, years back, on a beat-up radio that they'd taken from his parents' kitchen.

He almost misses the step of thin legs on the other side of the bike.

"Kade?" Felix says

Kade looks up, his chain glinting in the reflected sunlight from the driveway. His stomach drops.

Shit. Kade ducks his head, closing his fist around the ring. Felix isn't supposed to see that. He tugs the chain up over his head, shaking it from his hair, and shoves it into his back pocket. His jeans are smeared with bike grease; another few fingerprints aren't going to matter. Better that than reminding Felix of that failed proposal. "Hey."

"I brought the painting," Felix says, stepping into the garage, sunlight at his back. Kade squints up at him. "Sorry I'm late. Taylor was over, and we were distracted talking about the news."

"That's fine," Kade says, heart thumping. Felix has always been close to his brother, and Taylor's always out of town. Kade knows—he'd tried calling Felix's brother five years ago, when Felix had left. Taylor never returned his calls.

Felix catches him squinting, stepping around to his other side, into the shadows. "Sorry. I didn't mean to bother you."

But his gaze wanders down Kade's sweaty chest, to his crossed legs, and then away, to the bike. Now that he isn't in direct sunlight, Kade sees the loose black shirt hanging off his shoulders, the skinny jeans wrapped around his legs. Even if Kade had to wait days to see him, it's worth it, just like it was worth waiting five years for his omega to return.

"Thanks for bringing the painting," Kade says. "I could've just ridden over for it."

Felix shrugs. His gaze wanders around the garage, though, hovering on the tools and cardboard boxes lying around. "I didn't want to bother you," he says. But he's still looking over the place, his face pinched, as though he's trying to make a decision about the garage. "Nice house."

Kade glances at the scar on Felix's wrist. Still the one bite. He breathes in deeply, catching faint lavender and a hint of musky sweat. He wants to bury his face in Felix's shoulder, in his chest, down between his legs. He clears his throat. Felix didn't drop by for sex.

"It's not bad," Kade says. "I split the place with my mom."

"Oh! She's here too?" Felix looks toward the white door leading into the house, as though expecting her to step in. "I didn't think... you would be living with her."

Kade shrugs. Without Felix, he'd needed someone else to protect. So he'd returned to his mom when his dad died, looking out for her when he could. "She needed company."

"I should say hi," Felix says, biting his lip. He hugs the painting to himself. "Do you think she'll...

want to see me?"

Kade raises an eyebrow. Felix knows Kade's mom loves him. She's made him cookies, and he's sat at their dinner table countless times. "Sure, why not?"

And Felix's tentative look droops. Does he think she'll turn him away?

Kade frowns. "What's wrong?"

"Nothing." Felix sucks in a deep breath, then blows it out. Like he's hiding something.

Kade curls his fingers against Felix's calf. "You're lying."

Felix goes stone-still then, green eyes darting to Kade's. Kade feels his skin prickle. "I'm not lying," Felix says.

Kade sighs. "You know I can read you, right?"

Felix's knuckles whiten over the picture frame.

Kade nods to the side. "Put that down. Don't want you dropping it."

Felix sets the painting carefully onto the nearby stool. Kade catches his hand, pulling him over so his shoes bump into Kade's foot.

"Sit," Kade says. Felix tenses. For a moment, he thinks Felix will turn and leave, now that he's left his painting with Kade like he asked.

But Felix's fingers tighten around his hand. "On you?"

"Wherever. On the floor or the bike if you rather do that."

His omega hesitates, then turns his back to the driveway, crouching so his ass sinks lightly down against Kade's thigh. His elbow bumps into

Kade's chest, and he settles, a familiar weight. Their faces are less than a foot apart, and Kade picks out the darker flecks of forest green in Felix's eyes, the taper of his eyelashes. Felix squirms. "Like that? I'm not too heavy, am I?"

"Hell no, you're not." Kade slips an arm around him. Felix shifts, his ass grinding into Kade's thigh, and a flare of heat shoots through Kade's gut. He wants to touch between Felix's legs, but they have things to discuss first. Like what Felix is lying about. So he leans in, nipping on Felix's earlobe. "Tell me what you're hiding."

Felix's cheeks flush a dark scarlet. "I told you, nothing."

"I've known you since we were ten, Felix. Not gonna work." Kade noses down his jaw, breathing him into his lungs.

"I should go," Felix whispers. But Kade rubs his thumb over Felix's palm. Felix swallows loudly. "Kade—"

"Tell me," Kade says, kissing the corner of his mouth. It feels like he's showing Felix too much of how he feels. "I've kept your secrets."

"This isn't..."

Kade releases his hand, dragging his palm up Felix's inner thigh, to his groin. Felix's jeans bulge with his arousal. A light musk rolls off his skin, and he moans softly, spreading his legs when Kade cups his cock through his pants. "C'mon," Kade murmurs. "I won't tell."

"I can't—" But Felix bites his lip, tongue flicking out to wet it, and heat surges down to Kade's groin, makes him want to roll his omega beneath him, pin him and fuck him and make him his.

"You looked like you were scared of my mom," Kade says, catching Felix's earlobe between his teeth. He reaches further down, pressing behind Felix's balls. Felix's breath hitches, his jeans growing the slightest bit damp. Kade's pants tighten.

"Please don't ask," Felix gasps, his fingers digging into Kade's knee and hip for leverage. He pushes up into Kade's palm. "It really has nothing to do with you."

Kade stills. Felix is still keeping a secret from him. But if he refuses to share it, Kade won't force him to. "No one's going to get hurt, right?"

"No one, I promise," Felix says, his pupils blown. Kade relaxes, tugging his loose shirt up. Felix hisses, grabbing his wrist, pushing it back down against his cock. It grinds warm and solid through rough fabric, and Kade relaxes, lets Felix guide his touch, because all he really wants is Felix needing him.

And Felix needs him like this, when he tugs Felix's jeans open in the shadows of his body, and his cock juts out before them, a smear of precum at its tip. From the street, all anyone can see is Felix's back, not Kade wiping his hand on his jeans, grasping Felix's cock and stroking him. Felix's breath shudders out of his mouth.

"Kade," Felix whispers, his legs spreading wide. "Kade, more."

"What do you want?" Kade murmurs, sliding Felix's foreskin down his tip, then back up, slow, light strokes that make him squirm. Clear fluid trickles down Felix's cock. Kade smears it around his tip, then down to his base.

Felix trembles. "Inside. Please."

Which sends a pulse of heat between Kade's legs, because he likes being inside, likes fucking Felix and joining them, likes filling his bondmate with his cum. He slides his fist off Felix's cock. "Bend over the bike."

Felix shivers, eyes growing wide. "Over the bike?"

"Yeah. Pants down." Kade's own precum leaks in his clothes. He wants to see this again, Felix on his bike, squirming and hungry for him. He slips his hand under Felix's ass, squeezing so he gasps, and rolls him onto his feet. "Up."

Felix stands unsteadily, glancing over his shoulder at the sidewalk. Kade closes the garage door. It shields them from the glaring sunlight and the invasive street noises, leaving them in the shadowy, enclosed space of the garage. Felix leans over the seat of the bike, pushing his pants down with a wriggle of his hips. Kade's instincts roar at that sight.

He bolts the garage door, reaching down to free his own cock, sighing at the relief when it juts out of his jeans. Then he steps behind Felix, nudging the inside of his shoe. "Feet apart."

Felix spreads his legs. Kade tugs Felix's pants down as far as they'll go, until he exposes his pale ass, his slender thighs, and he leans in, biting lightly on his bondmate's ass, leaving teeth marks across his skin. Kade noses at his cheeks, licking between them, sniffing the damp musk of his arousal. On the other side of the bike, Felix's breath hitches.

With his thumbs, Kade spreads his smooth cheeks apart, and in the shadows, Felix's musk sends a searing desire through his veins. He pushes his tongue between Felix's cheeks, lapping, then spreads him to expose his hole, trails of slick trickling down his inner thighs.

Kade licks the salty rivulets up first, following them to his omega's hole, and slowly swirls his tongue around it. Felix shivers against him, relaxing, an invitation to push inside. But Kade doesn't, merely lapping over the pucker of muscle, sniffing at the heady scent of Felix's need. Felix pushes his ass up, his fingers digging into the leather seat. "Kade, don't tease."

"You don't order me around," Kade growls, biting his cheek again, leaving a darker imprint. Felix gasps. Kade licks over his hole, testing the give of it under his tongue, the pucker of its muscles, the way Felix trembles, expecting more.

So he pushes into the tight ring with the point of his tongue, licking up musky slick. Felix moans. He tastes like sex, like omega and *Kade's.* Kade fucks him slowly, so Felix gasps and squirms, his thighs trembling. "Kade, please. I want you inside."

"I'm inside," Kade says, sliding his tongue in deeper. Felix shudders.

"I meant with your cock," Felix groans, at the same time the door to the house squeaks open.

"Kade? I thought I heard..." His mom's voice slices through the shadows, and Kade wants to kill every single thing right now. His mom pauses at the doorway, squinting, and he's thankful that all she sees is Felix bent over his bike, not what he's doing to Felix's ass. "*Oh.* Hello, Felix."

Felix covers his face. Kade imagines red surging through his cheeks. "Hi, Mrs. Brentwood."

"*Busy.* See you later," Kade says, glaring when she smiles.

"I'll see you both later," she says, closing the door. Felix groans into his hands.

"That didn't happen," he says, voice muffled. "I'm thirty years old. I don't have people walking in on me having sex."

"Not thinking about it," Kade says, sliding two fingers into his ass. Felix jerks against the bike. "Want to hear you come."

"She—Your mom will hear," Felix groans. Kade hooks his fingers against his prostate, so Felix jolts, choking on his words.

"Yeah?" Kade smirks, slipping his hand up the front of his hips, grasping the velvety length of his cock. Felix ruts into his palm. Kade angles Felix's cock down between his legs, so it's caught against the bike's chrome tubing. Felix drips into his palm, a soft moan emerging from his throat. "I want to hear you," Kade says. "Hear how—how much you want my cock."

He almost says *hear how you're mine,* and bites his tongue, stroking Felix instead. Felix shoves himself into Kade's hand, a moan rumbling in his chest. "You're cruel," Felix says. Kade pumps his cock, grinding his fingers against his very tip. Felix shivers. Kade massages his prostate, so he pants and gasps, and his precum drips down the side of Kade's bike. "Kade—"

Kade ducks his head, tugging Felix's cock backward, wrapping his lips around his sensitive tip. Felix cries out. He shoves his cock into Kade's mouth. Kade sucks on him, swallowing his musky, salty precum, flicking his tongue just under his head. It makes him leak, when Felix pushes hard into his mouth, heavy and thick, like he can't control himself. Kade slaps his ass, the sound of it echoing through the garage. Felix jerks, hissing.

"Kade, fuck me," he groans, pushing back, his ass the slightest bit pink. Kade imagines the snug wetness of his body, Felix squeezing around his cock. He drags his lips down to Felix's tip, slipping his tongue just under his foreskin. Felix's breath shivers out of him. Kade kisses him right on his tip, sliding his tongue around him, grinding it against his slit. Felix swears, leaking onto his tongue.

So Kade stands, his cock taut, sliding it up against Felix's ass. Pleasure hums through his nerves. He squeezes Felix's cheeks together, pressing them around his cock. Then he grinds against Felix's hole, leaking into the cleft of his omega's ass. Felix rocks up at him, so Kade pushes his tip against Felix's entrance, rubbing over it. "You want this?"

Felix whimpers, rocking his ass against him. Kade pushes slowly against his hole, until it stretches against him, until it opens and takes the tip of his cock, sucking him inside. He slides out, and Felix groans. "Kade, fuck me, damn you."

"On the pill?" he asks, pushing in slowly, savoring the way Felix opens around him, his ass tight.

Felix squirms, looking at the floor. "Yes."

And Kade slides all the way in, Felix's ass

smearing him with slick. He rocks in steadily at first, into the tightness of Felix's body, and then he's fucking his omega hard, pinning him against the bike, swearing as Felix trembles, gasping, his nails digging into the seat. "How does it feel?"

"Fuck," Felix says, his voice jolting as Kade sinks home, and he chokes on his words. "Harder."

He grips Felix's hips, hauling him back against himself, thrusting in fast, and Felix shudders, reaching down to stroke himself. Kade lets him this time, Felix working his own cock slowly.

They build a rhythm, Felix pushing back, Kade meeting him, sliding to the hilt. Felix's body sucks him in. Kade groans, his thrusts turning feverish, his cock growing thick with each trembling mewl that rolls from his omega's lips. "Gonna come," he groans.

"Yes," Felix says, shoving himself onto Kade's cock, and his own strokes speed up, his breathing ragged. Kade imagines his flushed cock in his hand, leaking, then spurting milky white everywhere, and he slams inside, Felix squeezing around him.

Felix shudders, shaking, his arm going still as he moans, his back arching, his voice breaking. Kade imagines his cum streaking over the bike's chrome pipes, over the black paint, imagines Felix's *pleasure,* and he trembles, the pressure at his groin surging. Pleasure explodes in his body. With a roar, Kade spills into his bondmate, and he thinks about his omega filled with his cum, marked with his scent, his bites, his pleasure.

Kade leans in, covering Felix's body with his

own. He wraps his arms around Felix's chest, his abdomen, and Felix shivers against him, nudging his arm further down, to his hips.

They've done this a handful of times since the night with the lemonade stand. Back then, Kade hadn't wanted to fuck Felix and leave, so he'd pleasured his omega instead, and ignored his own need. The next time he'd visited, Felix had reached for him, sinking to his knees to suck him off, and Kade hadn't the strength to refuse him.

All it had taken, really, was Felix begging for him inside, and Kade had yielded. Has been yielding ever since.

His knot swells inside Felix, stretching him. Against his chest, Felix purrs, his body accommodating Kade, and it's intimate, them locked together like this. It keeps Felix close to him, gives Kade time to run his wrists along Felix's jaw, down his neck, along his arms.

"You're okay with this?" Kade murmurs, nosing into Felix's hair. Felix smells like sweat and musk, and a little whiff of lavender.

"Mm-hm." Felix sighs against him, and Kade slips his hands up Felix's shirt. Felix sucks his breath in. "Feels good."

"You like me inside you," Kade says. He rocks his hips lightly, just to feel the pull of Felix's body around his knot. Felix moans.

"Was there ever any doubt about that?" Felix chuckles lowly, arching his neck so Kade runs his wrists along his throat. Kade scents his temples, his chest, his hips, and it feels familiar, his omega against him, taking his knot, sweat mingling on their skin.

“Guess not,” Kade says. “Sorry about my mom.”

Felix groans. “No. I’m not thinking about that.”

“It’s not like it’s the first time she’s done it,” Kade says, then pauses. He doesn’t know how much of their history he wants to bring up, when he doesn’t know where he stands with Felix. Whether he can talk about the past, without Felix remembering the reasons he’d rejected him. *What part of me is not good enough for you?* “Remember that summer break? When we were in eighth grade? You stayed over for math homework and she opened the door.”

Against him, Felix sighs. “Oh, stop that. I still remember it. How can I not? It’s one of the top five embarrassing moments of my life. It’s not like we even had clothes on, Kade. I mean, how awkward is it to see your son kneeling in front of another boy?”

Kade winces. They’d remembered the locks since then, until now. “We’ll fuck at your place, I guess.”

Felix chuckles. “Yeah. But this wasn’t so bad. We were mostly dressed.”

“Now you are,” Kade says. He reaches down, rubbing his wrist down Felix’s cock, over his balls, and it gives him a thrill, marking his omega. Felix shivers. The last dregs of Felix’s release drip onto his fingers, and Kade rubs it into his own skin. *Mine.*

He bites lightly into the meat of Felix’s shoulder. Felix exhales, long and slow, his body warm against Kade’s. Then they fall silent for a while, Kade enjoying his bondmate's presence, combing his fingers through Felix's hair. When his knot recedes, he slides out of Felix, nuzzling his nape. "Get dressed. We'll show her the painting."

Felix whines, covering his face again. "Do I have to? I mean... She just walked in on us."

"It's not like she doesn't know we're fucking." *Or that you're my bondmate.*

Felix huffs. "I'm sure she saw you behind me. You shouldn't kiss her anytime soon."

That's how you change the subject? Kade wipes his mouth, clicking his tongue. "'Course not."

Felix pulls back from the bike then, glancing down. "Oh, crap. Your bike. Um. You might have to clean it."

Kade looks over his shoulder, at the smears of white streaked across the leather seat, down the gleaming inner workings and the exhaust pipes, and he can't help smirking. "Don't worry about it."

As he steps away from his omega, Kade reaches down, slipping his fingers into the smooth cleft of Felix's ass. He finds the smear of sticky fluids around his hole. Felix relaxes, lets him slip his fingers in, so he feels the ooze of his cum inside. Kade growls. Felix swallows noisily.

They dress in silence. Felix runs his fingers through his hair, and Kade zips up his own pants, pulling his shirt back on. Before they step through the door, he slips his hand around Felix's elbow, pulling him close.

"My mom loves you," Kade murmurs. "You know that."

Felix's gaze darts to meet his. "I... I guess," he says, biting his lip. "I didn't say goodbye to her before I left."

You didn't say goodbye to me either, Kade wants to say. In his pocket, the ring feels warm against his skin, satiny, and maybe Kade can settle for a friendship with Felix. He doesn't want to.

He dips his head anyway, pressing his lips to Felix's temple. "You're fine. Don't worry about it."

Felix smiles then, a little brighter, and it feels like he's warming up Kade from inside. "Thanks."

16
Felix

FELIX DOESN'T want to be here, not really. He'd taken a bus to Kade's house to drop off the bay painting, and maybe he'd hoped for some sex.

Then Kade had mentioned that his mom's also living in the same house, and she'd opened the door and seen... She'd opened the door and said "See you both later," and Felix doesn't want to see her at all. He can't face her after the bankruptcy, after the death of Kade's father, knowing that he had been the one to cause it all.

Kade nudges him through the garage door. "Get in."

Felix clutches the painting to his chest, pulse thudding in his ears. "You should be the one going in first."

Kade looks at him again, sharp eyes contemplative. "You're scared of something."

"No, no," Felix says, but it feels as though Kade can read him anyway. What else can he expect, after being together fifteen years?

He steps into the dim hallway, waiting while Kade shuts the door behind them. Kade eyes him, then turns, heading for a brightly-lit bathroom.

Everything in this house smells like pine, cedar and lilac, and it's almost familiar. In the home Kade had shared with his parents and brothers, it had been a jumble of smells—birch, hibiscus, cypress, layered on top of pine and lilac.

"You haven't been in heat," Kade murmurs, studying him.

Felix stops breathing. *I didn't think you noticed. Did you guess it?* Kade can't possibly know he's pregnant, can he? "I've been taking suppressants to skip them."

"Because of that bastard manager?" Kade frowns. "You shouldn't be working at that place."

"You don't have to worry about me," Felix says. But the questions light his nerves—of course Kade would notice. Felix's heat has always triggered his rut, and it had been a habit, Kade soothing Felix's heats every month. It had been something both of them looked forward to, when Felix would leave scratches down his back, and Kade would bare his teeth and smirk.

And maybe he misses being in heat with Kade. It hadn't been pleasant the past five years, looking for one-night stands with people he barely knew, going home with them. They'd fucked him and turned over, and he never received the satisfaction he'd sought.

Then he'd returned to Meadowfall, and Kade's touch has been *bliss.*

"I didn't know you can skip heats, though." Kade lathers soap in his hands, then up his forearms, before rinsing them under running water.

"There are some that do that," Felix says. He

doesn't actually know. Maybe Taylor has pills for that. He would have to, right, if he's concealing his identity all the time? "I got them from my brother."

"Can't be good for you if you miss your heats. Normal people just suppress them partially."

I would have suppressed it, Felix thinks, *if we hadn't met that night.*

Behind the framed painting, he cradles the bump of his abdomen, relief whispering through his limbs. At least Kade hadn't noticed it when he touched Felix earlier. "I'll probably be fine," Felix says. "It'll just be for a while."

"And then what?"

Felix shrugs, looking at the beveled edges of the bathroom mirror. "I'll find something else, I guess."

"Would be nice if your paintings take off," Kade says.

Felix sighs. The website has been doing better, but it'll still be a while before he earns a decent living from that. He rinses his hands and follows Kade out of the bathroom, down the hallway to the kitchen. Pots and pans clatter. Felix's stomach twists; he can't possibly face Kade's mom.

"I had Felix bring his painting over," Kade says, stepping in first. "The one Dad liked."

Felix braces himself, trying not to think about Kade's dad, or the old home, or bills and money and his own father's smile. He takes a deep breath, then rounds the fridge. "Hi again, Mrs. Brentwood."

Kade's mom beams, short and plump, her dark eyes lighting up. "Felix! It's good to see you again. I'm glad you found Kade."

"We bumped into each other." Guilt slithers through his veins, so he turns the framed painting around, showing it to her. "Kade wanted this painting. We thought you might like to see it."

Her face brightens as she scans over the glittering sea, the busy restaurant and its empty boardwalk, but her gaze returns to Felix after a moment. "It's a beautiful painting, dear. And how have you been?"

"Fine, I suppose," he says, but Mrs. Brentwood steps forward with a kind smile, taking the painting from him. What he doesn't expect is for her to hand the painting to Kade, and pull him into her arms.

She smells vaguely like food, like vanilla and lilac and loamy earth. The smells plunge him into a swathe of memories: a cheerful dinner table with six people, slicing carrots in a familiar kitchen, *home,* and his throat tightens, suddenly. He hadn't realized he missed her.

"I'm sorry," he says, and his voice cracks just a notch. Tears prickle in his eyes, flooding out through his lashes.

He hunches to hide his face in his shoulder, and he's holding on, thinking *I'm sorry your husband died. I'm sorry I caused you to suffer. I didn't want to hurt any of you.* Then he's shaking, crying harder than he should, and he can't stop it. He can't rein in the sadness that wells up in his chest. He hates that he can't even control himself.

"There, there," she says, rubbing his back. He sobs harder. How could she accept him, when she doesn't even know what he's done?

Felix trembles, and he feels another touch, a

warm, steady hand on his lower spine, and Kade's heat behind him. Kade's presence soothes him, provides an anchor he clings onto, and he drags himself away from those memories. *Kade's here. Things will be fine.* Even though they aren't, but Kade has promised him safety before, and maybe he will again.

He sniffles, pulling away from her. Kade's mom pulls a tissue from her apron. Felix accepts it gratefully, blowing his nose into it. He's only just met her again, and he shouldn't be breaking down into her shoulder. "Sorry," he says. "I didn't mean for that to happen."

"That's fine, Felix." Mrs. Brentwood peers at him over her glasses. "Are you feeling okay?"

He nods. Her nostrils flare, though, and he holds still, suddenly cautious of what scents she's picking up. He should only smell like Kade, and very slightly like himself, but... What if she finds out about the pregnancy? He reaches up to touch his belly, and catches himself midway.

Mrs. Brentwood eyes him carefully. "You smell different," she says, and he hears her measured tone, the way she's saying something other than *You smell like Kade.* "Did something change?"

She knows. His skin feels hot and cold at the same time. Her gaze fixes on his eyes, but it flickers down for a heartbeat, before darting back, and all the blood drains from his face. She can't know about the child. Even Kade doesn't know yet. "Nothing," Felix says, his voice high-pitched and scratchy. "Everything's fine, Mrs. Brentwood."

Her lips thin then, as though she

disapproves, and Felix's chest constricts. *Does she think it's someone else's?* He can't face her if she does, not when her son is his bondmate. His pulse thunders in his ears.

"I shouldn't be imposing." Felix tries smiles brightly, like his father always does in front of strangers, and both Kade and his mom can probably see past his pretense. "I should let you and Kade enjoy your Saturday."

"Kade says you have paintings for sale," she says, her eyes still on him.

Felix doesn't know what Kade thinks of all this, whether he's deduced Felix's secrets from his mom's questioning, but he needs to get out of here, needs to move out of Meadowfall. *Why am I always screwing up?* He backs away from her. Her arms fall to her sides, her expression drooping. Felix looks desperately for the exit. "I'm afraid I don't have the paintings with me right now," Felix says. "But I can bring some over the next time."

There's not going to be a next time. He won't step in here anymore.

Warm fingers curl around his arm, and Felix looks up to find Kade staring at him. *What happened?* Kade's gaze reads. His eyes are beautiful, reddish-brown and serious, and a strange meld of relief and guilt coils in his chest. Felix sags.

"I'll take you home," Kade says. "If you want, I'll show my mom the paintings on your site. Then I'll get you from the back porch when we're done."

"That'll be nice," Felix says. He just needs to escape their attention right now. "I'd like some fresh air."

So Kade steps over to the back door, pulling it open. Felix smiles apologetically at Mrs. Brentwood, then ducks outside. The balmy air caresses his skin, a relief from the closed, suffocating kitchen. "I'll get you in a bit," Kade says, pinning him with his gaze. "Wait for me."

When the door shuts between them, Felix twists his fingers together, his heart galloping. Kade's mom isn't going to tell him about the pregnancy, is she?

Because if she does, Kade would hate him, and he... he can't live with that.

Felix huddles into himself, wishing he were home.

17
Kade

"WHAT WAS that about?" Kade asks, turning to his mom. First Felix edges around his questions, and now his mom knows what his bondmate hides. How the hell can she read Felix better than he does?

She studies him, glances at the back door, and her expression falls. For a long moment, she stays silent, thinking over her words. His skin prickles. "Felix needs you," she says eventually. "More than either of you thinks he does."

"What?" Where the hell did that come from? He wants Felix to need him, but this... How did she know that from just a hug? "I don't get it," Kade says. Felix had burst into tears hugging her, when he had been shifty in the garage earlier. It's as though his mom knows, too. Kade growls, hating to be left out of the explanations. "He's hiding something. You know what it is, don't you?"

His mom sighs, pulling him into a hug. He forces himself to wrap his arms around her. He doesn't need comfort. He needs answers. Felix is his bondmate, and he deserves to know. *How can you keep secrets from me?*

"I don't think I know all of it," she says. "But you should look out for him anyway."

"You say that as though I haven't been seeing him."

His mom hesitates. "I think Felix has his reasons."

"And you know them."

"Partly, yes."

It burrows under Kade's skin, not knowing what his omega hides. Maybe it's his fault. Maybe it's Felix's. The uncertainty eats at him, and he swears, turning, about to pull the door open.

"Kade," his mom says. He stops. "Let him tell you at his own time. You can't rush this."

He breathes out slowly, gritting his teeth. There were never secrets between them. Maybe the proposal was one, but other than that... They had been best friends. "He's my... He was my bondmate. We're not... He doesn't owe me any answers."

His chest aches, saying it. Felix has been back for four months, and Kade's still trying to fix whatever went wrong between them. Still trying to work up the courage to ask why he left. If it's not something he can change, he'll never have Felix back.

The thought makes his heart clench.

"I'm sorry, Kade." His mother hugs him tighter. Kade takes a deep breath, closing his eyes. "I wish things were different."

"You think I don't?" He doesn't need her pity or shit like that. He needs to find his way back to Felix again, and maybe if they were better friends, or if he tried harder... He'll get nothing done hugging his mom. "Look, do you want to see his paintings? They're here."

Kade pulls his phone out of his pocket, tapping in the address to Felix's website. It looks better now, sleek drop-down buttons, large images flipping through the front page. He hands the phone over. "See, you tap on this button for the whole gallery. If you want to buy something, the paintings are under the Shop tab."

"I'll look through them," she says, giving him a small smile. He returns it, before heading out the back door.

He finds Felix standing on the back porch, his gaze drifting over the succulent garden. Birds flutter among the bushes. Sunlight shines on the sage and forget-me-nots, and part of Kade is thankful for this, that he gets to stand close to Felix again.

"That's a robin," Felix murmurs, "And a sparrow. And the crows are the bad guys. I'll teach you to paint birds."

Kade frowns. *Teach who to paint birds?* "Hey."

Felix *jumps.* "Hey," he says, fingers twisting nervously. Was he talking to distract himself? Does he think Kade's mom shared his secret? What has he done, that he's actually afraid of Kade finding out?

"How are you?"

"Fine." But Felix isn't, when he looks down at his hands, and he's still lacing and unlacing his fingers.

"She didn't tell me anything," Kade says. Felix's shoulders sag. "But I figure you'll tell me when you think I can handle it."

Felix bites his lip. nodding. "I'll try. It's really not important."

"If it isn't important, you wouldn't be crying," Kade says. He steps across the porch, though, slipping his arm around Felix's back. Felix melts against his chest as though he's meant to be there. "You know you can trust me."

Felix buries his face in Kade's shoulder, his fingers clinging to Kade's shirt. "I suppose. Sometimes I just... I don't think you should trust me."

"Why?" Kade sniffs at his omega, smelling the pine notes of his own scent. Something settles in his chest. "Do you remember the promise I made?"

Felix nods against his shoulder, red sweeping up his ears. "You shouldn't have."

And Kade strokes down his back, trailing his hand along Felix's forearm, to the scar he left when they were ten. He brushes his thumb over it; Felix shivers. "I swore to protect you," Kade murmurs. "Regardless of anything. Even if we're just friends now."

You're safe with me. You know that.

Felix trembles, sobbing into Kade's shoulder. Kade strokes his back, wishing he could ease his misery. He kisses Felix's hair, then his ear, his neck. *I swear I'll try harder. I swear I won't disappoint you anymore.* And strokes Felix's scalp, holding his narrow, slender frame against himself.

I love you, Kade thinks. *Always have.*

When Felix pulls away minutes later, his eyes red-rimmed, Kade leans in, pressing his lips to his forehead. "Feel better?"

“Yeah,” Felix croaks. “Thank you.”

Kade kisses his forehead again.

The kitchen door squeaks behind them. “I need help with the site,” Kade’s mom says.

Kade sighs, annoyance growling through his chest. “Are you just gonna keep walking in on us?”

“Walking out. You’re on the back porch,” she says. To Kade’s surprise, Felix chuckles.

“That’s funny,” he says, his voice flat from his stopped nose. “Sorry. I left a mess on you.” Felix pulls away, swiping at his cheeks. Kade just watches him, thinking about all the times Felix has smiled in his arms. “I’m sorry, Mrs. Brentwood. I shouldn’t have stepped out so suddenly. I’m feeling better now.”

Kade’s mom smiles, relief in her eyes. “I’m glad,” she says. “Would you like to stay for some tea?”

Felix leaves his arms draped around Kade’s waist, nodding. Kade feels his own mouth twitch. “Go on,” he says, giving Felix a tiny push. “Be right behind you.”

This time, Felix smiles brighter. Kade traces his gaze over Felix’s golden hair and long limbs, smelling that faint lavender scent under his own.

Things will get better, he thinks, trailing after his bondmate. He hopes fervently that they will.

18
Kade

"I'M SO, so sorry for interrupting you," Felix says two days later, when Kade pulls up to the curb by his house. "I forgot it was Friday. I thought it was Saturday and I didn't have to work."

Kade winces. *That must suck.* He shuts off the bike, handing Felix the keys to the trunk. Felix had called ten minutes ago. It's now 6:54 AM, and they'll only be there 7:12 AM or so. "No worries. We'll still be late, though."

Felix grimaces, pulling the spare helmet out. He hops from one foot to another as he buckles it, glancing down the empty street. "I need to remember not to shut the alarm off. Damn it."

It's the third time he's forgotten something. The first time, Felix had left his wallet at home and called Kade from the bus stop. The second, Felix had borrowed his headphones, and forgotten to return them. Kade had insisted he keep them, but Felix refused.

Felix slides onto the pillion seat behind him, his thighs clinging to Kade's. It's a common thing now, and maybe it's why Kade dropped his work the moment he received Felix's text.

They get to the gas station at 7:15. Felix peers over Kade's shoulder at the store entrance, their helmets bumping. "Oh, gods, I hope Rick isn't in there."

Kade narrows his eyes. That manager is a bastard, from the sneering jibes Felix has told him about. "Look, why don't I send you a text in the mornings? You better be up when you get it. Or I could send you to work."

"I can't trouble you so much." Felix chuckles wearily, sliding off the seat. He pulls the helmet off, and Kade follows him into the store, just to see he gets in safe.

He catches the scent of bitter-wood two steps from the door. Next to him, Felix winces. He steps around Kade, though, pushing into the store first.

Feet away from the counter, the manager props his fists on his hips, glowering. "What time do you think it is?"

"Seven," Felix says, circling behind the counter, his gaze lowered. "Sorry. It won't happen again."

"I don't trust you omegas." Rick flicks a speculative look at Kade. "You should train him better. He'll be late for seven days straight now."

The hell?

"This is the first time he's late. Stop that bullshit," Kade says, glaring. He doesn't want to leave Felix alone with this guy. It screams against his instincts, but Felix has decided to keep this job. Kade can't force his decisions.

The manager narrows his eyes. "You're a customer, sir, so I'll assume the best of you. But teaching your omega some manners would help us all."

"The fuck are you saying?" Kade glances at Felix, whose ears have gone red. *Why are you even working for this guy?* "Shut up about omegas, damn you."

Rick prowls forward, shoulders pulled back. "I've never heard of you before. Who are you to give me orders?"

"A customer," Kade says.

Rick sneers. "Unfortunately, I only yield to the highest-ranking alphas. Say, the mayor or the president. You, sir, are neither."

"Yeah?" Kade scowls. *So what if you don't know me? Rank isn't everything.* But Felix is watching, too, and *he* thinks money is important.

Rick's eyes glint. "There are alphas who think they're all that great. But rank matters, doesn't it? And you're a low-ranking alpha who can't even climb to the top."

Rick can't know that. But the taunt digs deep into Kade, makes him think about sprawling mansions and cool, dismissive eyes, and *You're not good enough.* His nails bite into his palms.

"Kade, don't," Felix says behind him, a note of worry in his voice.

"It's true, isn't it," Rick says, grinning like a smug fool. He's got something on Kade, and Kade hates it.

"Fuck you," he says. Felix looks like he'd be safe here. He's been okay for three months in this place, and the bastard manager needs a cashier. So Kade can leave him alone without worry.

He flips Rick off, fury thrumming in his veins. *Rank doesn't fucking matter. Neither does money.* And of course it matters, or he wouldn't have lost his omega in the first place.

Kade strides out the store, his heart thumping in his ears. He needs to hurt that bastard. But Felix said no. He straddles his bike, twisting the throttle. Then he stops by a gas pump, driving his fist hard into the news anchor on the display screen. The screen cracks under the impact, going black. Kade wipes the blood off his fist, revs the bike engine.

If it were Rick's face, that punch would have been a hundred times more fulfilling.

THE TEXT comes late in the afternoon, just after four. *I hope it wasn't you who broke the screen.*

Kade frowns when he receives it, settling on his bed. *Why? He deserved it.*

Sigh. You should have just left, Kade, instead of aggravating him further.

He growls. Ignore that asshole? Does Felix think he can do that?

He's been a bitch the whole day. Even the other customers were swearing at him.

I'm not surprised, Kade sends. *He's a POS.* But Rick has been a pain to Felix, even if Felix didn't say it outright. That wasn't Kade's intention at all. Did that bastard take it out on Felix? Kade's breath catches. *You okay?*

Because if Felix isn't, Kade will storm down to that gas station and beat that guy up.

I'm fine. Felix adds a sad face behind his words. Kade relaxes, wincing. His thumb hovers over the call button. He hadn't stopped to think what the consequences might be. He should have. And that was why Felix had left him, wasn't it? He wasn't good enough for his bondmate. Even now, he's not good enough.

Kade sets his phone down on the mattress, swallowing hard. His laptop screen glows, reminding him of the work he still has to do. Kade turns away from it. A minute later, he picks the phone back up. *Sorry,* he types. *Won't do it again.*

Then he hits the call button before he regrets it, pressing the phone to his ear. His heart hammers.

Felix answers two rings later, muffled street noise in the background. "Kade?"

"Hey," he says, his tongue fat and stupid in his mouth. "Look, I'm sorry."

Felix sighs. Kade winces. His omega sounds miserable. "Don't worry about it," Felix says. "He'll be better tomorrow."

"I didn't think—I was just pissed," Kade says. Hearing the weariness in Felix's voice makes it worse, somehow. "Sorry."

"Are you hurt? I looked at the screen. There was a bit of blood."

Kade looks at the raw skin on his knuckles. "I'm fine."

"I'm glad." Felix blows out a sigh, his voice right next to Kade's ear. "Don't go hurting yourself. I thought the screen might have shocked you with electricity, but Susan said it wouldn't. I'm... Well, I was worried."

Kade swallows. Felix cares? He presses his phone close, wishing he had his bondmate closer.

He doesn't want Felix to stop talking. "I won't do it again, okay?"

"Promise?"

As long as that bastard doesn't hurt you. "Yeah. I promise."

"Thanks. It might be best for you to avoid the gas station when Rick's around," Felix says. In the background, the bus tires squeal to a stop, and the bus hisses. The noise mutes, and coins tinkle into a collection box. "I mean, I'd feel better if you didn't butt heads with him."

"Fine," Kade says. "You have the times he drops by?"

"Mostly. But text me if you're coming over," Felix says. "I'll tell you if it's convenient."

Kade lies back in bed, closing his eyes. He imagines Felix on the bus home, squeezed between other passengers, his blond hair falling over his eyes. Felix is allowing him into his life, allowing him to listen in on what he's doing. And Kade is grateful for it, even now. He's spent years not knowing at all. "Yeah, that works."

"Thanks," Felix says, a smile in his voice. "I really don't mind if... well, if you drop by. Not saying you have to, of course."

You want me there? Kade's pulse thuds in his ears. "I'll see what I can do," he says. He'd be there every day if he could, except maybe that would make him seem too desperate. Maybe every two days. "Tomorrow?"

"Sure," Felix says, and his voice brightens. "I'd love that."

Something in Kade's chest eases, like it had when he first saw Felix again. "Sure. See you then."

19
Kade

KADE SETS a plush giraffe down at the cashier the next morning. "Think the giraffe has a problem. There's a murder on the candy aisle."

Behind the counter, Felix stares. So Kade leads him to the candy section, where an ugly Halloween monster from the year before lies face-down on the floor, surrounded by plush rabbits, tigers, and cows. Felix stops at the start of the aisle, jaw hanging open.

"Guess we have an audience," Kade says, his heart beating slow in anticipation. "You came too late. The murderer got away."

And Felix snorts, stepping forward to crouch next to the stuffed toys. Humor glitters in his eyes, and Kade breathes out, relieved. Felix picks up a stuffed cow. "I'm shocked, Kade. There was a murder on my watch?"

"You should have watched more closely. Dangerous people around these parts."

Felix turns to study him, his eyes gleaming. "And how would I know you aren't the murderer?"

Kade shakes the giraffe. "I have an alibi."

"You could be accomplices!"

"Do I look like a murderer?" Kade scowls, pushing his lower lip out in an imitation of a pout. "I was just drinking with the giraffe."

Felix clutches his stomach, his laughter rippling through the store.

Kade grabs a bag of cola-flavored gummies. "See, drinks."

Felix doubles over then, chortling silently, his eyes squeezed shut. "I can't—can't believe you did this," he gasps, shaking a cow at Kade. The toys aren't even hurt or destroyed, just sitting on the floor, but Felix wipes tears from his eyes anyway. "Plushie murder? Really, Kade?"

Kade shrugs, turning away. "Actually, the giraffe's the murderer. You shouldn't let them fool you."

"You're walking off with it? Aren't you afraid for your life?"

"Do you think I should be?"

Felix beams, gathering up the stuffed toys in his arms. "You scare people away, Kade. I'm sure lots of giraffe-murderers are afraid of you."

"What about you?" Kade asks before he can stop himself. "Are you scared of me?"

Felix's eyes glint, warm and grass-green. "Probably not. Do you think you'll frighten me?"

As Felix straightens, Kade steps closer, until his shoes bump into Felix's, and there's an inch between their chests. Warmth seeps through their clothes. Felix looks up at him, his lips slightly parted. Kade lowers his face, murmuring a hair's breadth above his mouth, "Are you scared now?"

"Try harder," Felix whispers. "You don't

scare me."

So Kade drags the tip of his tongue over Felix's lip. Felix's breath puffs onto his skin. "Maybe this weekend," Kade says. Felix opens his mouth, an invitation, and Kade swallows. "I'll test you again."

"No more murders?" Felix asks.

"Just a lot of fucking," Kade says, brushing his knuckles down Felix's chest. Felix's heart kicks against his fingers.

He turns, leaving Felix with musk rolling off him in waves.

THE NEXT week, Kade sets a bottle of lube down at the register. Felix smiles, meeting his eyes. "Another one? Are you already done with that first bottle?"

They both know it's still in the bike's trunk, unopened, but Kade shrugs anyway. "Need one for home. Ran out."

Felix licks his lips. "You must be a beast, going through lube so quickly."

"I fed it to the ants," Kade says. "To drown them."

"Oh?" Felix grins, raising his eyebrows. Kade knows his omega doesn't believe any of that. The last time he looked, there was half a bottle left on Felix's bedside table. They'd gone through a quarter of it this past weekend. "Don't you need any? Not that you're lacking, of course."

Kade raises his brows. "And you're a good judge of that?"

Felix squirms. His ass still stings, Kade knows. He smirks. "I'm not certain," Felix says, grinning. "We may have to try it out again."

"Sure."

Felix lets Kade take him home that night, and they spend two hours in the kitchen, Felix's moans ringing through the house.

THE WEEK after, Kade returns, saying, "Do I come here if I want to lodge a complaint?"

Behind the counter, Felix bites down his smile. "What would you like to give feedback on, sir?"

"The lube. It's gone too quick."

Felix snorts, turning and biting his lip, and over on the other side of the store, Susan groans. "Could you at least stop flirting while I'm here?"

"I have serious issues with the lube," Kade says, but he's grinning. "It doesn't last. You squirt it and it goes—"

"No! I don't need to know," Susan says, hidden somewhere behind the shelves. Kade imagines her covering her ears.

"*Where* does it go, sir?" Felix asks, gaze darting down to Kade's hips. Kade grins. Two nights ago, in Felix's bathtub, they'd smeared lube all over each other's thighs. Then they tried to wrestle, getting their shirts sticky. And Kade had pinned his omega down after.

"Inside," Kade says, quirking an eyebrow. Felix grins. Susan marches up, wagging a finger at them.

"Enough," she says, grinning. "Pay for your gas and go. Felix, you know better than this."

"Not how you treat a customer," Kade tells her. "Felix is doing better than you." He's smiling, though, reaching for his wallet. Susan shakes her head.

"I should be educated on lube," Felix says.

Susan groans. When Felix reaches for his cash, Kade rubs their wrists together, scenting him. Felix beams.

TWO DAYS later, Kade steps in with a small lavender bouquet.

"Where did you get that?" Felix asks, eyes widening.

"Across town," Kade says. "You don't sell them here."

"I know we don't." But Felix stares at the flowers anyway, pink fanning up his ears. "What are those for?"

"You," Kade says, pushing them across the counter. Maybe he shouldn't have assumed that Felix would want them, but Kade had glimpsed the bouquets when he walked out of his office, and it had felt *right,* getting one for his bondmate.

His omega stares up at him, his throat working. "You shouldn't," he says. But his cheeks turn pink, and he glances hesitantly between Kade and the flowers. "Flowers are expensive."

Kade shrugs. They're worth the fifteen bucks, if they light Felix's eyes like someone told him he sold a million-dollar painting. "Are you taking them, or not?”

Felix reaches out for the bouquet, his eyes glued to the tiny purple flowers, and he raises them to his face, inhaling deeply. “I guess they smell like me.”

“Thought of you when I saw them.”

Felix ducks his head, blushing up to his hairline. Kade smiles. It gives him hope that he has a chance with Felix after all, that he can still win his omega back, and maybe... they can have a future ahead of them.

“Thank you,” Felix mumbles, pushing his face so far into the bouquet that the plastic crinkles. “That’s very nice of you.”

“You don’t have to thank me,” Kade says. “You never need to.”

Felix hides his smile, and Kade watches as he darts to the backroom to tuck the flowers away.

When Kade walks out of the convenience store, it feels like things in his life are finally falling into place.

20
Felix

FIVE MONTHS into his pregnancy, Felix has a breakdown.

The tape measure around his waist reads thirty-four inches, up from twenty-eight. He drops the tape on the floor, sits back at the kitchen table, and tries not to look at the bills spread before him.

Instead, he pulls his lumpy sweater down, his skin prickling with sweat, and stares at the dark screen of his phone.

Kade still doesn't know. Every time his hand drags down Felix's chest, Felix links their fingers together, shoving their hands down on his cock. Kade's voice always echoes in his mind: *Don't wanna knock you up. That'll be a mess.* He doesn't want a baby. And that thought haunts Felix the most.

Once, Kade's hand had rested on Felix's abdomen, and Felix's heart had clenched. He'd kept absolutely still, picked off Kade's hand as calmly as he could, and pushed it down hard on his cock.

It distracts Kade, when Felix wants to be touched there anyway. Kade has never questioned why Felix wants his shirt on. Felix thinks Kade will find out, but he never does.

Kade has hardly removed his own shirt either, now that Felix thinks about it. Kade sometimes does, but his shirt stays on more often than not, and... it's not as though *he's* pregnant. He's never been shy about his chest before. Felix frowns, dragging his gaze back to the bills—the rent, the electricity, the water, his phone...

The water bills have been increasing. And so have the grocery receipts. Felix bites his lip, thinking about his half-stocked fridge and the baby needing more food, and the doctor's appointments that the internet says he should make, but he hasn't yet. In the living room, the pregnancy books Taylor brought along are hidden in some boxes, just in case Kade visits. Felix knows he should eat better, knows he should exercise and talk to other pregnant omegas...

It suddenly feels like looming mountain that Felix isn't fit enough to climb, and a nervous pang shoots through his stomach.

He's looked at a few post-natal websites—bottle feeding, teaching children to talk, teaching them about discipline. He wouldn't do what his own father has done. But is that good enough? Felix has other flaws, doesn't he, and what if his baby grows up resenting that?

"I hope you won't be disappointed in me," he says, looking at the bump of his sweater. "Your dad isn't all that clever, or brave like your other dad. I... I think Kade would do a better job raising you."

Except Kade had asked about condoms all

those months ago, and Felix hadn't remembered enough to get his BC right.

"I can't even pay these bills," Felix says, covering his face. "I'm not even out of Meadowfall yet."

In his belly, the baby shifts slightly, as though disapproving. An inexplicable wave of misery swamps Felix. He hates himself. Hates how he can't pull a mask on these days, when his hormones wreck havoc on his body. Felix wishes he isn't sobbing, but the tears spill down his cheeks like water from a broken dam.

He curls up in his chair, hands over his face, and thinks about Kade, about the unborn child, about his father and the cheerful family Kade used to have. He wails harder. What would his own mother have done? He doesn't know, because he's never met his mother at all.

He goes through handfuls of tissue, and when the misery finally washes away, Felix slumps into his seat, still faced with bills and still pregnant.

The phone buzzes. He reaches for it, feeling like a wrung towel, and his pulse skips when Kade's name flashes on the screen.

Thought about you, Kade writes. *Want a plushy?* Along with the text, he's attached a graphic of a stuffed giraffe. Felix laughs, his cheeks still wet. He scrolls up through their conversation, looking through the texts they've exchanged. Scattered through numerous *6 AM now, don't be late* texts, he finds *Are you busy tonight?* and *Was thinking that selling more cookies would help* and *I hate my boss.*

He flicks through the conversation, ending

up at the giraffe again, and he remembers *Are you scared of me?*

Kade had pressed close that afternoon in the convenience store, and in that heartbeat, he had thought Kade would reach for him, kiss him, squeeze his cock right there in the middle of the aisle.

Blood rushes down his body, pooling at his groin. Felix gulps, reaching down, rubbing himself through his pants. He wants Kade with him. He strokes his thumb down his cock, pretending it's Kade's touch instead, and he grows stiff, straining against his briefs and pants. The material chafes a little against his skin, mildly annoying.

He hooks his thumb into the waistbands and pulls them down over his cock, looking at its flushed red tip, the fine veins that stretch across his skin. Felix licks his lips, sliding his foreskin down, his eyelids fluttering shut at the pleasure humming through his body.

He closes his fist around himself, stroking slowly, thinking about Kade standing over him, about Kade's cock on his face, and wouldn't Kade like to see this now, Felix hard for him, all wet at his tip?

His pulse quickens, throbbing between his legs. Felix picks up his phone, tapping on the camera app.

In the incandescent lights of the kitchen, the image on the screen is far too orangey, but it's not as though Kade will judge that. Felix holds the phone up, angling his cock down with a thumb, and snaps one picture of it. He flushes. They haven't done this before. Five years ago, a picture message cost a dollar to send.

Am I being too needy? We haven't really been talking. He bites his lip, fingers digging into the phone. Before he stops himself, he attaches the picture to their conversation, and sends it. Then he sets the phone down, pushes Kade out of his mind, and strokes himself. *I'm not thinking about it.*

A minute later, the phone buzzes. Heat sweeps through his face. Felix groans, tossing his head back against the chair. "Tell me I'm a slut, why don't you?"

He avoids touching his phone while the wall clock ticks the seconds away. But curiosity sinks sharp teeth into his mind. Felix picks the phone back up, holding his breath. *1 new message from Kade.* He taps on the text notification, heart thudding.

Right beneath the too-orange picture is a too-yellow picture. It's Kade's denim-clad thighs pushed down low on his hips, and his cock jutting up hungrily, thick and big, pink at the tip.

Did you get hard because of me? The pressure at his groin magnifies. Felix moans, tightening his fingers, sliding his skin down, and he reaches into his pants to lift his balls out, letting them rest on cool fabric. Felix imagines Kade at home, stroking his own cock. Then he takes another picture, his fist pulling the foreskin away from his gleaming tip, and sends it.

Half a minute later, the phone buzzes again—another too-yellow picture; Kade's strong hand around his own cock. Felix's breath rushes out of him.

He brings the camera app up again: the next

picture is an out-of-focus shot, his finger stretching precum away from his tip, and he's stroking harder, hips rocking up, wishing Kade were here instead. Wishing Kade would suck his cock, his beautiful mouth stretching around Felix's tip, his tongue slipping under his skin.

Felix trembles, leaking onto his fingers. The thought of Kade getting off on his pictures makes him throb, makes him want to kneel and fuck his hand, imagining it's Kade's. He wants to slow down, wants to enjoy this with Kade, see how many pictures they'll send between them.

He pulls his hand off his straining cock, staring down at its flushed, hungry length. He flattens his hand against the cushioned seat of his chair, dragging his eyes to the kitchen cabinet, the wall calendar with its bright, colorful pictures of food: spinach quiche, a steaming bowl of minestrone soup, golden-brown puff pastry.

It gets a little easier to ignore the pressure at his groin, so he sits on his hands, squirming, thinking about roasted chicken, vegetable pizza, garlic toast.

His stomach tightens suddenly. He wants to taste an Italian soup, full of meat and tomato and spices, and he can't push the craving out of his mind when his mouth waters, and he steps over the kitchen to check his fridge. There's sliced pepperoni in the chilled compartment, bell peppers and tomatoes in the vegetable crisper, but no ham, or sausage to complete the dish.

Felix sags, staring down at his jutting cock, his pants loose around his hips. "This wasn't supposed to happen," he says. "I was jerking off."

But he's hungry for food now, and from his experiences over the past four months, he can't eat something else and hope the craving will go away. Felix sighs, picking up his phone. It buzzes against his palm.

Kade's next photo is of his fingers squeezing his tip, forcing his damp slit to open. Felix squirms, thinking about his tongue on it, lapping up salty precum. He winces. *I need some sausage,* he types. *And by that I mean sweet Italian sausage. I have a craving suddenly and I really am sorry to kill this conversation. I'm heading out of the house right now.*

He hasn't thought about walking to the bus stop, or waiting for a bus, but the thought makes him groan. Felix stares down at his belly, frowning. "The things I do for you," he says.

The phone buzzes seconds later. *I'll pick it up for you. Need anything else?*

You really don't have to, Felix answers, surprised. *I don't want to trouble you.*

Better than waiting for the bus. You'll be out for two hours just to get some sausage.

Felix bites his lip. It's nice of Kade to offer. And he can't stop scrolling back up to look at their pictures, Kade's cock heavy in his hand, looking like it needs a bit of care. Like it needs Felix's mouth on it.

He groans, knowing there isn't a faster way to go about this. *Fine,* he types. *I actually also need a bit of ham. I'll pay you when you get here.*

Be there in 40 min, Kade texts. *On my way out.*

Heat sweeps through Felix's cheeks. *I can't believe you're doing this for me,* he thinks, hugging himself. *I've hurt you so badly.*

But maybe Kade's hoping for some sex in exchange, and Felix won't say no to that. *Sorry for changing the subject,* he types. *I really didn't mean to.*

The phone buzzes again. *I still have some lube, so I'm not high and dry. But that lube goes quick. Gonna complain again.*

Felix dissolves into a fit of giggles. Kade is amazing. He's funny and handsome and strong. Felix can't possibly deserve his company. But his alpha will be here soon with a bag of sausages, and he can't wait.

Felix sinks back into his chair, cradling his phone in his hands.

21
Kade

KADE HAD been in his bedroom when the text arrived.

He'd bought the giraffe from a department store—Felix had liked the bouquet of lavender from the week before. Kade had wanted to surprise his omega, make him laugh with the toy. So he'd sent a picture of the giraffe, hoping he'd remember the plush toy joke at the gas station.

And Felix had sent another picture right back, except Kade never expected it to be a dick pic. Fifteen years ago, they had flirted on the phone, racking up phone bills until his parents yelled at him. Then they'd got their own phones, moved in together, and there had been no more need to stay up in bed, one hand holding the phone to his ear, the other shoved down his pants.

They haven't done that since Felix returned to Meadowfall, but this snapshot brings back memories. And the sight of Felix showing him his cock, well... Kade had grown hard. He'd wondered if they'd stay up late again, stroking and exchanging photos, and he'd had every intention of showing Felix streaks of his own cum on his chest, after he removed the chain and ring from his neck.

Then Felix had texted, *I need some sausage,* and talked about taking a bus, and Kade had cursed, his cock still throbbing in his hand.

It isn't so bad, he thinks as he flicks on the bike headlights, the garage door pulling open with a whir. *I buy stuff he needs, and I get to see his face. Even if we don't fuck.*

Although they probably will. All it takes is Kade shoving him up against a wall. Felix grows hard every time, and he'll roll his hips up, expectant, wanting Kade's hand on him.

At the brightly-lit store, he texts, *Need anything other than ham and sausage?*

Nothing, comes Felix's reply, *unless you want some garlic toast to go with the soup.*

Kade drops by the meat counter, then the bread section for some garlic spread, and heads to the registers. It's 9 PM when he's done buying the groceries, and when he reaches Felix's place, the living room lights shine through the window. Kade rings the doorbell.

Felix answers the door, his cheeks flushed, hair tousled. Kade leans in, barely stopping himself from kissing his bondmate. Felix smiles awkwardly. "Thank you. I'm sorry for putting you through all that trouble."

"It's fine," Kade says, following him into the house.

In the living room, stacks of packing boxes sit by the wall. Their presence scrapes at his nerves every time he visits. Kade stares warily at them as they pass, wondering if there are still things in those boxes, if Felix has just left them empty, or if he's never taken their contents out at all. Which means...

"You're really leaving Meadowfall?"

Felix glances over his shoulder, his eyes wary. "I've told you that, haven't I? I'm just here for a while."

I'm not good enough to keep you? Kade's chest squeezes tight. He shoves his hand in his pocket, setting the plastic bag of groceries on the kitchen counter. "When?"

Felix jerks his thin shoulders. "I haven't decided yet. Within the next two months."

"Why?" *Why are you leaving me?*

The plastic bag crinkles as Felix riffles through it, pulling out the packages of meat. "I just have to leave, Kade. It's... It's not right for me to stay here."

"I'm not right?" he blurts, pulse thudding in his ears. He shouldn't have said it at all. He doesn't want Felix to shut him out and tell him to leave, when he'd rather swallow his insecurities just to be near his bondmate again.

"It's... it's not you," Felix says, still looking down. "And as cliché as it sounds, it's really because of me. I'm not right for you."

"The hell," Kade says, incredulous. Felix thinks he's not good enough? That can't be right, because Felix is beautiful and funny and kind, and he needs Kade's protection. "Is that why you left? Five years ago?"

"Can we not talk about this?" Felix snaps, his shoulders taut.

Kade flinches. Felix hasn't snapped at him since he returned, and the thought of aggravating his bondmate, of Felix finding any reason to leave him... Kade swallows, his heart thumping.

"Okay. Okay, we won't talk about it," he says, looking away. But the question sits heavy in his heart, and Kade traces his ring through his shirt. He's still not any closer to getting answers. *Is it the money? Or something else?* "What're you cooking?"

"An Italian meat soup," Felix says, unwrapping the paper-wrapped packet of sausage.

When he looks closer, Kade realizes that the spotlights above the counters are on, that diced bell peppers and onions are piled on the cutting board. "Teach me how to make it?"

Felix glances up from the speckled sausages. "Why?"

So that I can cook it for you. So that you won't tell me to leave. "Just something to learn, I guess."

Felix chews his lip. "You've already done so much."

"If I'm eating, then I should help cook," Kade says, even if he doesn't really have any appetite for soup. "At least teach me something before you move."

"I... suppose." Felix sets the sausages back down on the waxed paper. "You want to cut the lining of those sausages first. Empty them in the pot. Then chop them up and brown them."

Kade washes his hands, then runs a knife down the length of the sausages. The sausages thump into the pot, and as the stove heats, the meat begins to sizzle, notes of oregano, marjoram and basil wafting into the air.

Behind him, Felix sucks in a deep breath.

"Mm. That smells good."

Kade waits while the meat browns, glancing at him. Felix has his eyes closed, pale lashes brushing over his cheeks. Kade still finds himself marveling at his beauty. At ten, Felix had stood out at the school playground—too blond, too pale—and Kade had somehow been attracted to him. That was before they'd even known he was going to be an omega.

It's strange how they're standing together again, here in Meadowfall, two decades later.

With his spatula, Kade cuts the sausages into smaller chunks, stirring them in the pot. Felix opens his eyes, blinking as he looks around. When he catches Kade staring, he smiles, and maybe the tension between them is finally dissipating.

At the cutting board, Felix quarters stacks of pepperoni slices. "Wish you could eat this," he murmurs, looking down. "It's the most delicious. I'll make it for you when you get older."

"What?" Kade frowns. When he gets older? Does that mean Felix is staying?

Felix tenses and looks over his shoulders, his eyes wide. "Nothing."

"You said something."

"I was talking to myself," Felix says, a scarlet tint sweeping up his face.

Kade frowns. Felix has been talking to himself lately. Mostly, it's things he doesn't understand, but it's not his place to question it. Above the sizzle of meat, he asks, "You picked this recipe up in Highton?"

"I had it at a restaurant there," Felix says, his knife slowing against the cutting board. "I was with a group of other artists. We had an exhibition at one of those large halls—there were so many people—and quite a few of us sold paintings. So we went out to a fancy restaurant to celebrate. I found this soup on the menu. It's... well, a meat soup. I think you'd like it."

"Sounds good," Kade says. "You're still talking to those artists?"

"Yeah. They're decent people," Felix says, smiling. "A little eccentric, but that's to be expected of creative types. I made a couple of good friends there, too, like Jared—he does oil nudes—and Tom, who's more of a sculptor, but he does metalwork too—"

"Oil nudes? With models?"

"Yeah. I've modeled for him."

Kade looks up, his mind whirring. Felix led a life without him those five years, and he's bound to have slept with other people, even if he never received a second bonding mark. Kade swallows. It's not as if he hasn't hooked up with random people, either, but Felix is—was—his bondmate, and part of him wants to mark Felix, wants him back. It feels as though he's lost part of himself all these years. "Huh."

Felix shrugs, dicing up more ham. "It never amounted to anything."

But it sounds like he maybe wanted something to happen. Kade clenches his teeth, a spark of jealousy streaking through his veins. His wrists prickle, and he swallows. "So you're going back to them?"

"Maybe. They may have some new networking opportunities," Felix says, stepping over to look into the pot. Kade wants to hold him tight and never let go. "You may add the onions in now."

Kade drops them in, and it's definitely the sizzling onions making his eyes water. He stirs the food, watching as Felix drifts off to rinse some tomatoes. He wants to say something to make Felix stay in Meadowfall, but he doesn't know what. His brother? "Taylor's gonna miss you if you go."

Felix shrugs. "Taylor's not around anyway. And it sounds like he met someone he likes... I just hope they're doing okay. They're working for different sides."

"That sucks."

"It does. But they're fucking, though, so that's a plus." Felix chuckles. He sobers a few moments later, scooping up the diced ham and setting it into a bowl next to Kade. "I'm worried for him. It's not as though they'll end up anywhere if they're on opposite sides."

Kade grimaces. He's met Taylor on a few occasions, but he's always liked Felix's brother. Taylor shouldn't have to choose between a mate and his job. "He knows what he's doing," Kade says. "You don't have to worry about him."

Unlike Felix, because Felix has always been a little less headstrong than his brother. He and Taylor may both be omegas, but Felix doesn't have the self-preservation instincts his brother does, and that's probably why Kade was drawn to him in the first place. Felix is someone he can protect, and Kade wants to be needed. It's not something he can ignore.

"Thanks," Felix murmurs. He leans against

Kade's arm, resting his head against Kade's shoulder. Kade wants to sniff at him. Right now, all he smells are Italian spices, onions, and meat, and it's not enough. Felix shifts. "I'm sorry for snapping at you earlier. I shouldn't have."

"It's fine," Kade says. "Don't worry about it."

"Add the bell peppers next," Felix says. "We'll drop all the meat in, then the vegetables and the chicken stock, and bring it to a boil. It's a pretty simple recipe, really. Oh, and don't forget the oregano and more Italian seasoning."

"Sure."

They take turns scooping ingredients into the pot, before adding cartons of chicken stock. When Kade cranks the heat on to high, Felix says, "I think you'll make a really good husband, you know. You cook so well."

Kade's stomach flips, and the ring sits heavy on his chest. "You think?"

"I don't think. I know," Felix says. He turns away, his cheeks flushing, and it steals the breath from Kade's lungs. Felix isn't... interested, is he? Because he had accepted the flowers, and he's talking about husbands now, and... Kade's heartbeat drowns out everything else.

"Really?" he asks, throat tight.

"Really." Felix wanders off across the kitchen, his back to Kade, and he's grabbing his phone, fiddling with it. "I mean, someone out there will be really fortunate to have you."

But not you? Kade's nails bite into his palm. He turns back to the pot, stirring the ham and tomatoes and oregano, watching as they swirl before him. "Really?"

"Because you're strong," Felix says, his face hidden. "And you're smart. And you love your bike. And you make all these silly jokes. And..."

Do you hear what you're saying? It feels like Kade's chest is gaping open. *You're interested, aren't you?*

"Come see if the soup is done," Kade says, trying to breathe. He wants his mate closer, wants them to be truly bonded again.

When Felix pads over, his hair falling into his eyes, Kade steps away, fetching a bowl from the cabinet. Felix ladles some boiling soup in, puckering his lips to blow on it. Then he sips the soup, eyelids fluttering shut, and a smile spreads across his face.

"This is delicious," Felix purrs, sipping again. "It won't be ready until it sits for another hour or more, but *oh,* gods this is good."

He stirs the soup, before scooping a full ladle of it into his bowl, then another. Kade follows him to the kitchen table, watching as Felix sets it on the clean tablecloth.

"It's not ready, but it's good?" Kade asks. The rest of the soup is now simmering on the stove, and it'll be a while before all the flavors meld together. But it does smell savory, like sausage and tomato and rosemary. Felix is almost through with his bowl when Kade reaches out for it. "More?"

"Mm. Yes." Felix hands the bowl over, dregs of soup swirling at the bottom.

Kade ladles more soup into the bowl. Before he sets it down at the table, he tries a spoonful of red-orange broth, tasting the faint spice of oregano and thyme, the acidic flavor of tomato, the meaty chicken stock. In a few hours, the soup will saturate with the rest of the flavors—the ham, the pepperoni and sausage, and maybe Kade should return for another taste of it.

"It's good, isn't it?" Felix asks, kicking his legs out. He grins, eyes bright. Kade sets the bowl in front of him, watching as he slurps it down with a spoon, a smile curving his mouth.

"Not bad," Kade says, but all he can think about is Felix's smile. "Probably will be better tomorrow."

"I wanted to eat it all now," Felix says, grinning.

"That hungry, huh?"

"Mm-hm." Felix tips the soup into his mouth.

Halfway through, he slows, licking his lips. "I think I've had enough to stop the craving," he murmurs, reaching up to curl his fingers into Kade's shirt. Felix tugs on it, pulling him down, and Kade kneels in front of his omega, breath catching in his throat.

Felix kisses him.

It starts off slow, Felix's mouth brushing over his, nipping at his lips. Kade slides his hand up behind Felix's knee, the warmth of Felix's body soaking through his pants. He tastes like tomato and basil, like chicken broth. Felix's tongue slips into Kade's mouth, insistent and hungry. Kade slides their tongues together, and Felix purrs, reaching down to fondle his cock.

"Hungry?" Kade growls against his lips, cupping Felix's knees to spread his legs.

"Maybe," Felix breathes. He slides forward in his seat, pushing his hips at Kade. Kade hooks his fingers around Felix's calves, heaving him forward so he's sitting right at the edge of his seat, his inner thighs pressing lightly against Kade's arms.

So Kade drags his fingers over the hard line in his pants, a touch just enough to tease. Felix groans, squirming in his seat.

"Gonna have to beg for it," Kade whispers, leaning in to sniff the musk of his cock. "I'll make you scream."

"Fuck yes," Felix says, and Kade smiles.

22
Felix

IT ALL happens in a whirl: Kade showing up at his door, Kade cooking for him, Kade being perfect husband-material in his kitchen. Felix has been half-hard the entire time, just watching his alpha move.

Kade's shirt stretches over his chest and biceps, and when Felix's craving for soup has been satisfied, he grabs Kade like a fool in love and kisses him.

And Kade responds. Which puts them in this situation: Felix's legs spread wide open, Kade's face pressed into the crotch of his jeans. Kade's smelling his arousal, dragging his nose along the line of Felix's cock.

Felix groans, squirming, needing to please his alpha, but he doesn't want to move, when Kade's pulling his pants open, his eyes dark, watching as Felix's cock juts up between them.

"I guess this is better than pictures," Felix murmurs, his throat dry. Kade's gaze rakes over him, heavy and hot, and Felix can't help the trickle of fluid that rolls down his cock, leaving a wet streak down his skin. He feels exposed like that, under Kade's stare, knowing Kade enjoys looking at all of him.

"Yeah." Kade leans in then, catching the droplet with the tip of his tongue, following it up along Felix's cock, a warm, wet touch. Felix sucks in a sharp breath. Kade laps over his tip, circling the opening of his foreskin, and pleasure winds through Felix's body. "Much better."

"I didn't think you'd send a photo back," Felix says, breathless. His cock jerks against Kade's lips, and Kade circles it with his hand, stroking it, so more precum trickles from its tip. He licks that up too, wrapping his pliant lips around Felix. Felix groans, trembling. Kade's mouth always feels so good, and he always knows what Felix wants.

Kade grins, meeting his eyes. "You liked my pictures?"

"You think?" Felix squirms, feeling as though Kade can see through him, anyway.

"Yeah." Kade licks over his tip, pushing his tongue under his skin, rubbing against his sensitive head. Felix hisses, grasping his seat for leverage, pushing up into Kade's mouth. Kade takes him all the way inside.

Kade sucks on him then, slow and even, and pulls off with a wet *pop,* his lips glistening. Felix groans, squirming further forward on the chair, pushing his cock at his alpha. "More, please. Suck it."

Kade smirks, meeting his eyes, and a jolt shoots down Felix's spine. "Really?"

"Yes! Don't just stop there," Felix says. Kade leans in by a fraction, opening his mouth two inches away from Felix's cock.

“Gonna have to do it yourself,” Kade says, pushing his tongue out. Felix groans, his cock throbbing. Kade wants him to fuck his mouth. Heat surges down his body, makes his cock jump. Felix flushes, reaching down.

Five months ago, Kade wouldn’t have allowed him to do this. They’d been separated so long, and Felix had had no idea how he should act around his alpha, how to avoid reopening those wounds. But Kade sits in front of Felix now, mouth patiently open. Felix carefully shuffles forward on the chair, angling his cock down with his fingers. The tip of it brushes over Kade’s nose, smearing precum over Kade’s lips and tongue.

“C’mon,” Kade murmurs, licking his head, sending another whisper of pleasure through his body.

Felix groans, dragging the chair closer. He pushes his cock into Kade’s mouth, and Kade’s lips close around his head. “Fuck,” Felix gasps, his hips rolling forward. Kade’s mouth is wet, snug, and it makes him throb to see his cock disappearing inside. Kade hollows his cheeks, sending a spark of pleasure down his nerves.

“That all you can do?” Kade asks, the words muffled around Felix’s cock.

So Felix bucks his hips, shoving into Kade’s mouth, grinding helplessly against his tongue. Kade’s throat works, his tongue dragging down his length. Felix shudders, needing more, needing to see Kade taking him in like he’s Felix’s.

He reaches up, winding fingers through Kade’s hair, pulling him closer. His alpha yields, until Felix hits the back of his throat, sliding out, then in, and this is far more intimate than Felix deserves.

He pulls out of Kade's mouth, panting, and Kade glances down at his spit-slick cock. Felix gulps. He lifts his legs, wriggling out of his pants, and Kade's nostrils flare.

Felix tosses his pants to the side, showing Kade his cock and balls, his hole. Kade growls, reaching down to rub himself through his jeans.

"Want something?" Felix whispers, wriggling off his seat into Kade's lap, straddling him easily, his cock dragging along Kade's shirt, leaving a trail of precum down thin fabric.

"What do *you* want?" Kade asks, looking between Felix's face and his straining cock. Felix reaches down for his belt, tugs it loose to pull Kade's pants open. His fingers tremble with how much he needs his alpha inside. The zipper rasps between them, and when Felix pushes his hand into Kade's pants, he finds his thick, silky cock, the same one he'd seen in those phone pictures.

"Just this," Felix breathes, pulling Kade's cock out, letting it stand between them, bigger than his own. He pushes his hips forward, rubbing their cocks together, and Kade sets one hand on his ass, hauling him close. Kade's cock is warm and heavy against Felix's own. Felix looks down between them, watching as his precum smears against Kade's cock. They slide against each other, their tips wet, his pleasure stroking up against Kade's.

"Fuck," Kade groans, his fingers dipping between Felix's cheeks, circling his hole. Felix relaxes for him, and he pushes in, pressing right against Felix's prostate.

Pleasure bursts through his nerves like fireworks. Felix jerks against him, crying out.

"Wanna hear you beg," Kade says, his fingers hooking inside, a firm, unyielding pressure. Felix clutches at his shoulders, his legs trembling. It's almost too much.

"Kade, please," Felix gasps, rocking up, his body squeezing around Kade's fingers.

Kade leans in, licking at the corner of Felix's lips. "You have soup here," he says, then licks the other corner, and kisses Felix deep and languid, pushing into his mouth.

Felix licks at him, tangling their tongues. Kade tastes a bit like soup, and a bit like *alpha.* His fingers work inside Felix. Felix bucks up, his cock aching, his body trembling and over-sensitive.

Then Kade pulls his fingers out, leaving Felix empty. He brings his hand between them, wipes Felix's slick on his cock, and whispers, "Now ride me."

Felix groans. With his hands on Kade's shoulders for support, he leans up, then carefully lowers himself, until Kade's blunt, moist tip nudges just behind his balls. He rolls his ass until it pushes right against his hole, its thick head spreading his cheeks.

Felix sits, biting his lip when Kade stretches him open, and he's inside, grinding against Felix's prostate, then deeper yet, until Felix takes him in to the hilt, and all he can think about is Kade inside him.

Kade bares his teeth, chest heaving, staring at Felix like he wants to devour him. And Felix wants him to. He rocks on Kade's lap, sliding him partway out, sitting back onto his cock, groaning as it presses into him over and over. Kade's nostrils flare, and sweat gleams along his throat.

"Feel good?" Kade whispers. He wraps his fingers around Felix's cock, holding still. When Felix raises himself on his knees, his cock slides into Kade's hand, into his tight grip.

"Yes," Felix hisses. He skims his hands down Kade's chest, over the nipples straining at his shirt, then down to his solid abs.

He wants to see Kade's abs, suddenly, feel the way they dip under his touch. So he curls his fingers into the hem of his shirt, rucking it up. Kade grabs his hands, eyes flashing.

He sets his own palms down on Felix's hips, pushing him off his lap so he lands with a thump on the kitchen floor. Kade follows him, flattens his hand against Felix's chest, pushing him down, one hand coming up to cradle his head. Felix's back hits the floor, knocking the air from his lungs.

"Gonna fuck you," Kade growls, leaning over him, their chests inches apart, his cock sliding wetly against Felix's ass, thick and hungry.

"Yes, please," Felix says, spreading his legs, wrapping them around Kade's waist. Kade pushes their cocks together once, trailing precum onto Felix, before he pushes back inside Felix's ass. Felix opens for him, ready, but he doesn't expect the vicious shove of Kade's cock inside him, and he arches, taking his bondmate's cock, his body humming with pleasure. "Kade, please, harder."

Kade barks a laugh. "Not hard enough?" His fingers curl into Felix's hair, and he hooks his other hand against Felix's shoulder, holding him down.

Then he withdraws, and *fucks* into Felix so hard Felix's entire body jerks up, and he cries out, needing more.

"Yes, oh gods, yes," Felix pants, his fingers catching in Kade's shirt, clinging to his sides. Kade's thrusts speed up, a steady rhythm that lights all of Felix's nerves, makes him aware of Kade inside him, Kade pounding him into the floor, and his own cock drips onto his shirt.

"Gonna make you scream," Kade whispers in his ear, plunging into Felix, fast and hard. Felix gasps, trying to hang on, the tension inside his body winding to fever-pitch, and he can barely breathe. Kade's hips snap up, his cock burying deep inside. "Gonna fill you with my cum. Make you take my knot."

And that makes Felix shudder, the thought of his alpha knotting inside him, stretching him open. He shudders, his cock pulsing, and Kade releases his hair, reaching between them to wrap his hand around Felix's cock. He thumbs Felix's tip, jacking him, and pleasure crashes through Felix like lightning, searing through his nerves, and a cry rips from his throat, and he can't breathe, can't think.

His body clenches around Kade, and Kade comes inside him with a bellow, his cock jerking. Felix feels him inside, filling him up. He shudders and groans, tipping his head back into the floor, and above him, Kade rests his forearm next to Felix's head, breathing raggedly.

When Kade stops panting, he nuzzles Felix's ear, nipping it with his teeth. "Forgot to ask. Still on the pill?"

"You don't have to keep asking," Felix says.

It's obvious that you don't want a child. His chest hurts. "Yes. I am."

Kade sighs, burying his nose in Felix's hair. His knot swells inside his body, a slow, pleasant stretch. He bites his lip and moans, his gaze catching on the thick, silvery chain around Kade's neck. It clings to Kade's skin, gleaming with sweat. *Does it have a pendant? You never wore chains before I left.*

Before he reaches for it, Kade closes his hand around Felix's, bringing it up to his face. Felix stares, and Kade noses at the scent gland at his wrist, nostrils flaring.

"You smell sweeter," Kade says.

Ice spears down Felix's spine. "I do?" he asks, hoping his voice sounds even. The scent suppressant should be working. Or is his scent getting stronger? "That's strange."

"Yeah." Kade sniffs at him again, his nose dragging down Felix's throat, nudging at the scent gland at the crook of his shoulder. Felix's heart thumps in his chest. "It's not a bad smell. Just that I can't—can't smell you properly these days. Not used to it."

"Really? But it's been months," Felix says, heat rising to his cheeks. Maybe Kade's just checking on him, instead of wanting to smell his scent. Maybe he's over-thinking this.

Kade sucks in a deep breath, his nose against Felix's skin, and maybe they shouldn't be doing this, splayed out half-naked on the kitchen floor. "When are you stopping the scent suppressants?"

"Maybe after I leave," Felix says. *After you can't smell me anymore. So you won't hate me.*

Kade sighs, burying his face in Felix's shoulder. For a moment, it feels as though his alpha is vulnerable like that, pressed against him, his face hidden. Kade hasn't been vulnerable with him in a long time. Then he pulls away, his eyes solemn, and maybe Felix didn't need to worry about him at all.

Kade slips out of his body, his knot receded, his cock still hard. He tucks it back into his pants, and Felix drags his eyes away from the bulge of it. "Guess I should go."

"Take some soup with you," Felix says, sitting up. "You haven't had any."

Kade's expression brightens slowly, like a growing flame. "You have containers?"

"Yeah. I'll look for them." Felix climbs to his feet, bare skin squeaking against the tiles. Kade's stare lingers on him, a warm, steady touch. Felix swallows. He pulls a microwavable dish out from a lower cabinet, his legs bare, secretly glad for the bulky sweater hiding his belly.

Kade grabs Felix's abandoned clothes then, holding them while Felix scoops simmering soup into the bowl. He fixes a lid onto it, sets it into two plastic bags just in case, and hands the bowl over to Kade in exchange for his clothes.

"Thanks for coming over," Felix says, smiling. His body aches pleasantly; he'll be feeling this two days from now.

Kade shrugs, his gaze flickering over Felix's face. "No worries."

At the door, Kade steps in close, leaving inches between them. Felix's breath snags when Kade leans in, kissing him on the lips. His breath puffs against Felix's cheek, their lips brushing soft and light. Felix's stomach drops. He doesn't know what this means, whether it's a *thank you* or something else, and he's still standing at the door as Kade pulls away on his bike, its engine purring.

Maybe he shouldn't still be in Meadowfall. His gut says he needs to leave, and he... doesn't want to.

23
Kade

20 Years Ago

THE DRIED blood stays a dark red on his wrist as Kade rides home with his mom. During the drive, she smiles, watching as he picks at his skin.

"I'm happy to know that you're an alpha," she says, glancing at the road. "But you'll have to remember: being alpha does not make you better, or worse than anyone else."

"Dad says it's a good thing." His dad has been grinning when he says, *I'm sure you're gonna be an alpha, kid.* Kade has smiled along with him, squirming with excitement.

"People see alphas one way, and omegas another. And betas are different, too. But that doesn't mean an omega can't be a leader. There will just be more work involved."

Kade thinks about Felix smelling like lavender. He doesn't know if it's because they've been friends so long, or if it's because he's exchanged bites with Felix, but Felix smells good to him. "Is that why Felix's dad doesn't like him? Felix says his dad isn't nice."

Mom looks over at him, her smile fading. "Felix's father is an important person. He's the mayor. People want him to fulfill their demands, and he has to make promises to different communities. As the mayor's son, people will expect things from Felix, if he chooses to follow his father into politics. I believe Mr. Henry is trying to groom him into that position."

It sounds like gibberish to Kade. "Show me your bonding mark again!"

She smiles, extending her left wrist to him while she drives. Kade holds his forearm next to hers, comparing the marks. Mom's scar is bigger than his, silvery, while his is still a dark red line. Felix hadn't bitten very hard at all. "That bond is for life, you know."

He grins with pride. "I know that. I said I'll protect Felix no matter what, just like Dad said to you."

Mom chuckles. "You're very sure, huh? Most people don't decide until they're much older."

Kade nods. He likes Felix. And Felix had felt warm, curled up against him. "Yeah."

"At some point, bondmates are expected to marry. Or at least be life partners. You'll fit into Felix's life just like he fits into yours, and in the future, the two of you may decide to have children."

Kade looks down at his mark, thinking about his brothers. Sam and Chris are enough—he doesn't want another baby he has to take care of. "Don't wanna," he says. "But I guess if Felix wants one, I don't mind."

She laughs, turning them into their driveway,

next to a tiny house with roses along the lawn. "Talk to Felix about it sometime. But you'll want to wait until you're at least twenty before making the big decisions, okay? Take your time to decide what you really want."

Kade nods, rubbing his thumb over the dried blood. "Yeah, okay. I'll talk to him."

24
Kade

6 Years Ago

IT ISN'T until they're twenty-four that Kade talks about children again.

They have their own little house now, a single-bedroom cottage with weeds in their front yard and a grassy patch at the back, shaded by some trees. Felix's father has visited them all of once, ever since they moved into this place. Kade never forgets his narrowed eyes, the contempt with which he glanced at their furniture.

Alastor Henry has never approved of this relationship, and it hurts most when they walk by a kindergarten with cheerful sunflowers painted on the walls, Felix sighing at the children on the slides. Kade wants Felix's father to be happy for him, like his own dad has been to Kade. Felix deserves more love from Alastor. Often, it seems the only way he can do that is by marrying a richer alpha. Which Kade isn't.

So when Felix asks, "What do you think of a daughter in the future?" Kade shakes his head. He doesn't have a bursting bank account. As Felix's alpha, he’s costing Felix his relationship with his father. Sometimes, he wonders if Felix regrets that they’re bonded, but he doesn’t dare ask.

“I don’t think we should have kids,” Kade says, guilt twinging in him when Felix’s expression falls.

“You don’t?” Felix looks at his feet, and Kade tugs on his hand, leading them to the nearby park.

“We shouldn’t.” Kade swallows, looking away. Kids would complicate their relationship. If they have children and Felix decides he wants a richer alpha, well. Why would he want that reminder of Kade? “I don’t think we’re suited for kids.”

“Oh.” Felix looks down, his fingers going limp in Kade’s hand.

Kade doesn’t know how to solve this, but his gut tells him that was the right response. Even if all the light has gone from Felix’s eyes.

25
Felix

Present Day

FELIX WAKES the next Saturday when his mattress indents next to his chest, like a weight settling beside him.

He's stirring, drifting in and out of sleep, snuggled under a thin sheet when gentle fingers touch his forehead. The fingers slide to his temple, warm and comforting, and they... shouldn't be there. He sleeps alone. No one is supposed to enter his house and sit on his bed.

Kade?

He springs up in bed with a gasp, eyes flying open, and Taylor stares a foot away, his hand retracted. "Felix?"

"Oh, gods," Felix wheezes, clutching his abdomen. "I thought—I thought you were Kade and I haven't taken my pills yet and I still smell like pregnant person and I thought I was going to die—"

"Hush," Taylor says, climbing further onto the bed. He pulls Felix into his arms, stroking his hair, but it doesn't quiet the thundering of Felix's heart. "Sorry. I didn't mean to wake you."

"You could have rung the doorbell," Felix groans, dropping his forehead onto Taylor's shoulder. He sucks in deep breaths of jasmine, trying to move his hands, and only realizes then that he's shaking. "I'm so fucking terrified of him sometimes, Taylor."

His brother stiffens against him. "You haven't told him yet?"

Felix shakes his head, looking at the translucent curtains, the stacks of sketchbooks on his tiny desk. "What do you think?"

"Oh my god. You're already five months along, Felix. And Kade still doesn't know?" Taylor slaps his forehead. "Are you serious?"

"Why don't you get a surprise pregnancy from an ex," Felix mutters, worrying the bed sheets with his fingertips. The child squirms in his belly again, an ever-present reminder. "Then tell me about it."

Taylor sighs, hugging him tight. "You can't hide this forever."

"I can hide it until I leave," Felix says. He wants to gather his stuffed toys close and pull the worn blanket over his head. They stare accusingly at him from the windowsill. "Then I'll stop with the pills."

"I think I should confiscate all your scent suppressants, Felix Henry." Taylor holds him up by the shoulders, looking hard into his eyes. "Kade loves you. I'm sure he—"

"What," Felix says. "You haven't even met him since you got back."

Taylor sighs, blowing his hair out of his eyes.

"And I'm also the one who got fifty voicemails from him when you fled. *Fifty,* Felix."

Felix winces. Had Kade left offended barbs that Taylor could show him? "Really?"

"Well, more like eighteen, spread over seven months or so." Taylor frowns. "He cares about you. You know that, right? I mean, you've been together forever."

"Not forever," Felix mutters, pulling his sheets around himself.

"Pretty damn close," Taylor says. He nudges Felix with his shoulder. "Or do you need me to tell him on your behalf?"

Taylor, telling Kade about the pregnancy when Felix can't even show his face? What kind of irresponsible omega does that to his bondmate? "That's worse!"

"Look, at least give him a chance to respond," Taylor says. "Then if he says he doesn't want the child, you'll pack your bags and leave."

Felix pulls the sheets over his head. It'll kill him, hearing Kade say he doesn't want the child. It'll feel like a rejection, and he deserves it for all he's done to Kade, but... "I can't. His dad's dead because of me."

Taylor winces. "The bankruptcy wasn't your fault. It was Father's—"

"Father asked me to draw those impressions," Felix wails, clinging to his sheets. "If people didn't fall in love with those houses... the bankruptcy would never have happened. And Kade's dad wouldn't have died."

"Drawing those impressions doesn't mean you caused the bankruptcy, Felix."

But Felix *had* drawn them, made them bright and colorful and classy, and prospective buyers had perked up when it slipped into newspapers and websites and every other advertising channel. If he'd never drawn those impressions, his father wouldn't have gotten the idea to clear out all his tenants.

Felix cringes. "Why don't you try having a death on your hands—" Taylor raises an eyebrow, and Felix sighs. "Well, a death of someone you love, at least."

His brother looks away then, his lips thinning. Felix tenses. "You haven't been in that situation, have you?"

"Once," Taylor says, his gaze fixed on the orange tree outside the window. "Years back."

"Oh my god." Felix glances at Taylor's wrists, then his neck—no bonding marks. What kind of relationship had it been? "Why didn't you tell me?"

"I was on an extended mission. Remember the time I left for two years?" Taylor meets his gaze, a deep ache in his eyes. Felix's ribs tighten. "I was mostly over it by the time I got back. I didn't want to talk about it."

"Oh, Taylor," Felix whispers, hugging his brother tight. "I didn't know."

They sit in silence for a while, listening to the birds chirping outside the window, the rumble of cars, the neighbors yelling for their children.

"You smell good," Taylor says suddenly. He leans in, sniffing at Felix. "I missed you. And I've definitely missed smelling you."

Felix cringes. "There's plenty other things for

you to smell."

But Taylor sighs. "You smell like home, you know? Like something familiar. There are... too many other smells when I'm working."

"I'm not taking the suppressants for long," Felix says, but he can't help remembering Kade's nose on his neck, and how he'd only pulled away ten minutes later. How would he react to this smell? He'd said Felix smelled sweet, but he hadn't realized why, had he? "Just until I'm out of Meadowfall."

"It's still too long," Taylor says. "I regret giving you the scent suppressants. You need to stop hiding."

"I'm not dealing with it," Felix says, and his brother shakes his head.

"Come on," Taylor says, rolling off the mattress, loose-limbed and agile. "Let's get some breakfast outside. I want something tasty."

"I still have leftover Italian soup," Felix says. "Kade came over and helped cook it."

His brother studies him for a bit, pursing his lips. "You were fucking in the middle of making soup, weren't you?"

"*No.* We fucked after." Felix pouts. "I know about hygiene, okay?"

Taylor snorts. He extends a hand to Felix, though, pulling him out of bed. "Fine. But I want to treat you to breakfast. Eggs Benedict, and maybe some pancakes. And some coffee."

"You have expensive tastes," Felix says, but he's smiling, padding out of the room with his brother.

"We don't live forever. Eat well," Taylor says,

winking. "But don't pop the suppressants today, okay? I want to smell you."

Felix frowns, pausing halfway to the bathroom. "I can't. I'm hiding."

"No one's going to look at you," Taylor says. "Just act normal."

"But what if we bump into Kade? That's the whole point to the suppressants."

"I'll look out for him. You'll be fine." Taylor squeezes his palm. His hand is small and warm, traced with scars, unlike Kade's.

Felix finds himself missing his bondmate, suddenly. He trudges to the bathroom, thinking maybe Kade will visit, figure he's out, and return home instead. They made no plans to meet today.

"Fine, I guess. And only because I want to see you happy." Felix will be fine smelling like himself, right? A few hours out with Taylor, and he'll be home. "I won't take them."

A BELGIAN waffle, an eggs Benedict, and a small stack of pancakes later, Felix steps into the department store with Taylor, the tension from his shoulders gone. "That was delicious," he says, clinging to his brother's arm. "I'm so happy we went out."

"I know. You haven't stopped grinning since we left the diner." Taylor leads them past the aisles of wicker baskets, stationery and gleaming kitchen appliances. "You're getting bigger. Do you want any clothes for later on?"

Felix winces, looking down at his belly. It

doesn't look like much from afar, but he's wearing a thin flower-print shirt, and if anyone looks closely, they'll see the faint bulge of his abdomen.

In another four months, he'll be swollen with child, and Kade won't be around to hold his hand. His throat grows tight. "I'm not... I don't know. I have clothes right now."

Taylor frowns, peering at him. "What about baby clothes? Do you know if it's a boy or a girl?"

Felix shakes his head. "Not yet."

"You've been to the doctor at least, right?" Taylor asks, turning them down aisles and tall metal shelves. Felix winces. "Felix! You should be visiting every month, so you know you're both healthy!"

"That's what the internet says," Felix mutters, looking at the shiny laminate of the floor. His borrowed cash has run dry, spent on food and bills, and a secret stash for moving. "I know."

"If cash is the issue, I'll just—"

"No." He can't keep depending on others to help him. "I'll find the time and money to go myself. Soon."

"If you say so," Taylor says, narrowing his eyes. "If I visit the next time and you haven't been..."

"I *know.* Stop worrying," Felix says, grimacing. "I worry enough for both of us."

Taylor sighs. He turns them around another corner, and Felix freezes at the piles of pastel clothes, tiny ones slightly larger than his hands. The baby clothes section stretches on for yards and yards, and this early in the day, few shoppers wander around the store.

He gulps, reaching out to touch soft cotton: little striped socks, egg-yellow onesies, shirts with animal prints on them. The clothes he'd wanted to look at when he was last here with Kade, shopping for lemonade stand items.

"We could get some that aren't gender-specific," Taylor says. "My gift as an uncle."

"Thanks, I suppose. I think it's finally sinking in. I'm going to be a dad." Felix trudges after him, staring at the unending piles of clothes. He sets a hand on the bulge of his stomach, thinking about the tiny life inside him, and how it'll grow into a walking, talking child. How had one night changed so much?

"There are parenting courses around. Sign up for one, you might learn something good." Taylor holds up a pale purple shirt, smiling. "Is this cute enough?"

On the front of the shirt, a bear sits with a pot, one paw coated with honey, a delighted grin on its face. Felix smiles. *You would look adorable wearing that.* "It's cute."

"What about these? I can't believe they're so tiny," Taylor says, picking up a pair of striped pink mittens, his eyes warm.

It's easy to soak up Taylor's excitement, when he sets the mittens against Felix's belly, his eyes wide. "I can't imagine you carrying such a big child... or will it grow to fit these mittens after it's born?"

"I don't know," Felix says, stretching the cuffs open on a pastel blue pair of mittens, the material flannel-soft against his fingers. "What do they need mittens for?"

"I think that's where research comes in," Taylor says, nudging him. "In case they accidentally scratch themselves? Seems like a good possibility."

"I guess I haven't thought about nails, either." It seems like a huge task suddenly, raising a child himself, seeing to all its needs while he tries to work and earn a living for them both.

"What about this? I'd love to see a baby boy in a sundress," Taylor says, lifting one off a rack of brightly-colored clothes. "This reminds me of your painting, the one with the field of flowers—"

Taylor goes still, his gaze flicking up as though he's just spotted an enemy. "Shit."

The alarm bells clamor in Felix's head even before he turns. Because they aren't hiding from secret agents right now. They're hiding from Kade, and Kade's ten yards away, striding across the linoleum floors to them, his eyes fixed on Felix, his lips a thin line.

Felix's stomach plummets to his feet. He can't breathe. They're surrounded by baby clothes, his shirt so thin the AC brushes over his skin.

I don't think we're suited for kids, Kade had said. *Don't wanna knock you up. That'll be a mess.*

And the ragged look in those mahogany eyes... Kade knows. Kade *knows,* and the tiny dresses around him aren't protection enough. They shouldn't be here, shouldn't have even left the house today. Kade's nostrils flare, and Felix knows exactly what he smells. The baby squirms inside him.

"Kill me now," Felix whispers, mind spinning. "You brought the gun in, didn't you?

Just—just make it a clean shot."

"I won't," Taylor hisses, his gaze darting between Kade and Felix. "I'm not shooting you. It's time you told him, Felix."

Felix whimpers, a soft, helpless sound. The exit's thirty yards away. He can run, but Kade is stronger and faster than him, and he can't move his feet right now. His body isn't cooperating. And Kade doesn't want a child at all. "Taylor, please."

Kade closes the distance between them, tall and looming. Felix curls his fist into soft, tiny dresses, and wishes he were a million miles from here.

26
Kade

WHAT KIND of tea did you want? Kade types, hitting the send button on his phone.

Of course his mom would forget the tea on her grocery run, when it's the only thing that'll keep her awake. And of course he'd offered to pick it up for her.

He strides into the department store, thinking about getting some brake fluid for his bike, and maybe some crackers. The last time he'd been here this early, it had been to get cups and straws for the lemonade stand. Felix had been with him. Kade shoves the phone in his pocket, winding through the empty store.

His attention drifts to the customers in the store—the sports mom with her baseball cap and two kids trailing after her, the plump old lady pushing a huge shopping cart, the two mops of flyaway blond hair behind some kids' clothes... It looks like Felix, actually. And his brother.

So Kade drifts closer, pulse racing. *What are the odds of meeting him here?*

One of the blonds looks up, and Kade can recognize his omega anywhere. *It's him!*

Taylor leans in, pushing two tiny mittens against Felix's abdomen. Felix stares contemplatively at the mittens, reaching for another pair. Kade slows his footsteps. Why would Taylor be sticking mittens on his brother's stomach?

Taylor turns to a clothes rack. Felix bites his lip, looking down. *Does he actually want a baby?* Kade thinks, following his gaze. Felix hasn't worn clinging shirts in a while, and his belly...

There's a bulge at his belly.

Air rushes out of his lungs. Had that bump been there all along? Kade doesn't remember seeing his naked abdomen recently. And they've been fucking countless times. How had he missed it?

Because it's noticeable, now that Kade's staring at it. Felix has never had a bump. How can it be anything else?

Felix is pregnant. Felix is fucking pregnant, and how the fuck had Kade not noticed sooner? *Thought you said you're on BC!*

All those bumpy sweaters he's been wearing, the lack of a scent, the time he puked... Kade tries to remember the last time he touched Felix's belly, but he comes up blank. Because... because Felix keeps shoving his hand away, and Kade had thought Felix wanted to be touched elsewhere. Instead, he has been keeping a secret. They've been fucking for *four months.* How the hell had Kade missed it?

Something roars in his chest. *Why the fuck did you lie?*

He swears at himself, his strides lengthening.

Felix carries his baby, and he wants to pull his omega against him, wants to kiss him, wants to know why the hell Felix thought it a good idea to lie.

Taylor glances up. His mouth moves, and Felix follows his gaze. Blood drains away from Felix's face. His lips pull down, and he's murmuring to his brother, looking frantically around.

Why is it a secret? Why don't you want me to know? It's... it's mine, right?

The thought sends a shiver of dread through his body. Felix hasn't once said anything about a relationship. He's talked about other people, maybe fucked other people, and... Kade's stomach twists.

"I'll be in the baking aisle," Taylor says, squeezing Felix's hand. He nods at Kade, then glances at Felix, his expression shuttered. Neither of them is smiling.

Maybe Kade was never supposed to find out about this baby. His breath catches.

He stops before Felix, leaving two feet between them so he sees the bump—because there *is* a noticeable bump. How could he have slept with Felix for months and not noticed? *I'm a damn idiot!*

The lavender scent hits him like a brick wall. Kade breathes it in deep, stunned, smelling the honey-sweet edge that wasn't there before. It should have been comforting to smell it this strong, but it only leaves him feeling empty.

"You're pregnant," Kade says, and the voice doesn't sound like his own.

Felix hugs himself. He bites his lip hard, glass in his eyes, looking as though he's about to cry. "I-I am. Sorry."

Sorry about what? Months of lying? Not telling his bondmate he's pregnant? That the baby might not be Kade's? *I trusted you,* Kade thinks, and the thought burns through his chest, restless and disbelieving. How could Felix do this? They've known each other twenty years. *We're fucking bondmates.*

Kade sucks in a deep breath, his pulse pounding in his veins. *How difficult is it for you to say "I'm pregnant"? Do I even mean anything to you?*

It's goddamn humiliating, finding out his omega is months along. When Kade has been sleeping with Felix, and he never noticed the bump. He should have read the signs, and they're so obvious now—Felix buying those bulky clothes, having late-night cravings, puking his guts out. They've been meeting for months, and Kade was clueless through it all.

"You never told me," he says, hating that his voice shakes.

"I couldn't, okay?" Felix snaps, his voice rising high, eyes glittering. His hands come up to cradle his belly, and he looks so damn vulnerable right now.

Despite the fury scalding his veins, Kade wants to pull him close. Because Felix is still his bondmate, Felix needs his comfort. Felix's fingers curl into the fabric of his own shirt. "You weren't supposed to know."

"Why?" His thoughts churn. Hope whispers, *Maybe he wanted to surprise you.* Before Kade regrets it, he blurts, "Is it mine?"

Felix's face crumples. He looks away, tears

welling in his eyes. And Kade hears it before Felix even says, "No."

It isn't his. *It isn't his.* Kade stops breathing, the thought clanging through his mind. Felix is his omega. Felix is *his,* Felix had been his for fifteen whole years, been his closest friend and his confidant. They've run and shouted and played, shared a home, shared their hopes for the future, shared their joys and fears, and this...

It feels like a knife turning in his gut when he thinks about Felix carrying a child that *isn't* his. Felix once belonged to him, and it fucking hurts when that child inside him *isn't* Kade's.

Vicious heat tears through his veins, whispering *It's not mine.* He can't stop thinking about that something *else* in Felix's belly, and it should have been Kade's, should have been *mine.*

It's not his. And the whirl of shame and anger and jealousy tears through Kade like fire consumes paper.

He turns, his eyes stinging.

The sun shines hot on his face, and Kade blinks. He's out of the store. He needs to get further away. Out of this town.

It's only when he slides onto the bike that he realizes his hands are shaking.

Felix isn't his anymore. Felix hasn't been his in a while, and Kade should have known better than to kindle his hopes into a flame.

He swipes the tears off his cheeks, jamming his helmet on, turning the key in the ignition. The bike roars beneath him, and maybe that's the sound his insides make, he thinks, when they're shredding apart.

27
Felix

THE RACK of baby clothes blurs. Felix buries his face in his hands, tears smearing over his palms.

Kade's eyes had burned with fury and betrayal. Then he had turned, walked out of the store, and Felix doesn't deserve to be here at all. He's hurt his alpha. Lied to him. Betrayed him.

Felix sinks to a crouch, trying to breathe, but he's sobbing and he can't stop it, can't stop the sudden chill in his limbs. *Kade hates me now. He shouldn't have found out. I shouldn't have been here.*

He bites hard on his lip, choking, and his nails dig into his skin. He shouldn't even be in Meadowfall at all.

I freed him of the responsibility. He won't be tied down by a child now. Felix holds his limbs still, trying not to shake, but the thought of Kade leaving breaks something in his chest. Kade has never abandoned him, and it hurts like the ripping of a jagged knife. Felix sobs, hating the pregnancy, hating his hormones, hating himself.

It'll just be you and me when we leave, he thinks to the unborn child. *Kade won't find us. He won't be disappointed. I don't think he'll come looking if he doesn't want us.*

As he struggles to breathe, a gentle hand rests on his back.

"Oh, Felix," Taylor whispers, hugging him close. "What did you do?"

Felix shakes his head. He doesn't have an answer. The truth will turn Kade against him, anyway. If he leaves now, Kade won't learn about the bankruptcy, about his father dying because of Felix, and maybe he'll be happier for it.

Taylor tugs on his elbow, but he doesn't budge. He feels his brother settling down next to him, draping one arm over his shoulders. Felix ducks his head, afraid to even look up. He doesn't want to see any pitiful stares or curious looks.

"Doesn't he want it?" Taylor asks some minutes later, stroking his back. "I thought..."

"I told him it isn't his," Felix says, his voice ragged.

Taylor's fingers still against his back, and he groans. "Felix, you *idiot.*"

But Felix has always been an idiot, hasn't he? He curls up against his brother, thinking about all the reasons why Kade would leave, why Kade *should* leave.

He curls into himself, breaking, and Taylor's embrace brings him no comfort at all.

28
Kade

KADE RIDES for hours, following random traffic off the highway.

He turns off an exit ramp, riding down empty asphalt roads, spiny shrubs skimming by to the sides. He makes a right at one crossroad, then left at the next, and he's riding in circles, getting further and further from Meadowfall, until all he sees are the mountains in the distance, and trees rising up around him, their pointed tips stretching for the sky.

Felix is pregnant with someone else's child.

Kade sucks in a deep breath, releases it. Then he inhales again, breathes out, and repeats the process. It doesn't ease the ache in his chest. Felix had lied to him, kept the baby a secret, never intending for him to find out.

He swallows, twisting the throttle. The bike speeds up, and it feels like he's flying along the roads, leaving everything behind.

WHEN THE sun crawls lower in the sky, Kade

remembers the work he left at home, the new program that needs coding done, and the minor fixes for another project. *Deadlines coming up. Someone needs to do them.* The thought anchors him to Meadowfall, to a purpose other than himself.

He reaches for his phone, plots a route, and heads back.

When he steps into the house hours later, he finds strains of classical music floating through the hall, and his mother in the kitchen. Kade pauses in the doorway.

She glances up from her crossword puzzle when he walks in, her forehead wrinkling. "You've been gone a while."

"Yeah."

"I was hoping for you to get the tea, but I drove out and bought it myself."

He notices the teacup by her side then, and the tea tag dangling over its rim. Tea...? He had been going out for tea. He'd gone to the store for tea, and found Felix in the baby clothes section instead. Felix is pregnant. It's not his child.

He swallows the ache in his throat, turning away. "Sorry. Things happened."

His mom watches him carefully. "Is it Felix?"

He flinches. Is he that obvious? "How did you know?"

"Is he doing fine?"

How the fuck would I know? Kade pulls the fridge open, looking over the yogurt cups, the rice in plastic boxes, the jug of filtered water. He's not hungry, but he should eat. It's 8 PM. "He's fine."

It hurts again, Felix keeping secrets from him, Felix with someone else's baby.

"He's pregnant," he says, cutting the words off before his voice breaks. His mom frowns, leaning closer. But she doesn't seem surprised, and it rankles. "You knew?"

"Yes," she says slowly. "But I felt it wasn't my news to share."

Kade sighs, shoving the fridge door shut. She's only seen Felix once since he's been back. "Am I the last fucking person to know?"

"There are signs and smells I recognize, Kade. It's not something I would expect you to pick up on."

He closes his eyes, wishing things were somehow different. Wishing he asked Felix why he isn't good enough, why he left five years ago. But Felix has someone else's baby, and that says everything, doesn't it? He doesn't need Kade around.

"Congrats?" His mom eyes him as though he's a feral dog.

"It's not mine," Kade snarls, and the humiliation burns through his cheeks, all through his face. He stalks out the kitchen. He doesn't know how to face his mom, or anyone who knows. No one else should. Felix has been hiding it.

But it doesn't erase the fact that Felix is his omega, that Felix should be carrying his child, and he isn't because Kade wasn't good enough to keep him.

"Kade," his mom says. He pauses in the painting-lined hallway, his back to her. "Have you considered that Felix may still... need you?"

"Why the hell would he?"

"Because you're still his alpha. That's not a

bond you can erase."

He wants Felix to need him, and the thought sends hope unfurling through his chest. Kade glances down at his own wrist, a faint scar left from a hesitant bite.

I don't want to hurt you, Felix had said, twenty years ago.

Kade clenches his fist, turning his wrist away. "He doesn't want the bond."

"And that's why you're still carrying that ring? You know we don't reuse rings for a second mate."

"I don't want to think about it," he says, looking at the glass cabinet with all her miniature teapots. "It's over."

She falls silent, and he takes the few steps to his bedroom. Before he shuts the door, she asks gently, "Do you remember your oath?"

Kade shuts the door with a click, pressing his forehead against it.

Yes. Of course he does.

29
Kade

20 Years Ago

"NOW, DAD had to work early, so listen up in class. And that boy, Felix? Don't get him in trouble," Mom says, kissing Kade on the cheek. The car engine purrs softly around them. "If I get another note about you and him sneaking out again..."

"It was just for ice cream, Mom," Kade says, scowling at Chris and Sam in the back seat. "And it was only four times."

"Four times is four times too many," Mom says, looking stern.

Kade's brothers wink at him. *They're* the ones always getting into shit, and Mom scolds *him* for buying ice cream with Felix. He's ten years old; he'd rather not play with his brothers' third-grade friends. "I'll be good," Kade sighs.

She leans toward the back, so Chris and Sam can kiss her too. Kade's brothers push their door open, scooting out of the car, and a medley of voices from the school courtyard drift in.

Mom settles back in her seat, her left hand

cradling the steering wheel.

There's a faint scar on her wrist, that Kade notices when she drives them to school. "Where's that from?" he asks, pointing.

"This?" Mom traces her finger over the silvery line.

Kade has patches on his knees from falling down, but the one on his mom's wrist looks different, like tooth marks. Did someone bite her? A surge of fury wells in his chest, suddenly.

"It's not something to be angry about," Mom says, a smile twitching at her mouth. "It's a bonding mark. A gift."

"A gift? How can a scar be a gift?"

"From your dad." The look in her eyes softens, as though she's remembering something precious. "He left it as a promise, to protect me no matter what. I gave him one, too."

"Oh." Kade scrunches his face up, trying to imagine his parents biting each other as a promise. It doesn't seem right. Only animals bite people.

"Now, this isn't something you need to know yet," his mother says, leaning in, her eyes warm. "Most people exchange their bonding oaths when they're sixteen, or twenty, or some even older than that. Usually, it's between an alpha and an omega."

"What am I?"

Mom leans back, studying him. "Probably an alpha. You're still young, so you haven't presented as either in particular... but you do have a temper."

"I do not have a temper!"

His mother glances at the digital clock on the dashboard. 7:18 AM. "We'll talk more about this when we get home, okay?"

Kade sighs, wriggling around in his seat. "Fine. See you later."

He slams the car door behind him, then the one his brothers left open, and trudges to the courtyard.

In the midst of pop quizzes and lab experiments about boiling water, Kade forgets about the conversation in the car. He moves with the river of students through the school, heading to Mr. Thompson's classroom for English, then the field for P.E., and Mrs. Mulberry's class for science.

By the time school's over, his backpack hangs heavy from his shoulder, full of assignments and books about the alpha wars. His brothers have another two classes before they're out, so Kade circles the classroom buildings, then the science lab ones, to the playground in the back.

This play area is half as big as the one by the canteen. Where the eighth-graders hang out at the wood-and-metal playground, surrounded by younger kids and clique-wannabes, Kade prefers the quiet of this one, where the outcasts hide away among plastic slides and monkey bars, kicking at the sand.

He finds Felix at the corner of the playground, sitting by himself amidst a cluster of dunes. Twenty yards off, Felix stands out: thin and pale, with a mop of wispy blond hair. He hunches over, fingers in the sand, building the next dune.

I found some cool stuff in the science lab today, Kade wants to tell him. *Wanna sneak in? Jones is hiding some plants in a cupboard. There's even a lamp in there!*

Before he thinks further, a handful of boys

steps out from behind the slides, their eyes fixed on Felix. Ben sneers, cracking his fists, and next to him, Alex and Tom laugh their high-pitched giggles.

"Go!" Ben shouts, punching the air. Kade's stomach drops. He's seen them lurking in the other playground, shoving at smaller kids, knocking out teeth and leaving bloody noses. Why the hell are they picking on Felix?

Kade shucks his bag, sprinting over the grass. He's ten yards away, and they're surrounding Felix. He runs right into an invisible cloud of faint lavender, like he's just stepped into a garden, but there's no time to think.

He plows through a gap in their ranks, among a flurry of fists and kicking feet, and someone cuffs him in the ear.

"Fucking get away," he bellows, swinging his fists. He punches someone in the stomach, and someone else grabs his hair, kicking him behind his knee.

Kade stumbles, breathing in a lungful of lavender. He throws himself over Felix, and the lavender scent coats his mouth when he gasps. Someone punches his head, a flurry of too many fists. Kade surges up with a roar.

Behind, Felix cowers, whining softly. Heat bubbles up in Kade's chest like an overflowing pot. Kade snarls, ramming his forehead into someone's face, clawing at someone else's eyes, and Ben scowls at him.

"What're you doin' 'ere," he squawks, and Kade slams his fist into his nose. It crunches against his knuckles.

He's seen things on TV, practiced these moves in his bedroom. It hurts more than he expects, his fists throbbing, and someone kicks him in the back. Kade stumbles onto Felix, swearing. Then he grabs a handful of sand, flings it in the bullies' faces, and while they're distracted, he punches them in the nuts.

The boys howl, hands on their groins as they stumble away. Kade watches them leave, Felix safe behind him, and adrenaline pumps heady in his veins.

"Sorry," Felix mumbles.

Kade turns, breathing hard, his fists covered in blood. "Why're *you* saying sorry?"

Felix shrugs, ducking his head. Dirty footprints cover his shirt, his arms, and his hair's all mussed, sand strewn over him.

On the other side of the playground, kids stare warily at them. The other students play soccer further away on the field. It looks safe right now. No more bullies. So Kade crouches next to Felix, swallowing. "They fucking attacked you."

Felix curls his fingers into his arms, shaking. "I thought they might someday. It... it was just a surprise."

"Fuck them," Kade says. The lavender scent is still strong in his nose, and he sits down slowly next to Felix, examining the torn skin on his knuckles. "I'll beat them again. Bastards."

"You didn't have to," Felix says. He looks at Kade's bloody hands, wincing. "I'm sorry you got hurt."

"It's fine," Kade says. He wipes them off on his clothes, looking at the small cuts on his knuckles. “They hurt you.”

“I’m okay,” Felix says. He peels back his sleeves, then his shirt hem, looking down at the pink splotches on his stomach.

Kade reaches out, poking a pink patch gingerly. Felix grimaces. But his skin feels warm against Kade’s fingers, and he smells even more like lavender up close. “What’s with your smell? Broke a shampoo bottle?”

Felix shrugs. “I don’t know. It just happened during break. Then everyone started looking at me like I was sick. Mrs. Mulberry said I’m blooming early, and I have to tell my father. He’s not coming to pick me up until five.”

“Huh.” Kade scowls at the shed the bullies disappeared behind. His mom smells like lilacs. His father smells like birchwood, and Kade doesn’t have a smell, himself.

He thinks about the bullies, and his mom saying *He left it as a promise.* He watches Felix rub his thumb over his stomach. Then he thinks about the bullies again, coming to attack Felix.

“They’ve been attacking the people who smell like flowers,” Felix says quietly. “I’ve been watching.”

It hadn’t even occurred to Kade to notice them. “They can’t do that.”

Felix shrugs. “I guess I’ll have to get used to it. It’s... it’s not so bad.”

Felix is his friend. They’ve been talking since last year, ever since they met in art class. How can Felix just resign himself to getting beaten up? How can Kade even let that happen, when Felix is the one he sneaks out of school with, chasing after ice cream vans?

"I can mark you," Kade says slowly. "Will that help?"

Felix's eyes widen, green as leaves. "Doesn't that only happen between bonded pairs?"

"Will they leave you alone if you're bonded?"

"I don't know."

They look at the shed again, and Kade thinks about his mother's scar.

"I'll protect you no matter what," he says. The moment he says it, he knows it's something he'll live by. He likes Felix. And so he'll defend Felix, no matter how difficult it gets. "If you want, I'll mark you. It better keep those bastards away."

Felix looks at his wrist, then the shed. "Okay." He wipes it on the front of his shirt, then extends it to Kade. "I can't get all the sand off. Maybe I should go to the bathroom first."

Kade shrugs; a bit of sand isn't gross. He takes Felix's warm, grubby hand in his own, and presses his nose to Felix's forearm, sniffing along it. The lavender scent fades toward his elbow, and wafts twice as strong at his wrist. It's the same place his mom has her scar.

"It'll hurt," Kade says. Wounds always do.

"I'll be okay." Felix gives him a wobbly smile. "Ben kicked me in the stomach. *That* hurt."

Kade bares his teeth at that image, heat rushing through his body. No one hurts his friend. And they won't again. "I promise to protect you."

He licks over Felix's wrist, salty sweat and grains of sand on his tongue. "I'm gonna bite," Kade says. Felix nods.

Then he presses his teeth against Felix's skin.

Felix swallows noisily. Kade drags his teeth down. But the skin doesn't break. His teeth slide against Felix's wrist, slippery with spit, and he bites down harder.

Felix's skin tears. He shudders, and the coppery tang of blood coats Kade's tongue.

"Oh," Felix gasps. He stares at Kade, lips parted, and Kade thinks, again, how pretty he is.

"You should bite me too," Kade says, pulling away. Crimson droplets well along the thin lines on Felix's wrist, and Kade licks them off. "So we're even."

"Okay," Felix breathes. He takes Kade's hand and sniffs along it. "How do you know where to bite?"

Kade looks at the reddish marks he's left on Felix's wrist, pointing to the same spot on his own. "You smelled really strong here."

Felix sniffs at his wrist, then along his forearm, and back to his wrist. "You smell like something here. I'm not sure what."

"Then you should bite there," Kade says.

Felix licks over his skin, a light, wet touch. Then his teeth press down, sharp, and he pauses, lifting his mouth away. "I don't want to hurt you."

"I'll take whatever hurt you give me," Kade says, nodding at his wrist. Felix replaces his mouth there, biting down.

Pain jolts through his body, along with a hint of something *else,* something delightful that sparks down his nerves. His breath rushes out of his body. Is this what bonding is? He hadn't felt that tickling, feathery sensation before, that sent shivers all the way to his toes. And he feels connected to Felix, somehow. Like they're best friends, or something more.

Felix pulls his mouth away, staring anxiously at him. "Does it hurt?"

"Not so much," Kade says. "Felt good."

"I'm glad." Felix leans in, his breath warm on Kade's skin as he licks the droplets of blood away. Then Kade brings his wrist to his own mouth, licking over it just to be sure.

They compare their bite marks after that. Kade's is straighter, and the one he left on Felix's wrist, a little slanted.

"So that's a promise," Kade says, linking his fingers with Felix's. "Wanna go to the science lab? I got something to show you. Jones has some secret plants."

Felix beams, and they head away from the playground.

AN HOUR later, after Mr. Jones shouts at them for opening his plant cabinet, Kade drags Felix to his mom's car. He swings open the front passenger door, Felix by his side. Mom raises her eyebrows.

"I'm staying with Felix until five," Kade says. Chris and Sam climb into the backseat, chattering between themselves. "I promised to protect him."

"You did what?" His mom leans over the center console, surprise darting across her face.

Kade shows her his wrist. At his nudge, Felix shows her his, too. Mom's jaw drops open.

"When... When I said that's what the bonding mark means, I didn't expect you to go out and get one," she says. "This is a life decision, Kade."

Kade shrugs. "I'm sure about it."

Next to him, Felix blushes a bright red, but he doesn't pull his hand away when Kade holds it again. "Nice to meet you, Mrs. Brentwood."

Kade's mom bites her lip, looking at the clock, then back at Felix. "You're Felix Henry, aren't you? The mayor's son?"

Felix looks down at his feet, nodding. "Yeah."

Mom closes her eyes for a brief moment, sighing. "Oh, Kade."

Kade glares at her. "What?"

"Nothing," she says, but her gaze lingers between them. "I'll pick you up at five. Okay?"

"Okay," Kade says. He doesn't know what his mom is hiding, but he squeezes Felix's hand anyway, just in case. Felix squeezes back. "See you later."

AT FIVE, Felix's dad pulls up in a huge black car. Its chrome grill sprawls out in an elaborate trellis, and its engine purrs, the sound of it vibrating in Kade's ribs. These cars are rare; he's only seen one before, in the workshop his dad works at. His dad had said, "That's an expensive mistress right there."

He can't see through the tinted windows. Felix steps forward, though, and the back door swings open. Inside, a burly man sits by the other window. An older boy, also blond, waves from the middle seat. Felix lets go of Kade's hand, angling a small smile at Kade before he climbs in.

"Father," he says in a small voice, almost drowned out by the car. "This is Kade. I exchanged bonding marks with him."

The man turns to look at them both. Kade recognizes his face from TV. Mayor Henry looks solemn, though. Kade hasn't been paying attention to what he actually does in town.

"Bonding marks?" the mayor says, nostrils flaring. He looks sharply at Felix.

Felix repeats himself, stretching out his wrist shyly. Both his father and the blond boy look at it. "Mrs. Mulberry says to tell you I'm an early bloomer."

The frown on his father's face deepens. He flicks a look at Kade, then Felix. "What do his parents do?"

"His father's a mechanic. His mother's a housewife," Felix says. Kade tries to grin, daunted by the size of the car, the austere man inside, how wide the expensive leather seat looks around Felix.

The mayor's mouth presses into a thin line. His gaze flickers across Kade, then Felix, and he looks out the other window. Kade bristles at the callous way Felix's father treats him.

"Close the door," the mayor says. "We're leaving."

Felix flinches. He turns back to Kade with a wan smile and wriggles his fingers, as though he's hiding it from his father. *See you tomorrow,* he mouths.

"See you," Kade says. Was this what his mom had been worried about? The expensive car, or Felix's father treating them both like disgusting midgets? Kade knows they can't afford anything expensive. But that doesn't mean the mayor can treat Felix like a mangy dog.

The car door slams. Kade tries to look through the window at Felix, but all he sees is a reflection of himself. Then the car rolls off, a sleek monster prowling out of the narrow parking lot, and Kade is alone once more.

IN THE following days, Kade and Felix realize that the bullies don't care about bonding marks. Nor do they care if someone gets hurt.

They haul Felix away from the playground into a bathroom. Kade chases after them, kicking and punching. They give him black eyes and bruised ribs, and Kade shoves someone hard into the wall, breaking his arm.

Felix apologizes after, when they're both huddled in a stall and shaking, and it's only the two of them, their breathing loud in the silence of the bathroom.

"It's not your fault," Kade growls, looking down at his own hands. He needs to get stronger. Better. So he can beat the crap out of those bullies and protect Felix, so they won't threaten his friend anymore. "I swear I'll trash them so hard they won't even *think* about touching you."

Felix sighs, leaning into his arm. "I'm sorry for getting you into this. You really didn't have to."

But Kade's mom had pulled him aside the night before, telling him about bondmates and staying by his mate for life. Kade will be damned before he abandons Felix. So he holds on to Felix's trembling hand, giving him a squeeze. "We're in this together. I'll swear it again if you want."

Felix smiles weakly at him, holding his hand tighter. "Thank you."

TWO YEARS later, they kiss in Kade's bedroom.

It's not something Kade anticipates, when all he meant by the bonding mark was to protect Felix. But as they sit side-by-side at a low table, doing their math homework, Felix sighs, and Kade has never seen anyone with greener eyes than him.

"So the bonding mark," Kade says, turning his wrist up to face them both. The scar Felix left is a thin, curved line now, tiny against his growing wrist. "You ever thought about what it means?"

"Other than we're supposed to be mates?" Felix laughs, then sobers. His brows draw together. "Do you regret it? I mean, if you find someone you really like out there..."

Kade stares. He's never even thought about anyone other than Felix. "Do you like someone else?" he blurts, suddenly uncertain. Because he still remembers the mayor's cool stare, the way Alastor Henry never seems to be satisfied with him. "Someone with more money?"

Felix laughs. "I like being here," he says, looking up at the dusty rafters of Kade's bedroom. "It's nice."

But Kade has been to Felix's house once—it's all marble, shiny and vast and expensive. When they got home, his dad had said, "We'll buy something like that if we shit gold bricks."

"This is a small house," Kade says. He looks at the worn covers on his bed, the chewed ends of his pencils, Felix's legs kicked out on a threadbare rug. "I'll get something better for us."

"You don't have to," Felix says, his eyes twinkling. "I have everything I want."

Really? Kade wants to ask. Because Felix is worth so much, and he deserves all the best things Kade can give him.

Felix leans in, his nose skimming Kade's neck to catch the pine and cedar scent. When he follows Kade's jaw up to his mouth, Kade freezes.

He's thought about it. Never really known if this is what Felix wants, because their friendship is fragile. He can't risk kissing Felix, and having Felix reject him. Not when they're bondmates. His heart thunders in his chest.

Felix brushes their lips together, slow and soft. Then his hand slips on Kade's thigh, thumping hard on the floor. In the next moment, he's sprawled across Kade's legs, giggling. Heat sweeps up Kade's cheeks.

"You call that a kiss?" he says, because Felix kissed him, Felix just *kissed him,* and he has been hoping for this to happen for *months.*

"Maybe?" Felix grins, pushing himself back up. "Should we try again?"

"Hell yeah," Kade says, hauling him close. Felix purrs, shoving him down onto the floor.

Against him, Felix is warm and delightful and safe. Kade can't imagine his life without this boy. He wants to spend years and decades with his bondmate, wants Felix laughing by his side, wants

to hold him close and never let go.
In that moment, he understands why his dad had given his mom that bonding mark. He will protect Felix, no matter what it costs.

30
Kade

Present Day

WHEN HE opens his eyes, Kade finds his fist clenched around the ring on his chain. He looks into the shadows, unfurling his fingers. In the glow from his laptop screen, the ring gleams a silvery-blue.

Once upon a time, he had promised Felix everything. Nothing is left between them now, and his heart aches for it.

Kade sighs, peeling himself away from the door. He settles down in his bed, staring up at the ceiling, and the same emptiness haunts his gut again. Felix is pregnant. The baby isn't his.

This happens in the news sometimes. *Famous Omega Carries An Outsider's Child.* Kade never imagined it would happen to him. It feels like he's a failure, like he never was good enough for Felix.

He piles other thoughts on top of it, trying to bury the reminder. He has promised Felix protection. He can't go back on his word, even if Felix is carrying someone else's child.

How had Felix even gotten pregnant,

anyway? He'd been in heat that first night. Kade remembers that sharp, musky scent, remembers the desperate hunger humming through his body, when Felix's heat had triggered his rut.

For a minute, Kade lingers on that night, the desire in Felix's eyes, the way he had lifted his chin, inviting Kade over. The way Felix had held his wrist, asking him to stay.

He swallows.

He has no idea how long Felix had been in heat at that point. Felix could have fucked someone in Highton before he returned. Does the baby's dad know? Had he abandoned Felix? Did Felix return to Meadowfall to recoup from that loss?

A chill slithers down his spine. If Felix had kept the baby a secret because it isn't Kade's, because he was abandoned by his previous lover... then by walking out, Kade has done wrong by him. And Kade knows how it feels to be left behind. He tucks the ring back into his shirt.

"I'm an idiot," Kade mutters. Hadn't his mom said *Felix needs you more than you think*?

The child Felix carries is not his blood. He wants to snarl. It should have been Kade's, just like Felix is his omega. He can't accept Felix carrying someone else's child; the thought sends another wave of shame through his body.

Get over it, he thinks. *Dignity doesn't mean shit. Felix needs protection, especially now.*

He tries to sleep, but he spends the entire night tossing in bed, thinking he shouldn't have left Felix at the store, thinking about the past, and how he could have changed any of this.

IN THE morning, he trudges to the kitchen, where he finds his mom with a hot cup of tea.

"Did you sleep?" she asks, looking up from her book.

"No," he rasps, pulling a mug out for coffee. "Sorry 'bout last night. Lost my temper."

His mom turns the page and studies him, her eyes kind. "I'm not the one you should apologize to."

He sighs then, thinking about Felix, wondering if they'll ever meet again. Felix had been planning to leave from the start. And this is why, isn't it? He had expected Kade's rejection. Kade shouldn't have left him at the store.

He turns the faucet on, watching as water fills his mug. "I know."

As soon as he calms, he'll visit Felix's place first, then the gas station. And hopefully, he'll be able to catch Felix before he leaves.

31
Felix

"THE NEXT time I see Rick, I'm quitting," Felix says as he steps out of the backroom, glancing through the store. It's empty here, anyway. "I'm leaving."

Susan blinks owlishly behind the counter. "What? That was sudden."

"I'm leaving Meadowfall tonight. I'm not staying here anymore," Felix says, touching his abdomen through the baggy maroon shirt. If he holds his hand still for long enough, sometimes, he feels the baby from outside. How big is it now? The last time he measured, he'd been thirty-four inches around. How obvious had it been to Kade? "So I suppose you could say your goodbyes now."

"What happened?" Susan tidies the stack of forest-themed postcards at the register, watching as he rounds the counter. "You look like crap."

Felix sighs. After a whole sleepless night, fatigue weighs down on his body. He's amazed at himself for even crawling out of bed. He shouldn't be here. He should be packing at home, where he can lock Kade out, and taking the bus out of Meadowfall. "I'm not surprised."

"Tell me already."

"What do you think happened?" He rubs his face, turning to the cigarette boxes on the back wall. Kade's haunted eyes flash through his mind. Felix cringes. How much more can he hurt his alpha? How much more can Kade hate him? "I fucked up."

"You mean... Oh."

"I'm a failure and a disappointment, Susan. Everything that could go wrong did go wrong."

"Surely it can't be that bad."

"It *is.* I met him at the store yesterday." Felix cringes. "My brother and I were looking at baby clothes. And he just... showed up. I can't even... The look on his face. Oh, gods."

"Oh my god. I told you, you should have said something to him before this." Susan clicks her tongue. "The baby clothes section? Really?"

"Really." Felix buries his face in his hands, moaning. How has his life come to this? "So he found out I'm pregnant, right? I told him it isn't his."

"What the fuck."

"I'm leaving Meadowfall. Tonight. I'm packing up and taking all my things and I'm never going to see anyone here ever again." Felix sucks in a deep breath. "It's been nice working with you."

"Can't you just... tell him the truth?"

Felix sinks behind the counter, burying his face in his knees. "No. I can't. I've thought about it for ages."

Because he's turned it over and over in his mind, trying to find a way to tell Kade everything without Kade hating every inch of him. Kade's father dying. The bankruptcy. The lies. The baby. Kade never wanted children. With each addition, it feels as though he's walking further out on a rotting bridge, and there's a river roaring ten feet below him.

Felix wishes he would fall, be swept away, so he won't have to worry about any of this again.

"Come on, don't give up," Susan says, crouching next to him. She sets a comforting hand on his shoulder. "I'm sure he'll forgive you."

He laughs, and it sounds broken in his ears. Kade hasn't forgiven him for leaving five years ago. Why would he forgive Felix for the baby now? "No, he won't."

The thought of it slices like a knife between his ribs.

"Put on a smile and stand up," Susan says, tugging on his arm. "We're working."

Felix sighs. He pushes to his feet, blinking when Susan leads him to the cramped back room and flicks the light on. There, she opens her locker, pulling out her brown canvas backpack, then her wallet.

"Here," she says, handing him a five-dollar bill. "Treat yourself to some ice cream."

He takes it cautiously, his eyes prickling. "Why?"

"Because you need some comfort food." Susan slides her bag back into the locker, turning the key. Then she grins, her gaze sympathetic. "And I never see you outside your shifts. It would be awesome if we could hang out somewhere that isn't this place."

Felix gulps, folding the note into his palm. It

feels like kindness. "That's too nice of you."

"You offend me." She holds his shoulders and steers him back out of the room. "Now, get back to work."

He laughs weakly, pushing the money into his back pocket. It'll help pay for his trip out of Meadowfall. To a new life someplace else, where no one has ever heard of him, and no one will know he left his bondmate behind.

The thought feels like escape, like freedom. Felix hangs on to it, trudging back to the counter.

A tall man steps through the doors, carrying a whiff of lemongrass with him as he heads for the fridges. The next customer—a lady with long black hair—steps in a second later, adjusting her purse. Susan nudges Felix to the register, grabbing the inventory list again.

"Do you have a basket?" the beta guy asks.

"Just behind the candy racks," Felix says, glancing past the lady to point at them. Who needs a basket at a convenience store? The things here are expensive, almost twice the grocery store prices. Felix would never buy any of them himself. He isn't paid enough for that.

The man waves his thanks. Felix turns to the omega lady when she sets two boxes of mints on the counter. "You smell wonderful," he says, grinning at her orange blossom scent. She smiles, and they wait as the card transaction takes forever to go through. "I'm sorry about the delay."

"Don't worry," she says, her gaze drifting down to his abdomen. Her lips twitch. "All the best with yours."

A wave of heat swamps his cheeks. Felix

ducks his head, hating how even his ears prickle. Has she noticed the bulge of his shirt? Is he that obvious now? "Thank you."

He needs all her well wishes, when he hasn't realized just how visible the baby bump is. No one had pointed it out, and maybe she'll be the only one. But it tautens his nerves to know that his secret is so thinly veiled. Of course he hadn't a chance of hiding it from Kade yesterday.

Another customer steps in—an alpha who smells like fir—and Felix frowns at the card reader, wishing it wouldn't take an entire minute to process the transaction. By the time it flashes the approval notice, the man with the basket is in line, and the new alpha steps behind him.

"I'm sorry about the wait," Felix says, handing the credit card back to the lady. "Have a great day!"

"Take care," she says, and it feels like he's losing a friend when she steps out the door.

The beta with the basket empties it carefully next to the register. Felix scans a variety of food—soda, beer, chips—and in the middle of checking his ID, someone else walks into the store.

He doesn't realize it at first, when he smiles up at the beta, wondering at the rarity of lemongrass scents. "Here's your ID back. I just have to get the rest of these scanned, so hang on..."

Until his skin prickles, and he looks up, meeting familiar mahogany eyes. His stomach *swoops.*

Who else could it be, but his bondmate standing just inside the door? Felix tenses. *Kade is here. Kade is here, and fuck someone help me I don't know what to do. I need to leave.*

Behind him, Susan heaves a sigh.

Felix looks back down at the things on the counter, ignoring the alpha standing six feet off, watching him with his hands in his pockets. His belly tingles. Kade's probably looking at his baby bump, thinking about how Felix betrayed him. Felix wants to die right here, melt into the floor, anything.

He fumbles with the soda bottles, realizing he doesn't remember which he's scanned. *Fuck.* He smiles up at the beta and taps on the register, doing his best to look apologetic. "I'm sorry. I'll have to re-scan the things. The register messed up for a bit."

Breathe. Keep breathing. Kade can't do anything if you're behind the counter.

But Felix also wants his alpha's touch, and he can't think right now, when Kade is still here. Kade watches as he scans the soda bottles again, then the beer, and approves the ID check. Why is he here? Does he want Felix to prove the baby's parentage? Or does he want to tell Felix what a slut he is, or tell him to pack his things and leave Meadowfall, or—Felix's ribs squeeze.

He sucks in lungfuls of air, his hands trembling as he accepts cash. He counts the notes under his breath, then the coins, and tucks them into the register drawer, waiting as the register spits out the receipt. Kade's eyes are still on him.

"Thank you," Felix chirps, handing the change and bag of things over, and everything about this is wrong, all over again.

Kade walks over, stepping behind the alpha

in line, and he's three feet away now. Felix's stomach knots into a lump. He turns to Susan, but Susan's checking the cigarette inventory, facing away from them both. Felix hates his life so much.

The alpha pays for a pack of beef jerky with his credit card, and the transaction takes another eon to process. Felix stares at the register, trying not to blink, trying to think about watercolor shades because he's going to break if he looks at his bondmate. The seconds crawl by, like a tortoise stepping toward a busy road.

"Thank you," Felix says again, handing the man his receipt. When the man leaves the counter, Kade steps forward.

Felix's entire body creaks with how still he's holding himself. He looks down at the counter, straightening the pens in their holder, checking the paper roll in the register, touching the damp sponge to see if it needs more water.

"Hey," Kade says, and his voice rumbles into Felix's ears, familiar and low.

Felix jerks, one hand coming up to cradle his belly. "Can I help you?" He stares at the plain blue shirt on Kade's chest. The fabric clings softly to his pecs. Felix drags his gaze away, unable to meet Kade's eyes. "I'm afraid some of our pumps are not accepting cards right now—"

"About yesterday," Kade says, still looking at him. Felix feels like a sheet of glass one second away from shattering. He doesn't want to talk about yesterday.

He turns, stepping away from the counter, brushing by Susan. He wants to say *Please help me with the register for a bit,* but his throat is glued shut and if he says anything right now, he'll break.

He strides past the shelves, along the fridges at the back, bracing himself for *I can't believe you lied to me* and *I wish you were never my omega,* and the soda bottles in the fridge blur into a mess of colors.

Kade follows. Felix feels him striding through another aisle somehow, and he's barreling forward to the back room, thinking about running out the loading entrance, thinking about locking himself up so he can hide and not be scared. *Three more yards and I'll be gone.*

Warm, callused fingers circle his elbow. His breath hitches, and Kade tugs him away from the backroom door, spinning him around.

Felix wobbles, yanking at his arms. Tears spill down his cheeks. He doesn't need Kade to see him cry. Doesn't need Kade to see any of this. He's put Kade through enough.

"Stop running," Kade murmurs, hauling him close.

Felix stumbles into the wall of his chest. It radiates warmth into his skin, and he shudders at that heat, needing to burrow closer, needing to get away. *Why are you touching me if you hate me?*

Kade's fingers squeeze. "About yesterday. I shouldn't have left."

Felix blinks rapidly, his chest so tight he can't breathe. He wishes desperately that Kade will stop talking, so neither of them will get hurt again. Kade had left yesterday. He hadn't wanted to know anything else.

Felix blinks rapidly, his chest so tight he can't breathe, and he trembles, wishing desperately that Kade will stop talking, so he won't get hurt again.

Kade had left yesterday. He hadn't needed to know anything else about a child that isn't his.

"Look, I don't care if it—if it isn't mine, okay?" Kade says, but his breath catches. He's lying. He cares a lot whose child it is. "I said I'd protect you."

Why are you doing this to us? Felix shudders, torn between pushing him away, and clinging on. *I'm leaving Meadowfall. You didn't want children.* "No," he chokes. "Go away."

"I swore an oath," Kade says in his ear, his hand slipping down to Felix's wrist where the bonding mark is. "I'm standing by it."

And Felix breaks against his chest, biting his lip hard to stop himself from sobbing. Kade can't do this to him. He doesn't want a child, he doesn't want a lying omega, and he doesn't have to remind Felix of what he'll be losing when he leaves this place behind.

Felix whines. Kade cups a large hand behind his head, pressing his face to his chest. It feels like warmth and safety. Felix wants so badly to stay, wants to be held and have Kade tell him everything's all right.

Kade holds him. He runs his wrist down Felix's spine, along his sides, marking his arms. It feels like forgiveness and belonging, like acceptance.

Felix crumples against him, shaking, wishing he could say *It's really yours.* But Kade doesn't want a child. Felix squeezes his eyes shut and shudders, his insides tearing apart.

When he calms, Felix realizes they're in the half-shadows of the back room, and the brightly-lit aisles outside feel alien to him, full of colorful rows of shampoo. He steps back, wiping his face on his sleeves, already missing Kade's warmth.

"Sorry," he croaks, his nose stopped. "I should get back to work."

But Kade catches his wrist again. Felix pauses, raw.

"I'm still here," Kade says, his voice low. His nostrils flare. Felix winces to think what he might smell. He's still using the scent suppressants. "And I'll protect the... the baby too. Just so you're aware."

Felix glances up, horrified that he's somehow influenced him. Kade, who didn't ask for a child at all. "You don't have to," he says. "I can manage."

Kade studies him, his eyes unreadable in the shadows. Felix looks at the tiled floor, afraid of what Kade might see in him. He pulls his collar up, wiping his face with it. When he steps out of the backroom, Kade follows, the heat of his body radiating through the space between them.

"What time are you getting off work?"

Felix bites his lip, glancing at the clock. He won't be seeing Kade anymore. He's moving out tonight. But Kade waits at the counter when he rounds it, and Susan raises her brows, worry in her eyes.

If he's not going to see Kade anymore... If he has one chance to feel Kade's warmth against him, Felix will take it.

"Four," he says.

Kade nods. His gaze lingers on Felix, and he turns, stepping out of the door.

32
Kade

FOUR O'CLOCK rolls around too slowly.

Kade can't concentrate on programming or debugging or any of the tiny details he's supposed to be cleaning up. The letters swim on the screen like a foreign language, so he sighs and jams his headphones over his ears, putting on a playlist.

The songs remind him of Felix. They've been to concerts together, squirmed in excitement when Kade's mom drove them to Highton for autograph sessions, and sung along to *When You Climb into the Clouds* on the radio. At twenty, Kade had expected that Felix would stay with him forever.

Felix is pregnant with someone else's baby.

Kade grimaces. The thought stings like a slap, and he pushes away from his desk, throwing the headphones down, stalking out of his bedroom. At the gas station, Felix had barely smelled like himself. Not like yesterday, when his scent had been intense, rich, like lavender and honey, and Kade's instincts had roared in his body. He needs to protect Felix.

He pulls on his jacket, his helmet, sliding onto his bike. It doesn't take half an hour to get to the gas station, but he can't stay home without those thoughts circling like vultures in his mind. So he twists the throttle, roaring down the street, leaving the visor open so the wind brushes by his face.

Kade rides out of town briefly, down the narrow, winding roads through the forest. Then he rides back out, rolling into the gas station at five minutes to four, and waits by the side door to the building, helmet under his arm.

He still doesn't know what to say to Felix. It had been reckless, offering Felix his protection. He doesn't even know if Felix wants it.

At 4:01 PM, Felix strides out of the convenience store. He glances around the gas station, at the dusty sedans filling with gas, then to the side, where Kade waits with his bike. Felix's gaze lingers at Kade's feet, until he finally drags it up, meeting his eyes. Kade's stomach jolts.

"Did that bastard harass you?" Kade asks. He can't help glancing at Felix's abdomen, though, and the bump is still there, less obvious with the maroon shirt on. Behind that shirt is a second life, one Kade didn't help create. It still feels *wrong.*

"No. Rick wasn't in today," Felix says. He drifts to a stop three feet away from Kade, his gaze fixed on the curb. His lavender scent is barely-there, unlike the heavy scent in the department store. "So that was nice."

"Yeah." Kade doesn't know what else he can say to his omega, so he leans against the bike, running words through his mind, tracing his gaze over Felix's slender, pale limbs, the smooth line of his jaw.

He wants to pull Felix close again. Wants to smell that heavy lavender scent. He'd fill his lungs with it.

"Look," he says, at the same time Felix says, "Actually, I—"

They fall silent, Felix's gaze flying up warily to lock with his. "You go first," Kade says.

Felix purses his lips, looking away. "It's not that important. I... I decided I'm moving later this week."

Kade swallows, his chest growing tight. *That's not important?* "You're still leaving?"

"Yeah... a few days from now." Felix hugs himself, his gaze downcast. "I need time to do some things."

Stay with me, Kade wants to say, but Felix isn't carrying their child. Why would he stick with Kade? "You need rides anywhere?"

Felix jerks his shoulders. "Maybe. Just to get some boxes, I guess. I threw some away when I moved back."

It hurts to ask, "Where are you going this time?"

"I haven't decided."

Kade looks at the baby bump again—someone else, something *wrong* between them. He doesn't know how to solve this. It's not like programming, where you delete some words in the code, and the app will run smoother than before. "If you need to bunk somewhere, I've got space in my house."

Felix nods. But he's still looking away, and Kade's skin feels too tight on him. They're bondmates. How could this even have happened?

Felix's arms drift to his belly. Kade blurts, "How long—When did you find out?"

Felix glances down at his abdomen, his fingers curving around the bump. In that moment, Kade imagines his future: cradling his child with a wide grin, marrying a faceless alpha, laughing with a new family. He swallows.

"A few months," Felix says. "I think it's due around December."

Kade sucks in a slow breath. "So all those times you said you were on the pill..."

"I wasn't, no." Felix's throat works.

Kade closes his eyes, breathing through the ache in his chest. They've been seeing each other for months, and he can't imagine Felix lying to him for that long. Kade has seen through all his lies before. "Okay," he says. "Okay."

It's still not okay.

"Do you have a name for it?" he asks, trying not to think about all this. Felix shakes his head. "Why?"

"I haven't been to the doctor," Felix says, hugging himself. "So... I don't really know what name to give it."

Kade stares. "Shouldn't you have gone? I thought... pregnant people visit the doctor. Do the ultrasounds and all that."

"Just haven't had time, I guess."

"You should make an appointment," Kade says. "I'm taking you there."

Felix laughs, low and raw, and his mouth twists halfway between a smile and a grimace. "Taylor said the same thing. Why do you... Why..."

He sucks in a sharp breath, blinking hard,

and he looks like he's going to cry again. Kade swears, stepping forward. It feels so natural, folding Felix into his arms. Felix trembles against him, tears glittering along his lashes. Kade smooths a comforting hand down his back.

"I hate... hate crying," Felix gasps. "I hate being pregnant."

Kade's heart cracks. He'd assumed that Felix wants the baby. And maybe he understands a bit of why Felix has lied to him, if Felix has never wanted to acknowledge the baby in the first place. He presses Felix's face into his shoulder, holding him close. Felix's hands tangle in his shirt, his entire body shaking.

"Why are you keeping it?" Kade asks. Felix sobs harder, tears soaking into Kade's shirt, and Kade regrets asking that. "Look, you're gonna be fine, okay?"

Felix shakes his head, his voice muffled. "I'm not."

Kade doesn't know what to say to that, because he wants Felix to be happy, and he doesn't know how to solve any of this. All he can do is hold him, help him however he needs.

He buries his nose in Felix's hair, breathing in deep. Under the musk of sweat, he smells faint lavender, and that *other* note of honey. Then he traces his wrist over Felix's nape again, down his back, and for a while, he pretends Felix is still his.

After a while, Felix's sobs taper off. Kade brushes his fingers through his hair, slowly rubbing his scalp. Felix calms. For long moments, they merely breathe, and Kade relishes the weight of his omega in his arms.

The air around them smells like vehicle exhaust, like a bit of freshly-cut grass. Kade thinks about bringing Felix out of town instead, somewhere they can be alone. After a while, he pulls his phone from his pocket, tapping out a search query.

"Here, this is a prenatal clinic in Meadowfall. Make an appointment now before they close."

Felix huffs into his chest, his shoulders shaking. "You're bossy, aren't you?"

"If both me and your brother are telling you to see the doctor, then you better see the damn doctor," Kade says, pushing his phone into Felix's hand. "They close at five. You've got half an hour."

"Fine," Felix says, thin fingers wrapping around the phone. He steps away from Kade, wiping his face, and peers at the screen.

Five minutes and one appointment later, Felix hands the phone back. "They only had the last slot left for tomorrow," he says, wincing. "But I guess it won't clash with my hours."

Kade pushes the phone into his pocket, watching him sidelong. "Need a ride there?"

"I don't want to inconvenience you." Felix bites his lip.

Kade rolls his eyes. "I've been picking you up from everywhere the last five months."

"I'm sorry about that, too."

"Jeez, you're an idiot," Kade says. Felix cringes. Kade swears inwardly. *Idiot* had been an affectionate nickname years ago. He hadn't thought it would hurt Felix now. "I'll pick you up from here tomorrow, okay? It won't affect my work."

"Okay. Sorry about that." Felix hugs himself,

his shoulders drooping.

Kade sighs, pulling him back into his arms. "I didn't mean you're an idiot. Just... you don't have to keep saying sorry. Okay?"

"I guess." Felix's arms slip around him, and Kade breathes him in again, savoring his omega's scent while he still can.

In some ways, Felix hasn't changed since he left. He's still apologizing. Still feeling guilty about everything. Kade sees the invisible tendrils of the mayor's influence on his son, and he wishes he could have changed that, some way or another.

"Need a lift home?" he asks.

Felix shakes his head, pulling away. His hands whisper along Kade's sides, and he takes a slow step backward. "I'll get home myself. Thanks."

"Okay."

Kade watches as he turns to the bus stop, his footsteps dragging down the sidewalk. But Kade will be seeing his omega tomorrow, taking him to the doctor, and maybe they can salvage a new normal out of this.

33
Kade

THEY PULL into the clinic's parking lot the next day. Kade turns off the ignition, unbuckling his helmet.

Felix slides off the bike behind him, his eyes wide. "Aren't you going home?"

"I'm going in with you," Kade says, checking the time on his phone. They're minutes early for the appointment—Felix had skipped out from work. "You expect me to leave?"

"I thought you wouldn't be interested," Felix mumbles, looking at the pastel pink signboard above the glass doors. His cheeks flush prettily, and Kade can't help staring at him, at this man he still wishes he could marry.

Instead, he sets the helmets in the trunk, touching the ring in his shirt. "Just making sure everything goes all right."

"Oh." Felix trudges to the door, peering through the glass. Kade joins him at the welcome mat and pulls the door open.

Inside, bright posters of babies cover the walls. Plastic mobiles dangle from the ceiling, and teddy bears and baby bottles sit on either end of the receptionist counter. A lullaby plays from the speakers overhead. Kade clenches his jaw, the jealousy in his gut growling again. That child should have been his.

The receptionist smiles up at them, smelling like roses. "Hello. Do you have an appointment with us?"

"Yes. I have an appointment under Felix Henry," Felix says, his smile brittle. Kade wonders if Felix would rather be alone for this visit. Should he have left instead? "It's my first time here."

"Welcome! We're glad to have you with us," the receptionist says, handing a clipboard over. "Mr. Henry, could you fill out this form for me? And you're welcome to bring your husband in with you when you see the doctor."

Felix tenses, and so does Kade. *I wish,* Kade thinks, and the thought sits bitter on his tongue.

He nods at the girl, grasping Felix's elbow lightly to steer him away from the counter. Felix sits woodenly on the sofa next to him. Kade stares at the carpeted floor, instead of the two other couples in the waiting room with them. The scar on his wrist mocks him.

Felix blinks after a minute, clearing his throat. "Sorry about that," he says, looking at the form. "Maybe... maybe you should leave."

Kade winces. Why would Felix be sorry that someone thinks they're husbands? Because Kade had been the one to propose, and Felix had rejected him. "You want me to leave?"

Felix squirms, red creeping up his neck. "I understand if you'd rather not go through this.

Things are fine here."

He's right. The baby in his belly isn't Kade's. But Felix is also his omega, and damn it if Kade isn't going to sit through this with him. "I'm staying."

Felix nods awkwardly. He fills in the form, leaving *Spousal Info* blank. Kade swallows, looking away. It hurts.

When Felix returns the clipboard to the counter, the receptionist glances over the forms. Kade knows exactly when she sees the blanks, because her eyes widen, and she glances at him, blushing. "I'm sorry about earlier, Mr...."

"Brentwood," he says. Heat washes through his face. Anyone can smell his scent on Felix. And if Felix is pregnant, and Kade isn't listed as a spouse, well. "It's fine."

It still isn't.

Felix settles on the couch again, his gaze on the floor. "I'm really sorry."

Kade blows out a breath. "It's not your fault," he says. He doesn't feel like talking about the past right now. "Just a routine check, right?"

Felix sighs. "Yeah."

And Kade feels sorry again, because Felix doesn't look excited at all. The other couples seem at ease—two men, a man and a woman—while Felix's mouth pulls down at the corners, his eyes shadowed.

Carefully, Kade reaches over, touching his palm. Felix doesn't pull away, but his gaze flickers down. Kade holds his breath, until Felix's fingers curl gently around his hand. He blows out a sigh. Felix doesn't mind him being here. "You're really keeping it," he murmurs.

Felix nods.

"And you're not staying in Meadowfall?"

"I... might be here for a few more days."

Better than none. In a lower tone, Kade says, "Didn't know you hate this."

Felix bites his lip. "It's not... not bad," he mumbles, trailing his other hand over his belly. "Just lonely."

And those are the most honest words Kade has heard from him in a while. Those, and the ones he'd said through his tears.

"You've got me," Kade says, immediately wishing he'd shut up instead. Five years ago, Felix had said, *You really aren't good enough, Kade. I need better.* How can he assume that he's worthy now?

Kade breathes out through his nose, looking at the pamphlets of wide-eyed babies.

One of the doors swings open, a nurse in pastel green stepping through. "Mr. Henry!"

"I'm here," Felix chirps, his fingers squeezing tight around Kade's. He's grinning and lying at the same time. And it consoles Kade to know that he can still read this part of his bondmate.

"Please follow me," the nurse says, her gaze darting from Felix to Kade.

"Want me to come with you?" Kade asks.

Felix hesitates, meeting Kade's eyes briefly. "If you want. You really don't have to."

"I'll come with you." Kade trails after them, watching as the nurse measures Felix's weight and blood pressure. Then she leads them both to a wooden door down the hallway, knocking twice before pushing it open. The room smells like hay.

Dr. Smith smiles at them both, tapping on her keyboard. She shakes their hands. Kade shifts on his feet, feeling out-of-place. *Why am I even here?*

Because Felix is here, and he needs a source of comfort. Kade settles in the chair next to Felix, so their knees bump together. Felix glances down at their legs, but he doesn't say anything.

"How are you, Felix?" the doctor says, her eyes warm.

"Good." Felix smiles a bit, but Kade's sure that the doctor can tell he doesn't mean it, either.

"Since this is your first visit, we'll do the standard tests," the doctor says. "Urine and blood, as well as an ultrasound to check on the fetus' progress. Will that be okay?"

Felix nods, his fingers curling into his thigh. The doctor taps on her keyboard, asking about Felix's medical history, and it's everything Kade already knows—good health on both his parents' sides, and no issues to date.

"When was your last heat?" the doctor asks.

Felix tenses, his fingers curling into his knees. He doesn't look at Kade. "The last week of March."

Kade remembers that week, remembers Felix beneath him. He shoves thoughts of the baby's father out of his mind.

The doctor checks the calendar. "So... you're twenty-two weeks in—just in time for the routine anomaly scan."

Felix smiles weakly. "Thanks."

"We'll do the ultrasound first, then the urine and blood later, since most of those will take some time in the lab. Now, climb onto the exam bed, please. I'll need you to pull your shirt up over your abdomen, and unzip your pants."

Kade glances at Felix. He's thought about Felix's belly since the revelation, but it's ironic how the first time he sees Felix's baby bump is at the doctor's office, not during one of the many times they've fucked. Felix's fingers curl into the hem of his shirt. He glances in Kade's direction, red creeping up his neck. Kade doesn't even know if he wants to see it.

The rolled-out sheet on the bed crinkles when Felix sits on it. His fingers clench and unclench, and Dr. Smith frowns, stepping over to him. "Are you comfortable with this?"

"Yes," Felix says, meeting her eyes.

Kade breathes in, a chill swooping down his spine. That was how Felix looked when he said he was on BC. He was lying the entire time, lying here, and he's not comfortable right now.

He swallows, bitter. *Felix has reasons for lying. No point getting angry with him.*

Slowly, Felix drags the shirt up, as though he's battling with himself. Kade gulps. He should look away. Felix isn't his anymore, and this feels too intimate. He hasn't seen Felix's belly in months. Instead of a flat plane, Felix's abdomen rises up, from his navel to his jeans in a gradual curve. *There's a baby in there,* Kade thinks. *It's not mine. It should have been mine.*

He glances at Felix's face, catching the way Felix's eyes dart away, knuckles clenched white. *You don't want me to see it,* Kade realizes, his stomach squeezing. *Are you embarrassed about the baby? Is that why you hate the pregnancy?*

Kade stands, stepping across the office to the

bed. Felix's eyes widen as though he's afraid. But Kade curls his hand into Felix's, squeezing lightly. Felix's gaze flies to meet his. "You're fine," Kade says. "Relax."

Felix sucks in a shuddering breath. "Okay," he says, his voice unsteady. "I'll try."

Slowly, Felix's grip loosens. He releases the hem of his shirt, setting his hands by his sides.

Kade looks at his abdomen again. It's still pale, with a new, darker line from his navel to his briefs. On the wall, a poster of a naked, pregnant woman shows the same line on her belly.

If Kade had seen Felix's belly constantly, while they were having sex... maybe he wouldn't even have noticed it swelling.

"Are you feeling better?" the doctor asks, pulling on her gloves. Kade steps back to allow her access, and she settles onto the low stool next to the bed, turning to the darkened computer screen next to it.

"Yes. Thank you," Felix says, his voice a little warmer. Kade smiles at him, the tension in his shoulders easing when Felix smiles back.

Dr. Smith pulls out a plastic bottle sitting in a machine, snapping its lid open. They watch as she turns it upside-down and squeezes, and a line of clear blue gel oozes onto Felix's belly. Felix gasps, his eyes growing wide. "It's warm."

"I hope it's helping you relax," the doctor says, smiling. She replaces the tube in the machine, unhooks the ultrasound scanner from the terminal, before pulling up a program on the computer. Then, she sets the flat end of the scanner against Felix's abdomen, on the pile of gel, and a speckled black-and-white image appears on the screen.

All Kade has seen are pictures of ultrasounds, rectangles of vast space with a tiny blob in the middle. The lines and spots move on the screen, changing when the doctor tilts the scanner against Felix's skin. But there's no disputing the shape in the middle of the ultrasound, the little curled body of a fetus. It's a baby.

After the disbelief and the shock over the past two days, Kade still hadn't thought the child was real. He's seen the bulge of Felix's belly through his shirt, sure, but part of him has remained skeptical, has hoped that Felix had been lying about having a baby at all.

The image on the screen makes it real. Felix is pregnant, and Kade wishes the child on the screen were his.

On the bed, Felix cranes his neck, looking at the screen the doctor turned to him. His lips pull thin, his face a whirl of emotions. Kade wants to help ease some of Felix's stress.

"Hello," Felix murmurs, watching the screen. Then he looks down at his own abdomen, fingers curling, as though he wants to touch his belly. "It's... nice to finally see you."

Kade sees the stark curves of its ribs, the thin lines of its arms, and that child is growing in Felix's abdomen. They'd fucked last week, Kade clueless about this baby. And Felix has been talking to it the entire time.

Through his omega's uncertainty, Kade glimpses a tiny bit of joy, like a bright spark, and jealousy growls in his body. Felix wants the child. Who did he love more than Kade?

"The fetus appears to be doing well," Dr. Smith says, checking the baby from different angles. "It's roughly ten inches from head to heel, which is normal at twenty-one weeks. All curled up, it's about six inches in your belly."

Felix stares down at his abdomen, his face contemplative, as though he's trying to gauge the size of his child. Kade looks down at his own hand—the baby is smaller than that right now.

"Would you like to know its sex?" the doctor asks.

Felix's gaze darts to Kade's, then away. He tugs at his pant leg, undecided, and finally shakes his head. Why would Felix look at him? Does he think Kade will have an answer? "No. I'll find out later on, anyway."

"Sure." The doctor zooms in on the ultrasound images, turning the screen away from Felix. Kade guesses she's checking to see that the baby's fine.

"Is it safe for me to have sex?" Felix asks in a tiny voice.

Kade's breath lodges in his throat. Felix is looking at the doctor, not him, but heat crawls up his cheeks anyway. Does Felix want sex with him, or someone else? Because he's leaving, and... and he probably means someone else. Not Kade. Kade looks away, his chest aching, thinking about stepping out of the room.

Dr. Smith glances at the ultrasound image, then Felix. "Your pregnancy looks to be normal so far, which means sex should be fine all the way until you go into labor. If you experience pain or bleeding at any point, consult a doctor before further anal sex."

"Okay," Felix says. He glances at Kade, and Kade can't read him right now. He doesn't know if Felix needs anything from him, even if he wants Kade to pull him close, cradle him so he feels safe. "That's good to know."

"Would you like to hold the scanner?" the doctor asks, glancing at Felix, then Kade.

Kade winces. Why would he want to touch a baby that isn't his? It's half of Felix, but... it still reeks of betrayal. Kade can't do this.

Felix looks away, his fingers curling into the side of the bed. "I'll pass this time," he says, smiling at the doctor. "These pictures on the screen are good enough."

"Right. We can also print the ultrasound image for a nominal fee," Dr. Smith says. "Would you like a copy?"

Felix hesitates. "How much is it?"

"Three dollars."

Felix lowers his gaze, mulling over it.

"We'll get one," Kade says, even though his mind reels with thoughts about touching Felix's belly. "I'll pay."

Felix opens his mouth, about to protest, but Kade shrugs. So Felix looks back at his abdomen, nodding. It feels wrong, because Felix wants a photo of a baby that isn't Kade's, but that's his choice.

The doctor talks to Felix about the baby's progress, lengths and weights and measurements that Kade doesn't really care about. He looks at the doctor's desk, the plastic roses in a vase next to her screen.

"Male omegas have a higher risk in pregnancies," Dr. Smith says.

Kade's attention snaps to her. "What?"

She meets his eyes. "There are more complications that can arise from male pregnancies," she says, handing a booklet over to Felix. "But ninety percent of fathers deliver their children with no problems."

"Oh," Kade says, her words echoing in his mind. There are risks to this. Why hadn't he thought about it sooner?

He doesn't know how they get through the rest of the ultrasound. Felix and the doctor discuss stretching exercises, things to expect during the pregnancy, and their voices rush past Kade's ears.

When it's over, the doctor pulls a clean towel from a cabinet, handing it to Felix to wipe the gel off. Kade keeps close to the wall, feeling as though he's intruding on this somehow. It isn't until they leave the room that he can breathe again.

"Sorry," Felix says as they head back to the receptionist. "You didn't have to get involved."

Kade shrugs. "It's fine," he says. "I'll send you home after this."

Felix nods, his shoulders hunching. Kade wants to kick himself. He needs to help his bondmate feel better. And even if the baby isn't his... he'll stay by Felix's side, for as long as his omega will let him. He'll get over this somehow.

34
Felix

AT THE counter, the receptionist prints out the receipt for their visit. "Five hundred and eighty," she says. "That includes the ultrasound, the tests, and the lab fees. Oh! And the photo."

Felix's stomach freezes into a block of ice. He's done some research, covering his eyes and huddling, but it's still painful to hear it listed like this. Even the cash he borrowed from Taylor wouldn't have been enough.

"Put it on this," Kade says next to him, handing his credit card over. Felix stares. He can't begin to imagine how many weeks he'll be selling lemonade to cover this bill.

"No," Felix says, grabbing his arm. "I'll pay."

Kade slants a look at him. Felix knows his alpha has seen through his hesitance, that he can't afford all this without skipping his meals for the next two weeks. "Pay me back later," Kade murmurs.

Felix gulps. Maybe Kade means *Pay me in cash over the next three weeks,* or maybe he means *Suck me off for the next ten nights.* And either is fine.

"I'll need to verify your ID for the

transaction, Mr. Brentwood," the receptionist says, smiling at Kade. Kade hands his driver's license over, his gaze flicking back to Felix. There's no expectation in his eyes, only calm, as though he's checking to make sure Felix is okay.

Felix loves this man.

He shouldn't be realizing this now, at a clinic counter, the baby fluttering in his belly. The child is Kade's. And he wants Kade to know, except Kade doesn't want a baby.

Kade takes his cards back. The receptionist hands the receipt to him, and Kade folds it up, giving it to Felix instead. It feels flimsy in his hands, not like something that costs five hundred dollars.

"We'll see you again," the receptionist says as they head out. Kade nods at her, holding the door open for Felix.

"Why are you doing this?" Felix croaks when he slows to a stop next to Kade's bike, his eyes prickling again.

"Why not?" Kade asks, then winces, as though he shouldn't have said it.

"Because..." *Because I've hurt you. Because I left you, and lied to you, and so many other things.* Felix twists his fingers together, sucking in a deep breath. *I can't cry right now. I've cried enough.* "Because you have no reason to."

Kade studies him, his eyes dark, and Felix wants to fall into his gaze, wants to lean into his chest and stop thinking about everything else. "I'm doing it because I want to," Kade says, and Felix's chest feels too small for his heart.

"Okay," he says. It feels like a weak attempt

at repaying the favor. “I have some cash at home. I’ll get that first, and as soon as I get my next paycheck—”

“I don’t care about the money,” Kade says.

Felix looks down at his hands. Kade did, in the past. He had tried saving up for a home for them, and together, they’d been frugal. Of course Kade doesn’t care about money now, when they don’t have dreams of a new place. That relationship had shattered when Felix left. “Okay,” Felix says. “I’ll pay you back anyway.”

Kade sighs, unlocking the trunk. “I didn’t know there’d be risks for you. If you carry the baby full term.”

Felix looks down at his belly, rubbing a hand over it. But the child is Kade’s, and he wants to bring a piece of Kade away with him, regardless of what it costs. “I didn’t know about it, either.”

“You’re still keeping the baby?”

Felix looks away, nodding. “Yes.”

Kade’s eyes darken, and he looks pained, somehow. He hands Felix a helmet, glancing up at the royal-blue sky. “Want to grab some dinner? It’s late. I’ll pay.”

“I guess it’ll be fine,” Felix says, pulling his helmet on. He owes Kade so much, and he needs to stop hurting him.

They ride to an old diner with frilly green curtains and neon signboards flashing above the doorway. When they step inside, Felix trudges behind Kade across the checkered tiles, sliding into a booth across from him.

“I’ll cook next time,” Kade says, nodding his thanks when the waitress leaves them with a couple of menus.

Felix blinks. "Next time?"

"The doc said you're supposed to visit every month."

I can't possibly set aside hundreds every month. Felix pulls a menu toward himself, scanning the bolded numbers on each page.

"Stop looking at the prices," Kade says.

It was something they did back when they had their own place—going out for meals, buying the lowest-priced things on the menu, and then grinning if the food turned out good. Felix cracks a smile, looking at the numbers anyway. "Or, what, you'll spank me?"

"Up to you," Kade says. Felix glances up so quickly he almost sprains his neck. Kade's eyes bore into his, solemn, and Felix realizes that Kade might still want to fuck him after all, despite the pregnancy, despite all that's happened over the past few days.

"Oh," he says, his throat running dry.

"Do you?" Kade asks. His gaze stays on Felix, and Felix feels exposed again, like he had during the ultrasound. For the first time, Kade had seen the extent of his pregnancy, the one secret he'd been trying so hard to keep. Felix had panicked. And Kade had held his hand despite all the pain between them.

It doesn't feel any different in the restaurant, because Kade's looking at another intimate part of him. Felix can't hide his need to be touched, especially if his alpha is the one doing it. He gulps, tearing his gaze away. "I-If you want."

Which means *yes.* Kade's attention lingers on

him, and Felix's pulse thuds in his ears. He looks back at the soups and salads on the menu, trying to figure if either will get him full. Or if he really wants to feel *full,* he should invite Kade into his bed.

His pants grow tight. *We're supposed to be having dinner.*

Across the table, Kade watches him, and Felix feels far too transparent in front of his alpha.

"Get something good for you and the baby," Kade says. "Eating salads is like eating air."

Heat sweeps up his cheeks. "Not if I get the ones with chicken," Felix says, but he's flipping the page anyway, to skillets and sandwiches and steaks, and his stomach growls.

"You probably need more meat."

Which sends his thoughts into another dirty spiral. Felix groans, covering his eyes and jabbing at the menu.

"Sausage is fine," Kade says.

Felix hides his face in both his hands.

Dinner drags along. After the waitress leaves them with drinks, Felix squirms. Kade asks about the website. Felix says he's been selling a painting every week, and Kade's eyes sparkle with triumph.

"You look better," Kade says when they're halfway through the meal, popping a sprig of broccoli into his mouth. "More relaxed."

"I didn't think you were looking." Felix blushes. Isn't Kade angry with him?

Kade shrugs, his gaze sliding away.

At the end of the meal, the waitress leaves the bill at the end of the table. Felix reaches for it. Kade slips it out from under his fingers, grabbing his wallet.

"That's cheating," Felix says, reaching out for the bill. Kade is already paying for the doctor's visit, and he wants to make this even, somehow.

Kade stares at him. Felix meets his gaze. *I'll swap his card out for mine when he sets it down.*

Instead, Kade slides out of the booth, striding toward the counter. "I said I'm paying."

His heat whispers into Felix's skin when he brushes by. Felix shivers, nerves tingling. He needs Kade closer, wants to be held against his bondmate. But it's still not fair that Kade's paying for everything.

So he stalks after Kade, a slew of protests on his tongue. All it takes is for Kade to rake his gaze down Felix's front, and Felix's thoughts sink back into the gutter, the heat at his groin a distracting pressure.

When Felix joins him at the bike, Kade glances over him once, his eyes lingering on Felix's hips. Felix turns, trying to hide his erection. Kade's gaze lingers on him anyway.

So Felix slides onto the raised passenger seat, leaving an inch between their bodies. Kade's heat radiates through that space, tantalizing, and their thighs bump when the bike pulls out of the parking lot.

Felix desperately wants to press closer to his alpha, wants to push his cock against his spine.

The bike vibrates beneath them, Kade's scent washing into his helmet as they fly down the streets; brief notes of pine and cedar. Felix groans, needing to adjust himself, needing to be touched.

The sodium lights cast their orange glow

onto the roads, but no one will look at his hands. So he reaches between his legs, squeezing his cock through his pants, trying to get into a more comfortable position.

Screw it. Felix unbuttons his pants and sighs when he wraps his fingers around his cock, pulling it out. The night air rushes warm over his skin, and he strokes his cock once, sliding his fist up its silky skin, catching the droplets at his tip. Kade doesn't know what he's doing. A thrill swoops down Felix's spine when he looks down, and his cock juts pale against Kade's leather pants, against his jacket, and the seat. They're riding in full view of everyone, and Felix has his cock out.

The light ahead of them changes from amber to red, and Kade brakes. Felix bumps into his back, their helmets knocking, his cock shoving against Kade's back. Pleasure jolts through his body. *Fuck.*

For long heartbeats, Felix doesn't move. His legs are spread around Kade's. If he doesn't budge, maybe Kade won't realize just what Felix is prodding him with.

Kade turns, but his helmet hides his eyes. Felix holds his breath. *Does he know?* Kade looks straight ahead, waiting for the cars in the cross-street to drive by. More cars pull up alongside them, streetlights glinting in their windows. Felix swears. He can't pull away from Kade now, or he'll be exposed to the passengers in either car. Kade shifts slightly, and Felix gulps when his cock drags across Kade's pants.

Kade moves his arm. Something taps against Felix's hip, and he realizes it's Kade's gloved hand, slipping between them. *Kade knows.* He felt Felix's cock shoving against his ass, and he isn't repulsed at all.

His fingers rub up the side of Felix's cock, nudging at it. Felix leans back a little, just enough for Kade's fingers to slip around his cock, squeezing. Pleasure hums through his body. But it isn't enough. He needs to fuck into Kade's hand, needs more pressure, and he grips the steel bars next to his seat, rolling his hips up so his cock slides through the circle of Kade's glove.

When the light turns green, Kade releases him. The night air rushes by his bare cock again. Felix squirms, sliding his foreskin down to expose his glistening tip. It looks lewd like that, dusky in the shadows moving over them. He swallows, slipping his skin up, then down, playing with himself, wondering if Kade will want to touch him, or bend him over again. The thought sends precum dripping down his cock.

The bike prowls into his driveway. Kade turns it off, pulling the keys from the ignition, and the bike's purr stops, leaving a ringing silence around them.

Kade slips off his helmet, reaching back to tap the keys against Felix's cock. They slide cool and hard against his skin, and he gasps.

"Take your helmet off, then open the trunk," Kade says. "Don't leave your seat."

Felix whines. The lube's in the trunk. They've never opened it, ever since Kade bought it from the convenience store so long ago. He fumbles first with the helmet, then the keys, reaching over the trunk.

Kade's warm hand circles around his cock.

Felix sucks in a sharp breath. *When did you shuck off your gloves?* Before he can think, Kade slides his skin down, rubbing his callused thumb around his head. Pleasure hisses through his nerves. Felix groans, his hips snapping up, and Kade rewards him with a squeeze. His breath stutters.

His alpha watches him sidelong. Felix bites hard on his lip, unsure if Kade wants sex or if he wants to punish Felix somehow, or...

Kade pumps his cock twice, fast then slow. Felix drips onto his fingers, trying not to moan. They're still in the driveway, and even though the neighbors' windows are dark, someone could still walk by. He shoves the key at the trunk, but it skids over the smooth plastic surface. Then it pushes into the keyhole, and it's almost like sex, finding the right fit.

The key turns in the lock. Felix lifts the trunk lid with a sigh, his cock throbbing in Kade's hand. "Grab the lube," Kade says.

"I'm trying," he mutters, fingers skittering through the trunk. He finds some cloth bags, some bottles, and finally the smooth cardboard box containing the lube. Kade pushes his thumb under his foreskin, circling his tip, and the air rushes out of Felix's lungs. "Kade!"

"What do you want?" Kade growls, his thumb sliding around Felix's sensitive head, flicking it. Felix groans, thrusting his hips up, wondering how no one is around to see them, even if they're mostly cast in shadow, the streetlamps only lighting his back.

"Need to come," Felix whispers, tearing open the box, the bottle of lube falling heavy into his hands.

"Squeeze it here," Kade says, tapping his cock with a finger. The vibrations hum through his body. Felix gulps, turning the bottle upside down.

Cool lube hits him like a shock. Kade smooths it over his skin, twisting his grip, slicking him up, until lube drips down Felix's pants, trickling down his balls. Then Kade turns to face the front, wiping his hand against the seat of his leather jeans, and the slope of the cushion against his ass.

"Push it in between," he says.

Felix stares. Kade wants him to fuck... his ass. And the bike. It's never happened before, and Felix doesn't know how to react, except he needs this so badly.

He angles his cock down, holding on to Kade's shoulder for leverage. They're not exactly touching. Kade's still in his clothes, but as Felix pushes his tip into that crease, the warmth of Kade's body soaks into his skin, and he slides in, moaning at the pressure. His hips snap forward, shoving him all the way down, until the tip of his cock hits the base of Kade's seat, and the leather caresses his cock, smooth and warm.

Felix gasps, hands trembling. He eases closer to his alpha, rolling his hips back, then forward, feeling the drag of his foreskin against leather, feeling it slip away from his sensitive head, and he's pushing back in, amazed that Kade's letting him do this.

Kade rolls his hips, leaning back against Felix's cock, and the pressure sends a thrill through his body. Felix shudders. He can't control his need, can't control the way his body jerks forward, pushing down into the snug space between Kade and his bike. He whimpers, one hand slipping down under Kade's jacket, curving around Kade's side.

Kade's heat seeps into his skin, and as Felix pulls himself closer, he slides his hand down to Kade's groin. Kade's cock is thick behind the leather. Felix wants it opening him up, wants it on his skin. He moans, squeezing it.

And Kade rocks into his hand. Felix wraps both his arms around Kade's waist, undoing his pants, pulling out his cock, whimpering at the smooth, heavy weight of it.

"Will you... will you fuck me?" Felix gasps, rocking his hips, pushing his cock against Kade, feeling Kade pressing down against him.

Kade glances away, hesitating. Felix's stomach plummets, and he bites his lip. *Of course, he's just doing me a favor.*

But Kade growls, "Yeah," and he slips off the bike, nodding at his seat. "Move up."

Felix's pulse thunders. *He doesn't hate me. He's willing to touch me.* And he shuffles up into the rider's seat, its lingering warmth radiating into his thighs.

Kade slides onto the seat behind him, squeezing Felix up against the bike's metallic tank. Felix leans up, hooking his thumbs into his pants. Except Kade grabs his waistband, pushes his pants down roughly, exposing his ass to the night air. Felix gasps.

Kade pulls away for a moment. The keys slide out of the trunk with a rasp. When he presses back close, the keys jangle in his hand, and he pushes it into the bike's ignition, turning it.

Beneath them, the bike rumbles to life, vibrating and smooth, a beast waiting to prowl. Kade slips his hands under Felix's thighs, moving him up further, until his cock presses flat against the bike's tank. Its vibrations shiver through Felix's cock, sending a hum of pleasure through his body. Felix moans, leaning into it, leaving his ass vulnerable to Kade.

Kade leans in behind him, his jacket open, the heat of his chest soaking into Felix's back, and he strokes his callused palm down Felix's thigh, lips brushing his ear. "You lied to me," Kade murmurs, and his hand pulls away.

It returns a split second later, a sharp *slap* against Felix's thigh. Felix gasps, pain jolting through his body. "I'm sorry," he whispers, trembling.

"Are you?" Kade sets a heavy hand on Felix's back, leaning him further forward, trapping his cock against the bike, and the next slap lands sharply on his ass, a burst of pain through his body.

Heat crawls through Felix's face, and his cock throbs. He deserves this, deserves to be punished, and he shouldn't be growing harder, or finding this pleasurable. "I am," he says, his voice almost drowned out by the bike's engine. Kade spanks him again. "Ah!"

"I don't want you lying to me," Kade murmurs in his ear, his breath hot. Felix shudders, jerking when Kade spanks him over and over, leaving his cheeks tender and burning.

"I know," Felix gasps, his fingers sliding against the bike's tank, his cock dripping onto it, knowing he deserves more pain than this. "You should... you should beat me harder."

"I should," Kade growls, squeezing his tender cheeks with his hands, spreading them open. Felix groans when Kade slides his cock between them, pushing up against his hole. "But that's not what I want."

And he thrusts inside, spreading Felix open. Felix shudders, his fingers scrabbling against the bike, and Kade slides further and further in, until he's completely buried.

"More," Felix says, rocking back. Kade pushes in deep. Felix shudders against him, pleasure heavy in his body. "I can't... can't hold on."

Kade pulls him away from the bike, one hand across his chest, so Felix's cock isn't pressed against the vibrating tank. It stands neglected in the warm night air, and Felix squirms, needing to touch himself.

Kade thrusts in a little harder, his cock thick, filling Felix, sliding out, easing back in. Felix's cock jumps, taut, and he's so close right now, having his alpha hold him, having his alpha caring for him and their child. Kade reaches around, sliding his fingers up Felix's cock with the faintest touch. Then he leaves Felix straining up, his hips rocking harder.

"Come for me," Kade rumbles, fucking into him, his hands anchored against Felix's groin, holding his legs open. Felix shudders, the pressure in his cock building.

He thinks about Kade's hands on him, Kade inside him, Kade tolerating him enough to want him close. Kade grinds up against his prostate, and despite Kade neglecting his cock, he comes hard, arching as pleasure floods his body.

Kade looks down at him. Felix is too far gone to be ashamed, when cum spurts from his cock, warm and sticky, leaving a mess on himself and the bike. Kade gathers it up in his fingers, lifting his hand over Felix's shoulder to suck it off.

Felix groans. Kade strokes him through the rest of his release, slowly thrusting in. Felix shudders.

"You can go harder," he says, grinding back down. Kade groans, fingers curling warm against Felix's chest. He leans Felix over the bike, hips snapping up, thrusting firmly, burying his cock deep, and he's coming with a roar, anchoring Felix against him, spilling inside.

Kade leans into his back, his hands falling to Felix's thighs, and for a while, they merely breathe. When Kade begins to swell, Felix pushes his feet under himself. Kade wouldn't want to knot inside him, would he? He should leave now, get home, and maybe Kade won't regret fucking him come morning.

He's sliding halfway off Kade's cock when Kade's fingers curl into his thigh, pulling lightly back on him.

Stay, his fingers whisper, and Felix's breath catches in his throat.

He had asked the exact same of Kade, that first night. And Kade had stayed. So Felix sinks back down on his alpha, pushing further so his body stretches around the beginnings of Kade's knot, taking him inside. Kade groans. And his knot thickens, locking them together.

Kade is touching him. He isn't pulling away with revulsion, and his hands cradle Felix's hips, holding him close, care in his touch. Felix's throat tightens.

After all Felix has done, this feels like forgiveness.

He looks down at the purring bike, wiping the splotches of white off its gleaming surfaces. He hadn't meant to dirty it. None of this should have happened, but little has changed: the baby still moves in his belly, he's still stuck in Meadowfall, and he's still hiding secrets from his bondmate.

Kade's palms flatten against his thighs. His nose brushes through Felix's hair, and even though Kade hasn't once touched his belly, he's still holding Felix close. Felix trembles, leaning tentatively back against his alpha. Kade slides his arm across his chest, a warm, heavy weight pulling him close, and it feels a little like coming home, when Kade runs his wrists down Felix's throat, across his collarbones, over his chest.

Mine, Kade used to say.

Felix exhales the tightness in his ribs, closing his eyes. He feels safest in Kade's arms, and that hasn't changed since he left.

"I shouldn't be asking 'Why?', should I?" he murmurs, looking up at the star-strewn sky. How much of this can be mended?

Kade's breath puffs through his hair. "Probably not." He noses at Felix's scalp, wrists brushing down his sides, then along his thighs.

"Still gonna take the scent suppressant?"

Felix bites his lip, remembering the manager at the gas station, his leering smirk and invasive stare. "Yeah. For now, I guess. I'd rather not let Rick know about the... the baby."

Kade snorts, and warm air rushes against Felix's skin. "You shouldn't be at that place. Work somewhere else. Paint something."

"I've been painting," Felix says, relaxing against Kade. That's what he's been doing at night, when he gets home early and Kade isn't around to distract him.

"Then put them up for sale."

"It's not that straightforward, you know."

Kade shrugs. "I still think you can do better. Need to improve your visibility."

"Okay," Felix says. He doesn't want to think about it. All he wants to do is burrow into Kade's arms, and forget about the world. "But I don't want to talk about that right now."

Kade slips his arm over his chest, holding him close. Felix sighs, leaning in to press his back against Kade. It feels as though Kade has made peace with him for the lie, and Felix feels a little more at ease, now that Kade knows he's with child. It's not such a big secret anymore, even if Kade doesn't know the baby is his.

At some point, Felix will still have to move. But that point isn't today.

35
Felix

"DID YOUR alpha propose and say he loves the baby?" Susan says the next day, eyebrows raised. "Because that's what you look like right now."

"Gods, really?" Felix winces. That's the best and worst way to describe it, because he'd love if Kade proposed to him. In another life, one where everything was perfect between them.

Right now, he's just delighted that Kade had visited last night, that things have settled between them. It had been a relief and a flaming mess of heat, and Felix had reeled with Kade's unending patience with him. He heaves himself over the counter and lands next to Susan.

"Oh, don't do that." She swats at his arm, wrinkling her nose when he grins. "Customer impressions and all that."

"There's no one in the store right now. But even if there were, Rick firing me is the kick I need," Felix says, wriggling in front of her. "So I'll finally start making the right decisions."

Susan rolls her eyes. "And how old are you again? Twenty?"

"Thirty. Shut up." But he grins anyway,

checking the spare receipt rolls around the register, the sponge, and the barcode scanner. "Kade stayed up late with me last night."

"*Ah.*" Susan shakes her head. She grins, glancing at his belly. "Things are okay now?"

"Mostly," Felix says. Kade had followed him into the house last night and bent him over the bed, as if once on the bike wasn't enough. And Felix had moaned himself hoarse. He clears his throat hoping his voice sounds normal now. "At least, you would hope."

"Mostly?" Susan raises an eyebrow. "Wait... He still doesn't know it's his."

Heat sweeps up his cheeks. "I'm leaving Meadowfall, okay?" Felix says. "He won't ever find out."

Susan sighs. "You're an idiot, honey. That guy's in love with you."

He flinches. That's what Taylor said, too, but neither of them has seen the way Kade narrows his eyes at Felix's belly, as though he doesn't want the child. Why would he?

"I'm not thinking about it," he says, covering his ears. Susan rolls up a wad of tissue and tosses it at him.

The morning passes slowly. Felix chats with Susan as they tidy the shelves. Then they clean the floors, the bathroom, and it's only after she steps out that Felix realizes he needs to pee.

He sighs, shoving his phone back into his pocket. He's not supposed to be taking breaks, or locking customers out for a few stolen minutes. It'll be hours until the teenage boy on the next shift appears, if he even shows at all.

Felix mutters, squirming at the pleasant ache in his ass. He'll lock the door, put on the 'Back in five minutes' sign, pee, and run back.

Except a lady steps in, her brows drawn low. She smells like wheat. "Pump four," she snaps.

Felix sets the sign down behind the counter, breathing out. "Yes, ma'am."

She pays with her debit card, and the transaction takes forever to process. By the time Felix hands over her card and receipt, another two customers are waiting in line.

One of those days, huh? He rings their purchases up, tucks crumpled bills into the register, and the customers flow in and out of the store like a stream: a man with three cans of dog food, a boy with tubes of mints, an older lady with a tub of ice cream. *Damn it!*

He's still at the register forty minutes later when Kade steps in. Felix hops between his feet, bladder full to bursting, his legs pressed together as though that'll help. Kade raises his eyebrows.

"I have to piss," Felix whines. "Hold the people back for me?"

"Sure," Kade says. Felix dashes for the bathroom in the back, sighing with relief when he locks the door behind him.

When he emerges three minutes later, there's a line at the cashier. Kade sets a stuffed elephant down on the counter. "Reserve this for me," he says, lips pulling up in a smirk. "Be back later."

Felix wants to laugh. The lady right behind Kade stares incredulously after him as he steps out of the store, but Felix smiles, the tension in his body washing away.

So maybe they're back to being friends. Felix can accept that, if it means Kade will stay with him longer.

TWO DAYS later, Kade strolls in, jacket slung over his shoulder. His shirt follows the muscled contours of his chest, down to his abs. When Felix drags his gaze to Kade's face, he finds Kade with a tiny grin.

"Found something you like?" Kade asks.

"Maybe," Felix says, grinning back. "You might be wearing too much."

Kade's eyebrows crawl up his forehead. "How much should I be wearing?"

Just about nothing, Felix wants to say. Kade's due for another visit in his bedroom, and maybe Felix will move out of Meadowfall next week instead. After he's had enough of Kade's hands sliding down his body.

"Oh my god, you guys." Susan strides out of the backroom. She pretends to frown at Kade, shaking a broom at him. "If you're not buying anything, get out."

"How much for the omega?" Kade asks, nodding at Felix.

Felix snorts, clapping a hand over his mouth.

Susan stops next to Kade, looking Felix over. "Five hundred bucks? I think that'll be enough."

"*Susan,*" Felix whines. "Five hundred? Do you think I'm cheap?"

Kade raises an eyebrow, his gaze dragging down Felix's body, from his throat to his chest to his hips, and back up. Felix's skin tingles. "How much is it gonna take for you to come home with me?"

Nothing at all, Felix thinks, and Susan sighs, shaking her head.

"Nothing," Susan says. "So five hundred was already too much. I'm right, aren't I?"

Felix groans. "I hate both of you."

Kade glances across the counter. "You hate me, but you still reserved the elephant?"

"Because you asked so nicely," Felix says. He can't help smiling, though. Kade's eyes rove over him, and Felix steps closer, reaching for his wallet. "I still have to pay you back, though."

Kade's smile flattens, and Susan turns away, humming to herself. "Pay for what?" Kade asks.

Felix grimaces. He's been counting his funds, trying to make everything work, but the only way he can pay Kade off is to dip into the money he'd saved for moving. "The doctor's fees from the other day. Remember?"

"Oh. You don't need to," Kade says, rolling his shoulders. "It was a gift."

Felix glowers. "Stop doing that. I still owe you so much."

Kade's shoulders tense. "You need the money more. Keep it."

"But—"

Rick waddles into the store, his beady eyes anchoring on Kade. Felix clamps his mouth shut. *Crap. I forgot to check the time. I should have told Kade not to drop by.*

The only time this job is pleasant is when Rick is far away from the store, his fat mouth offending somebody else. And now he's in the store with Kade again, despite Felix's attempts to keep them apart.

Kade turns, his eyes narrowing.

"Get to work," Rick snaps at Felix, nodding at the register. "Don't stand and stare."

"He was treating me like a regular customer," Kade growls. He steps between Felix and Rick, and Felix tenses. Kade had bristled the two times he and Rick argued; Felix can't tell why. *Did I forget something? Why would you care so much what Rick thinks?*

"He's my employee while he wears that uniform," Rick says. He nods at Felix. "Get to work. I didn't hire you to whore around."

"He's not a fucking whore," Kade snaps, eyes flashing. His fist clenches.

Rick sneers like he's about to attack with something dangerous. Felix holds his breath, hoping Kade will leave. But Kade stands stubbornly between Felix and Rick, and Rick says, "If he's working for me and flirting with you, then he's my whore, isn't he?"

Felix looks at the register, his stomach roiling. *That's disgusting.*

"Say that again," Kade snarls, stalking over to Rick.

Rick pulls his own shoulders back, eyes glinting. "You're a low-ranking alpha. That doesn't mean shit. 'Cuz even if you punch me, it'll be worth nothing compared to, say, the mayor. Now, that guy, I'd respect."

Kade's eyes flash. He pulls his arm back, bicep straining at his sleeve, arm quivering with violence. He'll hurl Rick across the room in an instant. As much as Felix wants to see that happen, he also needs his job. "Kade," he snaps. "Stop."

Kade freezes, glancing at Felix over his fist. Felix shakes his head minutely. *No.*

And Kade sucks in a deep breath, his chest heaving. He made a promise to Felix.

"That's lower than I thought," Rick says, smirking. "Controlled by an omega? You're embarrassing."

Pain darts through Kade's eyes, too quick for Rick to notice. But Felix recognizes it like a childhood ghost. *Why does that hurt you? Was it because of... me?*

"Say one more word about my omega, and I'll rip you apart," Kade growls, his face inches from Rick's, his teeth bared. Then he turns, keeping one eye on Rick while he storms out, leaving the store smelling like cedar and pine.

Rick watches him leave, his lips twisted in distaste. "Bastard's all bark," he mutters, glancing at Felix. "But he leaves you behind, doesn't he? And then what? He thinks he's so strong, running off like that?"

Felix forces a wide smile, adrenaline pumping through his veins. "He's killed a few people, actually. It was all over the news some years back. Didn't you see?"

It's a lie, but Rick's eyes bug out of his face. "Whatever," he says. "He doesn't belong in this store."

After Rick stalks off to the backroom, Susan edges around the counter, bursting with questions. "Did Kade really?" She glances at the door. "Kill people, I mean."

Felix shrugs, keeping an eye on the backroom door. "He came close. Some of them went to the hospital. One guy almost died, but that was from complications."

That had been when they were younger, and Kade had attacked the school bullies viciously. They'd left him and Felix alone after, and Felix never forgets those days, back when they were still ten, shaking together in the bathroom stall, Kade's hands bleeding.

Kade's hurt now, somehow, because of him. And their breakup five years ago still hurts, even today.

"He's loyal," Susan says, a note of admiration in her voice.

"He's mine," Felix answers without thinking. He freezes. Susan smiles warmly at him, and he looks down at his hands, his stomach flipping. He wants Kade to be his. And Kade had claimed him in front of Rick, despite all that's happened.

Felix looks down at his belly, smoothing his hand over their unborn child.

36
Kade

KADE PULLS into the gas station the next week, sniffing carefully at the air. No bitter-wood scent, but the faintest trace of lavender lingers, and his pulse quickens. After seeing his omega days in a row, he still hasn't had enough of Felix. Would never have enough of him, really.

In the store, he finds the counter empty. So he winds further inside, his heart kicking when he spots Felix crouched in the candy aisle.

"We'll probably have to put a limit on the amount of candy you eat," Felix says, tucking chocolate bars onto the shelves. He scoops more from a cardboard box, looking down. "And I know it won't feel fair if other children eat all the chocolates they want, but I think it'll be better for you not to have cavities."

Kade stills, holding his breath. He hasn't caught Felix talking to himself since learned about the baby, but to hear Felix talking like that... Kade wants to prowl closer, to protect his omega. Because Felix knows what he's doing, doesn't he? Even if hasn't learned it off the internet, he's caring for the baby on instinct.

And Kade loves him, damn it.

"But maybe you'll get candies every so often," Felix says. "My favorite is the chocolate wafer bites—"

"Hey," Kade says.

Felix jumps, turning to look at him. He pales, glancing down. Kade hasn't realized how much Felix feared him discovering the baby.

"It's fine," Kade says, his heart twisting. Felix shouldn't have to be scared of him. "Talk to it if you want."

Felix relaxes, smiling hesitantly. "You don't mind?"

Kade shrugs. "It's your child. Do what you want."

His omega looks away, but warmth grows in his eyes. When he smiles, Kade's breath catches in his throat. Yeah, he really needs to see Felix more often, see him smile.

"You're early," Felix says. "Is it already three?"

Kade glances at his phone clock. "Three-thirty, actually. Been busy?"

"Three-thirty? Wow." Felix sighs, leaning back. "It's been kind of crazy the whole morning—the gas prices dropped, so we had a flood of people coming in. It sounded like a zoo outside all day!"

"Yeah, they're still there." It's not surprising that people will flock to a station with the lowest prices. They'd done the same years ago, riding around to scope out different gas stations.

"There's a bit of a lull right now." Felix crams the rest of the bars onto the shelf. "How about you? Done with work?"

"Yeah, mostly. Still some minor things to clean up." Kade tucks his hands into his pockets, following Felix into the loading area. Cardboard boxes are stacked high on pallets, and a wall fan turns in a corner. "I'll look at it again tonight."

"Oh? No plans for later?" Felix asks, a tiny smile on his lips. "You've been busy the past few days."

They've *both* been busy the past few days, Kade picking Felix up after work, sending him home, and then staying for dinner. Felix's bed hasn't been made in a while.

"No plans," Kade says, his gaze clinging to Felix as he moves around the storage area. "Tell me if there's something you can't lift."

Felix smiles. "I will. Thank you."

Kade shrugs. Felix is pregnant, and he wants to help. He still hasn't touched Felix's belly yet, but thoughts of the baby don't grind on his nerves as painfully as before. "About the baby."

Felix tenses, looking over his shoulder. "What about it?"

"Does its dad know?"

Felix looks away, lip caught between his teeth. "No."

Kade sighs, rubbing his temples. How many people has Felix been keeping secrets from? "Why not?"

"Because."

"That's not an answer."

Felix thumps some boxes around, and noises echo around the storage space. "Because it'll be difficult. He won't want it."

Kade bristles. How could anyone sleep with

Felix and not want that child? Because he sure as hell does. "Then he's a bastard."

Felix shrugs, looking down.

"What are your plans for it?" Kade asks. "After it's born?"

"I haven't thought about it." Felix heaves the next box up, stepping toward the door. "It's... not due yet."

Kade buries his face in his hand. How is he in love with this idiot? He follows Felix back into the display space, to an aisle with household products. "You can't plan for it after it's born. Do you have clothes for it? I don't even know what a baby needs."

Felix sighs. "Neither do I."

Kade wants to shake his omega, but it wouldn't help anything. Parents are supposed to prepare for their children. "Wanna go get clothes for it this Saturday? Diapers? A cot?" Felix's expression falls, and Kade's two-hundred percent sure he's thinking about money again. "I'll pay for it."

"No!" Felix cuts the box open, pulling out bags of cleaning sponges. "I'll pay."

Secretly, Kade thinks he'll be glad paying off all of Felix's expenses. He's grown up thinking of them as a unit; everything they buy would be shared, and he'd pay for as much of those expenses as he could. "If you want. But you're free this Saturday?"

"I guess." Felix worries his lip again, and Kade wants to kiss him. Felix had said nothing about that one kiss, months ago, when Kade had stolen it on the night they did the lemonade stand.

Maybe he hadn't liked it at all.

The plastic around the sponges crinkles. Kade crouches down next to his omega, helping him stack the sponges together. "You free tonight?"

Felix's gaze darts up at him, surprised. Kade's pulse trips. Is it strange that Kade wants to see him again? He wants Felix to need him, and Felix needs him most when Kade takes him to bed. "Yeah," Felix says.

Kade checks his phone again. Felix smells like lavender and honey and a faint trace of musk, and Kade wants to push him down on the floor, kiss him and fuck him right here in the store. "I'll wait for you outside," he says. "Stop distracting you."

Felix quirks a grin, and Kade smiles. "Sure. See you later."

THREE DAYS later, Felix sends Kade a text. *Don't bother picking me up later. Tim's not making it into work.*

Kade sighs, shoving his phone into his pocket. Felix has been complaining about the kid on the late shift for months. Tim sometimes flakes off work, and it's usually Susan who fills in for him. *Looks like it's your turn today.*

He slides off his bike, glancing at the open garage door. It can't be healthy for Felix to work two consecutive shifts, especially if he's pregnant. And he wouldn't have anything decent for dinner, either.

So Kade replies with a text. *Dropping by*

anyway. I'll get you dinner. What do you want?

Felix's next reply takes five minutes, as though he's trying to let himself accept Kade's help. *An egg and mayo sandwich? That sounds really good right now.*

Okay.

Kade slides back onto the bike, glancing down. In the half-shadows of the garage, there's a smudge on the polished bike tank that he hasn't seen before—a splotch of something dried. Felix had panted over the bike last week, dripping, and it had been damn hot, just watching him splayed out, ready for Kade.

Kade swallows, scraping the stain off. They probably won't have time for sex today, if Felix is working until midnight. The thought brings him back to food and egg sandwiches, and he turns the key in the ignition, pushing out of the garage.

An hour later, he walks into the convenience store, carrying a plastic bag and a grimace.

"Your other—" Felix looks up, eyes growing wide, his hand hesitating on his belly.

"Go ahead," Kade says, setting the bag on the counter. *Your other what?* "Say what you have to."

Felix stares at him, gulping. He hesitates, then looks back down, as though self-conscious. "This is Kade. He brought us some food. When people do favors for us, we'll have to say thank you. Kade's favorite food is tuna sandwiches."

Why would you tell your child what my favorite food is? It feels odd. But Felix is including him in his life, Felix knows what his favorite food is, and that counts for a lot.

"Thanks for bringing food," Felix says,

smiling up at him.

"Sorry," Kade says, his heart thumping. "Store was crowded as fuck."

"I'm sorry for all that trouble," Felix says. He heaves himself onto the counter, inspecting the plastic bag. "Ooh, the chicken bisque smells really good. Better than egg-and-mayo sandwich."

Kade shrugs. He'd bought it for himself, but these days, Felix's appetite varies so much that he can't tell what his omega wants to eat anymore. "Take it. I bought extra anyway."

Felix pulls the containers out with a grin. "I can't decide which to eat first."

"Eat them all at the same time." Kade pulls the tab on his soda, sipping from it.

When he sets it down, Felix takes the can, sipping from it, too, and Kade can't help thinking it's sort of like a kiss. Except now he wants to kiss Felix for real. And Felix is sitting a foot away on the counter, pulling the lid off the tuna salad with a predatory look in his eyes.

Kade swallows, looking down at his meatball sandwich.

"I've not been sleeping well," Felix says. "I feel the baby moving."

Kade glances at the bulge of his abdomen, wondering if anyone else has noticed it. The bastard manager hasn't commented on Felix's pregnancy. If he does, Kade will break his jaw. "Didn't know it moves this early."

"It's been moving for a while now. Not often, but sometimes. Maybe once every hour, or thirty minutes. Like a little squirm, you know?" Felix cradles his stomach, looking down at it. His expression softens, and Kade wants him to look at their child like that, a baby they create together. "You could... I mean, if you wanted to touch it, you could feel it move, I'm sure."

A wave of scarlet sweeps through Felix's cheeks. Kade stares. So maybe Felix has introduced him to the baby. But Felix also knows he can't touch that baby. It's not his. Touching it would feel like accepting a betrayal. But Felix is his bondmate, and Kade can't abandon him, or his child. "You want me to touch it?"

Felix shakes his head vehemently. "No! No, I-I just meant it's possible for someone on the outside to feel it move."

"Oh." But Kade can't help thinking about touching Felix now, just setting a hand on his abdomen, feeling the heat of him through his clothes. He looks back at his seafood pasta, shoveling it into his mouth. It's not his baby. It's not his right, either.

They eat in silence, watching as cars pull in and out of the station, the occasional customer walking into the store. Kade drains the soda, then the next can, and he starts eyeing the slushie machines to the side of the counter. Orange slush would be good. Or cola or wild berry smoothies.

When they finish dinner, Kade drops the empty boxes in the bin outside. He steps back in, heads to the machine, and pulls a plastic cup from the stack.

"I've never tried those," Felix says, watching him. "But now I'm curious."

"Which flavor do you want?"

"Strawberry," Felix says, his tongue darting

over his lips. Kade shakes away his wandering thoughts, then pulls down the machine's handle.

The machine rumbles, something inside clanking and loud. He frowns, releasing the knob.

Felix rounds the counter to stand next to him. "It shouldn't be doing that. It was fine this morning."

Kade nods at the handle. "You do it, then."

Felix reaches over, pulling down the handle. The machine grumbles again, pink slush swirling behind its circular window. The clanking grows louder, like a train rushing toward a station.

In slow motion, the window of the machine breaks. Pink slush gushes out like a creature vomiting, pouring wet and icy over Kade's shirt, down his pants, and onto the floor at his feet. It steals the heat from his chest, sticky and goddamn *cold.* Kade turns to Felix, whose eyes have gone wide. The pieces of plastic window clatter on the tiled floor at their feet.

"What the fuck," Kade says.

"I don't even," Felix says, looking from the machine's whirring stirrer, to the bright pink splash on Kade's abs, to the puddle growing on the floor. "What."

Kade groans, pulling his shirt off. All he wanted was a drink. And now he needs a shower if he wants to feel clean. "This is a damn mess," he says, balling up the shirt to wipe down his stomach. "It broke like a fucking toy."

"I should clean it up." Felix steps away from the puddle before it reaches his shoes, hurrying to the backroom. Seconds later, he returns with a wad of paper towels. "Here, take this first."

"Is that bastard going to blame you for this?" Kade nods at the machine. "He was pissed when I broke the pump screen."

"He shouldn't. It was a malfunction." Felix studies it, frowning. Rick has been reasonable at times, particularly if Felix gets Susan to help with the explanations. But it's sweet of Kade, thinking of the consequences of this.

Kade nods, satisfied with his answer. Felix wants to hug him.

Felix wipes a paper towel across Kade's abs, the rough material of it catching on his skin. The paper tears. Felix grimaces, then moves the towel further down, dabbing at the bright pink stains on Kade's jeans.

"Looks like I pissed myself," Kade says. "Except it's pink."

"It's not coming off," Felix mutters. He grabs a thicker wad of paper towels, pressing it right over Kade's groin. "Think it'll soak up like that? You might have to take this off too."

"You think?" Kade asks, his voice dipping low. They're in a convenience store, and Felix's hand is a stack of paper away from his cock.

Felix's touch stills right over his groin. His eyes flicker up to Kade's, wide and green, and he flushes. "I shouldn't be doing this at work," he says, squeezing lightly. "I am, uh, caring for the customer."

Except his palm grinds down on Kade's groin, and Kade grows half-hard, despite the cold seeping into his body. "This is caring, huh?"

"This is caring," Felix says, smiling. "But you may have to clean up somewhere."

"Are you cleaning me up?"

Felix's nostrils flare, and he glances around the store. "You should probably do that yourself. But maybe somewhere I can watch."

Kade swallows, watching him. He wants Felix closer, wants them pressed skin-to-skin. "I need to strip if I really want to get clean."

"Then strip," Felix murmurs, his gaze raking over Kade's abs, to his groin. Kade rolls his hips, pushing into his hand. "But... maybe that won't be a good idea. Stripping in the store. Maybe you should do that at home."

Kade sighs. "Not sure how I'm supposed to get home," he says. "Either I wash the jeans here, or I get my bike sticky when I ride."

"It got sticky the other day." Felix glances up at him, eyes dark.

"Wasn't completely cleaned off from that." Kade sets his hand on Felix's, pressing his palm snug against himself. Pleasure whispers through his body. "Found some stains today."

"I'm sorry." Felix winces, his gaze darting to the door. "I should have cleaned better."

"Try again," Kade says, except the doors slide open, and a woman in yoga clothes walks in. Kade sighs.

Felix yanks his hand away, pasting on a bright smile. "Good evening! The slushie machines aren't working, so I hope you aren't hoping for some!"

"I'm just here for some cookies," she says, waving back.

"I should get the mop," Felix mutters, stepping away. "Be back soon."

Kade sighs. He rubs the bundled shirt over his abs again, grimacing at the sticky residue left on his skin. The slush melts into a pink puddle around his shoes, and he dreads the thought of leaving footprints everywhere—in the store, on his bike, back home. So he stands in place until Felix hurries back with a mop and pail, setting them down.

The woman steps up to the counter, and Felix rushes off again. Kade crouches, soaking up the spills with the towels. When Felix returns three minutes later, he crouches next to Kade, wincing. "I'm sorry about all this."

"You don't have to be sorry," Kade says, meeting his eyes. "It's not your fault."

He means all of it. Not just the slushie machine or the spill. He means the breakup, the baby, and everything wrong between them.

Felix looks down at the wads of crumpled paper towels on the floor, lips thinning. "Some of it *is* my fault. Maybe all of it."

He scrunches up a fresh tissue, dragging it through pink water. Kade reads the weight of Felix's regrets in his sagging shoulders. He reaches out, snagging Felix's hand. Felix stills, eyes flickering up to meet his.

"I don't care whose fault it is," Kade murmurs. Except maybe it's his, and he doesn't know how to correct this. But Felix is his omega, and he has loved Felix for too long for any of this to matter.

He leans in, closing the distance between them. Felix's eyes widen. Kade brushes their lips together, relishing the softness of his omega's mouth, the puff of warm breath on his skin.

I shouldn't be doing this. You didn't want me five years ago. What makes me think you'll want me now? Kade pulls away, his heart pounding in his ears. But Felix leans in, following his mouth, and he presses his lips to Kade's, sliding them over his, his fingers squeezing around Kade's hand.

So maybe Felix wants kisses. Kade can give him that, too. He drops his balled-up shirt, slipping his hand behind Felix's neck, holding him close, and it feels like redemption when Felix kisses him, slow and sweet. There's only him and Felix in this moment, and Felix feels like *home.*

When they pull apart, Felix glances away, a rosy flush spreading across his cheeks. "Sorry."

Kade sighs. Haven't they gone through this already? "Why are you saying sorry again?"

"Because." Felix runs the paper towels over the floor, then fresh ones up the side of the counter.

But Felix had returned the kiss, and... maybe there's hope for them. Maybe Kade needs to suck it up and ask the important questions. "We need to talk, you know."

"We're already talking." Felix wipes down the counter next, soaking up more pink water.

"I meant about five years ago."

Felix tenses, fixing his gaze on the slushie machine. Past the broken window, the machine yawns dark and shadowy, like a creature's maw. "Can we not talk about that?"

"What's wrong with me?" Kade asks, and he wishes he could take the words back the moment he says them. But he can't, and Felix doesn't move. "How do I fix myself?"

Felix turns, his mouth falling open. "What?"

Kade wets his lips, his heart hammering in his chest. "You said I—You said I wasn't good enough."

Saying it makes it feel real, and Kade hates that there isn't a simple solution to this.

"I did?" Felix blinks, frowning down at his hands. "I, um. I had... issues. We shouldn't be talking about this. I don't think I said you weren't good enough."

How could he forget? Kade stares at the silvery scar on Felix's wrist. "You said I could never afford the things you want." He swallows, shame burning through his face. "You said you were finding someone better for you. And I get it. I'm still working the same job. I can't buy a mansion like you used to live in."

Felix gapes, his eyes growing wide with horror. "That—I said that?"

"Don't you remember?" Kade scowls, wondering just how forgettable that day was to Felix. "You packed and left."

"You should go home," Felix says, his throat working. "Let's just... not talk about that, okay?"

"What about us?" Because it hurts again, Felix not wanting to patch their relationship back. *What about our bond?*

Felix glances at the door, as though he's thinking of running. "This is fine between us right now," he says, chest heaving. "Just dinner and sex. That's all I need."

He looks scared. Kade doesn't know what the hell he's thinking. If Kade pushes too hard, Felix might leave again, and he can't risk that. He needs Felix close. Why can't he have a relationship like his parents did?

"Fine," Kade says, looking down at his fists. He can't hold on to anything. And that makes him a failure, doesn't it? The thought feels like a lump of metal sitting in his chest. "We won't talk about that."

Felix nods jerkily, gathering up the crumpled tissues. Then he mops the floor, lets Kade wipe his soles off. Kade sighs, tucking away all his thoughts about the past.

When Kade steps up to the door, Felix says, "It was never your fault."

Kade looks back at him, but Felix has turned away, tidying things on the back shelf. Kade can't see his eyes through all that blond hair, and he stops himself from rounding the counter to pull his omega close.

"I'll see you tomorrow?" he asks instead.

"Yeah." Felix nods, his shoulders drooping. "See you."

When he rides away that night, it feels as though he's leaving part of himself behind.

HE FINDS Susan alone at the counter the next morning. Kade peers down the empty aisles. "Where is he?"

She sighs, eyeing the stuffed giraffe in his hand. "He took a half-day. No, don't look like that—he's fine. Just said he needed some time alone."

"Oh." Kade breathes past the sudden anxiety in his chest, relaxing his grip on the giraffe. Felix is fine. "Just thought I'd see him here today. That's all."

"Had a fight?"

He shrugs. "I guess." Except it wasn't really one. Felix hadn't wanted to discuss the past, and Kade is just now coming to terms with the fact that they might not ever regain what they had. "When's he coming back?"

"I don't know." Susan looks at the clock, pursing her lips. "Maybe one o'clock. He'll avoid Rick if he can."

"Yeah, I can see him doing that." Kade stalks back to the counter, looking down at the giraffe's innocent eyes.

It's the one he bought a while ago, back when they were texting pictures on the phone. It's been sitting on his desk, waiting for a good time to move into Felix's place. Kade brought it in today as an apology, hoping it would make Felix smile.

"If you want, you could leave it here. I'll hand it over. Unless you'd rather give it to him yourself." Susan shrugs.

Kade sucks in a deep breath. Maybe Felix won't have any use for him, or the giraffe. Felix knows what he needs. So Kade sets the toy on the counter, leaving it with the burden of his hopes. "Thanks."

"No problem." Susan picks the giraffe up, looking it in the eye. "It's cute. I think he'll like it."

If Felix remembers the plushie murder from three months ago, then yeah, he definitely will.

Kade turns, breathing in the heavy summer air as he steps out of the store.

37
Kade

18 Years Ago

THE FIRST time Kade thinks about kissing Felix, they're twelve, and Felix is lying flat on the lawn, a sketchpad of animals in front of him.

Kade has been watching movies at night, with his parents, and sometimes, the people in those movies kiss. Last night, an alpha had kissed an omega, and the omega had slapped him for it. It had made Kade cringe, pulling his knees up to his chest. He doesn't want to be slapped like that.

So he lies next to Felix on the cool grass, watching his omega sideways. Felix's mouth looks pink and soft. And Kade thinks about touching it, except he doesn't want Felix to look at him like some kind of sick monster.

Instead, he throws his head back and sighs. "I think boys are better than girls."

Felix glances over, kicking his feet in the grass. "How come?"

Because you're a boy. You're better than girls. Or any other boy. "They're just better," Kade says, his heart thudding like a drum. Will Felix want to hear it if he says *I like you*? But Felix already knows, doesn't he, if Kade hangs around with him so much? "I don't like girls."

"I like your mom." Felix grins, blond hair falling into his eyes. He sketches the finishing touches on a rabbit, then flips the page. "And I like your dad. And Chris and Sam."

Kade waits for him to go on, his pulse quickening. But Felix doesn't say *I like you.*

He deflates, plucking blades of grass from the ground, shredding them. *Maybe he just thinks I'm a good friend.* "Yeah?"

"It's better than being home," Felix says. "I like Taylor. And James, the butler."

"What about your dad?"

Felix looks down at his sketchpad, shrugging. "I love him, I guess."

"You guess? Don't you know?" Because Kade loves his parents and his brothers, and maybe Felix. He can't imagine not loving his dad. But the mayor also compares Felix to his brother, tells Felix he's not worth much if all he can do is draw. Kade doesn't like him. Alastor Henry doesn't like Kade, either.

Felix rolls his pencil in his fingers. "I love him," he says, but his eyes are dark. "Sometimes I think he doesn't love me."

Kade doesn't ask why. He scoots over to Felix, nudging his side. "I love you," Kade says. "Is that enough?"

His bondmate cracks a smile, looking down at his sketchpad. "I think so," he says, drawing ovals onto the paper. "I love you, too."

And Kade's heart soars into the clouds. He

lies on the grass, closing his eyes with a smile.

When he looks back a minute later, Felix has fallen asleep next to him. On the sketchpad are two boys, holding hands, and under them, Felix has written *Kade & Felix.*

Kade squirms up close to Felix, pulling him into his arms.

38
Felix

Present Day

FELIX DRAGS his feet into the store, sighing as he ducks into blessed shade. The AC brushes cool against his skin, and he sniffs—no sign of the manager, but there's a lingering trace of cedar and pine. His stomach squeezes.

"Kade dropped by earlier," Susan says, plucking a giraffe off the register. "He left this."

Felix takes the giraffe into his hands. It's soft, with bean-filled hoofs, and it smiles adorably up at him. *Actually, the giraffe is the murderer. You shouldn't let them fool you.*

Kade had left this for him. After last night, he wasn't sure if Kade would return, but the giraffe says everything he needs to know—that Kade cares, that Kade's reminding him about their jokes. "He left me a murderer," Felix says. He can't stop smiling. "That's... very sweet of him."

Susan raises her eyebrows. "Are you guys ever going to sort things out?"

Felix shrugs. He's made too many mistakes for Kade to possibly want him back. But he buries his face in the giraffe's flank anyway, breathing in its pine-and-cedar scent. It smells like Kade has been holding on to it for a while, like Kade is standing here with him, and he hugs it to himself, comforted. "Maybe."

"You should. It's only a few more months before you're due."

He winces, reaching down to touch his belly. It's still getting bigger, and the baby has been moving, a constant reminder of the new life inside him. Kade hasn't said anything about wanting a child.

But Kade had brought up the past, and Felix had deflected the conversation. Like a coward. There's a reason he'd repressed that memory from five years ago. He'd been focused on hurting Kade, making Kade stay in Meadowfall so he wouldn't follow him.

And the horrifying things Kade had repeated back to him last night... If Felix had said them to his alpha, then how could he possibly make up for that?

Felix brushes the tears from his eyes, hurrying to the backroom so he won't cry in front of anyone else. The giraffe presses soft against his chest, and he hugs it, breathing in Kade's scent, wishing Kade were here.

He wants everything to be right again. He wants to erase the awful bits of their past, so Kade's father will still be alive, so Kade's family will still be doing well, and his brothers and parents will still be living contentedly in the same house.

Felix tucks the giraffe into his locker. If Kade returns again, he can't reject his alpha. He'll make it up to Kade somehow.

TEN HOURS later, Felix opens up his email. *You've made some sales today,* the artist portal email reads. *Check out which pieces you've just sold!*

Smiling, Felix clicks on the email. There's been a sale or two every week, and one a day for the last two days.

What he doesn't expect to see is the list of sold paintings. He scrolls down the page, and half his collection is listed: *Ship at Sea, Goat in the Forest, The Kraken Attacks.*

He stops counting the number of paintings after a while, scrolling down to the order summary. *$5,230.41.*

His heart *thuds,* and Felix whimpers, his vision blurring. Someone bought his paintings. Someone bought half his collection, and he'll have money to pay for things again. He'll have savings now.

He sets his phone down, hugging his belly.

39
Kade

KADE RETURNS to the gas station the next day, feeling like he shouldn't be there.

Maybe Felix won't be around. Maybe he's swapped shifts with Susan so they won't have to talk. And it would be just like Felix to do that.

He steps through the doors anyway, expecting to see the giraffe on the counter.

Instead, Felix straightens at the register, his eyes hopeful, teeth biting down a smile. "Hello."

Kade's pulse trips. "Hey."

But the night before still stands between them. Felix doesn't want anything from him other than sex. Kade tucks his hands into his pockets, trying to look like he doesn't care, when his bondmate stands just four feet away.

Felix holds his gaze, squirming, looking like he's holding back a flood of words.

"How are you?" Kade asks. *Why do you look like you just throttled your manager?*

"I sold some paintings last night," Felix says, his words cramming together. "Half of everything. Someone bought forty pieces at once!"

"Really?" Kade stares. This isn't what he

imagined would happen. He'd pulled into the gas station, thinking he'd have to apologize, or edge around Felix. And here they are, Felix looking like he's bursting with sunshine. "How much did you make?"

"Five thousand," Felix says, wriggling.

"Holy shit." Kade grins. It's not something either of them expected to happen. Felix has groaned about his sales the past few weeks, and to have him sell so much suddenly... Kade thinks about jumping over the counter. He wants to hug Felix. "I told you, they'd sell!"

Felix does a little dance next to the register, his entire face suffused with delight. "It'll probably be a one-off event, but five thousand dollars, Kade! I can't believe it. I'll have it piled up and roll around in it."

"Gonna cash it in dollar bills?" Kade chuckles at the image, extending his hand.

Felix raises his eyebrows—they're a little past handshakes by this point—but he slips his hand into Kade's anyway, his fingers soft and warm. "Maybe some five-dollar bills. I want a bed of cash. Make a coat out of bills. Or maybe a painting. It'll be my thousand-dollar masterpiece."

Kade laughs, and it feels like a bit of relief, and a bit of joy. "Go ahead. You deserve it."

"I'm still walking around in a daze," Felix says, his eyes the brightest Kade has seen in five years. "I think I'll have to spend Saturday shipping everything out. I can't go out with you. Sorry."

Kade shrugs. He's happy for Felix, and if Felix has to take some time off to get his paintings shipped, he's willing to accommodate that. "It's fine. Want me to come over and help?"

Felix bites his lip. "Probably. I mean, I don't want to trouble you. But I don't know how else I'll get forty whole paintings packed. Some of them aren't even framed yet. I'll need frames for them. Oh, gods, there's so much to do."

"Relax," Kade says, rubbing the back of Felix's hand with his thumb. "I can come over tonight and help if you want."

Felix's eyes widen. "You don't mind?"

Kade clicks his tongue. "I've been coming over the past few days, haven't I?"

"Not yesterday," Felix murmurs, looking down. And Kade remembers two nights ago, when they'd crouched by the slushie machines and kissed. Felix's eyes had brimmed with regret.

"Don't worry about it," Kade says. He pulls his hand from Felix's, and Felix's expression falls further.

Kade rounds the counter. Felix watches him, eyes widening when Kade's almost in the "Employees Only" zone. He hurries forward, faltering two steps away. Kade closes the gap between them, pulling his bondmate into a tight hug.

"I'm proud of you," Kade whispers in his ear, running his palm down Felix's spine. He's always loved Felix's drawings: the peaceful mountainsides, the lush forests, the colorful, exotic streets. And Kade's glad and relieved that someone else recognizes the beauty of those paintings, that something good has emerged from all their efforts.

Felix's belly pushes against him, and Felix presses his nose into Kade's shoulder, hands curling into his shirt. "Really?" he mumbles. "I'm just... I..."

"Yeah. You deserve it," Kade says, holding his omega to himself. Felix's body fits perfectly against his, slender and warm. Kade buries his nose in Felix's hair. Felix smells like lavender and a trace of honey, and hugging him makes Kade think of home, of a cozy hearth and easy conversations.

"Thank you." Felix sniffles, hiding his face. "I can show you the sales on my phone. It's amazing. That is, if you want to see it."

"Sure," Kade says, pressing his lips to Felix's forehead. Felix's cheeks darken.

He slips out of Kade's arms, hurrying to the backroom. There's no one in the store right now, so Kade follows, his heart thumping in his chest. Maybe Felix can afford not to work for a few months, paint more, and take better care of himself.

Kade steps into the shadowy backroom after him. Felix turns the lights on, fishing in his pocket for his locker key. Kade can't help looking him over—rosy cheeks, baggy shirt, swollen belly. Felix is his omega, and protectiveness surges through his chest. He wants to pull Felix close, defend him, pleasure him. Make him cry out and shudder.

Kade slips his hand around Felix's elbow, flicking the lights back off. Felix glances up at him in surprise.

"Before you do that," Kade murmurs, turning his omega to face him. Then he shoves Felix up against the lockers, pinning him down with a hand on his chest. Felix gasps, his pupils dilating. Kade steps between his feet, lowering his mouth to Felix's, brushing lightly against his lips.

"Before that, what?" Felix whispers, his breath hot on Kade's skin. He winds his fingers into Kade's shirt, and Kade cups him between his legs, finding the hard line of his cock through his pants. *Mine.*

Kade huffs his laughter. "All it takes is that," he growls, increasing the pressure on Felix's chest, "and you're hard."

"Are you surprised?"

Kade snorts. After all these years? "No."

Felix rolls his hips. Kade covers his cock with his hand, and Felix groans. "But I can't—can't believe you're doing this here."

"You aren't saying no," Kade murmurs. Light from the store shines into the backroom, lighting a skewed rectangular patch on the floor, and the storefront is quiet. So Kade hooks his fingers into Felix's waistband, and Felix whimpers. "Consider it my way of saying congrats."

The zipper pulls open with a harsh rasp. Kade slips his thumb into Felix's briefs, easing it down to expose the silky skin of his cock. Then he lifts it out with his finger so it juts between them, flushed and hard. Felix pushes his hips up, needing more.

"Tell me what you want," Kade whispers, sucking on his earlobe.

"Touch me," Felix groans, rocking up against Kade's palm, his cock leaving a damp trail on his skin. "Don't just pull it out and leave it."

Kade smirks, grasping his foreskin lightly with his fingers, sliding it down to expose his tip. "What if I do?"

Felix trembles, his breaths stuttering. "Here?"

Kade traces his fingers down the underside of his cock, then back up. Felix is so big it has to hurt—and it's something else Kade remembers from their past—he likes being exposed like this, where someone can catch them. "You're so damn hard."

"Touch me," Felix hisses, bucking up, so his cock grinds helplessly against Kade's hand. "Kade, please."

And so Kade leans in, breathing in the musk rolling off his omega. He licks down Felix's throat, curling his fingers lightly around his cock, stroking him, and Felix fucks into the circle of his fingers. Kade squeezes him once, listening to the hitch of his breath, before he lowers his mouth to Felix's chest, biting lightly on his nipple through his shirt. Felix grunts, his hips stuttering.

Kade drops to his knees, at face-level with Felix's cock. He leans in, breathing in its heady scent, dragging his tongue slowly along it, leaving a wet trail on his skin. Then he slides two fingers against its base, angling it down at his face.

"Push inside," Kade growls, opening his mouth slightly.

Felix groans, rolling his hips. His blunt head rubs against Kade's lips, warm and damp, forcing them to open, and he's grinding thick against Kade's tongue, filling his mouth. Kade closes his lips around him, sucking him in. Felix whimpers, bucking, sliding all the way inside.

He needs Kade so much. Kade pulls away from his cock, letting it jut back up, gleaming in the light reflecting off the floor. Then he takes Felix back into his mouth, just listening to his ragged gasp, watching the way Felix's fingers scrabble against the plastic lockers. "Kade—"

Kade sucks hard on him, once. Felix gasps, thrusting hard into his mouth. It makes his own pants uncomfortably tight, just feeling the way his omega needs him, the way Felix doesn't quite have control over himself when Kade makes Felix fuck him.

"Hello?" someone calls from the front of the store. Felix whines. Kade glances at the splash of light coming through the doorway, his pulse thrumming. They can't continue this without the customer walking in and finding them. So he leans back, Felix's cock sliding out of his mouth, jutting hungrily at him.

"Guess you should go back out," Kade says, licking his lips. Felix swears. Kade tugs Felix's pants up around his cock, then presses its straining length down, sliding the zipper over it.

"You don't have to look so gorgeous doing that," Felix murmurs, his voice hoarse.

Kade smirks, meeting his eyes. "Get out there. I'm waiting."

Felix squirms as he pushes his feet under himself, his cock thick in his pants. As he leaves, Kade reaches down to stroke himself.

He'll be waiting for when Felix gets back. And when his omega returns, Kade will test just how well he can keep his voice down.

THE SECOND time they fuck in the store, Susan is at the counter, and Kade has to clamp his hand over Felix's mouth, holding him down while he plows into Felix's ass.

The third time they fuck, it's on a night shift, and Kade sits under the counter, Felix grinding against him until the next customer shows up.

The fourth time, Felix is bent over restocking a back aisle, and Kade tugs his pants down without even greeting him, before pushing all the way inside. Felix grows hard in seconds.

The fifth time, Susan walks in on them in the bathroom, Felix on his knees, and she rolls her eyes, closing the door behind her.

The sixth time, Kade bends Felix over the counter, keeping an eye on the cars outside, and Felix comes all over the floor.

The seventh time, Rick walks in, and they freeze.

THEY'VE BUILT a system by now: Kade checks the storefront and the cars at the pumps, and Felix will stop him if it's a bad time.

And this instance is the same: Kade steps in when Felix walks out of the backroom, adjusting his pants.

"Thinking of me?" Kade asks, smirking.

Felix grins. "If I was?"

Kade crowds into his space, cupping him through his jeans, and it takes just three squeezes before Felix is hard, his cock thick against Kade's hand.

"No one at the pumps," Kade growls, stepping behind his omega. He pulls Felix's pants open, letting his cock jut out at the snack aisle. Then he hitches Felix's waistband down, exposing his pale, smooth ass. "Get me hard."

Felix groans, slipping his thin hand past Kade's waistband. His cool fingers wrap around Kade's cock. Kade unzips his own jeans, so Felix eases his cock out, stroking him base to tip.

With an eye on the glass doors, Kade pulls his omega to himself, sliding between his cheeks, pushing his cock between Felix's thighs. They watch as its tip nudges at Felix's balls, pushing them up. "Don't tease," Felix says.

So Kade bends him over next to the end-cap of the shelves, sliding in halfway, then pulling out just to hear Felix whine. Then he shoves back in, and Felix shudders, his body opening around Kade's cock.

Kade walks them closer to the door, Felix shuffling in front of him, dripping onto the floor. Kade anchors him by the hips, edging them past the candy aisle, to the snack aisle, then the muffin aisle, seeing how far they can get to the door before someone steps in.

Except Felix whines when Kade fucks in, and Kade's attention fixes on him. He wants to hear that sound again. So he pinches Felix's nipples, angling his hips differently, shoving in. Felix cries out.

Something moves at the door. Kade stills, his breath rushing through his nose, and Rick steps into the store. His nostrils flare.

They've been lucky so far, avoiding the manager when they fuck. Until now. And Kade finds that he doesn't care. The bastard has been calling Felix names, crawling under Kade's skin, and it's about damn time something changed.

Their eyes meet over the shelves—Rick's narrowed, Kade's taunting. Felix straightens in a hurry, red sweeping up his face.

So Kade thrusts into him. Felix makes a little mewling sound, his cock jumping hot against Kade's hand.

"What the everloving fuck," Rick spits, his eyes bulging out. He stares from Kade to Felix, to their joined hips, and his lips twist in a sneer. "I always knew you two made a good pair. A slut and a measly alpha."

Kade growls. Maybe they were asking for it, doing this in the store, but he refuses to let Felix hear any more of Rick's crap. When Felix presses against him, his face paling, Kade slides his arms around him.

"You're not," Kade murmurs in his ear. But Felix's eyes are fixed on his manager. Kade slips out of him, tucking his bondmate back into his clothes. More loudly, he says, "He's my omega. If I want to fuck him, then I'll fuck him, your store be damned."

Like a tiger, Rick prowls toward them, his face turning puce. "This is my store," he snarls, elbows knocking wrapped muffins to the floor. "I didn't hire that whore to spread his legs! Especially for some puny alpha like you."

"Don't listen to him, Kade," Felix mutters behind him.

Heat sears in his chest anyway. Kade nudges Felix to the side, stepping in front of him. It reminds him of decades ago, back when they were in school, and it was Kade protecting Felix from his bullies, tearing into them before they attack his most precious person.

But Felix doesn't run. He freezes like a statue, eyes wide. Kade clenches his fists, staring down Rick.

"Just making sure he's getting treated right," Kade says, shrugging. Even though his heart thumps like a drum. "Needed to perk him up. You've been treating him like shit."

Three feet away, Rick leers. "Sons of bitches," he seethes, nodding at Felix. "Guess that sack of holes is good enough for you, if you rank so low. What's wrong? You're not good enough to get any better?"

Kade tenses. He's good enough. He has to be. But even that's not enough for Felix, is it?

Felix cradles his belly, and Rick looks him over. Kade wants to rip his eyes out.

"Huh. I never realized he was knocked up. Think he slept around? Were you gonna put a second one inside?"

It's not his child, and the reminder sinks its teeth into him, a nagging shame. He doesn't need this bastard, of all people, to know that. *You have no goddamn right to speculate whose child it is.* Kade growls, thinking about punching his fist through that mustached face, smashing his bones.

"Don't," Felix says, grabbing him by his shirt. "Kade, he's not worth it."

Rick swings a punch at him. Kade snarls, deflecting it with a sharp jab. He'll listen to Felix because Felix asked. Rick's arm swerves to the side, and Kade catches his wrist, gripping it and yanking him forward.

"Diss my omega again," he growls, digging his fingers into Rick's tendons, "and I'll rip your eyes out."

Rick sneers. Kade flings his arm against the shelves, hard enough to leave bruises. Then he turns to Felix. "We're going," Kade says, flipping Rick off. "If we come back, it's to crack his skull."

"Okay," Felix says, his face pale, chest heaving. He slips his hand into Kade's, pulling him out of the store. The entire place reeks of bitter-wood.

"You're fired, you omega slut," Rick yells after them. Kade almost turns back and punches him. Felix's fingers tighten around his.

It isn't until they've rounded the corner to Kade's bike, that Kade sucks in another deep breath, his hands shaking. Felix is fine. They're both fine, and they're going home now. It doesn't matter if he's not worthy, or whatever.

"Are you okay?" Felix steps in front of him, eyes darting over Kade's face. He brushes his fingers over Kade's forehead, down his cheeks, over his mouth. His eyes glimmer with worry.

"Yeah," Kade growls, baring his teeth. He needs to hit something, needs to make that bastard hurt. "Would've got him nice and bloody."

He would have thrashed Rick if Felix hadn't stopped him. Kade checks the store to make sure the bastard stays inside, before looking over his omega.

Felix is still pale, his pupils constricted, his hands trembling as he tucks Kade back into his jeans. Kade blinks. In the standoff, he'd forgotten that his cock was hanging out. "We're going somewhere else."

"I'm fired," Felix mumbles, looking down. "My things are still in there."

"Damn it." Kade scowls. He hadn't thought about that. And they aren't going back into the store right now, with that dick still in there. "Anything important?"

Felix shakes his head. "I've got my phone and wallet. It's just... the giraffe is still in there. In my locker."

Kade swears, but his heart thumps anyway. He'd seen the giraffe in the locker, but Felix liking his gift enough to want it back... "I'll get you another one."

"It's not the same." Felix shakes his head. "But it's fine. I'll get it some other time."

"Tell me when you want to go. I'll pick you up," Kade says, baring his teeth. He's not letting Felix in there alone again, not when Rick could be in there with his filthy hands.

"Yeah, okay." Felix breathes in. Kade mirrors him, sucking in a breath to calm down. They've got Felix out of the store. Felix doesn't have anywhere else to go, and Kade has his company for the next few hours. "So where do you wanna go now?"

Felix looks down at his hands. He's still trembling a little, so Kade pulls him close, tucking his head under his chin. Felix's hair tickles his jaw. "I don't know. My rent's due and I... probably still needed my pay, actually. The payments on the paintings don't process until the shipments arrive."

"That's a damn underhanded way to pay artists," Kade mutters.

They'd spent all of Felix's day off on the watercolors: buying frames, mounting the pieces inside, packaging them, then riding down to the post office to mail them off. With forty paintings, it had taken all day. It wasn't until ten PM that he'd left Felix that night.

Felix shrugs. "I was kind of counting on this paycheck. But Rick's probably not even going to process it."

"Fuck that bastard." But Kade was also the one to start all this. He was the one to slip up, not seeing Rick until it was too late. "Look, whatever you need for rent, I'll cover it. Look for another job if you want, but I'm not sorry that you're out of that place."

Felix grimaces. "I'm not sorry about leaving, either. It's just... you don't have to pay my rent."

Kade breathes his omega in—lavender, musk, honey. He wants Felix close to him, and he wants Felix... "How about you stay at my place? Rent's whatever you want to make it. Free if you stay in my room."

Felix chuckles against him, trembling slightly. "Free in your room, huh?"

Kade imagines Felix sleeping in his bed, curled up against him, and the thought sends warmth sweeping through his chest. So maybe the baby isn't his. But Kade will care for the child like his own, and that's the right way to do things.

Rick steps out of the store at that moment, looking in the opposite direction. Kade bristles. *Low-ranking alpha,* the bastard had said. As if it's anything important. "C'mon, we're leaving."

Felix catches sight of the manager, and nods.

THEY PULL into Kade's garage fifteen minutes later, the bike exhaust oily in their noses. Kade watches as his bondmate pulls his helmet off. Felix said it wasn't his fault that he left. But Kade also can't provide luxuries for him, and maybe he doesn't deserve to have Felix as his own, after all.

"Take my bed," he says. "I'll use the couch whenever you move in."

Felix looks away. "I'm not sure your mom wants me around. I mean, the child..."

"She'll be happy if you stay for a while." Kade sets their helmets into the bike's trunk, shutting it. "She doesn't have anyone else to talk to while I work."

Felix chews on his lip. "Okay. But I really don't want to impose on either of you. You don't have to sleep on the couch."

Kade sighs, wrapping his arms around his omega. The thought of Felix living with him makes his heart race. It's as though they're restoring their past, a little at a time. "It's not imposing. You'll be fine here. Just tell me when you want to move in, and we'll rent a trailer to haul your things."

Felix nods, pressing his nose to Kade's shoulder. Felix smells familiar, like warmth and home. "I'll think about it."

40
Felix

FELIX PICKS nervously at the rough maroon fabric of his shirt, twisting it between his fingers.

He's fired. It's oddly liberating. Terrifying, too, when he doesn't have the earnings from his watercolors yet. But he has Kade, and Kade has offered him and the child shelter.

He trudges behind Kade as they walk up the stairs, looking at the framed paintings on the walls—oil pastels, watercolors, inked sketches of a lake. He remembers Kade's family home from a decade ago, when his brothers squabbled over the TV, and his father sawed up planks in the garage. At the end of the hallway, his bay painting hangs on the wall, facing them as they climb the stairs. Felix gulps, tears prickling at his eyes.

How can he stay in this house for even a minute? He was the one who caused it all to shatter. He can't leave Kade and his mother ignorant for years, can he?

They find Kade's mom in her bedroom, folding some laundry. The child squirms in Felix's belly.

Kade's mom has known about it since his last

visit. Kade might have told her it isn't his. And Felix doesn't know how to talk to his alpha's mom, if she believes he's carrying someone else's child. They might think of it as infidelity. And it's just as bad, isn't it? Kade doesn't want a baby at all.

Kade knocks on the open door. Felix pauses next to him, working up a smile. "Hello again, Mrs. Brentwood."

She looks up, smiling. "Hello, Felix. Aren't you working today? Kade mentioned you're only free on Saturdays."

Felix cringes. *I was just fired* doesn't sound good any way he phrases it.

"I got him to quit his job," Kade says, looking at him from the corner of his eye. "Figured it would be better for him to focus on painting."

Mrs. Brentwood beams. "That's wonderful!"

"I guess," Felix says, his heart pattering. *That went better than I expected.*

"He's worried about rent, so I said he's welcome to live with us whenever," Kade says, slipping his hand into Felix's. It curls large and warm around his fingers, and Felix hangs on to it, glad for the whisper of comfort Kade offers.

"I really don't want to bother you," he says.

"Nonsense! You're always welcome here, as you were before." Kade's mom smiles, patting an empty spot on her mattress. "Would you like to stay for a chat?"

Felix hesitates. Twenty years ago, Mrs. Brentwood had welcomed him into their home, allowing him and Kade to do their homework together. It's very kind of her to extend that same hospitality again. His alpha nods toward his mom, and Felix breathes in deeply, stepping forward. A conversation wouldn't be difficult, would it?

"I'm going back to work," Kade says, glancing at Felix, then his mom. "I'll be downstairs if you need me."

"See you at dinner," she says. "Felix?"

His feet heavy, Felix trudges further into the room. Sunlight slants in through the curtained windows, and white drawers sit on either side of the queen-sized bed. He plants himself gingerly on the mattress, among blouses and skirts and towels.

"How are you doing?" Kade's mom asks, turning to hang a skirt in her closet.

Not that great. Felix swallows. "Okay, I suppose. I sold some paintings last week."

"That's exciting!"

"It is. Kade helped me pack them for shipping."

"So he said." She slips hangers into her blouses, turning back to her closet. "And how is the baby?"

Felix stops breathing. He hadn't expected her to ask this so soon, especially when she'd seen through his secret. He looks down at the bulge of his abdomen. "It's fine. Kade brought me to the doctor two weeks ago. I had an ultrasound done."

She brightens, pausing with a towel in her hands. "So... about twenty-two weeks along?"

"Twenty-four," Felix says, touching his belly again. The child moves inside, a bare flutter, and maybe he's more comfortable thinking about himself as a father now. And because he can't lie to her, Felix checks the empty doorway to make sure his alpha's not around. Then he murmurs, "It's

Kade's."

It feels like a boulder rolling off his chest. Felix breathes in deep, looking down so he doesn't have to see her reaction.

Mrs. Brentwood stills. Her stare prickles his skin, and Felix touches his belly, holding on to his child.

"Oh, Felix," she says. She sweeps away the jumble of clothes next to him, sitting by his side in a rush of lilac-scented air. He glances up—*she isn't angry that I lied?*—and blinks when she takes his hand in her own, looking into his eyes. "Do you know how upset he was when you said it isn't his?"

Felix looks down at their hands, guilt flushing hot through his cheeks. Kade had been furious. But wasn't it because Felix had lied to him? He had glowered back in the department store months ago, and Felix had shaken with terror. Kade's never touched his abdomen, or shown any sign of wanting the child. Maybe Mrs. Brentwood read him wrong. "Oh."

"You should tell him," she says, squeezing his hand. "It'll save you both a lot of pain."

But how does he tell Kade that the baby is his, when it's been almost a month since he spun that lie? He doesn't want Kade to know he's lying again, doesn't want to hurt Kade any more than he already has. "I'll try," Felix says, gulping. "I don't... don't want him to hate me."

"He'll never hate you," she says, slipping her arm around his shoulders. "You know him best, don't you?"

Felix shrugs, staring at his belly. Kade

wouldn't want this child.

"Come on, why don't you help me with these clothes," Mrs. Brentwood says, getting to her feet. "If you decide to move in with us, I'm sure Kade will be happy to help."

"You don't mind if I move in?" he asks. She doesn't know he caused the bankruptcy, either. Felix never wants her to find out.

"Of course not." She beams at him, crow's feet at her eyes. "You're my fourth son, you know."

His throat constricts. His own father has never smiled warmly and said *You're my son,* and it feels like he's returned to a home he hadn't realized he left.

"I guess I know that now," Felix says, his voice hoarse. He loves Kade's mom as his own, and it's sheer relief to know that she still accepts him.

Mrs. Brentwood pulls him into a hug, and tears well in his eyes.

41
Kade

KADE SITS down to dinner some hours later, his mother and Felix waiting for him at the table. Felix had knocked on his bedroom door ten minutes ago, poking his head in, and his nostrils had flared as he breathed in the scent of Kade's room.

He sits next to Kade now, his eyes very slightly red-rimmed. Kade frowns. "You okay?"

Felix nods, his mouth curving up. "Yes, I am."

Kade carves the steaming pork roast into slices, dishing it out: first to Felix, then his mom, and finally himself. Felix spoons peas onto his own plate. He hesitates, then dishes some onto Kade's, too. Kade stares. His omega hasn't done that in a long time. Not since five years ago, and his pulse quickens.

Felix looks away from him, cheeks flushing pink. He hands the peas over to Kade's mom, and Kade wants to kiss him, all over again.

"Felix helped with dinner today," Mom says, dishing some peas for herself. "He taught me a new recipe he learned from Highton."

"Really?"

Felix nods, meeting his eyes for a second. Kade wants to brush the slope of his nose with his fingers. "It's the pork. We roasted it with beef stock and powdered onion soup. I think you'll like it."

Kade bites into a slice. It melts on his tongue, savory and meaty with a hint of onion, and he could probably finish the whole damn roast by himself. How had he not discovered this earlier? "Not bad."

"Isn't it? We'll have you cooking more often, Felix," Mom says.

Kade can't help looking at his bondmate. *Are you...?*

Felix blushes. He pokes around at his food, scooping some peas into his mouth. "I think I'll take you up on moving in," he says, looking first at Kade's mom, then at Kade.

Kade's breath catches. "When?"

His mom laughs. "Finish your dinner first, at least," she says.

A wave of scarlet sweeps through Felix's cheeks. "Whenever you're free, I guess. It's not as though I have a job right now."

"So... you're sleeping here tonight?" Kade swallows, and maybe he's a bit too transparent right now. He doesn't care. His mom knows, anyway. And Felix can't tell how much Kade wants him here. "I mean, if you're moving in before your lease ends."

"I can stay tonight," Felix murmurs, glancing sideways at Kade, and he blushes all the way to his hairline.

Kade reaches up, running the back of his finger against Felix's cheek. Felix's skin is velvety and soft against his fingers, and he wants to touch his bondmate for days, hold him in his lap and kiss him senseless. "I'll take the couch."

"No!" Felix pulls away. Kade looks back at his food. Did he push too hard? "I-I mean, it isn't fair if I take your bed," Felix says. "I'll sleep on the couch."

"But you're pregnant." Kade can't help looking at the bump of his belly again, wondering how big that baby is right now. "You need to take better care of yourself."

"Just one night," Felix says, looking between Kade and his mom. "If the couch is bad, I'll sleep in your bed."

Something in Kade's chest roars. Felix will sleep in his bed, and that's the best thought he's had in a while—his omega curled up, safe from everything else. So maybe he can wait while Felix sleeps on the couch for a night.

"Sure," he says, a grin creeping up on his face. "We'll ride down and get some of your things tonight, then we'll get you moved in tomorrow."

Across the table, his mom smiles. Kade thinks there might still be hope yet for Felix and him.

THE NEXT morning, Kade steps out of his bedroom into a heavy lavender scent.

It washes over his skin, up his nose, lighting his mind. Then it goes straight down to his cock. *Felix.*

He hasn't smelled Felix's scent this strong in a while, since the day he discovered his bondmate was pregnant. Kade gulps, following the scent. And it figures—Felix hasn't taken any scent suppressants since yesterday. The scent is mellow, laced with honey. Kade trails through the hallway to the living room, searching for its source. He'd find Felix anywhere, just by his scent alone.

In the living room, Felix has curled up on the couch, one arm over his belly, his back to the rest of the living room. Protective. And Kade can't help stepping closer, admiring the peace in his face, the fall of blond hair over his eyes.

He slows at the end of the couch, wondering if he should wake his bondmate. Felix's eyelids flutter open.

"Hey," Kade says, his voice still husky with sleep.

Felix blinks, his attention fluttering around him—the couch, the living room—and his eyes snap open. But his gaze falls back on Kade, and the tension in his shoulders seeps away. "Morning," Felix rasps, sucking in a deep breath. "I forgot where I was."

"Slept well?" Kade steps closer, eyeing the spare pillow under Felix's head, the blanket he'd tucked under himself. It can't be comfortable like that, especially if Felix has been used to proper beds all his life.

"It was good," Felix says. He squirms around, his gaze raking over Kade, lingering at his hips. "Need something?"

Kade glances down at the tented fabric of his own boxers. He doesn't care about that, when Felix's scent is lush and heavy and *familiar.* He drops to his knees next to his omega. After months of barely-there lavender, it's now almost overwhelming. He wants to fill his lungs with it and hold it there forever.

"You smell good," he says, lowering his head to the crook of Felix's shoulder, where his scent gland is. It smells like fresh flowers and a hint of sweat, like days in the past when they'd tangled together and made love in the afternoons.

Kade runs his nose along Felix's throat, filling his lungs with his omega's scent. Felix's skin is warm and soft against him, his pulse fluttering against Kade's lips. So he licks it, and Felix gasps. The sound makes Kade's cock strain against his clothes.

"You smell good too," Felix whispers, shifting around on the couch to face him. His eyes are warm and forest-green, and Kade leans in, brushing their mouths together.

Felix's lips are slightly chapped, but soft. Kade slides into his mouth, growling when Felix opens beneath him, his fingers coming up to curve against Kade's nape. His tongue drags damply against Kade's, slow and welcoming. Kade slips his hand under Felix's thighs, squeezing his ass, pulling his legs open to stroke along his inner thigh, up the leg of his sleeping shorts. Felix's breath puffs warm against his skin.

Kade rolls his soft balls between his fingers, teasing the base of his cock with his thumb. Felix groans, shoving his hips up, trying to push his cock into Kade's palm.

"You like teasing, don't you," he gasps against Kade's mouth. Kade thrusts between his lips, tasting him, sliding the flat of his fingers up against his omega's cock, testing the heft of it.

"Should I come downstairs some other time?" Kade's mom asks.

Kade tenses, breaking the kiss. This can't be happening *again.* He pulls away from his bondmate, glowering up the stairs. "You have the worst timing."

His mom waves down at them. "I hope the couch wasn't uncomfortable, Felix."

Felix groans, his cheeks scarlet. He covers his face with both his hands, and Kade wants to hug him. He's adorable. "Good morning, Mrs. Brentwood. The couch was fine."

"We're going elsewhere," Kade says, scooping his bondmate up into his arms. "Do whatever you like."

His mom laughs. Felix hides his face in Kade's chest, his fingers curling into the chain behind his shirt. Kade's chest constricts. He forgot about the chain. And he can't risk Felix fishing it out, because that ring hangs at the end of it.

Felix tightens his fingers on the chain. "When did you start wearing this?"

Five years ago. "Sometime back. It's not important."

"Oh." But Felix picks at the chain, and Kade holds his breath. He can't drop Felix to yank the chain out of his fingers.

Kade shoulders his way into his bedroom, kicking the door shut behind them. Then he drops Felix gently onto his bed, rolling him onto his knees.

"Spread for me," he growls, slapping Felix's ass. Felix sucks in a sharp breath, his pupils dilating.

"Here?" Felix whispers. But he's wriggling out of his sleeping shorts, curling his fingers into his cheeks, spreading them to expose his damp hole. Kade throbs, at the same time relief feathers through his chest. He's got Felix distracted, now.

"Good," he says, slipping his own cock out. Felix gulps. Kade grinds his tip against his hole, sliding over it, up between his smooth cheeks, then back down. Musk rolls off his omega in waves.

Felix gasps, pushing back, and Kade rolls his hips, dipping into his tight, hot hole, groaning when Felix's warmth squeezes around him.

And as Kade sheaths his cock in his bondmate's body, dragging a cry from his lips, they forget about the past for a while.

THE MOMENT the bathroom door clicks down the hallway, Kade fishes the sweat-slick chain out of his shirt, pulling it up over his head.

The chain whispers into a dollop of steel in his palm, gleaming in the sunlight. What snags his attention, though, is the ring at the end of it. It's white-gold and smooth, its polish dulled after years against his skin, but it's still the same ring he'd held up before, the ring that had carried all his hopes.

Five years ago, Kade had offered it to Felix, holding his breath. Felix's face had crumpled, and he had slapped it from Kade's fingers, turning to stalk out of the house they shared.

Why did you spend that money on me? Felix had

cried. Kade still remembers the striped yellow wallpaper, the ugly second-hand couch they'd salvaged off a street corner. *You know we can't afford this.*

He still remembers the breathless anticipation of getting the ring: exhausting Felix with hours of sex, and when he'd fallen asleep, tying a twist-tie around his finger to measure his ring size. Kade had expected him to wake the entire time. He remembers going to the shop, twist tie cradled carefully in his palm, picking out a ring that would fit Felix's slim fingers. Then he'd collected the newly-forged ring a week later, engraved with their names, and it had sat heavy and important in his pocket for a day.

Kade swings his legs off the bed, tracing his thumb over the ring's edge. Now that Felix has put on weight from the pregnancy, would it still fit his finger? Would he even want to be with Kade?

His heart squeezes, and he closes his fist around the ring, the metal pressing an indent into his palm.

The bathroom door unlocks with a click. Kade swears, looks around. He needs somewhere to hide the ring. When Felix moves in, he may catch Kade asleep. Kade can't risk him looking at the chain then.

He can't stash the ring at the uncluttered desk, and the display shelves are open, with no secret compartments. He can't hide it on the bed.

So he tucks the ring and chain under the mattress, hoping that Felix won't start looking too closely at the things in this room. In fact...

Kade hurries around his bedroom, pulling off

the little photos of Felix behind his computer, the tiny plastic fire truck that Felix had given him on his fourteenth birthday, the yellowed picture of them that his dad had taken at a fair. These, Kade tucks into his desk drawer, under a pile of work folders.

When Felix pushes the door open, Kade exhales, looking up.

"I'll help your mom with breakfast," Felix says, smiling warmly. "Do you need anything from the kitchen?"

"No, but thanks." His heart thuds against his ribs. *I just need you.*

Felix shuts the door behind him, and Kade stares at where his face was, touching the empty skin on his chest.

42
Felix

BREAKFAST PASSES far less awkwardly than Felix expects.

He steps out of the house to let the musky scents dissipate from his skin. By the time he enters the kitchen, Mrs. Brentwood has diced potatoes going on the stove, and some eggs boiling in a pot. "I really do hope you slept fine," she says, looking pointedly at his belly. "Kade meant well when he offered his bed, you know."

"I know," he mumbles, looking at the floor. It would also save them some embarrassment if they keep all sex behind doors. "I'll think about it."

When Kade joins them in the kitchen, he looks sourly at his mother. The expression melts away when he glances at Felix, though, and Felix fidgets, wondering if he caused Kade to relax. If Kade truly wants him around, despite what Felix has done.

They sit down at the table, plates of potato hash and boiled eggs between them. Kade talks about the programs he has to adjust for work, and Mrs. Brentwood tells Felix about her garden.

"Feel free to paint in the backyard," she says.

"Some of the succulents are blossoming again."

After breakfast, Kade rides out with Felix to a strip mall nearby, where they hire a trailer for the day. It takes them an hour to pack Felix's things into boxes, and five trips to move all of it into Kade's garage. The baby squirms in Felix's belly as they unload the last haul, and Kade watches when Felix touches the curve of his abdomen.

"What should I name it?" Felix asks.

Kade fumbles a cardboard box. The plates inside rattle.

"Sorry," Felix says, wincing. "I mean, I don't know what to name it. I'm not good with names." Besides, Kade should have a say too, shouldn't he, if the baby is also his?

"We don't even know if it's a boy or girl," Kade says, but a dark red tint fans across his cheeks. "Why are you asking me, anyway?"

Felix lowers his head, pulling open a box of clothes. "I... thought you might have a better idea than I do."

Kade shrugs, his gaze lingering on Felix's belly. "We still have to get clothes for it, right? Maybe you'll have a better idea when we're there. Or you could ask my mom."

Felix sighs, tracing his finger over the tape on the box. "I'm glad about moving in." Kade glances up, his eyes bright. Felix shrugs. "I mean, your mom knows a lot about caring for children, right? I figure I could learn something from her."

"Oh." Kade hauls the rest of the boxes onto the garage floor, his fingers smudged with dust. His shoulders sag a little. "Yeah, she has plenty of experience with that."

Did I say something wrong? Felix cringes. Maybe he accidentally offended Kade's mom. "Anyway, thanks for helping me move. And for letting me stay here. I really don't want to bother you."

Kade rolls his eyes. "When have you really bothered me?"

"I... don't know." Aside from five years ago? Felix riffles through his memories, remembering the wrong-number prank calls he pulled on Kade, the ice cubes down his shirt, distracting him at work with silly farting noises... "The time I caught a duck and it shat on you?"

Kade laughs. He dusts his hands off, striding over to take the box of clothes from Felix. "I'll move your stuff in for you."

"This is light enough," Felix says, but Kade wraps his hands around the box anyway. Then he lowers his face over Felix, so his lips hover an inch away, and his warm breath feathers over Felix's skin.

When Kade kisses him, his lips slide soft and insistent. Felix doesn't know why he's doing this, but it feels good. Kade's kissing him, Kade's helping him move, and he'll never have enough of this.

He nips at Kade's mouth, sliding in. Kade's tongue tangles with his own. It feels like love and concern and affection, and it steals the breath from Felix's lungs.

Kade pulls away sometime later, his lips glistening. His eyes are dark, beautiful and mahogany, and Felix can't look away.

"You look good like that," Kade rumbles.

"Like what?" His pulse stutters.

Kade shrugs. His gaze rakes over Felix's face, though, and he pulls away, taking the box of clothes with him. "Go help my mom with stuff. I'll move your things inside."

"Okay," Felix says, feeling as though he should protest. But his body is starting to ache with the pregnancy, and maybe it'll be better to let his alpha lift the heavy boxes instead. "How about I follow you around and give orders?'

Kade snorts, but he grins, his eyes lighting up. "Yeah, sure. Whatever you want."

And so Felix follows him into the house with a smile, the unease in his limbs trickling away.

FELIX TOSSES on the couch late that night, drained and restless. His sleeping clothes catch and pull on his skin, uncomfortable, and the couch is too warm. When he turns, his skin sticks to the wooly blanket. Maybe he should have asked for a different one instead.

He squirms on the couch, sighing when he finds a comfortable spot.

Through the day, Kade had moved his things into the house. Three boxes of clothes in his bedroom, a crate of framed paintings in the guest room upstairs, and four boxes of painting supplies tucked against the garage wall.

Kade never once mentioned rent, or how long he'll allow Felix to stay here. Felix looks down at the shadowed bump of his belly, smoothing a hand over it. *I guess we aren't moving away from*

Meadowfall now.

And he doesn't want to, either. Kade has offered Felix his home. Felix isn't strong enough to reject him, when his alpha welcomes him in his arms, in his bed, and he has a family here that he hasn't expected to regain.

The living room yawns around him, full of empty furniture and shadows. The rest of the house rings with silence; Mrs. Brentwood has gone to sleep. Kade had said goodnight an hour ago, and Felix wonders if his alpha is still awake. If he should try texting Kade. Will he answer?

There's no point texting him if I'm just a room away.

Heat creeps up his cheeks. He could knock on the door and say hi, and Kade wouldn't mind. It'll be better than falling asleep alone. He's been falling asleep alone for years, and... falling asleep with his bondmate is a thousand times better.

Felix rolls off the couch, padding over to Kade's door. It swings open quietly.

Inside, the glow of the laptop screen shines weakly from the desk. Across the room, Kade lies on his side in bed, eyes closed, the little figurines on his display shelves behind gleaming in the white-blue light.

Felix pads into the room. "Kade?" he whispers.

When Kade breathes in and out, Felix tiptoes forward, sitting carefully on the edge of the mattress. The room smells like cedar and pine, like a faint hint of musk and lavender. This morning was nice, when Kade leaned over him in bed, running his wrists over Felix's skin.

It doesn't seem like he'd mind if Felix stays over for a while. So Felix lifts the thin sheet, climbing in next to his alpha, tucking his back against Kade's chest.

Kade stirs. For a second, Felix's chest squeezes. *What if he doesn't want me here?*

But Kade slips a hand around his waist, nosing into Felix's hair. His breaths puff evenly against Felix's scalp, gentle and warm. Felix moves Kade's hand further up, so it presses flat against his chest. The heat of his palm soaks into Felix's heart.

A second later, Kade's thigh presses against the back of his own—one of the ways they'd curled up in bed together years ago. Felix relaxes into his alpha's embrace, feeling far more at ease than he had on the couch.

He falls asleep without even realizing it.

43
Kade

KADE WAKES to a mellow lavender scent in his nose. His sheets wrap around him like a warm embrace, and he wants to sleep in, even though his alarm's beeping like a stupid cricket that needs to shut up.

He reaches over to slap it off, and freezes. There's something—someone—in his arms. Someone slender and familiar, and it feels like Felix. His eyes snap open.

The mop of blond hair kindles something painful in him. The fine, wispy strands, the way they curl just a little at the ends.

Kade hits the snooze button on the clock, five, ten times, his heart thudding in his chest. When had Felix climbed into bed with him? Because he's asleep, his breathing slow and even, his limbs loose.

Slowly, Kade curls back around his bondmate, his chest to Felix's back. Maybe Felix had been lonely last night. And it says something about them, doesn't it, if Felix can climb into bed with him and he never once woke?

It's been five years since Felix slept in with

him. Five and a half, if he wants to get technical about it, but it's been too long since he's held his bondmate. So he props himself up on an elbow, traces his wrist over Felix's forehead, down his temple to his cheek, his clavicle, his chest. Felix's shirt drags beneath his wrist, then rises up at his stomach. Kade pauses.

It's not his child. But Felix is his, and he should protect the child too, shouldn't he?

He follows Felix's belly with his fingers, the swell of it up to his navel, then down to his groin. There's a second heartbeat in there somewhere.

Felix stirs. Kade stills, his fingers low on his bondmate's abdomen. He should have asked permission first. But Felix sucks in a breath, his eyelids fluttering open, and it's too late for Kade to pull his hand away.

"Kade?" Felix murmurs, his voice raspy with sleep. His nostrils flare, and he slides his hand over his belly, bumping into Kade's fingers.

Kade stops breathing.

Felix blinks, looking down. Kade should really pull his hand away, except he's not hiding things, he's not lying. If he touched Felix, then Felix should know.

Felix sucks in a sharp breath, glancing around, then up, meeting his eyes. "Kade?"

He lifts his hand then, an inch away, his heart thudding. "May I touch it?"

His bondmate gulps, blinking rapidly. "Yes. Yes, of course you can."

And Kade gently sets his palm on Felix's belly, smoothing over the curve of it. Then he slips his fingers under Felix's shirt, trailing his fingers over Felix's warm skin, up over that dark line of his abdomen.

His bondmate has a child. It's not his. But he can touch Felix's belly without flinching, and he strokes his hand up, all the way to Felix's stomach. Then back down, over the bump, and there's a baby in there that Kade will accept as his own.

"I'll protect both you and the baby," Kade says, his hand gentle on Felix's abdomen.

Felix opens his mouth, as though he's about to say something, but no words spill from his lips. He swallows, choking, tears welling in his eyes. "Oh, Kade. I didn't think—I thought you'd..."

Kade reaches around, turning Felix over to face him. Then he pulls his bondmate close, leaning in to kiss his damp eyelashes. "I told you," he says. "I'll protect it."

Felix curls his hands into Kade's shirt. His face crumples, and Kade holds him close, stroking his hair.

THREE HOURS later, Kade follows his bondmate into the department store. He almost took Felix to a different one, but the one they arrive at is the biggest in Meadowfall, and they probably have the widest selection of baby clothes.

He breathes in deep and turns them into the baby clothes section, where he'd found Felix and Taylor a month ago. Felix had trembled, fallen apart when he said the baby isn't Kade's.

Next to him, Felix glances at the racks of tiny dresses, his eyes growing dark. He can't say *It's fine.* It's not. But the jealousy is a dull scrape in his throat now, instead of the angry simmer a month ago.

"I don't need too many," Felix says. "The baby will outgrow them really fast."

"So... three pieces?"

"I suppose. I read an article that said, 'When in doubt, buy a larger size.'"

They turn into the baby clothes section the moment they reach it, instead of walking further to the summer dress rack. Felix touches the shirts. "We're looking for the onesies right now, I think. I want something soft."

Kade reaches out for a striped one-piece outfit, with snap-buttons on the sides and flowers printed on its feet. And it's *tiny,* just slightly bigger than his hand. Can he even hold a baby that size without breaking it? Are all newborns that small?

Felix wanders over, raising his eyebrows. "Something wrong?"

"It's damn tiny," Kade says. He doesn't remember his brothers being this small. But the bump at Felix's belly is the size of the onesie in his hand. How much bigger will he be at nine months? Can his body hold a baby that size?

Pregnancies are riskier for male omegas, the doctor had said.

Kade swallows. Felix has been fine so far.

"It'll grow bigger," Felix says, a faint smile tugging at his lips. "If you look at the labels, you'll see them grouped according to their ages. Like these are for infants up to three months, and those are for children six to nine months old. See, isn't this one adorable?"

Felix holds up a pastel purple onesie, with a picture of a whale printed on its front. His eyes glow with warmth, and he looks more at ease, better than he had when he first walked into the store. To the bump in his belly, he says, "I'm sure it'll look great on you."

Kade sucks in a deep breath, then blows it out. Maybe they can put that day behind them, when Kade had turned and left Felix at the store. The pregnancy doesn't bother Kade now. He's touched Felix's baby bump. They're shopping for baby clothes. If the baby is as tiny as these clothes are, then Kade will be extra careful when he holds it.

"It's not bad," Kade says, picking up an egg-yellow piece. He stretches its tiny sleeves between his fingers, feeling the give of soft cotton, imagining it around a delicate, tiny wrist. "Think this will look better?"

"I like that too." Felix beams. He leans in, his shoulder pressing lightly against Kade's arm. Then he glances down. "What do you think? Do you want the yellow one too?"

"Are you making up answers for it?" Kade asks, nudging him.

"I'm not." Felix grins. "I'm just talking to it. I think it'll get used to hearing my voice."

And Kade can't help admiring his omega. Despite how he hadn't wanted his pregnancy, Felix isn't running from it. He's making decisions for the child, adapting to it in his life, and Kade is proud of him. For standing up, for being brave.

"You'll make a great dad," Kade says.

Felix blinks rapidly, a flush rising on his

cheeks. And Kade leans in, pressing a kiss to his temple.

THAT NIGHT, as Kade's pulling the sheets over himself, a soft knock comes at the door.

"Yeah?" Kade says, sitting up.

Felix peers into the dark room, meeting his gaze. "You're not asleep yet?"

"Something wrong?" Kade pauses, scanning him.

Felix is in a loose shirt and shorts, and his eyes are hesitant. He pushes the door open wider, and the soft glow of the laptop screen lights the curve of his abdomen. He steps into the room. "I wondered if I could maybe... share your bed?"

Kade's breath snags in his throat. "You have to ask?"

Felix takes a step back. "You don't want me to?"

Kade sighs, scooting over to make space for Felix. It's a queen bed—not big or anything, but they'll both fit on it. He pats the dip in the mattress. "Come over. I'm not saying it twice."

Felix smiles. He closes the door, padding over to the bed, and beneath the scent of his shampoo, Kade smells lavender. The mattress indents under Felix's weight. Kade holds up the sheets for him, and he burrows under.

Kade tucks the sheet around his omega, leaning over to kiss his forehead. "Better here?"

Felix's eyes widen, and red sweeps through his cheeks. "Yeah. I mean, the couch isn't bad, but...

it's better here."

With you, Felix doesn't say, but it hangs in the space between them.

You want this, Kade realizes. His pulse eases into a steady thrum, and he curves his arm around Felix, pulling him close. He's not sure why Felix is willing to stay with him now, but he's not questioning it, if it'll keep his omega by his side.

"A goodnight hug?" Felix slips his arms around Kade's back, careful. "I'll try not to bother you while you sleep."

Kade rolls his eyes. "What did I say about bothering?"

Felix laughs softly, looking away. "That I don't bother you, I suppose."

"Yeah, that. Remember it." But Kade's grinning when he settles into his side of the bed, pulling the sheets up over them.

For a while, they don't speak. The laptop hums, and Kade looks up at the shadowy ceiling, listening to Felix breathe.

"Thanks for buying the clothes today," Felix murmurs. He turns onto his side with a rustle of fabric, facing Kade. "You didn't have to."

Kade shrugs. "I'll help."

And Felix sighs, leaning in. He shifts closer, wrapping one arm around Kade's waist. The bump of his abdomen presses against Kade's forearm. "You deserve the very best person in the world," Felix whispers, nuzzling into his shoulder.

Which is you, isn't it? Kade wants to say, but he doesn't want to disrupt this new peace between them. So he turns, pulling Felix closer to himself. It feels as though he needs to say something, though.

After five minutes, Kade asks, “What about you?”

Felix breathes gently against him, his chest rising and falling.

“Felix?”

But his omega doesn’t answer, and a heartbeat later, Kade realizes he’s already asleep.

44
Kade

18 Years Ago

A FEW months after Kade turns twelve, he presents as an alpha.

It doesn't feel like much. He smells like himself in one class, and in the next, he smells like pine and cedar, and the kids around him start to look over. When he passes by Mrs. Mulberry's desk, she pushes her glasses up her nose and says, "My, we've got a new alpha here. When you get home later, remind your parents to go through the expected customs with you."

Kade grins, standing taller. His dad has been predicting it for the past few months, and his mom guessed it two years ago. He salutes and steps out into the hallway, heading for the art classroom.

When the wooden door opens, a stream of students flows into the corridor. Some glance over at Kade, but most are eager to head for home. Kade squeezes into the classroom, spotting Felix in the far corner, tucking his brushes back into his bag.

"Felix!" Kade calls.

"Keep your voice down," the art teacher says,

but Kade's running down between the desks, waving his arms.

"Guess what," Kade breathes. Felix's eyes widen when Kade's five desks away, his nostrils flaring. "Guess what, guess what, guess what?"

"Oh gods," Felix says, his mouth falling open. He leaves his watercolors on his desk, hurrying over to meet Kade halfway. "You have a smell!"

"I've always had a smell," Kade says, but he straightens his back, puffing his chest out.

Felix stops inches away, green eyes roving over him. "You don't look different," he says. "But your smell—you smell so good, Kade." He leans in, sniffing deeply, breathing out, sniffing again, and his eyelids flutter shut. "Mm. I could smell you for hours."

Kade brings his hand up, showing Felix the wrist with the silvery scar. "It's strongest here."

Felix presses his nose to Kade's wrist, his breath puffing humid against Kade's skin. "Oh, wow."

"I want to smell you forever," Kade says, grinning. Sure, he smells like pine and cedar now, but Felix's scent is still the best. "You smell like lavender," he says. "Sweet, but not like honey. Just right."

Felix blushes, lowering his gaze. He turns back to his desk and packs up the rest of his pencils. "You're just being nice."

"No, I'm not. And I can prove it."

Felix laughs. "How?"

"By marrying you."

Felix giggles, slinging his bag over his

shoulder. “Sure.”

“Just wait,” Kade says. “I’ll get you a ring.”

“Are we allowed to marry if we’re twelve?” Felix asks. They head down through the hallways to the playground, and no one bothers them. Kade has built them a reputation among the school kids, breaking the bullies who dare touch Felix. Felix is a lot happier for it—his cheeks rosy, his eyes sparkling, and he’s stopped hunching over.

“Maybe not twelve. But soon.” Kade slips his hand into Felix’s, savoring the way his skin clings to his bondmate’s, the way Felix steps closer and bumps into him.

“I’ll be expecting a ring,” Felix says. He pulls his hand out of Kade’s, running backward and blowing a raspberry. “Race you to the sand pit!”

“The race is on,” Kade yells, and Felix laughs, dashing away.

45
Felix

Present Day

OVER THE next month, they settle into a routine.

In the mornings, Kade turns off the alarm clock. When Felix wakes, he finds Kade at his computer, keys tapping away. That happens when Kade has a project due, or when Felix oversleeps. Sometimes, when Felix crawls out of bed, the sheets rustle off his skin, and Kade turns to look at him, a tiny smile curving his mouth.

When he crawls out of bed, Felix helps Mrs. Brentwood with breakfast. Kade eats with them, and when he shuts himself away to work, Felix weeds in the garden, or paints a new series of watercolors—flowers and succulents.

Twice a week, Kade accompanies Felix to the park. They bring along Felix's easel and watercolors, and while Kade taps away on his laptop, Felix paints.

"You never talked about rent," Felix says in the park one day, halfway through a painting. They've never mentioned it, and Felix has been waiting for Kade to demand payment, somehow.

"Do we need to?" Kade glances up from his screen, dappled sunlight falling on his face.

"Yes."

But Kade shrugs, looking back down. "Twenty bucks?"

"You're kidding."

"You asked. I decided."

Felix shakes his paintbrush at him. How can Kade not ask for more? "That's not fair to you. I should decide on a fair amount."

"The fair amount is zero," Kade says, meeting his eyes steadily.

"Why?" Because it doesn't make sense. Kade has put up with him, let him sleep in his bed, and... *Oh.* "The sex paid for it?"

Kade rolls his eyes. "No. I told you, it's free if you stay in my room."

Well, he'd forgotten about that bit. Felix grumbles, daubing aquamarine splotches for water under a bridge. The baby moves in his belly. He sets a hand on it, feeling it squirm, and his spine aches a little. "I've gained weight."

"You look fine," Kade says, glancing up from his laptop. His gaze rakes over Felix, as though he can see through Felix's loose shirt and pants. Felix shivers.

When they walk home after, the sun glares down on them, and the air around shimmers with heat. Kade hefts Felix's easel under one arm, his laptop in the other. By the time they step through the front door, Kade's skin glistens. Felix can't help sniffing at his musk, leaning in to lick at the fresh sweat on his throat. He wants Kade pressed up against him, wants Kade's scent all over his skin.

"I'm gonna shower," Kade says, setting the easel down just inside the foyer. His eyes darken. "Join me if you want."

"I'll grab a change of clothes," Felix says, staring when Kade strips the tank top off his chest, his pectorals flexing. "See you in a bit."

Kade smirks, reaching over to squeeze his ass, before brushing by in a whirl of cedar and pine.

I should hurry. Felix swallows, stepping toward the bedroom. *Kade's waiting upstairs.*

He grabs a change of clothes from the closet: pants and a shirt for Kade, and the same for himself. And maybe he should toss the bed sheets in the washer while he remembers; they'd stayed up late last night, Kade working him through three straight orgasms.

He pauses at the corner of the bed, thinking about the way Kade bent him over, sliding inside him, one hand reaching around to stroke his cock. Then they'd lounged around in bed, Felix almost nodding off, until Kade leaned in, taking his cock into his mouth. Felix shivers, reaching down to rub himself through his pants.

The bed sheets. They're stained, with bits of dried cum scattered around, and they really should be washed. It'll take thirty seconds to pull them off.

Felix sets the clean clothes on the desk, heaving one corner of the mattress up. Maybe he should have asked Kade for help, but they'll probably get distracted on the bed again, and the sheets are filthy. The corner of the fitted sheet comes off. He steps over to the other corner, reaching under the mattress.

His fingers bump into something cool and soft. Frowning, Felix slides his hand further along the bed frame, curling his fingers around the metal *thing.* It yields under his fingers like water, but there are ridges to it, like several tiny links.

It's a chain, he realizes, sweeping it up.

He crouches and pulls his fist out from under the mattress, his belly brushing against his thighs. Then, he uncurls his fingers, staring at the heavy chain in his palm. It's silvery like steel, the links thick and dense. Kade had been wearing it for the past few months. *Why did you take it off?*

Felix frowns, lifting the chain out of his palm. It falls into a loop. There's a ring at the end of it.

He stares at the plain metal band as it sways, his thoughts whirling. *Why were you wearing a ring?*

Light glints off the delicate carvings on the inside of the band. *Kaden,* the first word reads. Felix stares, his fingers shaking. People don't engrave names on just any ring. *Kaden Brentwood.*

The ring's too small for any of Kade's fingers. Maybe his pinky, but... It slips neatly over the tip of Felix's index finger. He rocks back onto his heels, sitting heavily on the floor. *You couldn't have...*

He slides the ring over to the chain clasp. The chain unhooks after a few tries. Felix slips the ring out, his throat tight.

It fits right onto his ring finger, cool and sturdy, stopping at his second knuckle because he's put on weight. But it would have been a snug fit otherwise, and—Felix can't breathe.

It's the ring Kade had proposed with five years ago.

46
Felix

5 years ago

THE HEADLINES blare in his mind.

One in Five of Meadowfall will be in Debt and Homeless.

Meadow Village Homes to Clear out Existing Tenants.

Sudden Rent Hikes Bankrupt the Community.

Felix clenches the papers in his hands, storming through the hallways of his father's mansion, his footfalls muffled by the thick carpets.

He hasn't agreed to be part of this. He hasn't thought the success from his illustrations would give his father ambitious ideas to fill his properties. He hasn't thought his father would use his drawings to throw out a huge part of his community.

Kade's family will be homeless in two weeks.

Felix has called his father's home rental company, asking to speak with corporate. He has told them, repeatedly, that as Alastor Henry's son, he has a say in the cooperation's practices. He wants to erase those debts, let people back into their homes.

All he's been met with are associates reciting scripts. *I'm afraid that the changes have been implemented. No, the tenants will be held to their contracts. No, we can't change that.*

He twists the knob of his father's study door, flinging it open.

At his polished desk, the mayor of Meadowfall glances up from his monthly planner, mildly curious. Felix slaps the newspapers down in front of him, his chest burning.

"You're evicting them," he snarls. How can his father do this? How is he even related to this man? "You're charging them for things they don't even owe. And you paid off the lawyers so no one will fight for them."

Alastor Henry straightens his shoulders, leaning into his high-backed seat. His cool gaze sweeps over Felix. "Yes."

I can't believe you're my father. "You can't do that." Felix jabs his finger at the papers. "You're the mayor. You can't just screw your people over!"

His father tilts his head, gray eyes calm. "I don't have time for tantrums, Felix. The wealthy will give Meadowfall's economy a boost."

"I didn't agree to this," Felix snaps. "Those were my drawings you used to sucker the new tenants in."

Alastor's gaze turns flinty. "You were aware what marketing images are for. This should have occurred to you before you handed them over. Or had you forgotten that while you were cavorting with that... what's his name?"

It still hurts, surprisingly. Felix wishes he

could wring his father's neck, wishes he could hurt his father just as he has hurt him. But he's never been able to. Father's always said he's helpless, and Felix *hates* it. "Kade," he says, his eyes stinging. "His name is Kade Brentwood. We've been bonded *fifteen years.* You knew that."

"Ah." His father looks back down at his organizer, a fountain pen perched in his fingers. "You should already know—the decision is irrevocable."

"At least make an exception for the Brentwoods' home. They're my family!"

"And I'm not?" The mayor narrows his eyes. "You're an embarrassment to the Henry line, and to me, Felix. Taylor has found success for himself. What about you? What can you do, other than caper with some forgettable boy?"

Felix flinches, shame dulling his fury. He and Kade live in a little cottage by themselves, saving up, and that's fine. They're happy. Kade is more than anything he can ask for.

But Felix is still a failure to his father, to everyone, and he has failed Kade and his family, now. The Brentwoods will be in debt because of Felix.

In two weeks, Kade's parents and brothers will be kicked out onto the sidewalks, too.

"Take your leave," Alastor Henry says, making a note in his organizer. "Come back when you have something of value to say."

Felix flinches, his ears ringing. He's Alastor Henry's son, and all he does is beg. His father's voice echoes in his head. *You could have done better. Taylor was named one of the top five employees in his firm.*

Heart thudding in his chest, Felix drifts along the winding driveway, past the iron gates. What had gone wrong? *Why can't I be better?*

He can't tell Kade about this. Kade has always known that Felix's family is rich, but Felix has never mentioned his father's position as a landlord. He hadn't wanted Kade thinking he needs to be wealthy too, hadn't wanted his alpha comparing himself to Alastor Henry.

What can he do to help Kade's family? Kade's parents had taken him in, treating him as their own; Kade's mom mended tears in his clothes, Kade's dad showed him how to score in basketball, and even Kade's brothers had shared their cookies with him.

They don't deserve to be thrown out on the streets. But they aren't welcome in his father's mansion, and Felix doesn't have much money scrounged up to help with their pending bill. Maybe they can all bunk in the rental home he and Kade share.

He doesn't realize he's home until the cottage comes into view. The tiled red roof burns into his eyes, and the curtains are drawn—Kade's home, maybe working on his laptop. Felix's stomach plummets.

At the door, he thinks about not stepping inside at all. If Kade has somehow made the connection between Felix and the evictions, he would be furious with Felix. That his omega could wreak so much damage on his parents and siblings. That his omega doesn't have the power to prevent it at all. The Brentwoods' rental bill hasn't shown up yet, but once it does...

Cold horror slides over Felix's skin. He can't ever let Kade know how he and his father are connected to the evictions.

I don't have to tell him anything.

Felix sucks in a deep breath, pushing the door open.

Inside, soft music croons through the hallway. Felix shuts the door quietly behind himself, trudging toward the study. Kade's at his desk, headphones over his ears, drumming his fingers as he scans the black-and-white windows on his screen.

Felix tiptoes into the kitchen, pouring himself a glass of water. He should eat. But he isn't hungry, and he sees the mansion in his mind again, his father's disapproving stare. Felix isn't good enough. How can Kade even tolerate him?

He twists the knobs on the stove, watching as the electric burner comes on, glowing red-hot. Waves of heat radiate into his chest.

He turns the burner off. On again, then off. On again, then off.

"Didn't think you were home already," Kade says behind him, his voice light.

Felix jumps, his heart slamming painfully into his ribs. "Oh! I didn't think I—I should bother you. You were busy."

Kade shrugs, the light in his eyes dulling. "Something wrong?"

"Nothing," Felix says, his pulse in his ears. Does Kade always read him this easily?

His alpha steps over, slipping his arms around Felix's waist, warm and strong. Felix's back bumps lightly against his chest. It feels safe in Kade's arms. Comfortable. Felix wants to lean into him, but he shouldn't.

Kade slides a hand up his chest. The heat of his hand soaks into Felix's sternum, and Felix allows himself to relax. Kade kisses his ear. "Sam said he'll be home this weekend. Said he won't mind taking us out to the coast for a dive. You wanna go?"

"Sure," Felix says, looking at the record covers on their kitchen walls, the ink doodles he had drawn that Kade picked out and pasted on the cabinet doors. "That sounds like fun."

Kade noses at his hair, then reaches up, kneading Felix's shoulders. "You're tense. You went back to your dad's place?"

Felix forces his body to relax. "Just had a bad run-in. It's okay," he says when Kade narrows his eyes. "I'm fine."

"Still tense." Kade trails kisses down Felix's neck, slipping his hands up under Felix's shirt. "Tell me?"

Felix shivers at his touch. It would be so easy to forget the visit, except he glimpses the wall calendar and the empty squares stretching out in April. Two weeks.

"Hey," Kade says, turning him around. He kisses Felix, pushing him up against the midnight-blue counters, cupping Felix's face in his large hands. "C'mon, tell me what's wrong."

Kade smiles encouragingly, handsome. Felix's heart squeezes.

He only notices then that his alpha's shoulders are tight, too, a soft light in his eyes slowly growing brighter. He focuses on that, desperate not to think about his own guilt.

"Tell me why you're all excited," Felix says, leaning into his bondmate, kissing up his throat. Kade smells like pine and cedar, and Felix loves this smell, loves this man.

"I've got something coming up," Kade says, grinning roguishly. "It's a secret."

When did you start keeping secrets? Felix squeezes his ass lightly. "You can't hide it from me like that."

"Sure can." Kade's eyes gleam.

Felix pretends to pout, to distract Kade from probing about the visit. "That's not fair. Tell me!"

Kade's breath hitches. He grins wider, reaching down to touch his pocket. "It's a surprise."

But Kade wants to talk about it, or he wouldn't even mention the secret. Curious, Felix slips his hand down to Kade's pocket.

Kade snags his wrist, his fingers callused and gentle. "No," Kade says, but his eyes shine. "Not yet."

"Please?" Felix whines. *What are you so excited about?* He makes a cutesy face.

Kade chuckles, pressing a kiss to his forehead. "You really wanna know?"

"Yes!"

Kade reaches into his pocket. Felix holds his breath, unable to help his smile. Is it a coin, or movie tickets, or maybe even plans for a trip somewhere?

Kade pulls his fingers out, a tiny piece of silver in his fingers. He lifts it up between them, his face tipped toward Felix's.

It's a ring.

Felix stares. Why would Kade's surprise be a ring? Because rings mean promises and marriage, and Kade...

Kade wants to marry me.

Kade's eyes are hopeful, expectant. Felix's breath punches out of his lungs.

"Why?" he gasps, a sickening dread coiling in the pit of his stomach. Kade can't do this. Felix has damned his family to debt, and he doesn't deserve to be married to Kade at all. He's still the failure his father says he is.

Kade frowns, his eyes darkening. "No?"

No, no, no. "I can't," Felix says, shoving him away, guilt exploding from that sealed-up well in his chest. *Kade will hate me. If he makes this promise to me, he'll regret it.*

Kade flinches like Felix has just stabbed him in the gut. "Why not?"

Felix inches away from him, pressing his back to the counter. "Because it's not right. I've been using you."

"You're my omega," Kade says, turning his wrist to expose his bonding scar. Felix cringes. Fifteen years ago, when they created that bond, he didn't know he'd help his father destroy Kade's family. If he could return and change everything... he would.

"I shouldn't be yours." It hurts to say it. He needs to leave. Free Kade so Kade can find someone else better for him.

"Why?"

"Because this was a mistake!" Felix backs

away from him, bumping into the fridge. "We've been happy together, and I appreciate that. But it really can't go on."

Kade scowls, stepping forward, the ring glinting in his hand. "What happened at your dad's place? You've never been unhappy with me before."

It strikes Felix, sharp as a palette knife, that Kade won't stop pursuing this relationship. Until he can see something wrong with them, Kade will hang on to him, because he knows nothing else. They've never known anyone aside from each other; Felix regrets that Kade has wasted so much of his life with him.

"I never meant it to last forever," Felix says, his voice wavering. At any instant, Kade will see through him. He'll find out about the evictions, and he'll hate Felix even more. *I need to leave.* "We're not right."

"I love you," Kade blurts. "I always will."

Felix's heart cracks. There's nothing but honesty in his alpha's eyes, and he wants to cry. *You can't love me. You shouldn't.* What comes out instead is, "You aren't good enough for me. I've been using you." Felix doesn't dare look up from the tiled floor of the kitchen. "I talked to my father. He said you aren't fit to be my alpha. He said you can't provide enough. That you won't ever rank good enough. And I—I agree."

If there's one thing Felix knows, it's this. Despite Felix's attempts at hiding his family's wealth, Kade compares himself to what he can see of the mansion, and Felix's father. He thinks that's what Felix would want. And Felix manipulates it now like a monster.

Kade stares, his expression lost. "Really?"

For all the times Kade has read through his lies, he can't now. Felix nods, sinking his teeth into his lip. "Yeah."

Kade looks down at the ring. Felix desperately wants to step in and hug him, soothe away his pain. But he can't. He needs to flee, needs to make sure Kade finds a better omega.

"If—If I try harder, will you stay?" Kade asks, stepping forward. He raises the ring, rubbing his finger over it, and he's vulnerable now, like a teapot perched on the edge of a table.

"No," Felix chokes. "You can't change this. You won't ever be enough."

Kade raises the ring anyway. Felix smacks it out of his hand. It bounces against the floor, skidding into a corner with paint peeling off the walls.

Neither of them speaks.

Felix spins on his heels, not breathing, not thinking, not hearing Kade shatter behind him, not hearing anything except the pounding guilt in his head. He doesn't want to. He needs to get out of the house, needs to get away so Kade can rebuild and move on. Kade needs to find someone better, needs to have a better life. He's out on the street, their house behind him.

Kade doesn't follow.

47
Felix

Present day

FELIX CAN'T move. The ring sits heavily on his finger, glaring up at him.

Kade has been wearing the chain for months. Years. Felix had no idea the ring was attached to it, had no idea Kade had attached himself to their past for so long.

He twists the ring off his finger, disgusted at himself. How could Kade still want him, when he'd told Kade he wasn't good enough? When he had abandoned his alpha, left him ashamed, lied to him...

Felix's cheeks prickle; he wipes the tears off. He doesn't belong in Kade's bedroom, or even in this house. He should have left Meadowfall when Kade found out about the child.

He looks down at his belly, nauseous. He has no right to touch the ring. So he shoves it beneath the mattress, then shoves the chain along with it, too, except the chain slithers back onto the floor, betraying him.

He stumbles into the kitchen, out the back

door, and sucks in a deep breath, trying to calm himself.

Do you know how upset he was? Kade's mom had said. *When you said it isn't his?*

Felix doesn't know if he should believe her. He's hurt Kade so much. But if she's right... If Kade wants the child, if Kade accepts both Felix and the baby...

Felix shudders, cradling his belly. It would be such a *relief* if Kade wanted either Felix or the child.

Felix curls into a tight ball on the back porch, burying his face in his knees.

48
Kade

KADE STEPS out of the shower, blinking when the bathroom walls stare back at him.

Felix was supposed to be here ten minutes ago. He'd promised to bring fresh clothes up, and Kade doesn't have anything but a bath towel. And a hard-on, too, but Felix isn't here to touch it.

Kade sighs, reaching for the towel. Two minutes later, he wraps it around his waist, grabbing his sweaty clothes as he heads out.

The radio croons in his mom's bedroom. Kade passes her door, heading downstairs. The living room is empty, and so is the kitchen. With a frown, Kade steps into the bedroom, grabbing a set of folded pants on the dresser.

Two corners of the sheets have been pulled up, exposing the quilted surface of the mattress. As though Felix was halfway through gathering the sheets to wash them, and—

The ring.

Kade swears, crossing into the room. If Felix pulled the sheets, then he must have found it. *Shit.* Something glints on the floor. Kade freezes, looking down.

The chain coils on the carpet like a snake. The ring's gone.

Kade swears, his stomach plummeting. It had slipped his mind, when Felix has been snuggling in his arms the past few weeks. The ring hadn't mattered anymore then, when Kade has been holding his bondmate so close. He hadn't thought about worrying, when he wakes up in the mornings, burying his nose in Felix's hair.

Kade drops to a crouch, gathering the cool chain in his hand. Felix is gone, too. *Where did you go?*

How could he have been so careless? Felix had been adamant about his reasons for breaking up.

Kade swallows hard, stepping into his pants as he strides out. He checks the garage, but the bike stands in the shadows, untouched. He jogs to the front door, but the street's empty. *If I asked, will you come back? You can't just leave.*

He hasn't checked the backyard yet. Kade hurries to the kitchen door. Why would Felix head there instead, if he's found the ring? But he has to check everywhere in the house, even if his hands are shaking. He can't lose his bondmate again.

Kade pushes the door open, and almost trips over the huddled figure on the back porch.

He swears, heart lodging in his throat. *Felix!*

But Felix isn't looking at him. He flinches as Kade stumbles across the floorboards. Then he pushes his face down against his knees, his limbs drawing tight against his body.

He's here. He's still here. Kade breathes out his relief, suddenly cautious. His omega hasn't left, and maybe this isn't such a big deal. Maybe Felix has decided to stay, unlike five years ago.

He kneels warily in front of Felix, needing to hold him. "Felix?"

"Go away," Felix rasps, like he's been crying.

Kade's heart cracks. He clenches his fists, shuffling closer. The heavy lavender of Felix's scent steals into his nose.

"You found the ring," he blurts.

Felix whines, a low, helpless sound laced with agony. "Why? Why did you even... I told you to leave."

But why would he be upset about it, when Kade's the one who wasn't good enough? Kade reaches for him, touching his arm. Felix flinches. It stings, Felix recoiling from his touch. Kade sets his hand down, swallowing. "But you stayed this time."

"I should go." Felix unfurls his limbs, trying to hide his splotchy face.

Kade tenses. He can't let his bondmate leave again. Five years of separation was too long. So he grabs Felix by his underarms, hauling him onto his lap, into the circle of his arms. "Don't go," Kade says, holding him tight. "Please."

He's vulnerable all over again, like Felix has all the power to break him.

Felix sobs. He shakes against Kade, a fragile, beloved warmth. "You'll hate me so much," he says, his voice cracking. Kade doesn't know what the hell he's talking about. "Let me leave."

"Tell me," Kade says in his ear. It feels like déjà vu, except Felix knows his secret now. A weight slips of his chest. "Tell me how to make you stay."

Felix shudders. "Y-You won't w-want me if you know."

"You don't know that," Kade says, because they've been through so damn much. He strokes Felix's hair, pulling him closer, careful not to compress his belly. "If I'm leaving, I'm leaving either way, right?"

Except he won't leave, and Felix should know that by now.

Felix tenses, hiding his face. "Your dad died because of me," he says, voice muffled. "I caused the bankruptcy."

"What the hell?" *What bankruptcy? We've been good for... for maybe four years. You couldn't have anything to do with the tenant mess.* But Felix curls into himself, and Kade strokes a hand down his back, his pulse thudding in his ears. "You mean the one five years ago? You weren't even here when it happened."

"I knew it was coming." Felix's voice rises, thin and helpless. "Why do you think I left?"

Kade swallows. The bankruptcy can't be what caused all this. "You said I wasn't good enough. You said I was too poor."

He hasn't been saving up as much as he should, and he doesn't have enough to buy them a new house, or anything like that. *Should've saved more money. I didn't think I had any chance left with you. Are you going to leave again?* His throat constricts.

Felix shakes his head, his hair catching on Kade's shirt. "It was never about that. I don't care about the money either. Except my father—he evicted your family. Do you remember that? My father used my drawings to get new tenants. So he could rebuild and have lots of big names move into those old homes."

Kade frowns. "Thought he was the mayor."

"He owns half the properties here. I just never told you about it." Felix huddles into himself. "Do you remember the first time you visited my father's mansion? For months after that, you said you wanted to buy one just like it, and... I couldn't persuade you away from that idea."

Kade breathes out, slow and deep. So on top of that grand mansion, Felix's dad is way richer than he thought. Great. "You've been hiding things from me."

That feels like a betrayal, too, and he thought it was only the baby Felix had lied about.

Felix breathes out, slow and heavy. "Yes."

Kade closes his eyes. He hadn't realized that Felix had hidden this from him for years. It's as though the earth beneath him has shaken loose, learning that about Felix. "Why?"

"Because I never wanted you to compare yourself to him!" Felix glances up, his eyes red-rimmed, and Kade aches to make it right. Felix sucks in a shuddering breath. "I don't care about the mansion, or rankings, or shit like that, okay? But my father—he had me draw artist's impressions for the marketing. And those homes took off."

Kade looks at the weathered grain of the floorboards. Can he believe this? That Felix doesn't really care? He'd thought that, once upon a time, but he's spent five years thinking he's not good enough, too. "So you're saying your dad screwed us over."

"Those were my drawings. Part of it is my fault. And your dad died when—when he had to work again." Felix cowers further, but at least he isn't trying to flee.

"That wasn't your fault," Kade says, pulling him closer.

"It is! And he succeeded in bringing so many new people to Meadowfall, Kade. B-Because of me, your parents lost their home, and your dad died, and I don't want you to hate me." His words dissolve into a mess of whimpering. Kade swallows hard, running his fingers through Felix's hair. Felix is just as broken as he is, if not more. How had they ended up like this?

"I don't hate you," he says. "I can't."

Felix shudders, choking on his sobs. "Y-you should. I've kept so many secrets from you. I'm not fit to be your omega."

Kade's heart splinters. How can Felix think so little of himself? He may have hidden things from Kade, and he may have hurt Kade in the past. But Kade understands why he's scared. Why Felix might have thought he caused the bankruptcy. And Kade can overlook the lies, because he understands why Felix told them. He might not be comfortable with his savings and ranking yet, but he'll get over that.

"Look, it doesn't matter," Kade says. "That's all in the past, okay? I don't think you're at fault for any of it. And... if you don't want that ring, I'll take it back."

Felix tenses. "I didn't... didn't think you kept

the ring."

Kade leans in, kissing Felix's hair. "'Course I did."

"But..."

"I love you, okay? That's all." He feels exposed, admitting that. But Felix hasn't shaken his head violently, or struggled out of Kade's arms. So Kade cradles him, breathing in his heady scent.

"You shouldn't," Felix says. "I don't deserve it."

Kade almost says *I'll love you no matter what,* but something in Felix's tone makes him pause. "You have other secrets?"

Felix stares at the floorboards, shadows in his eyes. "Maybe."

Kade gulps. What can be worse than the bankruptcy and his dad's death? Felix already carries someone else's child, and it's not like he's been sleeping with other people lately. They've lost most of what they had five years ago. But Kade can't help the dread creeping down his spine when he asks, "What is it?"

Felix swallows. "The baby."

"Yeah?" Something's wrong with it. It's deformed, or it stopped moving. Or... Kade holds his breath, afraid that something has happened to it, and Felix will break again.

Felix lifts his head, wet streaks covering his cheeks. Kade wipes his tears off. Then he traces Felix's lips with his thumb, and Felix meets his eyes fleetingly, before glancing away. "It's yours."

Kade stares. "What?"

"The baby's yours," Felix says, his shoulders sagging like he's relieved that Kade knows this, and... it's not sinking into Kade's mind at all.

"What do you mean, it's mine?" He pulls away slightly, just enough to look at the bump of Felix's abdomen. It stretches his shirt, but he can't see inside. There's no secret message on it. Nothing to prove Felix right. "You said..."

Felix buries his face in his hands. "I was lying then, too. I've been lying so much, Kade."

His voice breaks. Kade blinks, trying to process it. The baby is his. Really? He's spent weeks thinking Felix slept with someone else, trying to accept the fact that Felix carries someone else's child. And... Felix says it's his. "I don't.... don't believe it."

"It's fine if you don't," Felix says, pulling away, turning so he's not facing Kade. "I didn't think you wanted one—we aren't together or anything right now, and it's not fair for you to accept a child you don't want."

"What the hell?"

Felix looks at his hands, his mouth pulled down at the corners. He looks honest like this. It's not a joke. The baby is his. Really? But Kade had been convinced it wasn't his, and Felix had seemed so honest then.

"You were crying at the store," Kade says, remembering anger and shame and jealousy, all searing through his veins. He's spent weeks coming to terms with someone else's child. And that's fine. Felix can carry it. Kade has made his peace with the baby. "You said it wasn't mine."

Felix doesn't meet his eyes, but Kade reads regret in him all the same. And he wants to help Felix out of his misery. He never wants to see his bondmate in such pain. "There was a reason I left, Kade. I didn't think I deserved any of this."

Felix carries his baby. He's been lying to Kade for months and years, and to try and absorb it all now... His mind whirls. Felix had, in some way, helped cause the bankruptcy. And that's okay. He didn't mean to. Kade sighs. "I understand why you left. But it's not something that'll make me leave you."

"You said we shouldn't have a child." Felix hunches his shoulders, tears dripping down his chin. "Six years ago. At the kindergarten. Do you remember?"

Yeah, he remembers. But he didn't think... couldn't have known it would weigh on Felix for this long. "Damn it. Sorry. I didn't... I thought you wouldn't want my baby. I didn't think you'd stay—I can't afford all the rich things."

Felix's face crumples. "I told you, I don't care about that. I don't want our child to grow up thinking money is everything. But I've hurt you so much, Kade. And left you. And I'll understand if you'd rather have another omega. Someone who won't disappoint you."

Kade leans in, pulling Felix close so their foreheads touch. After all this time... Felix had left because he'd been afraid of Kade's reaction? Because he thought Kade could ever leave him? "I've been waiting five years for you."

Felix shudders, his hands trembling. "I didn't think you'd forgive me for all of this."

This close, the tears on Felix's lashes blur. Kade holds his hand, Felix's breath puffing on his skin. None of Felix's reasons are about himself. His fears all revolve around disappointing Kade, and... he's never had to worried about that. And maybe, just maybe, Kade can be good enough for his omega, too.

"You've been lying a whole damn lot," Kade says, still reeling from everything. The bankruptcy, the lies, the *baby*.

Felix flinches. "I won't be angry if you bond with someone else—"

"I know," Kade growls. "And I'm not bonding with anyone else." He holds out his wrist between them, the silver scar bright in the shadows between them. "The only person who gets to mark me is you."

Felix gulps, his gaze flying up to meet Kade's. "You aren't angry with me?"

"I'm damn annoyed," Kade says. "But I'm not gonna leave you because of that." He sucks in a deep breath, holding it. "The baby's mine."

"It is." Felix holds his stare, fear dark in his eyes. Kade sighs, pulling him close.

"It's mine," Kade says again, to himself. He still can't believe it. He tugs Felix's shirt up, staring at the curve of his abdomen, the dark line leading down, and there's a baby in there. *His* blood and bone. Not someone else's. "Really?"

"Really," Felix says, still hesitant. "You don't have to assume responsibility for it. I won't hold you to child support—"

Felix is carrying his baby. *Their* baby. Kade's chest fills to bursting. He cradles Felix's nape, kissing him softly. Felix gasps.

"Mine," Kade growls against his mouth, slipping his hand down to cradle the bump of his abdomen. The child in there is his. It's an alien concept. Fuck knows how long Kade has spent, trying to come to terms with that child. But Felix relaxes slowly against him, his lips opening for Kade, and Kade slides their tongues together, dragging his wrist down Felix's belly. "It's really mine?"

"I won't say it's yours again if you don't want it," Felix whispers, scarlet rising to his cheeks.

"My baby," Kade says, awed and disbelieving. "I thought... you were in Highton before you moved back. You were in heat when I picked you up. I thought... maybe you slept with someone and he dumped you."

Felix shakes his head. "My heat started only when you picked me up. When you asked about the baby's father... Well."

Of course the baby's dad didn't know about it. Because I'm the fucking dad. And the thought sends Kade reeling. "I'm gonna be a dad?"

Felix smiles up at him, suddenly shy, and triumph roars through Kade's chest. "If you want to be dads with me, I won't say no."

"I love you," Kade growls, fierce affection rumbling through his chest. Felix's eyes grow wide, and Kade slides his arms around his omega, dragging him close, blood rushing down his body. He'll be dads along with Felix. It's his baby. He wants to pin his omega beneath him, wants to mark him and fuck him and have Felix crying out, needing Kade.

Felix leans in, his hands coming up to curl around Kade's sides. "I've always loved you," Felix whispers, looking away. "I never wanted to leave."

His pulse misses a beat. “I want you in my life forever,” Kade says. “I've always been waiting.”

Felix whimpers, glancing back, his eyes yearning, and something in Kade jolts.

He's so hard it hurts. He reaches down between them, tugging his pants open. Felix's gaze drops to his cock, and his throat works. Kade slips his cock out. “Want you in my bed. Wanna be inside.”

Felix groans, musk rippling off him. He reaches down for Kade, his hands small against Kade's cock, and Kade wants to pin him right here and slip home.

“We shouldn't. Not out here,” Felix gasps, but he's stroking Kade's cock from base to tip, squeezing around him, squirming.

Kade drags him closer, and Felix's baby bump pushes against his abs. Kade hesitates, glancing down at it. “Have I been fucking you too hard? ‘Cause I don't wanna hurt the child. Our child.”

Just saying it out loud makes it different. *I'm gonna be a dad. I'm gonna be a fucking dad.*

“The baby will be fine,” Felix whispers, his eyes shining. Kade reaches down to touch the hard line in his pants. “So please, Kade, I want you inside.”

49
Kade

KADE SCOOPS Felix up in his arms, careful not to put pressure on his belly. Felix's legs spread around his hips. Kade turns them back into the house, kicking the kitchen door shut, then their bedroom door.

He drops Felix gently on the bed, tugging Felix's shirt off. Felix grins through his tears. "Impatient, are you?"

"Yeah," Kade says. He wants to kiss his bondmate all over, touch him, show Felix how much he wants his omega and their baby.

He kisses Felix's tears off his face, hating that they've spent so long apart. Then he kisses further down, sliding into Felix's mouth. Felix arches against him, his hands trailing down Kade's sides, up against his abs.

Kade smooths his hand down Felix's warm chest, thumbing his nipples. Felix moans into his mouth, his tongue sliding insistently against Kade's, his hand curling around Kade's cock. Felix wants him. Felix carries *their* child, and it's better than Kade ever imagined.

"Kade," Felix gasps. Kade slides both hands

down his omega's belly, cradling the child that's *theirs,* that is part of them both, and Kade's harder than before, his cock aching.

"Mine," he growls, pushing his tongue into Felix's mouth, tasting him.

"Yours," Felix groans. Kade drags his hands down to Felix's hips, and Felix spreads his legs, his cock a thick line in his pants. Kade breaks the kiss, trailing his lips down Felix's jaw. Felix tilts his head, giving him access. Kade needs to claim him. Leave marks on his omega, because *Felix is his.*

He presses little kisses down Felix's throat, sucking at his sweat, his fluttering pulse. Felix gasps. Lavender floods Kade's nostrils, and he presses his teeth against the scent gland at Felix's neck, hard enough to leave a mark. Felix cries out, his breath catching.

Kade kisses down his chest, licking his nipples, biting lightly on them. Then he nuzzles his way down to Felix's belly. Felix slides his fingers through Kade's hair, cradling him while Kade kisses down the dark line, the one that says Felix is pregnant, that he carries their child.

"Ours," Kade says, nosing at his belly. Their baby is in there, Kade's to love and protect. Kade growls, needing his omega, needing to pleasure him, needing to see Felix desperate for him.

So Kade kneels in front of his bondmate, pulling his pants open, letting the flushed length of his cock slip out. It's musky, glistening at the tip.

Felix rocks his hips, an invitation. But Kade only smirks, kissing down his abdomen, letting Felix's cock jut up hungrily. Impatient, he tugs Felix's pants off his legs, flinging them into a far corner. Felix chuckles, his eyes dark. He spreads his legs, a drop of precum trickling from his tip. "You're hungry."

"You think? What do you want?" Kade murmurs, kissing up the inside of his thigh, sinking his teeth lightly into Felix's groin.

"Fuck me. Please," Felix rasps.

Kade holds his omega's legs open, and Felix leans up to watch, propping himself up on his arms. Kade licks around the base of his cock. Felix whines, pushing his hips up. So Kade smirks, leaning in to blow a hot puff of air on his tip. "You didn't ask me to suck your cock."

"Suck it," Felix hisses. His cock twitches, bumping heavy against Kade's lips, and Kade kisses down the length of it, its heat soaking into his skin.

"Here?" Kade wraps his lips around his base, licking over it, sucking it, and Felix groans.

"Not just there," Felix says. "All of it."

Kade grins, pinning his omega's knees to the bed, spreading him wide. Felix whines, dripping onto his belly. And so Kade licks up his cock, takes his tip into his mouth, licking up salty precum.

Then he pushes Felix's foreskin down with his lips, exposing sensitive skin, and drags his tongue around his head. Felix swears, dripping into Kade's mouth, and Kade sucks on its heavy, velvety length. Felix has always liked this. And Kade knows the exact way to pleasure him, too. He strokes his thumb over Felix's balls, pulling away, pressing a kiss to Felix's tip.

Felix gasps, and Kade takes him deep, swallowing around his omega's cock. Felix writhes beneath him, trusting him, a cry tearing from his throat.

Kade pulls away with a soft, wet *pop*, releasing his legs. Felix's cock points at him, dusky and glistening. Kade lowers his head, licking over the soft skin of his balls, his own cock throbbing.

"Fuck," Felix says, his pupils blown wide. "Feels—Feels good."

But Kade hasn't had enough. He noses down to his omega's hole, kissing the pink pucker of it. Then he licks over it, slides his tongue in, tasting salty slick. Felix writhes, clenching around him, his cock jerking against his belly.

"Oh gods, Kade," Felix says.

Kade slides his tongue in deep, before pulling away, licking his lips. "Just seeing if you're ready."

"I'm always ready," Felix whispers, and Kade pushes two fingers into his hole, growling as Felix stretches around him, his ass hot. It'll be hot around Kade's cock, too. Kade groans, needing to feel his omega around him.

"On your knees," he says, slapping Felix's thigh. "Present yourself."

Felix groans. He rolls around, kneeling with his legs spread. Then he straightens, reaching down to pull his cheeks open, exposing his hole. He smells like musk, like arousal and need, and something ferocious kindles in Kade's chest.

Kade growls, leaning in, biting the soft skin of Felix's cheek hard enough to leave teeth marks. Then the other cheek, and when he climbs onto the bed behind his omega, his cock pushes up against the cleft of Felix's ass, grinding firmly against it.

"You're gonna take my cock," Kade growls,

sliding it against Felix's exposed hole. Felix groans, rocking back onto him, leaving a smear of slick on Kade's tip.

"All of it," Felix whispers. When Kade presses up against his back and looks over his shoulder, he finds the tip of Felix's cock jutting against his round belly, dribbling precum. Felix is pregnant with their child, and Kade wants all of him, wants to see how aroused he is.

So he reaches forward, wrapping his fingers around his bondmate's cock, angling it down to study the flushed length of it. "You're so hard," he growls in Felix's ear, licking down his neck. Felix's cock jumps in his hand. "Gonna fuck you so hard you cum everywhere."

Felix moans, rocking forward, thrusting his cock between Kade's fingers. It slides against the pads of his fingertips, smooth and solid. Kade slips his cock up against Felix's hole, pushing his head against it.

Felix sinks down onto him, and his hole spreads tight and hot around Kade's tip, taking him in. Pleasure hums through his body. Kade bites into Felix's shoulder, fucking in, and Felix cries out, his chest heaving.

"Kade," Felix chokes. Kade anchors his hands on Felix's hips, burying himself deep.

"So tight for me," he growls, sliding out, thrusting in. Felix trembles, dripping onto the sheets, his ass squeezing around Kade's cock. Kade sinks his teeth further down his bondmate's shoulder, reaching up to cup his abdomen. It's their kid in Felix's belly, they're going to be a family, and Felix is *his.*

"Mine," Kade says, shoving in deep, throbbing when Felix cries out, his entire body shuddering. So Kade hooks his arm over Felix's chest, rolling his hips to fill his omega, and he's already at the edge.

He trails his hand down to Felix's wrist, rubbing over the bonding mark. Felix's eyes widen.

"Can I?" Kade asks, his voice husky. "Do you want...?"

Felix nods, jerkily, a deep blush rising on his cheeks.

Kade growls, lifting Felix's wrist to his lips. He licks over the silvery scar, sniffing at the intense lavender scent, and when he presses his teeth against Felix's scent gland, Felix stiffens, his breathing coming short and fast.

"Gonna be my mate again," Kade whispers, dragging his teeth over Felix's wrist. With his other hand, he slides his fingers over Felix's pulsing cock.

"Yes," Felix whines. "Yes, please."

Kade sinks his teeth down hard, breaking skin. Felix cries out, his back arching, cock throbbing as he spurts all over the bed, his body tight. Kade barely tastes the metallic tang of blood. He's marking his bondmate again, and Felix is *his,* and Kade loves him.

He strokes Felix through his climax, savoring the heat of his body, the sweat between their skin. *Mine.* Desire surges hot in his body, makes the pressure in his cock spike. Kade fucks hard into his bondmate, cradling his belly. "Gonna come."

"I want your knot," Felix purrs, and Kade roars, fucking in deep, pleasure crashing through his body as he spills into his bondmate, filling him, marking him.

Felix moans beneath him. Kade leans forward, supporting his omega as he rolls them onto their sides. Before his knot swells, Felix squirms. Kade rolls over onto his back, and Felix shifts, so he's straddling Kade, his balls resting lightly on Kade's abs, his belly round, his lips curved in a smile.

"I love you," Felix says, his gaze warm.

"Love you too," Kade murmurs, catching his wrist. Blood glistens across the new bonding mark, and Kade licks it clean, a coppery tang on his tongue. How did they get from crying on the kitchen porch, to his knot swelling inside Felix, a new marking on his wrist?

Felix stretches around him with a moan, his eyelids fluttering shut. Kade swallows. Even though he's put on a bit of weight, Felix is still slender, his lips pink, his belly growing with child. Kade can't voice how much his bondmate means to him.

He curls his fingers around Felix's wrist, examining the line of dried blood crossing over the old silvery scar.

Felix blushes. So Kade exposes his own wrist, where Felix had left his own mark two decades ago.

"You wanna?" Kade asks, his pulse pattering. Felix could still decide not to, and—

"Yes," Felix says, his eyes gleaming. He curls his hands around Kade's forearm, and Kade's heart quickens when Felix licks over his scent gland, a soft, wet touch. His nostrils flare.

Their gazes meet. Felix sinks his teeth into

Kade's wrist, breaking skin, and pain and pleasure winding through Kade's body. Kade grunts. Felix marked him. Felix chose to mark him, and it means he wants Kade back in his life. Their eyes locked, Felix drags his tongue over the wound, his hands gentle around Kade's forearm.

Kade swallows, his throat tight. It feels like another part of their relationship clicking back into place.

"You're sure about this," Kade says, a little tendril of uncertainty whispering in his mind. For so long, he had believed himself unworthy of his bondmate, and this...

"I'm sure," Felix murmurs, setting Kade's hand on his belly.

Kade's heart expands, his chest too tight. He looks at his bondmate, Felix's body locked with Kade's, his belly swollen with their child. Kade sits up, cradling Felix in the gap between his chest and his thighs. His knot shifts in Felix, and Felix moans. Kade grins.

"I can't believe this," he says, brushing his thumb over Felix's abdomen. "I'm gonna be a dad."

"You'll be a good dad," Felix says, covering Kade's hand with his own. "I'm sure of it."

Kade closes the inches between them, kissing his omega slow and sweet. Felix cups his face, his lips gentle.

When they eventually pull apart, Felix slides his arms around Kade's shoulders, just holding him. "I'm sorry for everything," he murmurs. "I've put you through so much."

Kade kisses his shoulder, sliding his palm

down Felix's spine. Maybe they could have changed the past. But they're stronger now, better people for what they've been through. "Just don't do it again," he says. "I told you, I'm staying with you and protecting you. And our baby."

Felix draws a deep breath. "Really? Is that enough? Sometimes... it feels as though I've made too many mistakes. Sometimes I don't... don't know if our past can be repaired."

So Kade turns his wrist up between them, Felix's marking a thin curve of dried blood on his skin. "And I asked if you wanted to be my mate again. Says enough, doesn't it?"

Felix stares at the marking, his eyes growing soft. "You're more than I could ever deserve, Kade."

And that calms something in Kade's chest. Felix thinks Kade is enough. "I'm glad you came back," he says. "And I'm not sorry about the child."

He kisses along Felix's jaw to his chin, then up to his lips. Felix smiles, and Kade presses their foreheads together, enjoying their newfound peace. He never thought they'd return to this; their bond reestablished, Felix smiling, his gaze affectionate.

A little later, Felix pulls away from Kade, looking down at the bed. "Oh. I was going to wash the sheets."

"We don't really wash them," Kade says.

"That's because we've been using towels." Felix grins. "But we forgot last night, and there's dried cum everywhere."

Kade grins. "Want more?"

"Maybe later." Felix laughs, swinging his legs off the bed. Then he bends and scoops something off the floor. "I guess I shouldn't have poked under the mattress."

Felix hands him the chain. Kade sighs, looking at it. It had kept the ring safe with him all these years, and everything the chain set off had turned out better than he expected. "Where's the ring?"

Felix blushes. He reaches under the mattress, pulling the ring up after a moment. His expression turns pensive. "I never thought you held on to it."

Kade's pulse thrums. He takes the ring back from Felix, rubbing his thumb over its edge. Along its inner surface, the carved names glint in the sunlight. *Felix Henry. Kaden Brentwood.*

"Do you want it?" Kade asks. He holds his breath. Even though they've bonded again, and even though Felix carries his child, he can't help his jangling nerves. Felix could always refuse, like he did five years ago.

But Felix smiles, his eyes warm. "Is that any way to propose?"

Kade grins. Felix isn't saying no, so Kade takes his hand, leaning in so close their lips are a hairsbreadth apart. "Felix Henry, will you marry me?"

Felix's breath hitches. He kisses Kade softly, tears welling in his eyes, and Kade's heart pounds in his ears.

Against his lips, Felix murmurs, "Yes."

It feels like a balloon filling up in his chest. Kade grins, kissing his bondmate hard, breathing in his scent. He had once dreamed of this. And they're salvaging their dreams now, placing the pieces carefully back, weaving their lives together.

Felix kisses him just as hard, his fingers winding through Kade's hair, their bodies pressed close.

They break apart a while later, Felix glancing down at the ring. So Kade slides it onto his finger, blinking as it sits snug just before Felix's second knuckle.

"I put on weight," Felix says, his face falling.

"You're carrying our baby," Kade says, scooping his bondmate into his arms. "Wear it on your neck."

Felix blushes, suddenly shy. Kade kisses him. They're bonded again, and that's all that matters.

50
Felix

WHEN FELIX wakes the next day, he finds Kade's pillow empty. Instead, his alpha is curled up further along the bed, nosing at his bare abdomen.

"Hey," Kade murmurs, trailing his lips over Felix's belly. "Don't know if you can hear me. I'm your dad."

Kade grins to himself, pride and delight in his eyes. Felix stops breathing.

"I can't believe it either," Kade says, caressing Felix's belly with a finger. "Your other dad just told me yesterday. He's a jerk, but I love him. And I'll love you, too."

Felix's breath catches. He can't quite believe it, either. Kade loves him. Kade has looked past their history, has looked past his lies, and Felix is so grateful for this man.

"When you get a bit older, we'll play basketball," Kade says. "Or maybe dress-up. I don't know. Felix is the one who likes dresses. My mom made some for him when we were kids."

When they stepped into the kitchen yesterday, Kade's mom had smiled, meeting Felix's eyes. And then she had said, "You did great," and

Felix had cried a little then, too.

Kade nuzzles his belly. "We had a tree house when we were kids, though. Your other dad and I, we met each other when we were ten."

"Are you going to tell our child our life story?" Felix asks, his voice raspy with sleep.

Kade glances up, his cheeks flushing. Felix hadn't thought he'd be shy, talking to their child, but it's adorable. Kade kisses his navel. "Just saying hi."

"Well, go ahead and talk. I'll just listen over here." Felix grins, stretching out. Kade crawls back up the bed to him, wrapping Felix in his arms.

"I'll talk to it later," Kade says, nuzzling his forehead.

Felix smiles, burying his face in Kade's chest. He still can't believe that they're this close again, that Kade has marked him, that Kade wants to marry him. He takes Kade's hand in his, setting it on his belly. "If you keep still long enough, you'll feel it move."

Kade swallows, looking down at his hand. It's wide, almost spanning the width of Felix's abdomen. Together, they breathe in silence, Felix smelling the spicy pine notes of Kade's scent, Kade staying motionless, waiting for their child to move.

The baby shifts three minutes later. Kade glances up, eyes wide.

"I felt it," he says. "It fucking moved!"

Felix beams. Kade looks at him like he's just discovered a cool motorcycle accessory, and Felix leans in, kissing him on the nose. "It moves all the time, silly."

"Yeah, but this was the first time I felt it."

Kade sighs, setting both his hands on Felix's belly. "It feels real now."

His alpha wants this child. Felix breathes out the tension in his body, leaning closer to Kade. If he'd known Kade would be so excited... If he'd known Kade would accept him despite the things he's done wrong, they would have saved themselves so much heartache.

"Hey," Kade says, kissing him on the temple. "What's wrong?"

"Just thinking." Felix sighs. "We could have avoided all this—you could have touched the baby much sooner... and I'm sorry I didn't tell you earlier. I just... I thought you wouldn't want it."

Kade brushes their lips together.. "We're putting the past behind us, remember? I want you and the baby. That's all you need to remember."

And Felix relaxes, leaning into him. "I love you," he whispers.

Kade grins, and the light in his eyes fills Felix with warmth.

OVER THE next few weeks, they settle into a new routine.

In the little moments between Kade's programming work and Felix's painting, they pull a second chair up to the computer, looking up more articles on caring for infants. Kade says Felix needs more nutritious food. Felix protests, saying he has enough. Kade returns home from the store anyway, bringing fresh fruits and veggies.

On the weekends, Kade moves their things

upstairs. There are three bedrooms on the second floor: one for them, one for a nursery, and one for Kade's mom. They convert the room downstairs to a study, and together, they move into their new bedroom. Kade presses Felix up against the window, the doorframe, the closet, and they mark the room with their scents.

In the mornings, Felix finds Kade talking to his belly when he wakes. When Kade looks up to find him watching, he curls up around Felix, stroking his face. The engagement ring is at the jeweler's, getting resized. Felix forgets about it sometimes, until he looks at the new marking on his wrist.

Then he remembers: they're getting married. They're having a baby together.

These thoughts holds him through his hormonal swings, when nothing feels right, or he's sad, or angry, and he can't control his feelings.

"Work sucks," Kade says one day. "New deadlines coming up and no one thinks they're realistic."

"At least you're not pregnant," Felix answers. And Kade smiles, stepping over to pull Felix against himself.

"REMEMBER HOW I said that store manager waddles?" Felix says a little over eight months into the pregnancy. "Now I'm the one waddling."

"You don't waddle," Kade murmurs, rubbing his swollen ankles. "You move fine."

"I waddle, Kade. Don't lie." Felix pouts. Kade

massages Felix's calves, pressing his fingertips into Felix's muscles, dragging them down, firm and warm. Felix moans, his fingers digging into the bed sheets. "That feels good. But it doesn't mean you're right."

Kade grins. "Speaking of store manager, we never went back for the giraffe. Remember?"

"Crap. Yeah." Felix sags, smoothing his hand over his belly. After the rush of moving into Kade's place, unpacking, and getting his tenancy sorted out, he'd forgotten about the giraffe. "I never returned the key. Guess they hired someone else and they're using another locker. I should text Susan."

"Find a good time to visit," Kade says, leaning in to kiss his knee. "We'll grab the giraffe and go. Although I think you might be too big to fit on the bike."

The child's growing bigger now. Felix feels as though he's always full, or he always needs to pee. He looks down at his swollen belly, at his heavy thighs and arms. "I don't look that great now."

"You look like you're carrying our child," Kade says, warm eyes coasting up Felix's body. Felix has been wearing Kade's sweaters, their extra width fitting snug around his belly. Kade's nostrils flare. "You smell like it, too. Like a bit of honey mixed in with the lavender."

"Oh, good. I thought I'd smell bad."

"C'mon, you smell good."

Felix picks at the hem of his sweater. Does he really? Maybe he shouldn't be bothering Kade. They have things to buy for the baby, money to earn. He heaves himself up. "I should let you get back to work. Do a new painting for sale."

Kade leans up, catching him around the waist. "It can wait," he murmurs, pressing a kiss to Felix's forehead. Then he kisses Felix on the lips, a light, quick touch. Before Felix can move, Kade grabs his hip, rolling him onto his knees. "Heard being on all fours is good for you."

Felix laughs."Are you saying that just to keep me bent over?"

"You like bending over anyway," Kade says, a smile in his voice. He slides his hand down between Felix's legs, and Felix pushes into his palm.

"You might be making false accusations," Felix says, wriggling his hips. The baby kicks inside his belly. "Oh!"

Kade leans in, flattening his hand against his abdomen. "It kicked?"

"Mm-hm. If you hold still, you might feel it again."

Kade pulls a pillow over, tucking it under Felix's belly for support. Then he slips Felix's pants down, exposing his ass. "While I wait."

"I wasn't expecting you to multi-task," Felix says. Cool air brushes over his skin, and Kade rubs his callused hand over his cheeks, slipping down his inner thighs. "And I don't expect to tell any of our children this. 'Did you know? Your dad fondled me while he was waiting for you to kick.'"

"More than one kid?" Kade grins.

"Do you want more?"

"Sure. We'll see what you say after this one." Kade slaps his ass lightly, kissing up Felix's spine. Just as he reaches Felix's shoulder, the baby kicks again. Kade's breath catches. "I felt it!"

"I thought you might," Felix says, smiling. Sometimes, it still amazes him how Kade is still around, how Kade is just as excited about the baby as he is.

"Can't wait," Kade says, biting lightly into Felix's shoulder. "Want to see you with our baby."

"And you will." Felix grins, pushing back on him.

"Comfortable?" Kade runs his palm over Felix's belly, a warm, comforting touch, and Felix grows damp, just thinking about how much Kade cares.

"Yes," he say. Kade grinds up against him, holding Felix snug against himself.

Days like this are the best, Felix thinks. Just him and Kade, and their little bubble of safety.

51
Kade

"WHY DON'T you hand the key over, and I'll grab the giraffe for you," Kade says, pulling the connecting door open. "Not like you need to be there, right?"

"But I haven't seen Susan in months," Felix whines, following him into the garage. "I'll be stuck at home once the baby arrives."

Kade sighs. *Doesn't mean Susan can't visit you.* "You're nine months pregnant. And my mom just went out with the car. I'm not taking you on the bike."

"You've taken me on the bike other times." Felix waggles his eyebrows.

Kade rolls his eyes. He studies the swollen curve of Felix's abdomen, then the bike. It's a horrible idea. "If you get on the bike right now, it'll be a tough fit. I don't wanna squash you."

"It'll be fine," Felix says. "I promise. I'll hold you away from my belly."

"Still a bad idea," Kade says, clicking the garage door remote. The door rumbles up, and cool winter air rolls into the garage, so goosebumps march down his skin. Felix shivers. So Kade shrugs off his coat, pulling it over Felix's head. "Not gonna put you in danger."

The thought of his pregnant bondmate out in traffic sends unease coiling through his gut. They could face speeding cars, or trucks cutting into their lane.

"It's just a fifteen-minute ride," Felix says, shrugging into the oversized sweater. "If we take the back roads and go slow, it'll be safe."

Kade sighs. There won't be as much traffic if they wind through the housing estates. At 10 AM, few cars zoom down the roads. "You're due next week. That's a bad idea."

Felix rubs his hands down his belly, his eyes pitifully wide. "The baby has been kicking, but I haven't had contractions yet. See?"

Kade slips his hands under Felix's sweaters, cradling his abdomen. It's firm against his palms, warm, and their baby kicks against his hand.

Male omegas have a higher risk, the doctor said. The pregnancy has been fine so far, though. They've been through more doctor visits, and Felix has always checked out fine.

Kade swallows, sliding an arm around his bondmate, pulling him close. Felix's abdomen bumps into his. Kade looks at it, awed that they've created this life, that they'll get to meet their baby soon. They've got the nursery ready, got the diapers and baby blankets and a car seat, and snacks and more clothes for Felix.

"It'll just be half an hour," Felix says, smiling warmly. "Then we'll be back, and we'll have some lunch."

Kade slides his hand over Felix's belly,

kissing his forehead. "Don't wanna think about. I just want you safe."

"And I'll be safe, I promise," Felix says, rubbing Kade's sides. "You'll let me ride?"

Kade groans. Felix has always convinced him to join in his risky ideas. "Just today," Kade says. "And only the back roads. And we're not going to any other stores after this. Just the gas station and back home."

Felix brightens, his eyes gleaming. "Just that, yes."

"Are you even dressed enough?" Kade asks. It's winter. And even if they ride slow, it'll still be chilly. At least it doesn't snow here in winter. "This is a bad idea."

"If we stop arguing and start moving, we could be back home in half an hour," Felix says. He grabs another jacket from a rack, pulling his helmet on. Kade sighs.

When he's got his jacket and gloves on, Kade helps his omega onto the bike. Felix settles into the pillion seat, draping a blanket over his legs. His belly bulges out into the rider's space. Kade winces; it'll be a squeeze. He slings his leg over the seat, straightening the bike, careful to not bump into Felix. "Okay back there?"

"You're not squashing me," Felix says, rubbing his back. "We're fine."

Kade looks back to make sure. Felix is bundled up snugly, his cheeks flushed. *We're gonna be okay.* His stomach flops.

He rolls them out of the garage, turning the throttle. They head out at a slow pace, a cool breeze swirling into the helmets, and Kade double-checks for blind spots. Felix squeezes his thighs reassuringly around him.

The neighbors' houses slide by. Kade relaxes a little as they coast down wider roads, heading for the gas station. It feels like he's transporting million-dollar cargo, except it's Felix, and Kade can't lose him or the baby.

They pull into the gas station, parking at a corner lot. Felix eases off the bike and folds up his blanket. "See, I told you it would be fine."

Kade narrows his eyes. "We still have to get back home."

"And that'll be fine too." Felix pulls off his helmet, and Kade tucks their things into the trunk. Felix rubs his arms, staring up at the convenience store signboard, at the glass windows and the faded posters of hot dogs and slurpies. His shoulders sag, as though he's remembering the busy afternoons and his bastard manager. "Now that I'm here, I'm actually not that excited to be back."

Figures. "I told you."

"Oh, stop it." Felix elbows him.

Kade grabs his bondmate's hand, kissing his gloved fingers. "Love you too."

Felix grins. They tread slowly up to the glass doors, and Felix brightens when Susan looks up from the counter.

"Hey, you guys!" Susan waves, smiling.

"I'm sorry I haven't been back," Felix says, wriggling. He waddles over to the end of the counter, reaching out to hug his ex-coworker. Kade follows behind, ready to catch him if he wobbles.

Susan grins at Kade over Felix's shoulder.

She looks the same—warm eyes, bright smile—working at the station never took a toll on her.

"Oh, gosh, you're huge," she says, pulling back to stare at Felix's belly. Then she meets his eyes. "You told him, right?"

Felix blushes a deep red, glancing over at Kade. "Yeah. After a while."

Kade frowns. *Even Susan?* Felix had only told him after he quit the gas station. "How come everyone knew before I did?"

"Because this guy was afraid you'd reject him," Susan says, rolling her eyes.

Felix's gaze locks with Kade's. *I'm sorry,* his eyes read. Kade swallows. They've talked about this. Felix had been afraid, and Kade can't hold that against him.

"It's fine," Kade says. Felix relaxes with a tiny smile.

Susan takes Felix's hands in her own. "I'm so glad to see you're doing well! Are you due soon?"

"The Tuesday after next." Felix cradles his belly. His cheeks are flushed, his body swollen with their child. Kade hadn't expected this. But he had lost Felix, found him again, and he savors Felix's presence by his side. "We've got everything prepped," Felix says. "The nursery, the clothes—you should visit sometime."

"Definitely," Susan says, hugging Felix again. "So why are you back?"

"My giraffe." Felix grins sheepishly. He pulls the locker key from his pocket, handing it to Susan. "I guess I shouldn't be going into the back room."

"Right. I'll grab it for you. Be back in a mo."

Felix turns to Kade, smiling. "See, everything

went well."

"We're still not out of here yet," Kade says, glancing at the glass doors. There are fewer people at the fuel pumps now that it's winter, but that bastard manager could still appear. If they make it out of here without ever seeing that scumbag, Kade will be perfectly happy. "Gonna be better once you're home safe."

"I'll be *fine,*" Felix says, slipping his hand into Kade's.

"Yeah, well." Kade sucks in a deep breath, leaning in to kiss his bondmate. Felix purrs, and Kade slides his fingers against Felix's nape, breathing in his lavender scent. "Smells good."

Felix kisses him, slow and heady, and Kade slides his knuckles down his bondmate's side, slipping his fingers under the stretched opening of Felix's sweater. Then he brushes his wrist over Felix's skin, marking him. Sometimes, he still can't believe he's going to be a dad. Can't believe the baby will be here in a week.

"Got it," Susan says, stepping out of the backroom. "Oh, you guys. Come on, get out. Rick will be here in a minute. Just saw his car pulling in."

Felix jerks away, his face paling. Kade grits his teeth. How dare the bastard show his face? Months ago, Felix wouldn't have been afraid. But he's almost due, and Kade's omega is so vulnerable right now.

"I'll deal with him," he says, heat swirling through his chest. "Knock his teeth out."

The glass doors slide open. Kade steps in front of both Felix and Susan.

Rick swaggers in through the doorway, wrapped in layers of coats like an overgrown blueberry. His gaze locks onto Kade first, then Felix, and he sneers. "Look who's back? The slut and his sorry excuse of an alpha."

Kade's too far to stop Rick's gaze from dragging over Felix's belly. His omega's being violated, and Kade needs to stop it right now. He steps forward, fist clenched. "Fuck you."

"Take this and get out," Susan mutters behind. "Maybe through the back door."

"Got him knocked up good this time, huh?" Rick says, advancing on him. "Better make sure your low-ranking bastard kids survive."

The baby's mine, and rank doesn't fucking matter. Kade snarls. Felix grabs his arm, but he shakes Felix's hand off, striding forward. He's put up with the damn fucker for too long, and only because Felix was still working here. *Say what you want about me, but shut the hell up about my mate.*

"Say that again," Kade breathes, his pulse thrumming.

"And you'll do what? Flex your big muscles? You'll never succeed in life, in case you didn't know," Rick says, beady eyes glinting. Kade swallows. He still doesn't completely believe Felix about rankings, and money, and how can this bastard even say shit like that?

"Kade, we should go," Felix says, his voice low.

Kade isn't ever returning again. But he'll be damned if he doesn't punch this guy, either. "Later."

"Are you really going to hit me?" Rick steps

closer, his eyes sliding over to Felix.

Felix stands three yards away, Susan gone from his side. And Rick's leering sends an oily chill down Kade's spine, when the bastard looks at his omega like a plaything.

"Stay away from him," Kade snarls, striding forward.

Felix steps behind him, tugging on his shirt. "Kade, no."

"Or what?" Rick grins, raising his fists. "Are you going to stop me? I bet you'll like it, won't you, if I fucked that omega slut in front of your face? Put a few more up his ass? Cuz it'll be better than some alpha who's not even good enough for a whore."

"Shut up," Kade snaps, pulling his fist back, blood sluicing hot through his veins.

And as Felix nudges at his back, trying to push him out the door, Rick lunges for him, eyes glittering.

Kade swings his fist at Rick, punching him in the throat. The impact sends Rick flying sideways, toward the door, away from Felix.

Rick growls, staggering. The humor drops from his face, and he swings his fist at Kade, aiming for his jaw.

Kade blocks his strike and punches him in the nose, and cartilage crunches satisfyingly under his knuckles. "Do that again," he growls, "and I'll fucking murder you."

"Bastard," Rick cries, lunging forward.

Kade grabs his arm and twists it behind him, pressing it against his spine. He wants Rick to hurt, for all the things he's said about Felix, for all the insults, the humiliation. Rick shouts out in pain.

Kade bares his teeth, driving Rick into the corners of the metal shelves. The shelves rattle, and something in Kade's chest roars when Rick's body thuds into the jabbing metal, a corner smashing into his face.

He's been waiting to do this for *months.* And the violence hums in his veins, singing in his ears.

He grabs a fistful of Rick's hair, jerking his head back to expose his throat. Rick's eyes bulge, the whites of them stark on his face. He scrambles to his feet, slamming back into Kade. Kade falls against something warm. Felix yelps.

Felix!

Kade hurls Rick back against the shelves, turning away as Rick bounces off them, staggering to the side. Felix sits on the floor, his face pinched in pain. Kade's blood runs ice cold. *The baby. I shouldn't have done that. Shouldn't have got into that damn fight.*

"You okay?" Kade asks, his breath catching. Felix's face is pale, his hand cradling his belly.

"Yeah. I think so." But Felix winces, and Kade doesn't believe him right now.

"We're going," Kade says, glancing at Rick. The manager holds onto the shelves for support, his face a mess of blood.

Kade scoops his bondmate into his arms, striding out of the shop. He sets Felix gently down on the bike, his heart thudding. Felix winces. "I'm fine."

"No, you're not," Kade says, panic fluttering in his throat.

Susan steps out after them a moment later, her purse slung over her shoulder. She hurries over to the bike, her forehead creasing. "Felix? You don't look fine."

"That's what I said," Kade says, unlocking the bike trunk. Felix holds out the stuffed giraffe to him. "I'm taking him to the hospital."

"I should come along," Susan says. She points at her purse. "I quit, too."

Felix laughs weakly, and Kade manages a smile. "There's really no need to worry," Felix says. "I'll text you when we get home. It's probably just a bruise."

But Kade remembers *Risky pregnancy,* and his pulse doesn't slow.

"Text me your details. I'll drop by," Susan says. She gives Felix a quick hug, and Kade hands him the helmet when she pulls away.

"See you," Kade says. When Felix pulls on his helmet, Kade checks to see if he's ready. Then he starts the bike, his pulse thudding like the vibrations of his machine. *Felix is in danger.*

He twists the throttle, turning them onto the wide-open streets. Felix's thighs squeeze around him, and he leans forward, his helmet bumping against Kade's.

"Kade," Felix shouts.

Kade stops breathing. He pulls them down a side street, flipping his visor up. Was the fall worse than they expected? Did Felix break something? "What?"

Felix's fingers curl into his arm. When he leans forward, his belly pushing against Kade's back, he says, "I think my water broke."

52
Kade

KADE FREEZES, his thoughts stumbling. *Water broke. His water broke.*

They've read about the membranes breaking, and it should be fine. It *should.* But Felix's pregnancy still bears a risk. He can't help thinking *I can't lose Felix,* and the thought winds around his throat, constricting his breath.

"Hang on," he says unsteadily. "Gonna get you to the hospital."

Felix nods. Kade flips his visor down, urging the bike back onto the street. *Do I have ten minutes? Twenty? Should've remembered my temper. Should've just gotten out of the store.*

He guides the bike down the streets, the joy of riding evaporating.

Felix isn't due for another week. His water shouldn't be breaking now. Did the baby get hurt? Had it been crushed in the fall? Kade swears, his skin prickling. The fall hurt Felix. There are too many cars on the road, too many other things that can go wrong.

The trees and buildings brush by in a mess of colors. Kade pulls into the hospital parking lot, breathing fast. The second he shuts off the engine, he slips off the bike, cradling Felix against himself.

"C'mon, get your legs up. I'll carry you in."

"I-I don't think it's that bad," he says, pulling his helmet off. But he swallows, looking down at his belly. Kade wishes he could look into it, see if there's anything wrong with the baby.

"But your water just broke!" Kade swears, stepping around in a circle, his nerves jangling.

"I know, I know." Felix sets the helmet down, pulling his feet onto the rider's seat while Kade supports him. "But I mostly sheltered my belly. The baby is still moving. I think we'll be fine."

The moment he's ready, Kade scoops his omega into his arms, striding into the emergency department. "I need to know you'll be fine," he says, his voice catching. They've been through so much already. "Can't lose you or the baby."

Felix leans into his chest, cradling his belly. "Me neither."

Most of the seats are filled, and the scent of disinfectant permeates through the air. Kade swears, stopping by the receptionist. They can't wait three hours for the doctor. "My omega fell. He says he's in pain."

The nurse looks over Felix, and pulls a walkie talkie from under the counter, radioing a doctor. "I'll need you to fill in this form," she says, setting a clipboard down on the counter. "I'm having a doctor come over right now."

Kade bristles as they wait, scanning for an available doctor. They don't have time to fill in fucking forms. His omega needs to be examined right now.

It takes forever before a nurse appears. Kade follows her to a room, one with partitioned walls of teal curtains. There, he sets Felix down gently on the bed, the paper sheets beneath him crinkling. Next to them, the ultrasound machines remain silent—Kade recognizes the screens, scanners, and gel tubes.

The doctor steps in after a minute—a tall, built man smelling like mint. He takes the clipboard Kade has hurriedly filled, calmly scanning over the scrawled words.

Kade doesn't wait for introductions. "I walked backward into my omega and he fell. Says he's hurting."

The doctor nods, logging into the computer. He types as Felix talks, then listens to Felix's heartbeat and lungs. Then he asks questions like *Do you have difficulty breathing? Where do you feel pain?*

Felix says he breathes fine. Pain in his belly. Kade tenses, watching him, wishing he could help.

The doctor sets the stethoscope on Felix's abdomen, listening. Then he touches the baby bump, and Felix exchanges a look with Kade, smiling slightly. *I think we'll be all right,* Felix's eyes say, but Kade can't relax.

"Both your heart rates are normal—the fetus's is at 150. It's moving well, no fetal distress." The doctor takes Felix's blood pressure, then looks up. "Because Felix fell, we'll do an ultrasound to check for placental abruption."

Kade doesn't know half of what the doctor's talking about. "Did it break any bones?"

"It shouldn't have," the doctor says. "At this point, we're more concerned about tears in the placenta and bleeding."

"But he fell," Kade says. "That's enough to

break something. It broke his water, didn't it?"

"Minor trauma won't break the membranes," the doctor says patiently. "It was probably a coincidence."

Kade looks at Felix, who shrugs.

The doctor gets Felix to pull his shirt up, and they go over the ultrasound procedures again—the gel, the black-and-white images on the screen. "The placenta appears to be intact," the doctor says. "But we're going to have to admit you anyway. Both to monitor you and the fetus for any complications, as well as to prevent infections."

Kade sighs, slipping his hand into Felix's. They're going to be okay, right?

"I'll transfer you to our labor unit. We'll be seeing if the contractions start," the doctor says. "Kade, you may want to return home and pack an overnight bag."

Kade stares at Felix, his stomach twisting. "I can't just leave him."

But he knows that they'll need to get things ready for the baby. Felix can't be doing any of that. They aren't even ready for the baby yet.

"I'll be fine," Felix says, squeezing his hand. "Text me if you need anything."

"I should be saying that to you," Kade says, but the tension in his shoulders eases slightly when Felix smiles up at him.

"Leave the giraffe with me?"

"I'll get it," Kade says. He squeezes Felix's hand, heading out for the bike.

When he returns some minutes later, he finds Felix in the hallway in a wheelchair, cradling his belly, an ID tag on his wrist. Kade sets the giraffe on the crown of his abdomen, sliding his fingers over Felix's nape. "You okay?"

Felix beams up at him. "I'm fine."

"I'll drop by home really quick. Tell mom you're in labor. She'll probably have a better idea what to do." Kade chuckles. He's kind of glad, suddenly, that they're living with his mom. *She's* the one with three kids.

"Say hi to her for me," Felix says, holding the giraffe close. "Ride safe."

Kade leans in, kissing his bondmate slowly on the lips. "Be back soon. Take care of you and the baby."

Felix laughs softly against him, his breath warm on Kade's skin. "Will do."

53
Kade

KADE DASHES in through the front door, the oily scent of bike exhaust still in his nose. At the door slamming, Mom pokes her head out of the kitchen.

"Felix's water broke. Premature," Kade says, breathless. "I'm taking the car to the hospital. Gotta pack an overnight bag. But he said hi."

"Oh! How's the labor going?"

"Not started yet. Need to get back." He leaves her behind on the stairs, sprinting to the bedroom he shares with Felix. Bag. Toothbrush. Toothpaste. Sleeping clothes. Socks. Warm slippers.

"It might be better if you don't toss them all into the bag at once," his mom says, smiling from the doorway. "I'm sure you'll be fine."

"I don't want to miss it," Kade says, his breath catching. It's Felix, and it's their baby, and he wants to be there for Felix when he goes into labor. They're going to be dads. They're going to be *dads!* Is he going to screw up? Are they going to be good enough? He'll need to take some time off work to stay with Felix, and oh, hell, they'll be bringing a baby home. *Their* baby.

"Take some spare change with you," his

mom says. "For vending machines. It could be a long wait, since it's his first."

Kade groans. He doesn't want to wait anymore. "Sure."

He throws other things into the bag, like phone chargers and a camera, and sketchpads.

"Is Felix all settled in?"

"Yeah. They've got him changed into the hospital clothes. I left him with the giraffe." And it's kind of funny, Felix and that giraffe they joked about so long ago. Back then, Kade hadn't even known about the pregnancy. "Shit, I'm gonna be a dad. We'll have a baby here this time tomorrow."

"Nervous?" His mom smiles.

"Yeah." When he's got clothes for him and Felix, a pillow, and probably more things than they need, Kade looks around. "Never thought I'd be a dad."

"You'll do fine," his mom says, pride on her face. "So will Felix."

Doesn't seem like we need anything else from here. He relaxes a little more, stopping by the doorway to pull his mom into a hug. "Be back soon. Get your sleep in. I'm sure it's gonna get busy around here."

She laughs. Kade sucks in a deep breath, wishing he could be as calm as she is.

AT THE hospital, he checks his phone again. *I'm in Ward 63A,* Felix texted. *Things are fine.*

Kade weaves through the corridors, brushing by nurses and people strolling around. There are too many people in here. He needs to get to Felix.

He barrels into the ward, almost knocking down a nurse. Felix smiles up from the cot. The sheets are pulled over his hips, and he's in a purple hospital gown, tiny in the wide bed. "You really didn't have to rush."

"You weren't waiting for me?" Kade grins, slowing down when he reaches his bondmate's side. "I brought you things."

Felix wriggles the giraffe at him. "I had company. It smells like you. It was comforting."

Kade sets the overnight bag at the foot of the bed, relaxing. Felix scoots over the mattress. Kade squeezes beside him, gingerly holding his belly. "It's fine?"

"It is. You really don't have to worry," Felix says, folding Kade's hand into his own. "I just had the first contraction a few minutes ago."

Kade's breath catches in his throat. "It's starting?"

"Seems that way, yes." Felix snuggles close to Kade, leaning his head against Kade's shoulder. "But it might be many more hours yet. I hope you won't get bored."

Kade laughs. "Bored? With you?"

Felix grins. "Oh, sure. I'll just be here being bitchy and pregnant for the next several hours."

Kade kisses him. "Then I'll wait with you," he says, gingerly touching the baby bump again. It moves against his palm, and his heart skips. "Go ahead and bitch."

"Ha!" Felix leans in and kisses him, his eyes glowing with warmth. "You're the very best, Kade."

And those words light Kade up from inside.

THREE HOURS in, Kade's nerves twist together, like live wires trapped in his body. "It's not coming out yet?"

Felix winces as he breathes through a contraction, squeezing Kade's hand. "No. It's supposed to take longer than this."

The midwife checks on them. Kade sighs, leaning in to smell the lavender of his bondmate's hair. "Guess I should've expected this."

"You think?" But Felix grins. He slaps Kade lightly on the thigh. "Go read your bike magazines," he says. "You're more worried about this than I am."

Kade sighs, grumbling as he pulls his phone out. "Fine."

FIVE HOURS in, Kade paces on the floor around the bed. "You'd think it'll be out faster," he says. "Breaking the water and all that. What the hell is it still doing in there?"

"It's waiting for you to calm down," Felix says, his tone dry. He cuddles the pillow from home, tossing the giraffe at Kade. "Looks like you need a snuggle buddy."

"I'm fine," Kade grumbles, his heart still pattering. He plucks the giraffe out of midair. "It's just taking a lot longer than I expected."

"You need to sit down," Felix says, patting

the bed again. "Maybe the doctor should order you some bed rest."

Kade barks a laugh. "Me, bed rest?"

"Why don't you get pregnant next time?" Felix says, his eyes twinkling. "You'd be so calm about it."

"Maybe. Guess I'd try getting pregnant if I could." Kade frowns. They've been here for *hours.* "I don't get how you're so calm now."

"It's built into me, I guess." Felix laughs, shrugging. "Come on, quit stomping around and kiss me."

Which doesn't sound bad at all. So Kade steps over, settling into the bed next to Felix, pulling his omega into his arms.

AT TEN hours, Kade's ready to snipe at something. Break a wall. Felix pants through a contraction, his fingers squeezing the life out of Kade's hand.

"Breathe," Kade says, sucking in lungfuls of air to demonstrate.

"Tell me to breathe one more time, Kade Brentwood, and I'll wring your neck," Felix wheezes, flipping him off. "Fucking hurts."

Kade winces. "It should help, right?"

"No!" Felix shudders again, his face paling. Kade holds his hand, and Felix squeezes the life out of Kade's knuckles. A minute later, Felix relaxes, his entire body going limp. He flops back onto his pillow, sucking in breath after breath.

Kade brushes the hair out of his face, dabbing the sweat off his forehead with a towel. "Sorry."

"You better be," Felix mutters, his skin damp with sweat. "Didn't think it would hurt this much."

Kade winces. He didn't mean to put Felix through this. "Sorry. Does that mean we're having just the one child?"

"Maybe. Quite possibly. We'll see if I've murdered you by the end of this."

Kade chuckles. "Right."

Felix tips his head back into the pillow, his eyes fluttering shut. "Gods, I'm so done with the pregnancy."

"Ready to meet the baby?" Kade leans in, smiling when Felix curls his fingers into his palm.

"Yes! I'm sure she'll be lovable." Felix smiles.

"She? We don't even know that yet."

"It's just a feeling I've been getting lately," Felix says, pulling Kade closer. "I still love you, by the way. I'm not killing you."

Kade smiles, relieved. "That works," he says. "If you love me but kill me, at least I found out first."

Felix laughs, punching his arm.

AT FOURTEEN hours, Felix pants on the bed, his hair damp with sweat, and the midwife slides her fingers out of Felix's hole. Kade bites down a low growl. If she were anything but omega, he'd be itching to yank her away. Felix is *his* to touch.

"Almost fully dilated," the midwife says, washing her hands before bustling around the room

"You look like you're about to murder

something," Felix pants, tapping on Kade's wrist.

"Want to bring you home," Kade says, possessiveness clawing up his throat. "You and the baby. Then you're all mine." *Enough of strangers putting their hands on you.*

Felix laughs weakly, and Kade wipes his forehead down with a damp towel. "That works. I'd love that."

But they're still waiting, and as the seconds tick by and nothing else changes, Kade sighs. He rubs their wrists together, then trails his scent all over Felix. "Mine," he says again, scenting his bondmate.

Felix looks up at him, smiling. "All yours."

"PUSH," THE midwife says. Kade echoes after her.

"C'mon, push," he says, stroking Felix's hair off his face. "Just a bit more. Squeeze."

"I know what I'm doing," Felix snarls, arching off the bed, his teeth bared. Sweat beads across his forehead. Kade holds his hand tight, wishing he could take all of that pain away. "Argh!"

"Almost there," the midwife says. "You've got the head out now. And the shoulders. Just a little more!"

"Keep pushing," Kade says, kissing his forehead. Felix's grip squeezes like a vice around his fingers, and he pants, his pupils constricted, his eyes shadowy green in the dimmed lights.

"I told you, Kade," Felix hisses through gritted teeth. "So help me, but if you tell me to push one more time, I'm going to fucking murder you."

"Push," Kade says, a tendril of adrenaline shooting up his spine. He knows his omega, knows Felix's boundaries, and this will rile Felix up just enough...

Felix growls, his eyes flashing, his teeth bared. He heaves again, his entire body shaking with the effort, and Kade knows his omega will kill him in another life, if they were ever on opposite sides of a fight. But that life isn't theirs, and Felix is his bondmate, his love.

"It's a girl," the midwife says. Kade turns, staring at the mess of red and wet and *baby.* "She's beautiful."

Felix drops back onto the pillows with a whine, gulping deep breaths, his eyelids slipping half-shut. "Oh, gods, that was difficult."

But he smiles, his cheeks flushed. As the midwife wipes the baby down and hands her over to Felix, Kade leans in. He wants to memorize this: Felix with his golden hair damp, his eyes bright as he gazes down upon their child. The baby is tiny in his arms, her skin flushed, her eyes still shut, a dusting of hair on her head.

"You did great," Kade says, his throat suddenly tight. Felix looks up at him, tears in his eyes. So he leans in, kissing Felix softly on his forehead. "Proud of you."

"You did great too," Felix murmurs, sagging into the pillows, their baby cradled safely against his chest. "I'm exhausted."

"Rest," Kade says. He reaches down carefully, touching their daughter's tiny curled fingers. She wraps them around his own. As though she knows who he is, and she's saying, *Hi, Dad.*

Five years ago, Kade wouldn't have dreamed of this. Felix had left, and Kade had thought he'd lost his bondmate for good. But Felix is back. They've marked each other again. They have a home together, and a beautiful daughter that Kade will protect. And they will get married soon, when Felix is ready.

"Love you," he murmurs in Felix's ear, kissing his temple.

"Love you too," Felix whispers, his eyelids fluttering shut.

Kade cradles his family close, thankful for everything in his life.

Epilogue

3 months later

FELIX LOOKS up at the mansion looming above them, drawing a deep breath. This visit is long overdue, and he's been putting it off for... what, almost a year now? Perhaps that has added to his growing dread, but he can no longer put this off.

"You're sure about this?" Kade asks, parking the car at the end of the driveway, by the circular stone fountain. He reaches over for Felix's hand, cradling it in his own. He smooths his warm, callused thumb over Felix's ring. "I'll talk to him alone if you want."

Felix shakes his head, smiling fondly. "It's about time I did things myself, isn't it? Grow a spine and all that. Besides, you can be the backup muscle."

Kade mulls over it, narrowing his eyes. "Fine."

They step out of the car. Felix unstraps Bethy from the car seat, smiling when she grins toothlessly at him. "We're going to meet your grandpa," Felix says, kissing her on the nose. "And hopefully we'll all come away intact."

"I'll punch him if he disses you." Kade locks

the car doors, stepping close to slip his arm around Felix's waist. His eyes dart over the rows of windows along the first floor, and the turrets at either corner of the mansion.

Felix leans into him. Years ago, Kade had thought that he needed to provide a sprawling house like this for Felix to be happy. It's taken him a while to shake that impression. "I like our home," Felix says quietly. "It's feels like family."

Kade looks back at him, a tiny smile curving his lips. "I believe you."

They walk up the stone steps together. Shifting Bethy to his other arm, Felix unlocks the door, pushing it open.

Inside, the butler looks up at them, raising his eyebrows. Then his gaze flickers over Bethy and Kade. "Mr. Felix," he says, dipping his chin. "Your father was not expecting you. You've caught him just as he was about to leave."

The butler glances to the side. Felix finds his father standing at the foot of the grand stairway, briefcase in hand. Felix swallows. This was less time than he had to prepare.

Alastor Henry scans them over—Felix, Kade, the baby girl in Felix's arms. His eyes widen.

"Father," Felix says, his pulse jumping in his throat. "I apologize for not dropping by. We've been caught up lately."

By *lately,* he means *the past half year,* but his father doesn't answer. The mayor of Meadowfall steps forward, his forehead crinkled. "You birthed a child."

"A daughter," Felix says, lowering his gaze. "Bethy Brentwood."

His father stops two feet away, staring at the blond curls on Bethy's head, her mahogany eyes. For a long moment, he stares at her, lips pressed thin. Then he sags, ever so slightly, and in that moment, he looks *old.*

Felix thinks about handing the wedding invite over and leaving, but his father reaches up, and pauses. "She reminds me of your mother," he says, his voice barely audible. And Felix's heart quickens, because his father has never talked about his mother. She'd died when he and Taylor were infants.

"She's a great child," Felix says, his voice shaking a little. Anytime now, his father will tell him what a failure he still is. And it will hurt again. "We've been reading books to her. Her favorite is 'Big Rabbit and Little Rabbit'."

Alastor Henry drops his hand, his shoulders sagging. "Your mother would have raised you better," he murmurs haltingly. "She was far kinder than I am."

Felix stares at his father, his eyes stinging. His father has never acknowledged the way he treated Felix, either.

"You could have shown him some kindness," Kade says, eyeing Felix's father. "That's all I ever hoped to see from you."

That, and a proper acknowledgement. But Felix knows Kade won't ask for it.

Alastor glances at Kade, nodding. Then he looks back at Felix, his eyes dark and contemplative. "I raised you in the hopes that you would take over my businesses someday," Alastor says. "Taylor did well with that. I wondered why you didn't. And I hope you won't make the same mistakes I did with your children."

Felix gulps, his throat tight. It sounds like forgiveness, and he hasn't thought he needed to hear it that much. "I'll try not to."

Kade lifts the ivory envelope in his hand, glancing at Felix. *Do you want me to hand it over?*

Felix nods. So Kade presents their wedding invite to Alastor, meeting his gaze. "We're getting married in June. Thought you might like to be invited."

Alastor takes the envelope from Kade. "You can expect me to be there."

Felix smiles. It's a victory, that his father would even want to witness their marriage.

And a heartbeat later, Alastor adds, "I regret my decisions about the estate, sometimes. For the impact that they caused the people of Meadowfall. My wife—your mother, Felix—I think she would have thought the same you did."

It's the closest he'll get to apologizing for the bankruptcy. Kade breathes out, dipping his chin. *Fine.*

Felix doesn't know what to say to all this, himself, how to even respond to the man he'd grown up fearing. So he nods, holding Bethy closer to himself. She gurgles. "We'll be leaving," he says. "See you at the wedding."

His father nods solemnly. "See you then."

THEIR WEDDING takes place on a balmy morning in June.

At Meadowfall park, children run and shout and play in the shade of spreading trees. Swans glide across the distant lake, and ripples spread through the water's surface. Under an intricate iron gazebo, Felix and Kade join hands before their families, facing each other, and their audience holds its breath.

To Felix's left, Taylor cradles Bethy in his arms—she's six months old, dressed in bright yellow overalls—and next to him, their father watches on, the butler James at his side. Felix swallows. His father's presence isn't enough to make him tense, though. There are other people around, family and friends who have been kinder to him. Kade squeezes his hands, and Felix shifts his gaze to their other guests.

To his right, Mrs. Brentwood smiles, her eyes shining. Kade's brothers stand with her—Chris and Sam—and just past them, Susan grins, mouthing, *Go on, kiss him.*

Felix smiles. He looks back at Kade, and his breath catches again.

"You always look so handsome," he murmurs, warmth settling in his chest. For the past months, Kade has been taking a day off work each week to help with Bethy. Together, they've taken turns staying up through the nights, changing her diaper, feeding her, playing with her when she doesn't sleep.

Sometimes, Kade's mom steps in to babysit, and they get a day to themselves—time they spend idling with each other, kissing on the back porch, tangled amongst the bedcovers.

Sometimes, they take Bethy out on strolls to

the park, looking at the swans, the laughing children, the rustling leaves.

"She'll grow up coding the computer games," Felix will say.

"She'll start doing crayons and oil pastels," Kade will say.

They'll end up looking at Bethy, and she'll fling a dried leaf into the air, giggling.

Kade rubs his thumbs over Felix's hands. Felix focuses on him again; Kade's dressed smoothly in a blue-grey suit, its lapels curving gently over his chest, his pants clinging to his thighs. Felix's suit is a shade darker, and from the way Kade's gaze trails over his body, it won't be staying on long after the reception.

"I never thought this would happen," Felix murmurs. After all that they've been through, and after all the times he doubted they'd ever get together again, this still feels a little like a dream.

Kade rubs a gentle thumb over his wrist. The new bonding mark has become a silvery scar, matching Kade's and that is a reminder in itself. They've lost some, gained more, and Felix can't regret the things that have blossomed between them. They have a beautiful daughter now, a cozy home with warm smiles and joyful laughter.

"And the most important questions of them all," the minister says, an elderly man with twinkling eyes and half-moon glasses. "Kaden Brentwood, will you take this omega to be your husband, to love and to cherish for the rest of your life?"

"I do," Kade says, his eyes locked with Felix. Felix's breath hitches.

"And Felix Henry, will you take this alpha to be your husband, to love and to cherish for the rest of your life?"

"I do," Felix says, and it's the easiest promise he's ever had to make. He's always loved Kade, and he's Kade's for the next twenty, forty, hundred years.

Kade's face lights up. He leans in, brushing their lips together, and in that moment, there is only them, and the brightest future ahead.

ABOUT THE AUTHOR

A huge fan of angst and bittersweet tension, Anna has been scribbling since she was fourteen. She believes that everyone needs a safe place, and so her dorky guys fall in love, make mistakes, and slowly find their way back into each other's arms.

Anna loves fine lines on her notebook paper, and is especially fond of her tiny glass globe. She is currently living on the west coast of the US with her husband and a menagerie of stuffed animals..

Printed in Great Britain
by Amazon